Fresh Men
2

New Voices in Gay Fiction

INTRODUCED BY Andrew Holleran

SELECTED AND EDITED BY Donald Weise

CARROLL & GRAF PUBLISHERS
NEW YORK

FRESH MEN 2
New Voices in Gay Fiction

Carroll & Graf Publishers
An Imprint of Avalon Publishing Group Inc.
245 West 17th Street
New York, NY 10011

AVALON
publishing group incorporated

Contents

Foreword

The *Fresh Men* series was launched last fall because it seemed to me that new gay writers didn't have many venues for publishing their work. In fact, I continue to be surprised to see so few vehicles—both in print and online—devoted to gay fiction, much less committed to publishing fiction by emerging gay writers. The readership for gay fiction is there, of course. Maybe not as vigorous as it once was—gay culture along with the rest of the world seems no longer to rank books high on its list of priorities—but there nonetheless. As someone who publishes fifteen to twenty gay titles at Carroll and Graf every year, I can attest to the market's strengths as well as its weaknesses.

For me, one of the most important and satisfying functions of my job as editor is introducing new writers. Thus, all of the contributors to *Fresh Men 2* are emerging authors; that is, none of the writers has published a novel or story collection. Whereas gay anthologies like the *Men on Men* series mixed emerging talent with veteran authors, the *Fresh Men* series showcases new writers exclusively. Of course, some of the contributors have published online or in anthologies and journals, most notably *The James White Review*. However, all the authors in this book are in the process of breaking out—and breaking out, I'd like to add, regardless of one's age. Indeed, the *Fresh Men* anthologies challenge the notion that emerging authors are young men, even if the majority of emerging writers might fall within this demographic.

As you'll find, *Fresh Men 2* offers honest, unapologetic, often surprising depictions of gay life that speak the truths of each author's experience. I selected and edited these stories: later Andrew Holleran generously agreed to introduce them. Perhaps unsurprisingly for a book of gay stories, coming of age is a big theme. But so are issues surrounding the complexities of adult heartbreak, friendships, and family. Sex is as important as ever and drugs come into play from time to time. Not everyone lives in the big city, not everyone is gay. In fact, not every gay man is a gay man, as you'll see. Yet despite its diversity, the book doesn't attempt to represent a full cross section of gay life. Instead *Fresh Men 2* weighs heavily on the merits of the writing. Within that criterion, however, readers will discover a wide array of gay experiences covered.

At the risk of overstating its importance, the *Fresh Men* series and gay anthologies like it offer us a window into the next wave of gay fiction. But don't take my word for it: consider the contributors to last year's *Fresh Men*, who have since published (or are about to publish) a first novel or story collection: Vestal McIntyre's *You Are Not the One*, Keith McDermott's *Acqua Calda*, Scott Pomfret's *Hot Sauce*, Barry McCrea's *The First Verse*, Matthew Fox's *Cities of Weather*, Robert J. Hughes's *Late and Soon*, and Patrick Ryan's *Send Me*. The future of gay fiction is as exciting as we choose to make it.

—Donald Weise
July 2005

Writers who would like to submit stories to *Fresh Men 3* can send work to my attention at Carroll & Graf, 245 West 17th St., 11th Floor New York, NY 10011.

Introduction

By Andrew Holleran

Last autumn I went to the gay bookstore Lambda Rising in Washington DC to hear a friend read from his latest book. The bookstore seemed to be divided into three zones that evening: Behind us, customers were flipping through a new picture book of a French "rugby team" at the front of the store. In the middle, we fans huddled listening to my friend read. Behind him, over his shoulder, other customers were leafing through the porn magazines at the back of the room.

Ah, I thought, gay publishing really is over—and gay bookstores have returned to their original function, a place where men can find pictures of hot guys!

It's banal by now to say that the gay publishing boom that occurred in the late 70s, early 80s, has been succeeded by what is called a postgay culture. If the theory that a movement dies the moment it constructs its biggest monument is true, then perhaps the beautiful store A Different Light opened in New York in 1994—a high-ceilinged, polished-wood affair with its own auditorium downstairs for readings—should have been a warning. Since then it seems to have been downhill. Not only has that store closed, but Creative Visions, the bookstore that took over A Different Light's original small space on Hudson Street, just closed too, and it looks as if this particular institution has now gone the way of the hippy coffee house:

another item in the ravenous maw of American culture, which eats, digests, and moves on with such incredible speed.

Even during the boom, of course, people asked if gay literature was a good idea. Why ghettoize gay writing? Didn't that make it second rate, provincial? It wasn't long before novelist Michael Lowenthal claimed in a subversive essay that gay books had become a synonym for mediocrity; which did not stop people from still gathering at gay literary festivals to hear panels discuss questions that, toward the end, seemed more and more tired: Is there such a thing as gay literature? A gay sensibility?

The cultural assimilation that followed AIDS—not to mention America's penchant for moving on—mooted these questions. Whatever the answers, you can now find gay books in Border's and Barnes & Noble, or on Amazon.com. And now there's *Will & Grace*, *Queer as Folk*, and the new gay channel Logo, to make gay writing even less crucial. I'm not sure these stories on celluloid answer needs the printed word can. But in a recent article in the *New York Times* about two men in Boston who write gay romance novels, critic Michael Bronski said the future of gay fiction is not promising for a simple reason—once upon a time, gay people could not find representations of themselves, and now they can—in lots of places.

So why this anthology? For a long time George Stambolian, and then David Bergman, edited a series called *Men on Men* that, in the boom days of gay writing, provided a place where gay writers could get published and gay readers find stories about their lives. I don't think this desire has vanished. But now the question is: What happens when gay subject matter is no longer taboo? It would be hard to dispute the fact that fiction with gay elements is now entitled to "mainstream" attention. Last year Alan Hollinghurst's *The Line of Beauty* won the Mann-Booker Prize in England—and *The Master*, a novel by Colm Toibin based on Henry James, was very warmly received. The culture does change, of course, and in this collection of tales I was curious to see how it reflects that history. I was curious about two things primarily: literary style, and the approach to gay subject matter. Sometimes it seemed the first was much more important to the author than the second; sometimes the reverse. In the best of these stories one quite forgets the issue, and one is given the pleasures any good short story provides. "The Oryx," "Psychic Rosemary," and "Thirds" are classic Gothics. Others eschew realism in favor of a postmodern irony. Three of the latter— "All The Young Boys Love Alice," "Cotton Candy," and "A Separate Reality"—even use other works of art (an Alice Munro story, *The Wizard of Oz*, Carlos Castaneda) to establish a certain distance.

Oddly, it is the most traditional—"Ephemera," "An Ideal Couple," "Jax City Limits," and "Difference"—that are arguably the gayest. "Ephemera" reads like a classic tale by Joyce. "An Ideal Couple" manages to depict with no frills or sentimentality what a novel often tries to capture: two lives across a span of time (in this case, friends who drank together). "Jax City Limits" slyly and wittily uses memory (and a female narrator) to look back and try to understand relationships between two boys in high school. "Difference" follows a man as he walks around Manhattan one day trying to understand why his lover left. Only the short story could do this.

Others, like "Sunday Morning," compress life to a single moment (how does one gracefully leave the apartment of the two lovers with whom you've had a threesome?).

In some that moment contains a lifetime: In "A Bright, Shining Place," a white man witnessing the confirmation of his black lover's son in a homophobic black church comes to a point of no return. In "Sucker," a man must take a gamble on moving a purely sexual relationship to another level—or destroying it completely. In "The Oryx," a gay man finds himself in a sinister Texas hunting lodge with a too-butch boyfriend; in "The Lost Coast," a settled gay couple find a baby in the strangest way.

While two of these stories—"Ephemera" and "Last Summer"—

deal with death, "My First Story," and "Manboobs" deal with the comedy of desire. In several a single speaker carries us vividly along. "Yesterday's Nihilist," "My First Story," "Ofelia's Last Ride," "Romeo's Distress," and "Manboobs" (a pecs protest piece), we have monologues by two Manhattan queens, a Mexican mama's boy, and two punks (one in New York, one in San Francisco, the first hilariously critical, the second furtive and depressed).

In more than one of the stories being gay seems to no longer be an urgent matter; we now have the freedom to be bored. Some seem to lack an ending—as if they are not sure themselves what the point of being gay is anymore (though this may have more to do with modes of writing now than gay life). With assimilation comes a certain blurring of identity. Indeed, "Ofelia's Last Ride"—a pitch-perfect, hilarious evocation of Mexican culture—asks the question "Is this really a gay story?" (Its gayness lies in its, yes, sensibility.) But that too reflects the present situation: Gay life is now so familiar a cultural phenomenon (though it may still be a tremendous matter in the lives of individuals) that assimilation has led gay people to the same cultural dilemma integration presented blacks: Where do I belong? These tales illustrate perfectly the vague, transitional, post-assimilation zone in which gay writers and readers find themselves now

Of course, all those years when people were wondering if there was a gay sensibility, or a gay literature, the question should never have been "Is this a gay story?" but "Is this a good story?" Oscar Wilde said the question is not whether a book is moral or immoral, but well or badly written. From this anthology you will come away, I think, with your own opinions and responses—and the feeling, perhaps, that I had, that for all the assimilation and its consequence (the mundane quality of gay subject matter), there is still a need for the subjective, intricate, ruminative, and dense evocation of (gay) life that only the short story can provide. *Will & Grace* is a farce, *Queer as Folk* a soap opera. These stories convey a reality they cannot.

Ephemera
By Michael Wynne

SENAN DIED, AS at last he'd planned it, on his fifty-first birthday. His passing came with that of the day itself. For it, his mouth wore what looked like the semicomic exaggeration of a non-smile, with the corners turned pronouncedly down in a face that had with his fading imperceptibly tautened and tilted toward the sash window, past which had flown and still flew on the daylong gusts leaves from the apple tree that stood between the house and the streetlight bordering the sluggish canal.

When he saw it was over, Pierce watched intently for several minutes, his mouth shielded by the frame of his fingers. Then he bent across the bed and, holding the sinuous and pulseless wrists of hands that curved like parentheses around the hip bones beneath the old quilt, kissed lightly the lids of eyes that in life had, because of some never-discussed condition, oscillated constantly, as though their owner sought without rest to keep track of and register every varying element his world presented. Next, he went around to the window and drew the lank, unlined, corpuscle red drapes, and lit with a Bic lighter he took from the breast pocket of his shirt a stout plain white candle in the spiral-stemmed holder by the bed.

Circling the bed, he went to a beveled-glass dressing table that

had served as a desk. It stood before an alcove opposite the left side of
the bed. The alcove was lined with shelves holding antiquarian ref-
erence books, antique mathematical instruments of tarnished brass,
and a small phrenological bust, punctuated by gaps made to accommodate framed maps of the ancient world fixed to the intervening
wall spaces. He lit a single candle stuck in a steel candle stand of
twisted, asymmetrical branches standing before the left wing of the
mirror, and with the reflection of his dead lover's profile before him,
sat at the dressing table, littered with several significantly empty
tablet phials and a glass jug of water, and picked up a thin hardbound
notebook whose cover was almost the same shade of red as the
drapes. It was Senan's journal—not a journal in the conventional
sense that it documented chronologically his day-to-day doings and
preoccupations, but a commonplace book full of random quotations
and aphorisms, gathered often as potential material for the poems he
wrote, but mostly for their own sake. He'd begun keeping it several
months previous, in this old ugly logbook he'd saved for a special
purpose, when finally the growth, stealthy and pervasive, his body
carried in its depths settled him on a decision he'd edged toward since
its busily consuming nature was confirmed the spring before they
met. It was a decision from which there was no moving him, a decision Pierce never gave the least indication of the confused resentment
he felt about being invited to witness.

Realizing he did not wish after all to read anything contained in
the journal, he closed it abruptly and laid it squarely before him.

Over his shoulder in the slanting wing of the mirror Senan's
slightly inclined profile was outlined nimbuslike from the candlelight
beyond. His desire for death, his very will to die, had, in Pierce's
mind, as he now realized, given Senan a delusory immunity; the
enormity of his having reached and passed into the state he had for so
long and so clear-sightedly discussed and weighed up and made
arrangements for was almost dizzyingly inapprehensible to Pierce.

He got up, left the room, descended the narrow stairway of the dark, silent house, and went out into the front garden. He lit a cigarette and, standing against the wall of the house, turned his eyes toward the black, dense canal. Facing fully into the teeth of the wind, which whipped away in broken swirls the first outpouring of smoke from his mouth, he looked up at the candlelit window.

Picturing Senan's shell above, he experienced again the harsh ungraspableness of the fact that, having brought forward his own end with such conscious preparation, that very consciousness was now effaced so absolutely. He felt a dull desolation at the finality, not only of the death of his helpmate, his lover, but of the disbelieving horror and all the grimly thrilling expectancy that Senan's decision fomented. He wondered who it was that said that grief feels like fear, and when, or if, he'd feel the proof of this.

He'd been to this house for the first time on an autumn evening as pitch-dark as this particular night, a week after their initial meeting. He arrived on his old mountain bike and went directly around to the trellis-bordered side door, as Senan had instructed him. Leaving his bike against the stone wall of the house, he entered directly to find Senan stirring in a deep copper pot the ratatouille he was preparing for them, while running his free hand continually over his helmet of close-cropped iron-gray hair. He'd turned to Pierce with a calm smile and kissed him neatly on both cheeks and then, surprising Pierce, both casually and precisely on the mouth.

Six nights previously they'd met by accident, above a center-city pub where a weekly writers' group Pierce attended regularly was held. Senan, wandering in for a pint on his way from a north side book fair, had stumbled on the literary gathering when he took himself upstairs to get away from the frantic din of the crowd watching an All-Ireland match below. Pierce was conscious of the lofty gray-haired man standing back, motionless, discreet, hyperattentive-seeming, in a darkened area of the room, as he continued his not-so-sure-footed reading of what, with some embarrassment, he had in his preamble described for his fellow writers as "an extract from a patchwork of set pieces I ambitiously call 'a novel under construction.'" After the last poem was read and critiqued, Senan ambled over to where Pierce sat alone with an empty coffee cup on the table in front of him and lowered himself onto an opposite stool, saying, in his kind, intimate manner, "I was taken by the obsessed note of your story."

"Were you? *'Obsessed* note'?" Pierce echoed, a little confused, a little bit indignant, but curious, attracted.

When everyone else had gone, they stayed on chatting and ended up going to a late-night coffee bar off Grafton Street that Senan liked. Here Pierce—mystified by those irises of his new friend that moved ceaselessly over and back while remaining unwaveringly intent on his own face, his eyes, his mouth—vented some of his mounted-up criticisms of the writers' group, that "coven of scribblers and poetasters," as he'd come to call it, that fixed unyieldingly in his craw. His main gripe was simply that new blood was kept away by the elder core members' intolerance of adventurous criticism ("reading too much into things" was the parochially worded condemnation). But in the absence of other outlets, which he'd felt at the time he needed, Pierce had put up with it, week after week, for many months. At Senan's suggestion, he never went back to the pub but instead now took himself every Monday night to Senan's place, to read new or reworked parts of his projected book and to listen in turn to Senan's latest poetic outbursts.

On the morning following the ratatouille dinner, Pierce had come away with an ardently inscribed galley copy of Senan's latest published volume. He had disliked it for its prosaic dispensing of imagery, and for its dogmatically insisted-upon theme, as he saw it, that the evil in our natures that can destroy us, or destroy others, or blight the quality of our lives, is, paradoxically (it was this business of the paradox that especially irked him), necessary, if we are to *evolve*—

a concept of which his possibly increased appreciation when he got to know Senan barely endeared him more to the poems themselves.

When he finished his cigarette he went back into the house to phone the hospital, and Senan's only relation, a Cork-based older sister.

The next day he moved out of the canal-side, semidetached house where Senan had lived all his life, the last half on his own, after the death of his father. Pierce had stayed there for the past year while, in order to have his own space to write and study, keeping a bedsit on the South Circular Road, whose nominal rent a monthly check from the health board covered most of. It was here he now returned to live in the ordinary way, taking with him the red logbook. Over the following two or three weeks, he flipped randomly through it between studying for his master's in English and carrying out seemingly endless revisions and amplifications on his ever-expanding, ever-more-convoluted and irresolvable-seeming novel.

At the end of the month, as a fitting substitute for the custom of the month's mind, Pierce organized a reading of Senan's work by some of his closest sympathizers, at a new, recently launched arts center in a fashionable part of the city. He himself made a brief opening speech that afterward he guiltily felt was a failure—facile, overflippant, a total washout when it came to doing justice to the decency and depth and humor of its subject, with its too-clever and possibly (he feared) scathing-sounding references to Senan's "racing," "voracious" eyes and his penchant for merciless dissection of character. As he listened to what Senan's friends had decided made up an illuminating selection of his work, he found himself thinking, with no great cause as he knew himself, that they understood as little and misinterpreted as much of the poetry as they had the man himself. He sat at an angle to the podium, facing them on their plastic stack chairs, full of self-distaste for thinking this now, at such a time.

As he sat there, cross-legged, uncomfortable, a bit bored, he recalled how once, not long into their involvement, Senan, after consuming single-handedly a large bottle of Powers, remarked with an embarrassing philosophic sentimentality typical of him when he was drunk, "Remember, Pierce, the goodness that exists in you is testament to the goodness in the universe." At the time Pierce guiltily felt Senan was a fool to so idealize him. But now he wondered, with some discomfort, whether the words hadn't carried an irony he'd been in the habit of missing altogether throughout the short time they'd been allied.

The morning after the reading, a Saturday, he awoke so depressed he was unable to get down to the moderate quota of work he'd set himself, and was more depressed still when, later that afternoon, he answered the phone in the drafty hallway below his room to a man whose personal ad in the local queer rag he'd responded to during a spell of intense loneliness at the end of the third week after Senan's death. He was unable to remember the precise wording of the classified—he'd thrown the paper away almost as soon as he replied to it—just that the hopeful was in his fifties, and that gallant mention was made of a good physique, a choice of information Pierce had half-sneered at even as he'd reeled off his lust-driven but blandly phrased reply. Now, as he lifted the handset, he sensed the nature of the call, sensed also it would be utterly wanting.

Without making sure who exactly was at the end of the line, the aged male voice, phlegmy, apologetic, went headlong into a rambling, quietly manic speech about how, yes, he had a good body, and was, like Pierce, creative (he helped design backdrops for all the big productions for a local theater company in his southeastern town) and into "developing" himself—Pierce had to ponder what it was he himself had said that prompted these guarantees—and how he'd "kicked football" for years but didn't anymore because, though it wasn't something he mentioned in the ad, he'd some trouble with his hip, though it wasn't that bad, his body by and large was still good. . . . The faltering, clapped-out, hope-filled spiel went on. As it wound down, the man suddenly added, "I've spent all me life down here, all me life. There's not that many places to go—ya know what I'm saying—not that many chances to, y'know, meet others like meself, like, and I'm, I'm—" He paused, sucked in a quick, rattling breath. "Y'know, well, I'm not gettin' any—any younger, put it that way."

"We're all in that boat, aren't we?" Pierce winced, imagining, as the words left his lips, how full of youth and seemingly unimpeded promise his voice must sound.

"Aye, well, I could go up and see ya some weekend."

"That'd be grand, grand."

"Do ya want to see me?"

"Give me your number and I'll be back to you," Pierce hated his own voice, the smooth, crushing insincerity of his words, despising himself for having allowed the exchange to happen, with all the stale craven deceit it demanded.

He put down the phone swearing to himself it was the last time he'd be responsible for kindling hopes he hadn't the remotest intention to fulfill, and grim with distaste at his own carnality, that propelled him into such fraudulence. It was so often in the end such a grossly inconsiderate, ill-considered, muddying, meaningless routine, this casting about for sex partners. But he couldn't help himself. In this, he was so banally unexceptional. It made him feel very nearly worthless.

When he returned to his room, he eyed Senan's notebook lying flat on top of the bookcase that stood at the end of his bed. He went across to the window and looked out over the roofs of adjacent rows of houses. There came to his mind the thought of a review of Senan's last volume, a viperish piece by a poisonous crank named Ambrose Manning, an overambitious poet and inveterate committee member who had, for whatever reason, appointed himself an enemy of Senan's, and who, what's more, had with outrageous mendacity

printed a eulogy of Senan in a national paper the week of his funeral.
After the appearance of the odious review, he could remember precisely Senan saying, as they sat in the kitchen of his home, "Yes, he's
pompous and spiteful and inflated, but I don't hold a grudge because
I see his mired strivings behind these unpleasant facets of his."

Pierce could almost feel again the pang of scorn this display—
so generous, so sincere—had activated in him, while Senan, as if
sensing this, had with deliberate lightheartedness added, "Lack of
generosity makes terrible devils of us, Pierce. But there can be no
helping it, can there?"

With his arms hanging limply and the tips of each finger
touching the cool wood of the high window ledge, Pierce whispered
slowly to himself, ironically and yet not ironically, and as if testing the
sense and the relevance of the words, "The kindest of men . . ."

All the afternoon and on into the evening, as he tried to work,
thoughts recurred to Pierce of the day Senan told him of his intention, his wish. It had been the height of summer, cloyingly warm.
Senan had just come through a course of treatment and was feeling,
as he put it, anything but human. That morning he explained that
he'd thought it through, that his last day would be his birthday this
winter, that he wanted Pierce to bear witness.

Pierce had shed wild tears—highly unusual for him. He did not
want to be privy to this—was disgusted, frightened, at hearing it.

"How could you think of this—and, and lay it on me? How,
Senan? It's selfish, calculating," he'd said.

"Then forget it, forget it," Senan said gently, soothing him.

He'd left Senan alone in the small front room, and gone upstairs
to calm down. When he went back down, a little later, Senan was still
sitting at the window. A noisy, disoriented, dazed, possibly dying
bluebottle kept banging against the glass of the sash window, open at
the top the mere fraction its age allowed.

"Doesn't that sound annoy you?" said Pierce, coming over and touching his shoulder.

Senan looked up at him, his irises vacillating excitedly, a kind of dim joy in the weakness of his smile.

"I was busy drawing analogies," he said.

"Were you?" said Pierce, maybe not so interested.

"Look at the way it's got itself into a head-banging frenzy, as it seeks a way out there. It throttles backward down the glass, then darts away, then back again, to throttle upward this time, covering the same space over and over, silly little eejit. If it broadened its scope a little, it'd find a way out, it would find release. All it has to do is stop protesting uselessly, obsessively, against the barrier of its chosen sphere, and move just a little higher, just exert itself that extra bit to break out of its chosen limits, and there it'd go, free to fly in the unbounded garden and live and expire under the wide sky."

"Does it put you in mind of a poem?" said Pierce with soft irony, caressing the rather stiff gray, close-cut hair.

"It puts me in mind of what *I* can discern, what *I* might do," Senan replied, reaching up and taking Pierce's hand with wonderful tenderness.

Weeks after this, Pierce gave, with less and less ambiguity, his guarantee of supporting in love what it was so plain Senan ultimately desired.

Sickened by the feeling of inadequacy his fruitless struggle with his writing brought on, and keen to obliterate the aftertaste of the stranger's phone call with a plainly, cathartically abandoned sex encounter or two, he escaped that night to a sauna, the first time he'd been to one, after years of frenetically regular attendance, since moving in with Senan.

When he got there, he undressed quickly and donned around his waist the thin milk-white towel he was given as he was buzzed in.

For the first fifteen minutes, he sat where the coffee bar angled, eyeing the two impossibly young-seeming boys tending the bar who complained animatedly between themselves that the stereo kept failing to read their CDs. One of them absently gave Pierce the coffee he asked for. He sipped it gratefully and smiled bleakly around at the other patrons in their improvised sarongs.

There were three, all in their forties, sitting in a cramped huddle to his right, including a striking man with dramatically moist, bulbous lips, tattoos, and sideburns each angled and shaped like the brandished blade of a dagger. They were having a jocularly philosophic chat—about death, apparently.

One patron only occupied the entire length of the counter to his left, an older, but not really very much older man whose dark brown rinse actually managed not merely to physically age but to efface him. All the same, something about him—something tense, compulsive, concentrated, spectacularly unself-conscious—held Pierce's attention. Before him sat a side plate with a scone and a knife, and a coffee cup. Blinking elaborately, contemplatively, he leaned over these, his fingertips resting together as though over a shrine, then suddenly whipped his fingers apart and elaborately, finickily, lifted the cup by its sides.

At the same time one of the men on Pierce's right said, "And when you're aware of it, when you accept it, *level* with it, it's just there, like it's your best friend, the only friend you want, the only guide, like—do you know what I mean?"

Pierce sipped his coffee, eyeing the trio over the rim of his cup.

The man went on. "It's just there, and you don't—you don't want it to go, you won't want to forget it, like."

"It defines you," said one of his friends, as if providing a summary.

"It does is right—it fucking does," said the first man, as if this assessment were a small, neat miracle, pulling excitedly once, twice, on a cigarette.

"So, you're saying you should walk hand in hand with your mortality from the get-go, like, is it?" offered the attractive one with the distinctive locks.

"Too fucking right. You should be taught it at school, so you should," insisted the first man.

Pierce took this in, now with half an ear, now with all ears, while returning his gaze to the lone man to his left.

He had set down his coffee cup in its saucer fastidiously and moved on to his knife, cleaning every centimeter of both sides of its blade with a licked forefinger and napkin. Then it was back to the cup, whose rim he cleaned in the same way, circling it around with a moist forefinger as far as a centimeter from the handle on both sides, then, with a tiny flourish, drawing the napkin along it for good measure. Then back to the knife, giving its blade one last wipe with the napkin for luck, and sinking it into the broadest part of the scone, dividing it into two neat hemispheres, each of which he spread butter on evenly, ever so evenly.

For some reason, the sight of this little ritual put Pierce in mind of his first encounter with Senan, in the long room above the center-city pub, and his soft-spoken words about the obsessive tone of his prose. His remembrance of that comment had only lately stopped rankling.

Meanwhile, the three to the right of him were more and more excitedly immersed in their philosophic talk.

"That's the point, that's why we're put here, it's why we're sitting here, to learn to live with it, to live *through* it, and make friends with—with that fact—that's the point, that's the secret."

"Yeah, it's a bit like that saying, what's this it is, ahm, you should live every minute like it's your last, and at the same time like you'll be around forever and ever."

"Right, right, isn't that your man, Alexander the Great, that said that—or rather the writer, the American, what's-her-face?"

After his coffee, Pierce took an unhurried shower on the second floor and went up by a spiraling staircase to the third, where the maze of cubicles was. Stopping at the top to transfer his locker key on its band of faded, flaking plastic from his wrist to his ankle, he padded down the narrow passageway lined on either side with booths whose doors, each one pushed out and seeming to shield an anticipatory hush, were painted a glossy black that gave a sketchy, liquid reflection of his towel-girt torso in transit. A monitor showing silent pornography was perched on a single bracket a few feet from the ceiling on the end wall, and at Pierce's approach the shot switched to one of perfectly shaped spheres of gleaming butter-yellow buttocks pumping with blind, even, determined diligence.

In the erratic light shed by the television screen Pierce could make out a pair of smooth, bulky calves that had just emerged from one of the pair of end cubicles. He deliberately took his time in reaching them. When he did, he saw they belonged to the sideburned man from downstairs, both of whose thickish biceps were encircled by tattoos in a once-but-nowadays-not-quite-so-in-vogue serpentine Celtic design, and whose eyes, Pierce now noticed, were large, drooping, supremely nonexpectant.

Pierce lingered near the doorway for a moment, glancing with conscious detachment from the screen above to a point close to the man's eyes, which watched him steadily, with that near-hopeless worn-out expression. At last, deciding to take as a signal an apparent deepening of their despondence, he leaned tentatively toward and then entered abruptly alongside him.

At once the man closed and locked the door behind him. As they collapsed together onto the vinyl mattress, Pierce's mouth closed hungrily on the other man's. He responded for the first minute with an indulgent, almost put-upon air; then, leaning back against the bolster, he let the towel fall from his hips and pushed Pierce down. Tentative, Pierce licked the low-slung, rather meager balls. More committedly, he drew his tongue along the underside of the jutting synthetic-tasting cock, tongued the swollen purple rim of the glans lovingly. He smeared his lower lip with a globule of precum that oozed out, glinting, before his eyes, and took the smooth-shafted penis halfway, then fully, in his mouth, glancing up to see the mouth of his companion contort in a grimace of gratification that looked remarkably like nausea.

Inspired somehow by this, Pierce reared up and, walking on his knees on each side of the man's torso, he whipped off his towel, brought his crotch directly in front of the man's face and hissed at him to lick his balls.

At once Pierce could see the spell was broken for the other man: The strong body wilted instantaneously beneath him, the face lost its expression of tense queasy craving and took on instead a small sour smile, filled with a mild repulsion and dismay. Sure enough, when Pierce looked down, the erection was gone.

The man lay silently looking at him, his eyes enlivened now by a glow more sardonic than lustful.

"You all right?" asked Pierce.

"Tired," he said offhandedly.

They sat in silence for a minute, smoking cigarettes from Pierce's pack.

"I caught some of your conversation in the coffee bar," Pierce said. "It was very articulate, very . . . pertinent."

The other man grinned, radiating indifference, but a bit shame-faced, a bit annoyed, all the same. He shrugged one solid shoulder. "That's the kind of bollocks you come out with when you're full of aftershocks, isn't it?" Crushing his cigarette in a plastic dish, he left the cubicle with a perfunctory "Seeya," which Pierce answered with a stiff little wave.

He stayed on for another few seconds, rolling the butt of his cigarette in his fingers thoughtfully. Then, binding his towel around him and wedging his cigarette pack between the cloth and his hip bone, he left the booth and went back down the passage, past two men humping in a dark corner at the top of the stairs, which he descended, entering the steam room just off the coffee bar.

A tall, shaven-headed man sat facing the door on the tiered benches, his towel draped on the pine slats beneath him. When Pierce entered, his large, open features looked alert as an owl's in the light that fell on him. Awkwardly, Pierce hoisted himself onto the same bench and sat against the wall with one knee pressed against his chest. The minutes passed as they sat like this, Pierce's head against the wall, the other man's hanging as though in contemplation, the only sounds those of the odd snatch of distant chatter or the occasional creak of the slats beneath them.

Then the man lifted his head and, as though continuing after a pause in conversation, said in a Belfast accent that he'd come straight to the sauna from the theater: he was in a performance made up of dance and monologue in which he'd a part as a satyrlike entity personifying, he divulged with a wide smile, *la petite mort*. He'd hopes that later it might go on a small countrywide tour, said it was possible they could do it at Galway, Sligo, places like that. Had Pierce seen any of the theater-festival shows, he wondered. Pierce hadn't seen any, was barely aware it was on.

For several minutes they chatted like this, all the time aware of their humbly nude, firm-fleshed bodies tensed toward each other with the will for release. To the man's Northern accent Pierce was sensually attuned: its plangent, carrying lilt described for him a world of seductive secrets—secrets feral, thrilling. At the sensuous music in it, Pierce smiled purely, blatantly, right into the man's eyes. Perhaps he missed at points the surface gist of the words the stranger spoke, but he was all the while carried willingly with their seductive underflow, slow, liquid, elemental. Caressingly, with hushed, quiet excitement, their wills flowed and conjoined in a wonderful mutuality and with an urgency, hushed and pleased and eager, that carried them, caressingly, elementally, toward pure bodily merging, a coming together in fast, vital lostness.

"Don't stop talking," Pierce whispered when they were in the stall he'd occupied not ten minutes previous. "Please, keep talking." He lay balanced on the small of his back at the edge of the thin mattress, the soles of his feet planted square on the clammy wall of the booth. The Northerner stood between his legs, holding, now lightly, now tightly, the raised thighs. Shuffling forward, lurching at first, in one thrust he plunged with welcome depth into him. Pierce gasped, and listened in wonder to the other gasp and murmur something continuous, something mantra-like, primal, senseless, in reveled-in obsessive obedience, as, moisture dripping from his jawline, he tipped forward over him and they rocked in rhythmic unison, the Northerner all the while maintaining his masterful depth, then easing, easing back, and arching his lithe frame to sheathe himself fully again in the other; then back, withdrawing, again; and again forward, faster now, in supremely smooth, full, full movements. In an absolute pure synchronicity of lost sensation they moved, rocked, each pair of eyes held on the other in mesmerized concentration, the Northerner's mobile mouth moving, emitting its grave continuous murmurings, its mantra-like, soft, strong, knowing, sensuous music, bereft of ordinary sense but drenched magically with the sensual. By this sound, as if almost it seeped from their full connection, both clenched and smooth, within him, Pierce was utterly, powerfully lifted, and lost from himself.

Afterward, when the Belfast man wrapped him in his arms and told him he was beautiful, Pierce was embarrassed and felt a discomforting twinge of derision; at the same time, he was moved enough to reply, with a level of sincerity unusual for him in these situations, "You're beautiful," while realizing with a jolt it was something he'd never told anyone before.

An awkward moment followed, not straightaway but gradually, in which it was difficult to know how to proceed from this tenderness. Pierce, irritated by the tension and moved by an overwhelming urge to go back to his bedsit, kissed the dancer on the lips hastily and slipped out of the cubicle without another word.

When he'd showered and dressed and was on his way to return his locker key, he went by the stairwell where the Northerner was sitting cross-legged in an alcove. Pierce flashed him a conspiratorial grin as he passed on, but he was grabbed back by the crook of his arm, and into his hand was pressed a slip of paper—a fragment of the flyer for the dancer's show. On the blank side he'd written, "I would like to take you out for a drink. What do you think?" with his number scribbled underneath.

When Pierce returned to his room, he lay down and slept deeply for hours.

He rose late and ate something meager, then wrote for an hour without stopping, while on a clothesline strung across the lawn below, a bedsheet, peripherally visible from where he sat, flapped irately in a new-sprung gale. He felt he could finally see, if still hazily, to the end of the novel, which ultimately was about the perhaps-fortunate aspects in the failure of the relationships of two pairs of men, each made up of a younger and older man, all of whom have been friends and occasionally sex partners.

At the end of the hour, he lit a fire and sat watching the flames flicker, tentative, around the briquettes. Unconsciously, he took up from his lap Senan's logbook, which he'd leaned on as he wrote. The lined notebook opened loosely in his hands at a filled central section. His eyes skimmed the controlled, cursive script in which the notes and observations, each one about five to eight lines and separated with characteristic regularity by a single line; aside from Senan's own personal thoughts they included quotations from Pirandello,

Schopenhauer, Wittgenstein, and many others, one under the other. Pierce had to smile at these collected insights from such an array of intellectual heavyweights. It was ironic, in light of the strong suspicion of pure intellectualism Senan always had when it came to the sphere of poetry. His own poetry Pierce still did not like; he still thought it overstated, too didactic, certainly too intellect-based for a poet who so distrusted the intellectual approach when it came to his chosen medium. Senan once had called himself a minor poet, and Pierce, in guilty secret, had wondered if he had overrated himself.

He turned a page to a place where he'd inserted in recent weeks a number of notes Senan had written. Most of these were inconsequential, affectionate little communications he'd been in the habit of leaving around the house for Pierce. One, however, was the valedictory note he left when he died; another was a passage cut from a longer letter Senan sent him one weekend from his sister's house at Skibbereen, months after they met—a passage inspired by an intermittent anxiety of Pierce's. It read:

> When death comes finally, you won't be the same person you are now, but rather—if you've the will, as I believe you do, to acquire real peace of mind—one whom life has modified with a radicalness as subtle as it will be gradual, so that, even despite the last desperate residues of instinctive resistance, there'll be a deep-seated preparedness for, and acceptance of, your passing.

He'd saved this more for its eloquence than its power to reassure. Now it seemed redundant and, for some reason, it shamed him; without a thought, he leaned over and let it slip from his fingers into the fire. He sat back in the tatty, sunken armchair, glimpsing his young face suffused with strange, confused resentment in a hand mirror propped on the window ledge, and thinking of how understanding

Senan was, of his sad, wise humor—and how oppressive he, Pierce, sometimes found these qualities. Impulsively he stood, the open note-book in his hands, and, suddenly slowly and ceremoniously, he placed it facedown also on the fire.

He watched the flames slowly take hold, and felt purged, or rather, enjoyed the anticipation of feeling purged. He had held this logbook as a sacrosanct thing; but that was illusory. His life, his being, whether young or aging, long or short—that was sacrosanct.

The other notes had fallen free onto the rug when he stood up. He picked them up. They were the occasional love notes, begin-ning, "Darling Pierce," "My lovely Pierce . . ." With a feeling of necessary brutality, he dropped them onto the hard covers of the commonplace book, which the flames were slowly lapping and edging around. There was one more at his feet, lying faceup, the vulgarly called suicide note. He hesitated before picking it up, then stood with it in his hand.

> TO ALL CONCERNED,
>
> I CHOOSE TO MAKE MY FLEETING LIFE THE MORE FLEETING STILL, BEFORE MY SICKNESS GETS TOO DREARILY UNMANAGEABLE—AND BECAUSE EVEN THE THINGS THAT UPLIFT LIFE I FIND TOO HARD AND SUPERFICIAL TO BEAR.
>
> FORGIVE WHAT MIGHT SEEM MY WEAKNESS.
>
> SENAN

Pierce read it again, then again, coolly conscious it was to be for the last time. Then, to ensure it didn't lie lingeringly in the fireplace waiting to be reached by the flames the notebook for the most part obscured, he lit it with the lighter he took from on top of the cigarette pack on the mantelpiece, and let it burn almost to his fingers, then threw away the remaining scrap.

He wanted to get out of the room, to go for a walk in the open air. He picked up the cigarettes, made to put them with the lighter in the breast pocket of his shirt. But something impeded them. He took it out. It was the fragment of flyer with the dancer's number.

He moved to throw it into the fire but, reflecting, stopped himself, put it on the mantelpiece after a moment, and cast a last protracted look at the logbook smoldering by degrees on the grate.

2. An Ideal Couple
By Jim Cory

THEY MET IN a hustler bar the year Tom came out. The establishment, called Roscoe's, consisted of one windowless room in which there were to be found from mid-afternoon onward a besotted assortment of middle-aged disability cheats, pocket-picking drag queens, trust-fund drunks, and the skeeviest male prostitutes on Spruce Street, all of whom used it for a headquarters. It was the clientele, more than anything, that drew Tom. That and the cheap beer.

On the evening in question, Tom had just finished using the ladies' room, which no female person had probably ever entered, and where a Quaalude or a small quantity of coke could be bartered for a hand job or a five-dollar bill. There he ingested a line of snowy powder and, conspicuous in gray flannel slacks, a blue cotton shirt, navy blazer and patterned red tie, was bustling toward the door, trailed by many eyes, some lustful, some venomous.

Tom was on his way to a concert. Halfway to the door, a hand closed on his shoulder. The hand tugged him, almost lifting, in the direction of the bar. A thrill of imminent adventure transcended the panicky millisecond of indignation he experienced. Tom found himself yielding. A pair of slightly protuberant eyes the color of seawater, under a shock of gray brown hair, stared into his own.

"BUY YA A DRINK?" shouted the chubby apparition. It was a command as much as a question.

Whether it was the sheer brazenness of this maneuver—Tom had long since learned to deflect free drinks at Roscoe's—or because he really would've preferred getting drunk on top of the cocaine to squirming through another Philadelphia Orchestra concert in the far reaches of the leg-constricting Academy of Music, Tom acquiesced. "I'M STEVE," shouted the bloated benefactor, who raised a ten spot above his head and waved it back and forth, like a gleeful child.

Two Budweisers appeared. They were off and running.

Tom, twenty-three, thought anyone older than twenty-six was not only over the hill but so far past it as to have disappeared into the horizon. Steve, he figured, was . . . forty-five? fifty? Age alone ruled him out as a sex partner.

Tom lived at home with his parents in the suburbs. He told Steve all about Penn State and what he planned to do, which was get a job with an arts organization. Normally, Tom's discourse on ambition—thoroughly laced with an unself-conscious arrogance—bored people after three minutes. Steve actually paid attention. Not only that, he kept buying beers. At one point late in the evening, it occurred to Tom that politeness dictated he reciprocate. This gesture surprised and pleased Steve. It seemed to seal some kind of deal. When the mustachioed barkeep bellowed, "Last call!" at 1:49 A.M., the two of them were just starting on the four extra Budweisers they'd had the "prescience" (Tom's word) to order.

"'Tis a pleasure to have many," Tom said, quoting Chaucer on the subject of books. Steve howled.

Tom woke the next morning on a sofa in the living room of a Center City town house. His brain had morphed into a glutinous mass of frog's eggs. He felt some vital energy leaking away through an invisible orifice and stuck his fingers in his ears. He removed them a second later and opened an eye. "Ugh," he said. He heard water splash somewhere behind his head.

On the wall opposite the sofa, a handsome young man, maybe twenty-five, with blond-brown hair and startling green-blue eyes, stared down out of a large painting executed in accurate if splashy fashion. Tom peered at it through a filter of pained brain cells. It took a full minute to recognize the figure as Steve. Some wholly different incarnation gazed out from that canvas: radiant, preppy, thin.

"HAVE A BLOODY!" Steve emerged from the kitchen in a blue terrycloth bathrobe, a glass in each hand. The glasses sprouted pale and slender celery stalks. Wedges of sliced lemon graced their brims. Tom squeezed the lemon over the textury red surface—pure politeness—and took a big gulp of what tasted like damn near raw vodka. He polished it off in five minutes.

Tom's visits to the town house on Juniper Street grew frequent. He and Steve became drinking buddies who cruised, or cruising buddies who drank—it wasn't quite clear which. The relationship seemed wholly uncharacteristic of Tom, who distrusted older people, especially men. Tom and Steve launched their weekend evenings with beers in Steve's living room before proceeding to the round of bars, which began and ended in Roscoe's. From Roscoe's they repaired once more to Steve's, where Tom took to sacking out on the sofa in the finished basement, one morning even emerging "naked as a jay bird" (Steve's description) with an overnight guest in tow, though that practice ended when Steve laid down the rules. ("Tommy, you can crash here whenever you want. *But no numbers.*") Steve, it turned out, was finishing a long-delayed dissertation in psychology and working as a staff psychologist at a social-services agency. Tom, who'd majored in English, had settled for waiting tables and working in bookstores after trying, and failing, to land a white-collar job. He thought at some point he might return to school for a graduate degree.

They made an odd, if complimentary, pair. Steve enjoyed Tom's beer-fueled self-assurance and wit. He could see right through the smart-ass know-it-all-ism to the naïveté underneath. He chalked Tom's little romantic dramas up to age. Tom liked it that Steve was open to being teased. In warm weather, for instance, Steve always wore extra-large shirts that he never tucked in. These masked a considerable, and growing, tummy. "I see you're wearing your muumuu," Tom would say. Or, "Been to the gynecologist lately?"

Steve would frown in mock annoyance, tap his cigarette at the ashtray and snicker, "Oh, fuck you."

Some evenings they would down an entire case of Budweiser while recalling exploits from their drinking careers. In Steve's case, the worst thing that had ever happened was the time he got fired from a teaching position at a local university for propositioning a student when drunk. The student, invited to Steve's for dinner, filed a complaint, insisting Steve had come on to him. Steve maintained that the student had come on to *him,* that the whole thing had been—in one of two versions Tom would hear over the years—either a setup or a misunderstanding.

"Once his father got involved, I never had a chance." Steve said, stubbing out a Marlboro.

Fairly soon in their relationship, use of terms such as "blackout" and "dry drunk" caused Tom and Steve to realize they were both AA dropouts. Neither planned to stop drinking again. Steve genuinely preferred inebriation to sobriety, and Tom now had Steve to bail him out whenever his own drunken escapades resulted in disaster. As, increasingly, happened.

Like the night Tom, half in the bag, rolled his station wagon in a field. He crawled out of the car and saw a factory in the distance. Tom stumbled to the factory gate and knocked at the guardhouse door. "Call the police," he said. "There's been a terrible accident." He woke in a cell, wearing his Academy of Music finery minus tie, belt, and shoelaces. Released on his own recognizance, he took a bus to City Hall.

Steve was having a party that afternoon. Tom walked to the town house and knocked on the door.

"Can I come in?"

"Tommy! My God, what's happened to you?"

Steve filled the tub and brought Tom a Bloody. Two hours later, the party was on and Tom was the center of attention.

It's hard to say if they were like-minded spirits or similarly damaged souls. They never went to bed together but the relationship grew to resemble that of lovers who evolve into genial, if sexless, companions. The difference in their ages—almost a generation—conferred on Steve the Grumpy Uncle role. When Tom moved to a small, one-room apartment in Center City, Steve helped him furnish it. When he set out to take a graduate degree, in spite of having no savings, Steve wrote a check to pay the bursar.

They talked about everything, or it seemed that way to Tom. Parents, schools, siblings. Steve had grown up in New London, Connecticut and still had family there. He especially liked to hear about Tom's love life. Tom was in and out of relationships large and small in search of the Ideal Mate. His Ideal Mate, he told Steve, "has a perfect ass and reads Pound and Plato." Steve, who'd never read either, was always anxious to hear about what Tom did in bed with these revolving-door lovers, but Steve never, as far as Tom could remember, talked about his own relationships.

When Tom finally "met someone"—a big-lipped blond named Brian—Steve seemed almost as excited as Tom. Steve liked Brian, though he didn't like the way Brian controlled Tom by nagging, and, later, provoking arguments in public once Tom had a few under his belt.

About a year after Tom took up with Brian, Steve's sister died and Steve moved from Philadelphia back to New London to be near his

father. He bought an old apartment house a block from Ocean Beach
Park. Steve invited Tom and Brian to New London for a long
weekend. Brian, bored with their drinking, left Tom and Steve sitting in a bar called Frank's and went off to explore the town on his
own. Tom and Steve ended up drinking all weekend.

Tom's relationship with Brian, fragile enough when Tom was
going out and getting drunk every night, didn't survive his newfound
sobriety. After he went back to AA and stopped drinking, Tom began
standing up to Brian's nagging and confrontations. They decided to
end their relationship, and Brian quickly found another drunk to
take up with. He continued living with Tom for a few months, and
every night Tom heard Brian and his new lover, Michael, screaming
and throwing things at each other through the wall between bedrooms. *It's like being an extra on the set of my previous relationship,* he
thought. Finally Brian moved out. Tom phoned Steve in New
London to tell him the news. Steve told Tom that he, too, had quit
drinking.

"I was getting started on the beer every morning around 10:00,
Tommy," he explained. "The tenants knew that if they wanted anything done, they had to get hold of me before noon. Otherwise, I'd be
potted."

It had reached the point, Steve told Tom, where one day he had
found himself unable to urinate. The day stretched into a day and a
night, and then into the next day, at which point he became concerned. The doctor he went to see directed Steve to lie down on the
examining table, then plugged a stethoscope in Steve's ears and set the
opposite end of it to his stomach.

"Hear that sloshing around? That's all the fluid your body can't
eliminate 'cause your kidneys have shut down."

The doctor scratched out three prescriptions.

"If you'd come in here even twenty-four hours from now, it
might've been too late," he said. "And here's a piece of advice,

whether you want it or not. If you drink again, and I mean *at all*, it will be too late."

So Steve stopped drinking.

That year, Steve started teaching psychology at the University of Rhode Island. The next year he got a part-time job as a youth counselor at a social-services agency, specializing in substance abuse and AIDS services. The year after that, he started buying real estate. He bought a duplex in New London, a house in Mystic, then another New London duplex. He took on mortgage after mortgage.

Tom came up to New London several times in the summer and fall, usually with his newest lover.

"Tommy"—Steve said, steering him aside on one occasion—"I hope you're taking precautions."

"What do you mean?"

"Are you using condoms?"

"No."

"Can I ask you a question?"

"Go ahead."

"Do you want to die young?"

Tom started using condoms.

Tom and Steve, and whatever new lover Tom had in tow, would go out to dinner at a waterside restaurant, the kind serving cheeseburgers, french fries, or fried clams in greasy paper holders, to be consumed at splintery picnic tables by a dock. Once Steve signed them up for a riverboat excursion on the Thames, complete with Dixieland band. Steve liked playing social director. He took pictures and sent Tom copies. Even though Tom sometimes found these occasions a little "gin and Judy," he went along without complaining.

Steve without booze seemed a bit strange at first, but then Tom realized it was because his friend was forced to fill up what had been his drinking time with other activities. He still loved going to bars

and restaurants that served alcohol, where, as in the old days, he eye-
balled the crotches of all the young waiters passing by. This had
amused Tom when, sodden and uproarious, they rolled from bar to
bar in downtown Philadelphia. Now, however, he noticed Steve's
lurid glances earning hateful looks from waiters, restaurant man-
agers, and other customers.

One early evening, as they sat facing each other at a restaurant
in Mystic, a hawkfaced waiter with slicked-back blond hair
emerged from the kitchen, balancing a loaded tray. Steve turned to
his left, then swiveled to the right, in an effort to "check out the
basket." He repeated this gesture when the waiter came out of the
kitchen again.

Tom felt himself flush. "Steve," he said, clearing his throat.
"Work the mirrors."

"What?"

"Work the mirrors."

"What do you mean?"

"OK. This mirror behind me?"

"Yeah."

"You can use it to see everything you need to see. And a lot more
discreetly."

"Was I being too obvious?"

"Uh, let's just put it this way. You were practically inside his
pants."

Tom rotated his spoon in his hands. "If you want a good look
without drawing attention to yourself," he said, "you gotta work the
mirrors."

"What if there isn't a mirror?"

"There's always a mirror, Steve. There's a mirror behind the
bottles on the bar. Use the windows; they reflect everything. Pull out
your fucking compact, for Christ's sakes."

They both laughed, and that was the end of it.

Steve talked about sex a lot. Driving through New London in his BMW, or the Jeep Cherokee he bought to replace it, he sometimes nearly steered into stop signs watching hot guys walk down the street. Being engaging, he often developed friendships with men far younger than himself. Sometimes they were current—or former—clients who'd been referred to him by a court on account of substance-abuse problems. Some were guys he hired to cut lawns or paint. Some were young academics, who looked to Steve as an authority on adolescent psychology.

One day Steve called Tom to tell him about his latest piece of real estate, a condo in Provincetown. The two-bedroom third-floor apartment on Freeman Street overlooked the town library at the corner and had a view of the harbor.

Steve furnished the condo the way he furnished his house in New London: homey and haphazard. A chair and ottoman of tan-colored leather. An overstuffed cream-colored sofa bed. A Colonial rocker. A fake bearskin rug. He placed his dining-room table next to the window overlooking Commercial Street and the harbor. Post-it Notes ("Call Dad." "Pick up shoes.") littered the table. Mail and other bills sat stacked on the windowsill.

Tom became Steve's regular condo guest, coming up for a week at least twice a year. He had the room facing Provincetown Library and was free to come and go as he pleased. ("Just don't bring back any numbers," Steve said.) On Tom's arrival, the two of them would drive to the A&P where they bought six-packs of Diet Coke, assorted pastries, Baby Ruth bars, ice cream and—Steve's concession to a healthy diet—cantaloupes. A typical Steve breakfast consisted of a bowl of carefully sliced melon wedges speared with toothpicks stuck on miniature seashells, a cherry or apricot danish glistening with sugar, and a pint of chocolate or strawberry ice cream, consumed between cigarette puffs.

Steve liked to watch the comings and goings on Commercial

Street. He was especially enamored of a restaurant opposite the library called Big Walt's. He ate lunch there daily and grew chummy with the rotund Walt and his lover, Jimmy, who between them owned a half-dozen restaurants and considerable real estate in Provincetown. Tom and Steve would eat breakfast on the condo deck overlooking the library. Tom marveled at the dish Steve collected.

"See that guy?" Steve said one morning. "He got fired from the Gifford House."

A round-shouldered figure with a monk-like fringe of brown hair slouched down the street, hands in pockets.

"What for?"

"Didn't come to work 'cause he was drunk. Second time. So they canned him."

The man halted, looking from left to right.

"Then," Steve continued, "the idiot phoned in a bomb threat."

"You're kidding?"

"No. He called up at about nine on a Sunday night and told who-ever answered that there was a bomb in the building."

"What'd they do?"

"They evacuated. They have to."

"What happened?"

"They called the cops and the cops traced the number. Right now he's out on bail, awaiting sentencing."

The figure glanced up at Tom and Steve, scowled, then hurried on.

It was early September and chilly. Steve wore a bathrobe, Tom an oversized gray sweatshirt. Steve lit a fresh cigarette. A brown-haired woman about thirty-five appeared walking a golden retriever.

"Oh-oh," Steve said, pushing the first spoon of Häagen-Dazs in his mouth, "there goes Betty."

"She doesn't look happy," Tom observed.

"That's because she's drunk and on coke every night."

"How do you know?"

"She owns the first-floor condo. I see her coming in at two in the morning."

He paused. "She had sex with her dog at a party."

"What!"

Betty dug in her pocketbook for something while her pet lifted its leg at the library Dumpster.

"She was drunk and started making out with it."

"'Oh, c'mon, Steve. Where'd you hear that?"

"Jimmy. Him and Big Walt know everything that goes on in this town."

After breakfast, Tom would pack his knapsack and bike to the beach. Steve spent the day doing chores or sitting at the table by the window, smoking, punching numbers into a calculator, scratching notes to himself. At night the two of them would walk to the video-rental store on Commercial Street and rent a tape. Steve kept his eye out for live entertainment and two or three nights during Tom's visit they'd hit the Town House to catch a drag act or go to The Moors to hear a piano playing comedian named Lenny with whom Steve had gotten to be pals.

As the years passed, Steve went out less and less. Apart from lunch or dinner at Big Walt's, he rarely left the condo. A recession had substantially reduced the value of his properties, and Steve was fending off banks and creditors. Instead of going out, he sat by the window shuffling through bills and mortgage statements. When he and Tom did venture forth, Steve would have to sit down and rest every other block. He'd gotten that big. The last time they went to the video store, Steve had had Tom call a taxi. After that, he simply sent Tom to get the movie. He'd also developed a racking, phlegmy cough.

Tom began to notice a certain distance, an irritability, which he suspected wasn't limited to himself, and which he thought might be related to Steve's finances, or health. Steve became obsessed with his weight and started taking diuretics. Tom stopped kidding him about it. Steve also grew openly suspicious of people and their motives. If one of his houseguests offered to take him to lunch, it was because they were trying to maneuver him into buying them dinner. When Tom and the newest love of his life, Jeff, borrowed the condo for a weekend, they left behind a pound of French coffee with a thank-you note. Tom phoned later to ask if Steve liked the coffee. "Oh," Steve said, "I just thought it was leftover coffee you didn't want anymore."

Steve also became quick to take offense, even cutting off people he'd known for years. When Glen, one of Steve's friends from college, came to visit with a new and much younger lover, Steve took them both to a well-known restaurant on the water.

"We'd only just been served," Steve recalled to Tom, a few weeks later, "and all of a sudden this fucking New York queen sort of tilts his head back and starts sniffing. 'What's the matter?' I said. He says . . ." Steve pursed his lips and tilted his chin a fraction of an inch. "'Sewage.'" He paused. "'Sewage.'" he repeated, rolling his eyes and stamping out a cigarette. "You'd better believe they're not staying *here* again."

Tom began coming up once a year instead of two or three times a season. He did that for two years in a row. Steve was quiet a lot and seemed to have run out of funny stories to tell. The next year Tom decided to make it a four-day weekend instead of a week. Steve didn't say anything, but the atmosphere became strained. One afternoon during his visit, Tom stood at the sink scrubbing breakfast dishes. Steve came up behind him and screamed: "Tommy! YOU'RE WASHING THE DISHES WRONG!" Tom left a day early, with Steve in a sulk. They barely said good-bye. Six months later, when Steve called to invite him up, he told Steve he couldn't make it on account of a business trip.

The next summer, Tom and Jeff were staying up the Cape in Orleans, with Jeff's brother. Feeling guilty about turning down yet another invitation to visit Steve, Tom suggested they drive to Provincetown and take Steve to dinner. Surprised and pleased to get Tom's call, Steve said he'd be ready at 8:00. When Tom and Jeff arrived, there was no answer. They knocked again.

A light appeared. Steve opened the door, wiping his drained face with a washcloth. "I'm sorry," he said. "I fell asleep."

It was Labor Day weekend. A line of people stood outside Big Walt's, waiting for tables to open up. Steve complained to the waitress about lukewarm coffee, then to Jimmy about the waitress. He smoked nonstop and kept asking Tom questions about Orleans. Where were they staying? What were the good places to eat? When it was time to leave, he tried to persuade Tom not to leave a tip. Tom was happy and relieved to walk Steve back to the condo.

"When he answered the door I thought for a moment he was drinking again," Jeff said, when they were back in the car.

Tom agreed that Steve looked pretty bad.

"And his paranoia is completely out of control. It's just raging."

"Do you think so?"

"All those questions about where we were staying and what we were doing in Orleans. I mean, obviously he didn't believe we were *in* Orleans. He thought we'd been in Provincetown the whole week and just never called him."

"I don't think he's well, frankly."

"How could he be? He smokes constantly. He's at least a hundred pounds overweight. He can hardly get up those stairs. At some point he's just going to drop over."

Three months went by. Tom got a Christmas card from Steve but neglected to send one back. Then, in the early summer, one of Steve's hand-scrawled-in-ballpoint notes arrived. "Tom," it read. "Hate to be the bearer of bad news, but I've had to sell the condo. Health's not good. I need to rest a while + get my strength back. Steve."

Tom decided to phone.

"Steve," he said, "what's going on?"

"Tommy, is that you? Where are you?"

"Philadelphia. What's the matter with your health?"

"It's not good. I've got congestive heart failure."

"What does that mean?"

"I'm not sure, but they tell me it means my circulatory system is compromised. On a practical level, it means I can't walk across the room without having to sit down and catch my breath. I had to stop teaching. I'll probably have to give up my practice."

"Are you still smoking?"

"I'm cutting down," Steve said. "How are you doing? How's Jeff?"

"Jeff . . . left. He went to New York to take a PhD in social work."

"Well, scratch another one. How long were you two together?"

"Five years."

"I'm sorry," Steve said.

Tom didn't want to talk about Jeff with Steve. Jeff had been the one Tom was going to spend his life with. For three years, everything seemed fine. People described them as an ideal couple. Then, strained by the need to hold down jobs they both hated, by the death of one of Tom's closest friends, by the terminal illness of Jeff's mother, and by what the therapist Tom finally engaged told him later was his own selfish and demanding nature—their relationship unraveled.

"The problem with you is that you don't know how to love anyone," Jeff said and started packing. Tom, furious, at first disbelieved Jeff would ever leave, then grew impatient for Jeff to be gone, then convinced himself Jeff would return. But months went by. The mornings he woke by himself in the bed they'd shared were the worst he'd ever had. He became convinced he was going out of his mind.

Six months later, in mid-August, Tom received a letter stamped with Steve's New London return address. His own name was inscribed in a blocky, unfamiliar hand. *Steve's dead,* he thought. He tore the letter open.

"Dear Folks," it began. "We are sorry to inform you that Steve has terminal lung cancer. It was diagnosed about a month ago and the prognosis was that he would live another year or so. However, on Friday, August 1, he was told that the cancer was rapidly spreading to other vital organs and that, barring divine intervention, he had maybe a week or two or three at most to live."

The letter was signed by Steve's cousin, Rick, and his wife, Sheila.

Tom reached Steve by phone at the hospital. Steve assured him the letter was "somewhat alarmist."

"Listen, Tommy," Steve said. "My cousin and his wife and some friends are taking me to Provincetown for my birthday. They're going to drive me up in an RV. I want you to come."

What in the world are they thinking? Tom thought. He considered the whole idea of the trip foolish and began rehearsing excuses not to go.

At the end of the week, Tom flew to the Cape and took a taxi to the Truro motel where Steve and his friends had made reservations. Steve's group hadn't arrived yet and he had a few hours to kill. He decided to rent a bike. He rode the bike into Provincetown, then back to the motel.

The RV arrived hours later. Steve lay in a foldout bed in the back, tethered to a canister of oxygen. He had lost about a third of his weight. His hair, now thoroughly white, stood out in tufts and cowlicks. *He looks like a corpse,* Tom thought. *Except for his eyes.* The eyes held all the life that seemed to have deserted the rest of his body. They also lacked the hard squint of suspicion.

"Tommy," he said, "get me my slippers, wouldya? And that walker!" It amazed Tom how quickly he fell back into doing Steve's bidding.

Using a special wood ramp he'd built, Tom's cousin Rick, a contractor, unloaded from his pickup truck a three-wheeled scooter with a chair on it. Steve inched his way to the scooter with a walker and climbed into the seat. He started the motor, gripped the throttle, and glided across the parking lot toward the motel-room door. Steve's New London friends—all staying in rooms above and next to Steve's—hooted and clapped. Steve waved to them before dismounting. Steve quickly made himself the center of attention, issuing orders and wisecracks from his gurney in the room. He directed Tom to wheel the gurney to the sliding glass doors, so he could see the water.

Later, Tom excused himself, mounted his bike, and rode into Provincetown for something to eat. He parked the bike in front of a pizza place. The late afternoon sun divided the patio out front into zones of light and shade. Tom bought two pieces of cheese pizza and sat on a bench to watch the crowds pass. It was mostly guys in their twenties and thirties. He was now forty-three, a few years older than Steve had been when they met. Middle-aged. He remembered watching men in their forties when he was in his twenties, trying to guess what they might've looked like when they were young, wondering what he'd be like at that age. Impossible.

After Jeff left, Tom thought of himself as ready to retire from dating and sex. Six months later, when he began going out again, he found he attracted a different kind of man. Or men, since there had already been several. They were mostly in their early to mid-thirties, looking for a strong, seasoned guy who took care of himself. *I guess I'm what they call a Daddy*, he thought. He imagined Steve's mirth on hearing the term as applied to him but then considered that Steve had more pressing concerns. Still, Tom thought, *I'm back where I was in my twenties. That revolving door of dates and convenient little relationships. At some point I'll be too old even for that.*

Shirtless men in shorts or cutoffs walked past, some holding hands. Tom noted lots of couples, many dressed alike. Two guys went by in baggy khaki shorts, white socks and construction boots that looked as if they'd never seen a building site. Another couple, in their sixties, strolled along arm in arm. One of them was bald and had a thick white mustache. The other wore glasses and marched along on spindly, hairless legs. Tom studied the legs, fascinated, thinking how odd it was that guys in their twenties shaved off the leg hair that guys in their sixties would kill not to lose.

Someone was sitting next to him, balancing a paper plate with pizza on it. Someone attractive.

"Hello," Tom said.

"Hi," said the guy, whose name was David. David worked in a jewelry store in New Jersey. He had dark hair and a great tan. It was David's first visit to Provincetown and he and his best friend, Anthony—"The Ant"—were having a "fabulous" time. They'd been there a week and were leaving tomorrow, unfortunately.

"How about you?" David said.

"Actually I'm just here for the weekend. I'm staying in a motel in Truro," Tom said.

Tom heard a slow, thudding bass coming from down the street.

"How was the tea dance?" he said.

"Kind of boring. I like the beach better."

Tom bit his crust in half and noted, out of the corner of his eye, David inspecting his crotch.

"Where are you staying?"

"Ant and I rented a condo."

"Where?"

"Freeman Street."

"Really? Which building?"

"I don't know the number."

"Is it by the library?"

"Right across from it."

Steve must've sold the apartment furnished. Everything he'd had there—the overstuffed white couch, the brown leather chair with ottoman, the rocker, the VCR and TV, even the fake fur rug—remained. Brown bottles of tanning lotion and a pile of rainbow beach towels lay on the table by the window where Steve used to sit with his bills and mortgage payments.

The Ant emerged from the bathroom, toweling himself off. Unbelievably cute, Tom thought. Especially that rubbery butt that bounced to the back-and-forth swing of the towel. Tom and David disappeared into the room where Tom had always stayed.

David unbuttoned his blue-jean cutoffs and let them fall. A lime green Speedo glowed against his brown skin. "Ummmmm," Tom said, rolling the tip of his tongue across his upper lip. Barefooted, David kicked his shorts away. A long, slightly curved cock lay horizontally to the right of the crotch under the bathing suit. Tom walked over and drew two fingers along its length, pausing to caress the head, which took the shape of a fat acorn. He slipped a hand under the bathing suit and squeezed the whole plump package. David grinned as if there were not a thought or feeling inside him except that of anticipated pleasure, and Tom smiled back into David's smile, then pulled his own T-shirt off and flung it on a chair. He unbuttoned his khaki shorts, let them fall, kicked them away. Naked but for his boxers and black boots, he tugged David's Speedos down and kissed his mouth hard, eyes closed, his mouth a perfect seal over David's and they breathed each other's air while tongues pushed, touching teeth, cheeks, gums, throats.

Tom heard the door open slightly and opened his eyes. In the mirror above the dresser, he saw The Ant, nude but for the strawberry-colored bath towel around his neck.

"Mind if I join you?" he said.

When Tom got back to Truro he found Steve in his motel room, alone, alert, watching CNN. Steve hit the mute button. "Rick and Sheila went to the A&P," he said.

Apart from the fact that his days were, literally, numbered, something seemed odd. Tom realized it was because Steve wasn't smoking. He couldn't remember fifteen minutes when Steve hadn't been lighting up, smoking, or stabbing out a cigarette.

"I gave it up right after they diagnosed the cancer," Steve said.

"Was it hard?"

"I just threw 'em away, Tommy."

A giant dollar sign came on the screen next to a chart of some kind, both superimposed over a black-and-white photo of Wall Street.

"I went into therapy, too," he said.

"How come?"

"Lots of reasons. It's too much to go into." He paused. "Well, maybe not."

They sat without saying anything for a minute or so. Somewhere in Southeast Asia a ferry had capsized, spilling dozens of people to their deaths. A shot from a helicopter showed lifeboats struggling through rainy swells.

"You know," Steve said, "I was never good at relationships. That's my biggest regret. I never really had anybody in my life. Well"—he thought about it—"I had one relationship. With this guy, Gary. It lasted nine months."

"When was that?

"In my twenties."

Steve looked from Tom toward the glass doors that opened to the beach. A woman trudged in the direction of the motel, tugging two blond boys with plastic pails. Tom thought of the portrait in the house on Juniper Street, that picture he'd seen the first morning he woke on Steve's sofa.

"Where'd you meet him?"

"In graduate school. At UConn. He was a knockout, Tommy.

But we fought all the time." He paused. "I was drinking. He was still dating girls. I don't think it was meant to happen."

Then Steve changed the subject.

"Tommy, I want you to know you're the first person named in my will. I'm leaving you some money. It's not that much. Five thousand dollars. Find some way to use it."

"Thanks, Steve, that's very generous of you."

Steve stared at the TV screen and frowned.

"All the other people I left money to told me I didn't really have to do that for them," he said.

"Well, I don't know what they said, but what I'm saying is thank you very much. You've always been generous."

Steve snorted. They both laughed.

"OK," he said, "now go fuck yourself and get me a Diet Coke, would ya?"

Tom retrieved the cold can from the fridge under the sink, popped the top, and handed it to Steve.

"Steve," he said, "I had sex in your condo."

"Oh, c'mon, Tommy, that hardly matters now."

"No, I mean a half hour ago."

Steve rose on his back, almost jerking away the tube of oxygen clamped to his nostril.

"What!? You're kidding me!"

"No. I met this guy and started talking to him, and he suggested we go back to his place. It turned out to be the condo on Freeman Street."

"So you finally got laid there?"

"I finally got laid there."

"Whore!"

They both laughed. Someone knocked and Steve's cousin and his wife came in with bags of groceries, including cantaloupes, cookies, pies, Baby Ruths, and danish.

Later that night everyone went out to dinner. They used Rick's portable ramp to get Steve's scooter chair into Big Walt's, where Steve and his party occupied the premier table for the better part of an hour and a half. Then they loaded the chair into the truck and drove to The Moors, where Steve's friend Lenny was still the entertainer-in-residence. Steve was able to go down the ramp and into the bar, where Lenny kept throwing him jokes.

Sunday afternoon, as they helped Steve into the RV, Tom hugged him good-bye.

The pilot pushed the throttle of the Fokker steadily forward as the aircraft approached the end of the runway. It hopped into the air, jerked, righted in a split second, and climbed. The plane ascended to what Tom assumed must be five or six thousand feet. At 6:47 A.M. the Cape's end was the sand-covered sliver of a dying moon, tufted with pine canopies and tied with strips of gray asphalt, the stone phallus of Provincetown Monument rising above it.

I almost didn't go, Tom thought. *Imagine what you'd feel like if you hadn't gone?*

The plane leveled off over the broad, flat expanse of the bay. Someone behind him in the cramped nine-seater swung a camera at the window and clicked the shutter button. Someone rattled the pages of a *Boston Globe*. Most just stared out the window where, off to the right, a trawler spilled its foamy wake into the sea and, a little farther out, a pair of sailboats floated, seemingly motionless.

He probably wouldn't see Steve again. Steve had . . . weeks at most. Whatever he might think. *Steve,* he thought. Moving back and forth between poles of generosity and bitterness. Expecting to be betrayed. Making the same mistakes again and again. How not to repeat them? Anyway, he, Tom, had made worse ones. *What does that mean, that I'm flawed? Of course you're flawed. Who isn't flawed? I've done things that were so stupid, so selfish, so inconsiderate. . . .*

Steve. Whose pleasures had killed him without providing any real enjoyment. Who used pleasure to displace time. Who filled up his time with anger. Killing it, really, with anger.

Then the thought came to Tom that Steve, who'd lived as if it were a chore, and always by himself, who'd seemed so far from the reach of love, had loved him, Tom. Had always loved him. From the beginning. And had, somehow, chosen never to state it.

Why don't I ever think about love, Tom wondered. *I think about everything except that. I think about money, work, sex, people I hate. I never think about love. You don't even know what it is. You've never even seriously thought about it.*

Was it, he wondered, something beyond his reach? No, in fact, he had loved. He couldn't define it, but he had felt it with some people. It was there, or had been. Lately he had come to understand that it wasn't the instant attraction he'd believed in for so long, but something more subtle, something long term, a connection between two beings that was larger than either of them, that had to put down roots and grow. Jeff, for instance. Steve talking about someone named Gary, a name he'd never heard mentioned in twenty years. What held that in place? That mirage.

The plane made a wide turn over Boston Harbor and descended toward the runway at Logan. Tom looked at his watch. The twenty-minute trip had passed in seconds. Wheels hit the runway. The craft slowed, braked, fell in behind a jet taxiing toward the concourse. Another small plane came up behind them.

"Please wait till the plane is safely parked at the gate before unfastening your seat belts," said the pilot, without turning around.

And then they were parked and Tom was lifting his bags off the carousel to get the airport bus for his flight to Philly.

The memorial service, in New London, took place two months later in a bar on the Thames River. Lenny officiated from the piano. Tom was supremely grateful for Steve's decision not to have it in a church. A church would've been so un-Steve. At one point, while Lenny pounded the keys, enacting some bawdy song, he saw, reflected in the wall of windows behind the piano, a submarine moving downstream toward Long Island Sound from its base farther up the Thames. *How odd*, he thought. *That's what happens when you work the mirrors.*

And laughed out loud.

After Lenny finished, someone told a story about Steve's outrageous behavior in a New York bar. Tom liked hearing the stories people told, which were mostly about Steve's humor and kindness. They each seemed to know a different Steve, but nothing he heard that afternoon surprised him.

We hope this bookmark serves as a reminder to display the flag from sunrise to sunset on all days the weather permits, especially on...

New Year's Day
Inauguration Day
Martin Luther King Jr.'s Birthday
Lincoln's Birthday
Washington's Birthday
Easter Sunday
National Day of Prayer
Mother's Day
Armed Forces Day
Memorial Day *(half-staff until noon)*
Flag Day
Father's Day
Independence Day
Labor Day
Patriots Day
Constitution Day
Columbus Day
Veterans Day
Thanksgiving Day
Christmas Day
Election Days
State and Local Holidays

Disabled American Veterans
P.O. Box 14301
Cincinnati, Ohio 45250-0301

120085

A PRAYER FOR LUCK

If you think you can't,
You really must
In God and our soldiers,
Please keep the trust.
To keep us safe,
Day and night,
To stand in front
And faithfully fight.
In the name of freedom
And even love,
I pray for Grace
From the stars above.
That soon one day,
We can live in peace,
When fears subside,
World wars will cease.
With hope shining
From my eyes,
I ask for gifts
With the bright sunrise.
May luck and joy be
With all who know
That what you reap,
Is what you sow.

3. Manboobs

By Michael Van Devere

ON AUGUST 1 he moved in and by August 2 I was in love. Manboobs was in a state of metaphysical transition and needed a place to room. I needed a roommate. Days before, my fiancée had moved back to Minnesota. She didn't know why she was going there. She only said she was being forced from New York and our apartment by impending events, a repeat performance of sudden calamity visited upon an entire city. I forbade her to go—then helped her pack. And when we kissed good-bye, I felt estranged from all of womankind, as if her sudden departure was an act of treason.

It was a careless and immature reaction toward her instinct to survive, I confess. Explained in masculine terms: It confused me. We're safe, I assured her; we live in midtown Manhattan, here nothing grows and nothing dies. Perhaps she realized this already; saying so only confirmed her fears. My words, painted like an obtuse poet, acted as wind in her sails. She fled, and I, like a creeping vine, held on to the old habitat, asking, how will I pay the rent?

In the months after the Twin Towers collapsed, many New Yorkers grew troubled whenever they stepped outside of their apartment, including Miss Mouse. She dreaded crossing the avenues, which gave a clear view, if she looked south, of nothing. She didn't like nothing; the concept frightened her. New York was about everything, or at least lots of something, but never nothing.

In my way, I comforted her. I offered soothing advice like a sponge bath, cleansing her troubled nerves. It was a pragmatic exercise, and it worked temporarily. But when she saw nothing staring back at her from that gray space nearest Battery Park, she ran home and filled our apartment with blue. Gloomy blue. Bleak blue.

Blue saturated our existence. Everything in the apartment shared a blue tint: the couch, the bed, the walls, the floor. Blue sedated her. It calmed her nerves and impaled any instincts to breed. When the present altered its appearance, when I suggested a floral arrangement in autumn colors, Miss Mouse went berserk, injecting aquamarine into her veins.

The couch she took with her to Minnesota (soft blue Minnesota) had been reupholstered five times since we shared our apartment, blue shades flashing across it in dizzying tides until an aqua that belonged on the facade of a Miami hotel finally stuck. We were poor, constantly in the red, wearing postmodern threads; but Grandmother's chaise lounge was pampered like Cleopatra, given face-lifts on the dime.

The day Miss Mouse exited my life, she wrapped the couch in a blue sheet that made it look like a giant tampon. Two beefy movers carried it downstairs and into the moving van. They glowered with sweaty pride as if anticipating a scene along the road when Miss Mouse would oblige their burly lusts with a tour of her family pad. These thugs operate out of Queens, I warned her. Queens is worse than midtown! Look at them, nurtured their entire lives with animal sinew. They're treating the Mouse couch with false dignity, sheathed delight!

It's sad how Miss Mouse slipped through my fingers, the only person that really mattered, that fit perfectly. Worrisome thoughts swarmed me in her wake, pestering me, and for the first time, I trembled. I actually shook. That first night, the telephone rang at three in the morning. I hesitated, suspecting it was her. I envisioned her somewhere in Ohio, crying and wanting to know if I had changed much in the last twelve hours, if my behavior had somehow become original without her. Calling me that late was her way of testing me.

But it wasn't her.

A man spoke on the other end in a masculine tone gradually fading. Perhaps he called too late, and was tired, that he chose to employ only basic speech patterns. Or maybe, like me, he avoided language at three in the morning. He asked me if a room was available in my building. He lived in Queens and worked for a moving company. That day, a friend on a job had given him the heads-up that someone had just vacated my apartment. Since I lived in New York, maybe I planned to do the New York thing and rent out a room.

It hadn't occurred to me to rent. In my untested isolation, I thought only of Miss Mouse and her Mouse couch moving with speed through the womb of America. I needed to heal, reacquaint myself with the urban crowd, stand alone, surround myself by trends and pretty people and lots of drugs! The solitude gig would be my healing agent. But his voice, steeped in late-night manhood, severed all previous thoughts and I agreed. His offer to rent on a month-by-month basis suited me fine. Eviction was at my discretion. We hung up.

Do you believe in concrete happiness?

Do you believe in sex as a means of utilizing human space?

I do.

Thirty-sixth Street sits in midtown Manhattan like a boomtown on the Barbary Coast. While essentially industrial, the buildings lining its westernmost reaches are inhabited by hungry artists escaping the rent wars of the Village and Chelsea. They find midtown accessible to their interests, close to the theater district, the television studios, Fashion Avenue. Three years ago, I had selfishly insisted we move here, against Miss Mouse's suburban plea. She dreamed of Park Slope, but I didn't see the point of living in Brooklyn. We must strive to be authentic New Yorkers, I told her heatedly. Live on the rise, stress it out in the bigger pot, the fatter jungle. Morning to night, we'll trample the sidewalk until it ejaculates us. I meant "ejects," but she liked when I said that.

I aired out the small room the next morning and said a few prayers, hoping for a fresh start with no rude bumps. I went to work, leaving a set of keys in the mailbox and a note, cheery and borough-friendly, asking my new roomer for quiet when I was home and a small amount of consideration in the kitchen and bath. Miss Mouse had beset the apartment with hundreds of such messages during her occupation. My late twenties were spent deciphering these doily-designed memos, each maddeningly brief and charged with feminine authority.

Naturally, when facing new challenges at home, one reaches for the familiar art form with its sadistic persuasions. But where was the masculine mythology in memos between men? Impractical! So I drew a manly face on the back and assumed that my unseen partner in this exchange could detect the irony. In fact, courteous doodle aside, I was hoping to inspire a moment of truce.

I finished work and returned home. There, I was greeted by a confusing silence. Summer silence, willful silence, oppressive and intense. There was little difference to my living space so far as I could see, though I knew something had occurred between dawn and dusk because the keys had been removed from the mailbox and the note unfolded. The kitchen sink was empty, the bathroom left intact; not a drop of water languished in either. The only suggestion of change became apparent when I entered the living room.

The wasteland, as I called it after the female factor had vacated, spread before me. Wood floors lay bare and wires on the walls dangled without anchors. My crowded bookshelf gloated in one corner and a long-suffering sofa crouched in another. Had I been robbed? No, that's how Miss Mouse left me. Nothing in between and nothing new. I thought selfishly that I should have purchased a loft full of storeroom product and stuffed the apartment with ugly crap, modern interpretations of old appliances, if only to impress apprehension in my new roommate from seeking to decorate things himself. But he wasn't an interior decorator; he was an interior *mover,* which meant he was sick of furniture after hauling it around all day and didn't care to see it when he got home.

Slowly, my eyes turned to the second bedroom door.

It was closed.

How morbid it looked, closed. It was never closed. Miss Mouse and I refused to get into the habit of closing doors. Now a shut door decided my fate with the knowledge, in my mind, of a strange man lurking inside.

I busied myself that evening, quietly cleaning the kitchen, organizing the shelves, keeping my activities ordinary, not too feminine, eyes focused on the shut door. When did he go to work? Did he ever piss? Were we fated to cross paths at inconvenient hours of the morning or night, each of us on our way to separate lives, while living just a few feet apart?

I had heard strange stories described of opposite lifestyles pressed together in the seams of this city. They were prevalent in our packed wilderness. I wasn't afraid to live in that tradition, and I refused to hold a grudge against anyone inclined toward this custom. However, courtesy suggested that *new* housemates might at least meet at the very outset of cohabitation even if they intend to avoid one another for the duration of their stay together. This was a trial run, wasn't it? Eviction was always on the horizon.

At once, the front door unbolted. The key jiggled in the lock. He's home! I hurried to hide, but the Mouse couch—the only appropriate hiding place—had been removed. Curse her! I made a mental

note in my panic to buy a Japanese screen, when the door banged shut
and I was alone in the apartment with *him*.

Terrified, I lurched from side to side. I needed to piss, expel the
tightness. What if he sees me and doesn't approve? What if he thinks
I'm too bureaucratic looking, too thin, too short, too pale? Worse,
what if he thinks I've been expecting him, sitting past my bedtime
just like his mother in Queens? He's probably used to women knit-
ting accusatory thoughts. I know I am. . . .

"Headstrong boy, disobedient boy, intransigent boy, I ought to
spank you to your room, lock the door, and dial your dead father with
my cruel thumb while you obstinately procrastinate to sleep, making
loud grunting noises, moaning and wanking just to show your
mother what a stupid old woman she is!"

I heard his heavy footsteps through the kitchen.

I knew then that it was true, what he said on the telephone, about
his job. He stepped deliberately, weighed down by the numbing
memory of hundreds of pounds of furniture on his back. His boots
met the linoleum without regard, scraping in their masochistic
nature, unintelligible beyond this. Each step sounded too lumbering
to be a discreet lover, a carefree dreamer, or a thoughtful thief.

He was a *mover*. Gloriously burdened with other people's possessions and bearing them through this city like an urban ox, sacrificing
his spine, never saying hello, never sticking around for a modest chat.
Maybe my new roommate was moving furniture right now, balancing a large TV over his shoulders, a king-sized bed, a stolen
couch. That's why his steps sounded stilted and ungraceful. I should
be more sympathetic, more welcoming.

I spun in a circle like a fly in a jar with nowhere to go. He
stopped at the entrance to the living room and that's when I saw my
new roommate/housemate/kitchen companion/bathroom alter ego.
He reeked of his heritage of the hardworking male. His body filled
his clothes like a red-blooded rig, occupying the doorway as a virile

contraption. Every limb spanned in every direction for every mechanical purpose. Even his shadow, which fell on the floor, filled the living room automatically.

I stared at him, my eyes blistering. When finally he stepped into the light, I saw the great weight he carried, the burden fate condemned him to move, clinging to his torso and suffering his stride.

He had a Chest Magnificent: two towering pectorals, that is, gigantic breasts or man boobs attached to his upper ribs, each giant and defiant, tremendous and immeasurable. Athletic-minded men call them pecs, for they are foreign to average physiques. They are built in spartan gyms and showcased in professional competitions, at boxing matches or in paying arenas. They are fashioned, I am told, under incredible acts of resistance against crushing amounts of weight. Men labor long hours for these impossible trophies, pressing between their grips all manner of mechanics or lifting infeasible elements while lying on benches, then christen their achievements in the locker room with lots of baby oil. In Central Park, I have seen them bulge in the summer heat beneath shorn tank tops. And I know a handful of men in the West Village who worship their ideal like priests worship the Madonna.

While I acquitted life with the very basic assortment of muscles, I was no slouch in suspenders. Nor did I act the invalid, settling for the formless nature of a gummy body. In fact, I was fit enough to entertain Miss Mouse every night on her couch. Nevertheless, I hadn't what he had, those manful boobs! They were bigger than my sister's, bigger than my mother's, bigger than my ex-girlfriends'. As he lingered in the lamplight, his chest yielded its seductive bosom to my gaze, astounding in its presence as they filled my living room, my street, my city, substituting sex for religion, one breast a blessing, two a holy crusade!

I backed away as he neared me, feeling the air escape through the holes in my chest. My lungs had withered, pierced by a sudden bout of self-hate.

What manner of nutrients and how many mountains climbed does it take to inflate skin like that? I wanted to pinch the secret out of him. Maybe they were implants. Maybe, like Miss Mouse, they were foam rubber. Or maybe they were wholly industrial, the product of years of rigorous exercise and strict dieting.

"My name is—"

"Manboobs" was all I heard and all I heard after that. He captivated me with his boobs, aroused me with his bearing and bade me accept his hand as it met with mine. And he forced me into conversation for nearly an hour. Excruciating! He was sadistic, offering small bites of personal history in disproportionate lumps. In fact, he refused to shut up. Did I laugh? Did I respond? Did I tell him anything meaningful about myself? No!

He stretched out on my sofa completely relaxed. I watched his boobs rest beneath his chin in sculpted stillness, never bouncing, never jiggling. They remained perfectly poised, redefining the skyline in my apartment, bidding me to send for pizza as we were going to have a good time.

I stood before him, nodding, doing my famous fly-in-the-jar routine, maintaining my anxiety while tipping my head. This seemed to amuse him; but anything would amuse a person who stares lustily at his own chest for hours on end. I entertained him, demonstrating the relationship I had with my self, and he thanked me for welcoming him into my space.

"Anything for you, Manboobs," I said, or something to that effect. And I really meant it.

An encounter like this with a man twice your chest size usually ends disastrously, with one person beaten and raped while the other walks away, smirking through his nose and cleaning off his hose. I refused to play into that West Side scenario. So at the end of our first meeting, not wanting to appear prewounded, I opened my mouth and asked him, "Do you like roasted nuts?"

"Sure," he said.

"I have a jar in the cupboard, mixed, no peanuts, please help yourself."

And I quickly fled to my room.

The distraction of magnesium and protein, I admit, was a cheap ploy. It's a known fact at any dinner party that almonds, cashews, and hazelnuts act as decoys while your hosts excuse themselves to quarrel or make love. The truth is, after talking to Manboobs for an hour, I found myself starving. I wanted the nuts to myself. But the roasted nuts were an inexpensive offering, the first of many I had hoped would seal a good bond. After feasting on my roasted nuts, his gut would inform him that I had passed the cohabitation test with rich flavors. I was a listening roommate and a generous landlord, agreeable to his labored senses. We will survive together in New York City by the slimmest of margins provided his boobs and I got along. His muscular appendages were part of the apartment now, family fixtures; they, like Miss Mouse, would have to obey.

The size and firmness of a man's pectorals, boobs, breasts, I defer to you, suggests that a similar robustness resides elsewhere on his person, in appearance or, at the very least, in bed. Read: penis. But a man's chest is the vital pocket for his most insecure organs. His very purpose for being is contained within this primitive structure. To eat, to digest, to breathe; these are the rules.

Never mind the intellectual complaints of his head, which hoist meaning out of every moment. Forget his lower realm, which urges him to thrive in pleasure. His legs may appear thick around the thighs, good to go fast, or lean for the long race; nevertheless, he uses these, as he uses his arms, as tools for movement and progress only. They are helpful, yet they are not vital. The torso is *vital*. How wonderful a statement of respect for the processes that sustain him when a man, with the aid of a few barbells or a hard wood floor, adds a

visceral metaphor to his natural provision, making his daily act of
being appear more abundant, more real.

I sat in my room and brooded. Manboobs was marvelous. His
flesh was abundant. I wanted to touch him. I wanted to be him. I
wished to open the door to his room and fall into the well-maintained
space between his pecs and use them as pillows, dribbling on them
like a baby and asking him silly Seussian questions like, "Doo wee
pap tooey?" and "Ma wow nen woodle?"

I wondered how he'd respond to playing crib games with a lonely
thirty-year-old male, the kind of fun that made Miss Mouse infamous
in her fun house. Was the door to his room strong enough to slam in
my face if it made him uncomfortable? Were his man arms as powerful as his man boobs, capable of punching a hole through my heart?

Munching on a fantasy macadamia, I explained to my inner child
that a late-night appearance by me wrapped in a blanket and reciting
gibberish would overwhelm if not intimidate my new roommate.
Yet, I half-expected a knock on my door: Manboobs afraid of the
dark, afraid of living with a stranger, needing to know if I was upset
that he'd eaten the entire jar of roasted nuts without sparing a cashew
for me. It's your home, too, Manboobs. Don't fret. Why don't you
come in here? Bring your boobs and rest them beside me. Here's a
towel. Wipe those tears, one tit at a time.

For the rest of August, the man I called Manboobs, the man who
restored masculinity to 36th Street, became a one-manned mystery.
He disappeared the day after our first encounter, and I didn't see or
hear from him, neither in the morning nor at night. His door stayed
closed, the apartment perpetually still. Everything felt cut in half
without him.

In high spirits, I aired out the apartment, anticipating fall. Dark
particles floated inside; New York City was crumbling apart. All the
while, I imagined the wonderful things Manboobs and I would do
together as winter approached.

Being near the breakdown stage by his prolonged absence, I picked up the telephone one morning and called his employer. I cleverly faked a job. Like a new client who was also his roommate, I requested Manboobs, saying how a good friend recommended him. I described him in breathtaking detail:

"The one who's young and smooth with wide thighs, thick arms, and enormous pecs. I understand he's firm in bed and potentially violent," I said.

A pause.

"Yeah, I know your guy," responded his boss. "Bench-presses obsessively, calls himself—"

Manboobs was moving through Columbus, Ohio, delivering office furniture for Phase II of a customer relocation. He's expected back on the fifth of September, barring delays. Of course, there were delays and he came back on the thirteenth.

"Mister, you have things to explain!" I said to his closed door.

I rehearsed all day, searching like a poet for the correct words. In a rampant monologue I exclaimed my suffering and loneliness: checking his door every day, riffling through his mail, wandering the Lincoln Tunnel in a pectoral fog. I was in a state of high alert on 36th Street with no help from him! Then, at the end of this tirade, I'd tear off his shirt and slap him on the breasts.

He made me mad, impossibly wrathful, targeting my ego with deliberate and unnecessary cruelty as his means of forcing me into the kitchen to roast ten jars full of his favorite mixed nuts for his arrival. I set them around the living room in two pectorals, I mean ovals, leading ceremoniously to his door; and I said a prayer that Interstate 78 should bring him back to New York generously healthy.

That evening, I fell asleep on the sofa sampling a handful of his nuts and dreamt of the Perils of Manboobs. One early September day, Manboobs climbed out of his truck somewhere near the Pennsylvania Turnpike. Tired and lost, he lay down in a field to rest his boobs.

Immediately, danger called. A herd of hungry calves captured Manboobs and dragged him through the menacing landscape, uttering his name with growing hatred.

"Manboooobs! Manboooobs!"

Apparently, their mother had been slaughtered two months before to package the beef that Manboobs consumed after his intense workouts. The grams of protein and iron he fed his pecs had belonged to her. They wanted their mother back, thank you, and devoured his boobs!

The key to this dream jiggled in the lock.

Mechanical sensation? A burglar? No, Manboobs!

I awoke and tripped over a jar. The rush of scattered nuts sounded loudly. I hurried nowhere. Fly-in-the-jar panic absorbed me. I managed to organize the nuts in a pyramid outside his door as the sound of boots scraped through the kitchen. When I thought I saw his chest materialize through the kitchen door, I dove into my bedroom, but fell short, hit my head on the door frame and passed out. . . .

Baby cows, Jersey cows, Belted Galloways, like gigantic caterpillars with multiple rib cages and one hundred hooves. They drank milk from a thousand manboobs in the sky, rigged in the overhead of a celestial gymnasium. Drinking milk and masticating mixed nuts, they lived in udder peace.

"Wake up." Manboobs banged my head over the kitchen sink. Cold water jostled my senses and I sprung out of his arms.

"Hey, you drunk?" he asked.

Now was my chance! I slobbered, with his wrist to my mouth.

"Doo wee pap tooey?"

Manboobs leaned an ear forward. "Huh?"

"Ma wow nen woodle?"

The fury of his pecs stared back at me and I crawled under the towel.

He apologized for finding me sleeping on my exercise break and he mentioned his long trip. Something about getting paid big bucks and running over a calf in Lancaster County, PA. The mini-cow put a dent in his radiator and caused a three-car crash. The truck needed major repairs. A local was hospitalized. And Manboobs was temporarily out of a license and a job.

"What a misfortune," I said, counting my blessings.

After that, I saw him every day. We exchanged greetings once in the morning and once at night. My remarks were usually bookish, his self-concealing. He found work as a personal trainer at a midtown gym and spent the weekends at his girlfriend's place in Flushing. When he was at home, he called her constantly, though she rarely called.

When the phone did ring, it was the gym scheduling appointments. Apparently, Manboobs was a hit. Our telephone became a major business. 1-800-Man-Boob. Famous people called, everyone sounded healthy, some spoke Norwegian.

By late fall, after whisking past him in the bathroom and worshiping the progress of his pecs from poised predicaments to heaving monstrosities, I worked up the nerve to touch him. I wanted to draw near enough to sample the elixir he applied to get his boobs to stand up and burst from underneath his skin, in cycles it seemed. I thought it was a fair request on my part to be included in the wider orbit of his pecs. If I could not be his girlfriend or workout partner, I should at least be a welcomed tourist, traverse the terrain, maybe even take a few pictures.

So one afternoon I found myself sitting in the living room, quietly stationed at one end of the sofa with Manboobs tagging the opposite end. The sound of fire engines swept through 36th Street; an accident had congested the Lincoln Tunnel. We were at home at the same hour and celebrated the fact with strained dialogue. He chomped on the last of the roasted nuts and talked about his girlfriend. Every Sunday she made him leave before her bitchy sister got home. As I understood from his description, Bitchy Sister hated

Manboobs because his tits were larger than hers and that made her speech obscene. But I know women. While Bitchy Sister disapproved of Manboobs on the way out, she secretly missed him when he was gone. It's the old routine: what women say versus what they mean!

"Look at this."

Manboobs put the jar aside, unbuckled his belt, and rolled up his shirt. Rolled up his shirt, I repeat. He was bathed in his own man light; his skin radiated a Middle Eastern tone, bronze glowing in the egress of summer. His arm extended toward me, revealing cords of muscles bound thickly to bone. I felt my own sinew tightly knot. His biceps converged under his skin where not a hint of hair contradicted the spectacular flesh binding him. He nudged me with his elbow to pay closer attention to his abdomen. There, eight muscular steps climbed up his torso to the principal feature of his pecs. His naked boobs at last revealed! They jounced in succession, one at a time, dangerous to witness, like an avalanche of flesh.

My hand reached to catch their fall. I've got you, little ones!

"What is this?" he asked.

My hand swayed guiltily. A finger unfurled from my palm and felt the striking curve of his right boob. The skin, like a marsupial pouch, protected its offspring. My eyes drowned in desire as I stroked his pectoral.

"Don't touch the trunk," he said.

It was a warning. He said it with cool remonstration. I was forbidden to enjoy the spectacle. I removed my hand. It fell into his lap. Sometime thereafter, I made stupid owllike sounds and tugged him playfully.

Manboobs went to his room and slammed his door.

My nerves scattered about the wasteland. How to fulfill the expectations I had only moments before entertained? To squeeze his whole pec, that's all I wanted. I had touched him with only a knuckle, yet I had experienced with only a knuckle the awesome power of a male bosom. The boob was heavy and breeding with invincible tissue.

Understand, the pec had greeted my mercenary knuckle with ambivalence, but the thing had discovered my presence. I was no longer invisible. I ran to my bedroom and cried, "Nothing but the thing itself!" The weight, the proportion, the elasticity and texture were now my good friends. All these were cataloged instantly in the folds of my left index finger to be summoned in the night like faithful bedfellows.

I jotted down my impressions like empty shells at a rifle show. The information for future desires had been sufficiently ascertained with one stolen touch. Imagine a whole universe converging at the point where one knuckle met God; then you'll see the beauty of my deed and the urgency of my note taking. If only I had used my whole finger, probed a little further for deeper meaning, then I could fill the pages of eternity.

But at what cost? I got a slap on the wrist. A single warning never to touch his trunk again. It made me laugh. So shallow! Distraught mortal, fear not. No one could expect me to obey that. It was a playpen warning of an infant; the spoiled song of a bully in his crib. He couldn't possibly be taken seriously. No one is ever taken seriously. Not about their own flesh, their body. It wasn't like I had taken advantage of him, them. No one could take advantage of him, them.

Manboobs protested my assault by remaining out all night. And the next night. And the night following that. It was already November, the city was getting cold, but I didn't see him again until December.

When he returned, he acted sour toward me and wore the suspicious trouble-down-the-road expression of wives and ex-lovers. He inquired if I had been in his room while he had been away.

"No," I lied.

I stood at his door as he gathered his gear into his gym bag, sorting through a pile of unwashed garments, assorted fabrics, and male fragrances that I had cataloged only hours before. Notepad in hand, I had dived headfirst into his laundry seeking to find a sacred relic, a holy T-shirt, some ruined shroud that mystically possessed the image of his pecs painted with perspiration on the inside. The Turin of Thirty-sixth Street, I called it. But my search had been fruitless and it served as the second act of betrayal.

Mind you, outside New York, roommates obey silent codes of civility toward their partner's possessions, never investigating their private space unless invited. But in a city where everything is gargantuan, where human nature acts out in proportion, I felt I was more than behaved. Manhattan is a battlefield. Hourly, the territory is shifting and the personal is temporary.

Surely Manboobs saw the magnitude of our story: perfect strangers living together in humanity's failed vestige, sharing a streetlamp, dividing an address. Who would dispute that I had a self-preserving right to inquire about my mysterious housemate?

"I'm leaving," Manboobs told me right before Christmas.

"You can't," I said.

"Watch me," he replied.

Manboobs, to his credit, tormented me by packing his things all day, which meant stuffing his belongings in garbage bags and propping his futon against the doorway to his room. I sat on the sofa the whole time, watching him glumly. His pecs heaved as he angled his mattress out of his room. They pulsed, silently playing a little drumroll. They wanted to stay, the twins. But I had no right to take them away from their father. How silly he'd look without them after he climbed off me, finishing me off in a beating frenzy. I mourned their disaffection, innocently helping father sow the seeds of estrangement.

"Thanks," he spoke at last.

Manboobs patted his trunk, saluted, and left.

I sat there stupidly.

*   *   *

These days I've gotten into the chest craze that seems to be possessing modern American males. That is, the need to acquire large pectorals at the expense of true health and longevity. It's extremity really, and really silly. So much time spent packaging one's masculinity above the waist where it doesn't even exist. But I'm a sucker for trends, vain pulses, the buzz of life. That's the way of progress in the city, get it? Making modest things grand.

If she saw me sitting on her aqua couch, Miss Mouse wouldn't recognize me. I've become tanned and rather athletic. In the wasteland sits an armchair facing the entertainment system. There I watch my favorite weight-lifting videos and compare my endowments to the professionals. Of course, they're much bigger than me, but I don't sweat them. They've got nothing compared to Manboobs. Extraordinary Manboobs. Colossal Manboobs. I saw you in my house, Manboobs.

I honor Manboobs every day of my life. The small bedroom has become a shrine. The bench press is in there; I moved it in myself. A pile of derelict shorts rests in a corner, and a mirror stands ready to capture each moment of growth. I can't keep up this pace much longer, not past forty. Unless, by surprise, I see Manboobs staring back at me, telling me to touch the trunk . . . don't touch the trunk, my name is Duncan, sure, wake up, look at this, what is this, I'm leaving, watch me, thanks.

4. Romeo's Distress

By Aaron Nielsen

"SO, WHAT DO you want?" Blake asks me, again. I stare up at the menu above the cash register and decide that I'm not hungry anymore.

"I'm not in the mood, I'm not really hungry." I tell him.

After he orders, we sit down at a sticky table in the middle of the crowded pizza parlor. Blake's eating a piece of cheese pizza that is covered with red pepper flakes and dripping orange grease. I drink some of his soda—it's Sprite, I think. "Do you want me to get you one?" he asks.

"Nah, I just wanted some of yours."

He smiles at me and wipes his fingers with a small paper napkin. I smile back as I stare past him and out at the street, where it has started to drizzle. It's Saturday afternoon and Telegraph is overflowing with tourists and street vendors peddling their home-made wares.

I feel happy, but in a melancholy sort of way. I'm just glad to be here with Blake, watching him eat, watching the rain. Once he and Tina broke up, I was afraid that we wouldn't hang out anymore, but lately we've been seeing each other a lot.

After he finishes most of his pizza, he looks up at me, gets really sullen all of a sudden and asks, "So, um, how's Tina doing?"

"All right, I guess."

Blake sighs, before muttering, "Well, that's good, then."

"Yeah, I guess."

"Has she asked about me?"

Does it matter? You dumped her, remember? "No, she hasn't, not that I can remember."

"Oh . . . is she still—"

"Yeah." I say, before he can get the sentence all the way out.

I bite my bottom lip, nervous habit. Outside, a dirty man holds out a dirty paper cup to passersby. Blake goes back to eating.

I get agitated all of a sudden, like there are too many people around and so I get up and go to the bathroom. It's pretty gross. I try not to breathe too much, but the fluorescent lights keep flickering on and off and so I get distracted. I pick through my pockets looking for the small blue pill with the punched-out V in the middle. I find it mingled with lint and almost drop it on the floor. Almost. I swallow it dry, look at myself in the mirror. Hate how washed out I look, decide the mirror was a bad idea and go back out to Blake. He doesn't notice me at first, just stares down at his stained plate, shredding a napkin.

"Hey?" I mumble.

"Hey." Blake repeats back.

"If you want, we can stop by your place, pick up your stuff?"

"Is Tina home?"

"No. I haven't seen her in a few days."

He contemplates this for a minute, looks down, runs a thin hand through his dirty blond hair then looks back up at me and through pale blue eyes and asks, "You sure she won't be there?"

Outside, people bustle about in the rain. Merchants start pulling tarps over their tables in an attempt to protect them from getting wet. Blake walks really close to me, our shoulders occasionally brush against each other. He looks over at me and smirks. I try to light a cigarette, but it gets too wet and ends up breaking. Dismayed, I toss it onto the ground. I think about lighting another one, but it'll happen again, I know. So I don't. It starts to rain harder, faster.

"I don't know if I really want to do this." Blake says as we walk up the stairs to my apartment. I look down at the ground, I don't really have that much to say. Blake keeps talking. "I just don't want"—his voice trails off—"can't you just bring my things over to my house?" I plug my key into the lock and turn to Blake, "Nothing's gonna happen. If she is home, just ignore her. I do." As we walk inside, Blake's the one who looks down at the ground. Tina's on the couch smoking, the volume to the TV is turned down, and the stereo is turned up. She's listening to the Dead Kennedys. She looks over at us, blue-eyed; suspicious, then decides we aren't that interesting or something because she goes back to watching the TV. Blake and I hurry into my room.

"Dude, I'm sorry." Blake looks at me all teary-eyed, either that or it's leftover rain, "You're an asshole. You knew she was going to be home," He sniffs. I shake my head, "No, I swear to Christ. If I knew she was here, I wouldn't have *come*."

"Whatever." Blake whispers, to himself or to no one.

I pat him on the shoulder because it's supposed to be comforting, but Blake doesn't seem to be too into it, so I stop.

"I'm really wet." Blake mutters as he looks down at himself.

"Here." I say as I hand him the bulging plastic grocery bag stuffed with a sweater, two T-shirts, dirty socks, and the mix tape he made Tina.

He pulls his soggy shirt over his head. I sit down on my bed and light a cigarette but they're damp, so it burns funny. I try not to watch Blake. It's a strange thing to see someone naked—well, shirtless—because there's nothing to hide and so they're really vulnerable looking. Clothes are such a way to hide. I look out the window but Blake's form is reflected back on the pane all thin and translucent. I exhale a slow plume of smoke, rub my forehead, and pretend like I'm not watching him. Out in the living room the phone starts to ring. I don't get up to answer it. Blake puts on a faded Tom Verlaine T-shirt and over that a brown sweater, all from the bag. I don't think I like the way he looks in clothes, I liked him better vulnerable.

The phone stops ringing and then Tina starts pounding on my door. When I open it, she thrusts the phone in my face and walks off. I put it to my ear cautiously and listen for a second before asking, "Hello?"

"Are you coming tonight?"

"Oh sure, yeah, I think so."

I look over at Blake. "Hey do you want to go out tonight? Sonoko is deejaying . . ."

He scrunches up his face and shakes his head in a violent *no*.

"Yeah, I'll be there, just me."

Click.

I shuck off my sweater and trade it for a jacket.

Tina's watching some lame slasher flick. On the TV this busty blonde wearing a pink teddy gets her throat slashed and thrown off the balcony of her sorority house. I stop for a second and watch it until Blake starts tugging impatiently or uncomfortably at my arm. Tina never looks over at either of us. Which is just as well, I suppose.

It's still raining when we get my car. Neither of us have much to say, so I turn on the stereo, because it's just too calm. I hum along to the Cocteau Twins as best I can and get slightly hypnotized by the lobbing of the windshield wipers, and the Valium. Blake says something to me as he gets out of my car, but I don't catch what he says, so I just nod like I understand. He seems satisfied. I wait until he's all the way inside his building before I drive off.

"I don't care if he comes over here; just let me know first, so I can leave or something." Tina looks at me more disappointed than upset.

That's fair enough, probably, so I tell her OK and walk off. "It's your turn to do the dishes, too!" She yells after me, but I've already shut my bedroom door, which means, I'm officially ignoring you now.

I start to get ready to go out, but it's still too early, so I take another Valium and lay down. I bury my face in my pillow and unfurl. The rain keeps up its steady beat outside and then the front door opens and I hear muffled voices. The stereo gets turned up and all I want to do is sleep for a while, just a while. I pull my blanket over my head and try to ignore the commotion in my living room. Fucking drug addicts.

Sleep falls away slowly and I can still hear people in the apartment. I regret that I told Sonoko I would go out tonight. It's already after midnight and so I don't want to. But I get up anyway. Start to peel away my current ensemble, while trying to negotiate a new one. Black, of course, black. It's night so my room is black and all the clothes hanging in my closet are black, so of course black. I fumble around feeling for textures, since it's all black, but the moonlight makes everything look watery in this way I hate and I really hate all of my clothes and I don't want to go, not at all. I stick my hand in my under-wear for inspiration or something but it doesn't really work out too well. My balls feel too loose so I just end up grabbing a button-down shirt and some pin-striped pants I bought a while back but have never worn. There, whatever, I'm done.

They all look at me when I get out there. Carey and Sheila and Tina, all amped, cigarettes dangling from lips and traces of crystal still filmed on the coffee table. The Baggie isn't empty yet though. I grab my jacket—not the one from earlier, a different one—velvet i.e., expensive, and walk out the door. Fucking drug addicts.

Driving in Berkeley sucks, bottom line. It's not so bad now, because it's pretty late and so people are asleep or at home, but I hate it still. The rain stopped and the wetness makes the streetlights reflect

all . . . "glittery" seems to be the right word, but that's cliché. Everything is shimmery, sodium oranges and faded green, on darkling
black surfaces, *slick*. That kind of works. But I sound pretentious
now. Who cares what the fucking pavement looks like anyway?

My car pisses me off, I want to punch through the windshield. I
wanted a BMW. I had it all picked out and everything; 540i, V8,
silver. But, my parents bought me a *Saturn* instead. A hunter green
one at that. I seriously will punch the fucking thing someday. I light
a joint and it takes the focus away from my anger so I can drive, albeit
erratically.

I hate driving in Berkeley because I got a ticket for driving the
wrong way down a one-way street. If I had a BMW that wouldn't
have happened, since I have a Saturn, I was pretty pissed. So that
night after I got the fucking ticket I went back to the street and kept
driving up and down it the wrong way, for like a long time it seemed.
In the end I felt vindicated, but not really.

By the time I get onto the freeway I kind of wish I had made
Blake come with me. I contemplate turning around, but he's probably
asleep already or something. Traffic is pretty light and for this I'm
thankful. When I roll down my window, to hand the tollbooth
person my money, a cloud of pot smoke drifts out and I'm suddenly
embarrassed. The lady who takes my money just looks at me with
contempt. So I turn my radio up louder and try to sing along, but I'm
still listening to the Cocteau Twins so I can't. I smoke the joint down
'til it burns my fingertips and I have to put it out or eat it or something. I just drop it into the ashtray and let it burn itself out.

The bridge is pretty lit up, and as I make my way across it San
Francisco blinks into view. No fog obscuring anything, just pointy
buildings with glowing windows. The movie-esque scene does
nothing for me, I'm pretty jaded, I guess.

When I get to the club there's a doorman there that I don't recognize. He's wearing black army pants, an overly starched dress shirt,

and a black beret with a Nazi Death's Head pin on it. I start to wonder if I'm at the right place, I turn to leave, but the Nazi guy asks me in a really irritated, effeminate voice, "Can I help you?"

I want to bolt, but I hear myself tell him. "Yeah, I should be on the guest list, my name is Spencer, Spencer Dalten."

Mr. Nazi Fistfuck flips through the papers on his clipboard and says, "Found you, OK go on in." The whole experience was creepy and now I really want to be at home, but I told Sonoko that I would come. I shouldn't have woke up.

The inside of the club is dark and smoky from the fog machine, the walls are painted black and there isn't much to the decor. At the back of the club there's a small stage that a few people are dancing on and a bar and the stairway up to the balcony. I head upstairs because that's where the DJ booth is and probably Sonoko. There are a lot of people here, more than I'd like. I guess I just hit the peak, hopefully it'll start to wane soon.

She's standing outside the DJ booth smoking a slim cigarette or joint, I can't tell which in the gloom. When I walk over to her, she stands on her tiptoes and kisses my cheek. Sonoko is slightly over five feet tall, I feel so awkward, so gangly around her since I stand at six-one. Her outfit: a high-collared short-sleeved black silk dress that comes to the middle of her slim thighs, fishnet stockings, and very tall Doc Martens boots. Around her large almond-shaped eyes she has meticulously painted purple eye shadow and liquid eyeliner, so that she looks like some sort of Egyptian goddess. Her lips have also been stained purple and her long ebony hair has been trussed up into a series of small buns splattered across her head. The first thing out of her mouth is, "You're late!" I try to come up with an apology, but I'm too stoned to think of one. Sonoko finishes her cigarette, throws it on the floor and pulls me into the DJ booth. The room is small and dark, it's cluttered with arcane switchboards and cords and other electronic gizmos. I flip through a crate full of records and Sonoko puts on an old Siouxsie and the Banshees track, "Metal Postcard." Out on the dance floor this guy with thinning hair and a puffy pirate shirt tries to dance to the song. He's easy to spot, even in the crowd, because he looks so awful. He must think he's really cool, but if he could see himself he would go home and slit his lame wrists.

Right before the song ends this really drunk kid wearing a black suit and sunglasses requests a Christian Death song, but the one he wants Sonoko to play is a Valor song, so she doesn't. Instead she plays "Romeo's Distress," just to piss the guy off. Such are the petty politics at Goth clubs. Jay, one of the club's other DJs comes up to the booth to relieve Sonoko. He's wearing leather pants, with no shirt, and both his nipples are pierced. He has a huge black mohawk which makes him seem infinitely tall to me. As soon as Sonoko and I leave the booth, he puts on some overplayed Coil track.

Back downstairs Bat, who looks scarily like Genesis P-Orridge, except with a lazy nasal lisp, pulls us into the women's bathroom. The guy is such an old pedophile, he thinks just because we do his drugs that he's entitled to sex. Wrong, asshole, but as long as you keep offering we'll keep snorting 'em.

We cram ourselves into the last stall. The handicapped stall. Bat pulls out a tin full of coke. Oh, excellent. Sonoko starts to roll a ten-dollar bill giddily between her petite fingers. Bat licks his lips and gives me the eye. I look up at the ceiling casually and pretend not to notice, it's creepy.

> Bat: Spenther, you look just like Peter Murthy. (Sniff. Sniff.)
> Me: (Sniff.) Thanks.
> Coil: Measure the extent of the dizzying descent/ Down the Anal Staircase.
> Sonoko: My turn! (Snoorrrt!)

Her eyes start to glass over, she rubs her nose, snorts again, and then dabs at the corners of her eyes, so as not to disrupt her makeup. Bat inhales more blow and then shoves the tin into his jacket pocket. When we leave the stall, Sonoko checks her nose in the mirror and then touches up her face, even though she doesn't need to.

On our way out of the bathroom two girls come in, one with maroon hair and a black velvet dress, the other with black hair and a maroon velvet dress, and they both go into the stall that we just came out of. Bat, Sonoko, and I exchange glances. Sex? Drugs? Both? We make our exit before we have a chance to find out.

Bat disappears, which is fine, but then we run into Jared. Oh, excellent. *Him.* He's wearing a navy blue velvet frock coat with a white button-down shirt underneath and a pair of black pants that are tucked into his knee-high boots. He isn't wearing any makeup, he's already pale enough naturally, and his bleached blond hair is sticking up in a zillion different directions. He gives us a wide cheesy grin and fidgets with the small silver hoop in his left nostril. "Hey, guys, guess what?" He doesn't wait for us to ask what. "Last night on *Daria,* they showed Trent's room and he had Sisters of Mercy *and* Bauhaus posters on his wall, isn't that cool?" I stick my hands in my pockets and look at the floor, I want to ask him why in the hell was he watching *Daria,* but remembered that I watch it too. I just have the good sense not to admit that I watch MTV, in public. Sonoko on the other hand comes back with, "Yeah, at the end of one episode they played a Bauhaus song and at the end of another episode they played a Love and Rockets song." Goddamn, my life is now complete having found this out. "Cool," is all Jared says, cool. Such are the sad drug-induced conversations at Goth clubs.

We all end up going over to the bar together. Jared and I sit down at a red-upholstered booth and wait for Sonoko to come back with our drinks. Jared sits way too close to me. I keep trying to slowly edge away from him without seeming too rude about it, but he seems

totally oblivious anyway. I pretty much just ignore him. I start to mess
with the small votive candle that is sitting in the center of the table. I
pour melted wax on the tabletop, wait for it to harden, then pick off
the hard white glob. Jared asks me what's wrong and I tell him
nothing and so he scoots *closer* to me. Yeah, there *is* something wrong,
you are fucking *touching* me. I don't say this though, and if I move
over any further I'll be sitting on the floor.

I notice Sonoko walking toward the booth juggling three drinks
in her hands and so I rush over to her, my salvation. When we sit
back down, I sit across from Jared. I'm drinking a Long Island iced
tea, Sonoko is drinking a rum and Coke out of an impossibly small
red straw, and Jared is drinking an Absolut on the rocks and after
each gulp he grimaces. More fake fog descends upon the dance floor
and people twist and swirl in it and to me they look like they are
drowning, they look like long strands of brown seaweed, being
manipulated by the cold, dark ocean.

> The Cure: Sometimes I'm dreaming/Where all the other
> people dance/Sometimes I'm dreaming.
> Jared: I'm gonna go dance.
> Sonoko: Yeah, I think it's almost my turn to spin again.
> Me: I want a cigarette.

I set my glass down on the table and we all separate like roaches.
Jared to the dance floor, Sonoko upstairs, and me outside. After I get
my cigarette lit, Jay appears, still sans shirt. He nods in my direction
and then starts to walk toward me. Oh, excellent.

"Hey."

"Hi. Jay."

"Hey, do you think I could maybe get a cigarette?" People with
mohawks and nipple rings shouldn't try to act coy, it doesn't work.

"Um, yeah, sure."

"Thanks, man."

"Oh, hey, wait. Did you bring any Current 93 with you? Sonoko didn't and I wanted to hear a song."

"Sure, just come up to the booth later and remind me." With that he saunters back into the crowd of smokers mulling about. I snuff out my cigarette and as I walk back inside, the faggot doorman with the beret checks out my ass. I don't actually see him do it, I can just feel it.

First thing, Bat grabs me by the collar of my jacket and pulls me back into the bathroom, except this time with Jared. Oh, excellent. I do another line of coke and feel really uncomfortable in here with both *Jared* and *Bat*. Luckily Bat's preoccupied with trying to get into Jared's pants.

> Bat: Thared, your hair lookths totally Robert Smithh.
> Jared: Actually I was going more for a Birthday Party–era Nick Cave look.
> Maybe, but Bat's right, it's totally Fat Bob.
> Bat: You hathve cool hair.

Jared blushes and looks down, Bat starts to rub Jared's neck, in this unnerving dirty-old-man kind of a way. I don't like Jared, but this is so not right.

> Me: Oh, shit. Hey, Jared, I forgot Sonoko was looking for you.
> Jared: Yeah?
> Me: Yeah. C'mon.

With that I grab his hand and we leave Bat all alone in the bathroom. I ditch Jared once I know we've lost Bat for the time being. Jared isn't my favorite person, but the last time Bat took an interest in him . . . somewhere on the Internet there are pictures of Jared in a leather thong, fellating Bat. Jared was also seventeen at the time. The kid is a dumbass and too passive to know any better.

Jay goes on to DeeJay so I go up to the booth, because I want to hear Current 93. I sneak up behind him, he has headphones on and is busy shifting through a pile of records, so he doesn't notice me until my hand sneaks around and tugs on one of his nipple rings. The muscles in his back tense and he turns to face me.

"Oh, Spencer, hey."

"Hey." I smile. "So, uh can you play a song for me now?" And I twist my finger through the ring and yank down. Jay bites his bottom lip, but not out of pain, no, not really.

"So, uh, um, what song do you want me to play?"

"You pick, it doesn't really matter." I whisper and pull *harder*.

Jay sucks in a breath, quick and taut, "Spencer, you really need to stop." (Translate as: Or I'm going to have to fuck you.)

I unloosen my finger, Jay shifts his hard-on around in his pants, flushed. I bite his earlobe and then leave. A few songs later, he plays, "This Carnival Is Dead and Gone."

Bat is dancing next to Jared, they're snorting coke, right out on the dance floor. Passing a tiny spoon back and forth, nostril to nostril. Bat never gives up and Jared, well, Jared's probably going to get raped. I find Sonoko at the bar, talking to some guy I don't know, so I don't feel bad about interrupting the conversation.

"Sonoko, do you need a ride home?"

"Uh, what, oh, yeah, that would be nice."

"Okay, you know Bat has been like all over Jared all night."

"Oh, fuck." She mutters and rolls her eyes. "I'll be right back," she tells the guy she was talking to. He just turns back to the bar, and his drink. I follow Sonoko.

They're still on the dance floor, Bat has his face buried in Jared's neck, and Jared's standing there, swaying to the music, trying to ignore Bat, I guess. I stand back and watch. Sonoko wends her way through the dancing throngs, pushes Bat away, and drags Jared to safety. She makes him spend the rest of the night with her in the DJ booth.

Legendary Pink Dots: "And though we wanted to change things/The fact remains we never tried . . ."

I end up, not only taking Sonoko home, but also Jared *and* Jay. Oh, excellent. *Them.* I drop Jared off at Sonoko's, so at least he's finally out of my hair, finally. Jay's 'hawk is so tall that it's smashed to one side underneath the roof of my car and he's too fucked to notice. It really isn't sexy, and kind of makes him look like a jackass but he thinks that it's cool, so whatever. I put on Psychic TV, but have to take it off, because whenever I hear Genesis sing, I see Bat's face, Bat touching Jared, Bat staring at me, et al. Okay, Cabaret Voltaire then, no not them, Joy Division? Aw, fuck it, where does Jay live, anyway?

"So where am I taking you?"

"I don't know, I don't want to go home."

Oh, excellent. "Well—"

Jay cuts me off, "Can we go to Denny's? I'm hungry, I'll pay for you, since, you know, you're driving."

"Whatever."

"Cool."

Oh, excell—aw, fuck it.

Our waiter is totally gay, like with the ugly mustache and all. Jay keeps fucking with his mohwak trying to get it to stand back up, it's now bent to one side. As if this were a punk beauty pageant or something. I just get a Coke, because I'm still really spun and the idea of putting food inside my mouth doesn't really make sense to me. Jay has no problem with that, though—he's probably stoned. It just doesn't look right to be putting things like french fries into your face. I need a cigarette. The Coke is too cloying and its flavor

lingers in my mouth. I think the cocaine was cut with speed. I hope
I don't puke.

"Do you want to come in? I never get to show people my record collection." Jay asks, but his eyes say, You touched the nipple rings,
wanna fuck? Reluctantly I agree, I'm still amped, and I need something to do, but I'm not sleeping with anyone who has a mohawk.
Yuck. I turn off my car and my hands drop, exasperatedly into my
lap. "Sure, why not?" I smile.

An hour or so goes by, I'm buried in piles of records in Jay's dingy
living room. He keeps handing me LPs and the stories that go with
them—i.e., where he obtained them, how limited they are, etc. . . .
We've been smoking pot though, so I can't complain too much. I just
nod, like I care. Feigning interest is so easy. Thank God I'm on drugs
or I couldn't handle this at all. He lights another joint and then leans in
close to me. Instinctively I move back, I hate people. He just passes me
the joint and I take a hit, then decide it's time to go. I am so not going
to fuck anyone with a mohawk. Yuck.

I lay in bed until the morning light illuminates my miniblinds. I feel
really aware and I can't fall asleep and so I just stare across my room
at the black-and-white Bauhaus poster and I just stare at Peter
Murphy and remember Bat's words, "Spenther, you look just like
Peter Murthy." I get the chills, I can't help it, my teeth just knock
together and I can't stop shaking. *Spenther, you look just like Peter
Murthy.* Now I remember why I stopped doing dirty street drugs,
because my heart is lobbing around in my chest like a washing
machine on the spin cycle and I totally think that I'm going into car-
diac arrest and I convince myself I have a pain shooting down my left
arm, but then I just end up slowing down.

*   *   *

"What? Wait."

Blake is silent for a long time, then he finally says, "What the hell am I waiting for?"

"I thought I heard something."

"Where?"

"The living room."

"So what do you think you heard?"

"I don't know."

"You do too many drugs."

"Probably."

"I gotta go, Spencer."

"Sure, later."

Click.

I dial Sonoko's number. "Something's going on out in the living room."

"Huh?"

"Sonoko?"

"Yeah?"

"Never mind. I just thought I heard something out there."

"It's your roommate, isn't she always out there, on drugs?"

"Definitely. The living room is totally persona non grata."

"It's the drugs."

"I liked her better on coke."

"She was still a bitch then, too."

"Not to me," I say. "Not to me." I had to say it twice, for dramatic effect.

"So is there a point to this conversation?"

"Not really."

"Well, call me later when you like have a point."

"Sure. 'Bye."

"'Bye."

I decide to go out into the living room, where I find Tina sitting on the couch sipping a generic diet soda and I don't know where she got it from because I don't buy that generic shit. Or anything diet. She looks weird and I'm not sure why, but then I figure it out, she's all dolled up. Her bangs are gelled and barretted down, the rest of her hair is ratted and spiked out at awkward angles. She's wearing pink eye shadow that matches the pink two-sizes-too-small T-shirt she had on. There's also a black felt skull ironed onto the front of her shirt, placed strategically between her tits so your eyes are forced to look there. And rounding out her ensem: a pair of black Vivian Westwood bondage pants she picked up in London a year ago. As of late Tina hasn't been too preoccupied with her appearance, so seeing her out of pajamas is kind of jarring.

"So what's going on?" I ask.

She lights a cigarette then says, "Mitchell's coming over. He's back from Europe." And with that she turns the volume back up on the TV.

Mitchell is Tina's younger brother and at the mention of his name I remember this one time in high school; Tina told me this story about how she caught him jerking off to Internet porn. She told me while we were getting high. She said his dick was really small, too. But, it was pretty fat; that's what she said. Later that night we ended up over at Tina's house. Mitchell was home and all I could think about was him whacking it to Internet porno and how he has a short, chubby cock.

I try not to think about this while he sits across from me. Hopefully it's grown some. They creep me out when they're together because they look so much alike. Same hazy blue eyes, same blond hair, same high, fragile cheekbones, etc. The only real difference is that Mitch dresses more preppy or whatever than Tina; jeans, button-down shirts, sweaters, et al. She's the "black sheep" or he's the good kid, I guess. Whatever, at least my dick is pretty long. And for that I'm thankful.

They sit next to each other on the couch, Mitchell occasionally waving cigarette smoke out of his face, Tina oblivious. They talk about relatives I haven't met and what Mom and Dad, whom I have met, are up to. I'm bored, I'm bored, and I'm bored. Their inane chatter goes on for almost an hour before Mitchell changes the subject,

"I think I want to get stoned."

Tina turns to me, "Hey, Spence, what's Sonoko up to?"

Well, whatever, I guess it's better than sitting here all day, staring at the TV.

It's basically the same scene at Sonoko's, except now we're all on a different couch getting high with her roommate. We order pizza because no one wants to cook or get up and go get anything to eat. So we take bong hits and wait for the pizza, not much else to do. When the pizza guy finally comes he looks really antsy and keeps peeking into the apartment. As Sonoko hands him the tip, he sheepishly asks, "Can I have a bong hit instead?"

She just opens the door all the way and lets him follow her inside. He's not bad-looking, if that's what you're thinking. I mean, as far as stoner pizza guys go, he isn't bad-looking. He sits down next to me and sort of nods, hey, or whatever. And his knee rests against mine, bony, knoblike, but obviously human. Weird.

Sometime later, the pizza guy staggers off, bleary-eyed and less than lucid. He's stoned. Period.

Sonoko clicks through the channels, settles on Nick at Nite, they're showing reruns of *The Addams Family* so we watch that for a while until it's time to smoke more pot. We ditch the bong, Sonoko rolls a joint and then hands it to me and then I pass it off to Tina, who gives it to Mitchell, who starts choking and coughing almost to the point of seizure. Hate that.

"Are you OK, man?" I ask.

Mitchell sniffs and then wipes his eyes, "Yeah, I think so."

"Drink some bong water, it'll make you feel better."

"Uh, no." Pause. "That's really foul, Spencer."

"No, seriously, you'd like it."

After that no one really says much else, so we go home. There's no point in hanging around anymore, really.

I sit down on the couch, turn on the TV, Tina goes to bed. Mitchell, I think, runs to the bathroom to puke, someone's puking back there, regardless. I flip the channel, more crap, surprised? Not really. Mitchell swaggers back into the living room, flops down next to me, slightly sour smell hanging around him, he puked. I should have taken him home, whatever, too late now. I flip the channel again, Mitchell sighs, audibly: Pay attention to me, basically.

"So how was Europe?" I ask, trying to make small talk, but not really caring.

"It was, I dunno, it was Europe. People smoked a lot and listened to a lot of bad dance music. I watched a lot of shitty American television, with subtitles. That's all."

We sit there silent for awhile, both of us just staring at the TV, until Mitchell breaks the silence by asking if I've ever been.

"Ever been what?" I ask.

"Have you ever been to . . ." His voice trails off. He starts to repeat himself again, but stops.

"No, I haven't ever been." I tell him, but it doesn't really matter because he's passed out.

* * *

The next day I'm sitting over at Blake's reading the paper. For some reason he gets the *San Francisco Chronicle* and for some even stranger reason, I'm actually interested in it. I pick through it, disappointed mostly. That is, until I find this one article in the back of some section, about this gay porn star that killed himself in Las Vegas or Los Angeles or Orlando, or someplace that isn't here. And the story kind of bothers me because he was only twenty-three and, I'm only nineteen, and when they did the autopsy they found coke and heroin and alcohol and some sort of prescription painkillers in his system. This also bothers me because I've done all of those drugs, too, except for heroin. I get really scared because I wonder if I'm going to kill myself too, but then I remember that I'm just hung over, not a gay porn star. I'm relieved, a little.

"So, what'cha reading?" Blake asks.

"Hmm, oh nothing, some porno guy shot himself or something."

"That's pretty morbid, Spence."

"Yeah, I guess so, it is."

I grab an old dog-eared issue of *Playboy* from Blake's nightstand; it's the one with Drew Barrymore in it. I don't know why he has this, it was so disappointing, her hair looked awful. Well not that awful, I cross my legs to conceal my swelling crotch. She does kind of look like Tina though, at the recollection of that, the tension in my pants recedes, slightly. I put the magazine back where I found it.

"Hey!" Blake shouts.

"Now what?" I ask.

"Let's go to Starbucks. I want coffee."

"Do we have to?"

"Yeah, c'mon, it'll be fun."

"Whatever. Just give me a second, OK?"

"Sure, why?"

"I can't really stand up right now."

"Are you all right?"

"Oh, yeah, fine. I was just you know, looking at Drew and stuff . . ." I trail off, hope he gets the gist of what's going on here.

"Drew?"

I motion to the nightstand, to the *Playboy*.

"Ohhhh, riiiight."

I really hate Starbucks. They give me the creeps. They're every-where, like the Big Brother of coffee or something. Blake loves it though. I get bottled water, how yuppie. Blake gets a mocha-caramel-frappa-latte-blah-blah-blah. Right after we sit down, this spaced-out hippie chick that was in my English class last semester comes in. She seriously thinks she's Janis Joplin or something. I hope she doesn't notice me, I sink lower into my chair, try to hide, pray Blake's obstructing her view. I loathe going out into public and seeing people I sort of know and having to make polite small talk with them.

"Spence? Something wrong?"

"Huh? No, yes, sort of." I lean close into Blake, "See that girl over at the counter?"

Blake grimaces. "Yeah, she was in my American history class. Total burnout."

"I hope she doesn't see us."

"Just shut up and don't look over there."

"Deal." I look down at the shiny, brown, overly lacquered table. Press my finger onto it, leave a smudge, wipe it away, hope she's gone.

At a table across from us, a middle-aged, overweight fag lets out a high-pitched cackle and it really pisses me off when people laugh in public; it should be illegal or something. I need a cigarette. Instead I opt for a few Percocet; I stole a whole bottle from my mom. She has so many pills, she won't miss them. Blake looks at me as I swallow, like a disapproving parent.

"What?"

"*Prescription,* they're prescription."

"But, whose prescription?"

I shake my head, like I don't understand the question. Unscrew the water bottle, watch carefully as the hippie chick leaves. The coffee stink is making me nauseated. I drink some water, try to ignore it. At least the stupid hippie is gone. Blake starts picking at a fingernail, then looks up at me and smiles, "This is nice." I have no idea what he's talking about, so I nod, like I understand. Cigarette. That's all I want right now, a cigarette. That'd be nice.

"Spence, are you OK? You look really pale."

"Yeah, it's all right." I make a flippy hand gesture so he can understand just how OK everything is.

"What were those pills you took?"

"Oh, um . . . pills?"

"Yeah, what were they?"

"Pills . . . white ones."

"You're starting to look really flushed. Are you sure you're all right?"

"Mmmhmmm, OK. This is nice." And it is. I'm not lying, no.

Blake stands up; he's tall. "We're going, come on, before you pass out or throw up or something."

I stretch my arms out to him, like a child or someone who is on drugs that are a lot stronger than he expected. Blake grabs one of my hands and pulls me to my feet. I put on my sunglasses and stare at Blake. He seems bright through the dark tint of the lenses, almost like he's backlit by some sort of blond angelic light. I sort of lean into him, trying to be coy, i.e., acting like I'm on drugs. And either way he doesn't mind. He just guides me out of the coffee shop, arm around my shoulder. Awww . . . this is nice.

Outside I light a cigarette, but I feel too dense, so I'm not sure if I'm smoking it. I have to sit down a few times because it gets really overwhelming. I want to take another pill, but Blake keeps watching me and I know I'd be too slow, in my current state, to get one out and eat it before it was intercepted by him. I'm OK.

I land in Blake's recliner, he sits down on the bed. We aren't talking. He starts to look at the *Playboy,* I'm annoyed. I pretend to act interested in the liner notes to a Clash CD. Which was probably Tina's—

she always leaves her stuff everywhere, almost like marking her territory. I light a cigarette; Blake looks up at me. He doesn't say anything though, so I don't put it out. I pick a book up off the floor. *Wuthering Heights* by Emily Brontë; I hate this book. But I open it anyway. A wiry blond hair falls into my lap, it looks like a spider leg. I toss the book back down on the floor, brush the pubic hair off me, then get up, go into his bathroom. I run my half-smoked cigarette under the faucet before throwing it away in the trash can. Eat another pill.

Blake's still engrossed in the nudie magazine. I watch his crotch, I think he's hard, maybe. God, I'm bored. I grab *Wuthering Heights* and throw it at Blake. It lands on his chest. He lowers his pale gaze at me, chiding, but not threatening, from across the room. I give him the finger, and try to light another cigarette. Blake, however, chucks the book back at me, knocking the lighter out of my hand. Smug, and satisfied, he returns to the naked chicks. Asshole.

"Hey, Spencer, come here."

I get up and walk over to the bed, "What?"

Blake's hand slides down his stomach and under his jeans. *Ohhhh, riiiight.* Without really thinking, I strip off my shirt, but leave my sunglasses on.

The *Playboy* is spread open between us. Blake's eyes are closed, he's biting his bottom lip. Drew isn't wearing any underwear; I still think her hair looks like shit. He never lets me touch it, him you know, his dick. I don't know why either. He gets off on this so much, us jerking off side by side. Weird. He makes this whimpering noise, bites his lip harder.

"So, does her pussy look like Drew's?"

Blake stops midstroke, "Huh?"

"Tina's pussy, does it look like Drew's? They look sort of the same—I was curious."

Confusion settles over Blake's face, he jerks himself, like in contemplation, "Yeah, kinda, I guess. But, you should know, though—

didn't you and Tina in high school? She told me that." Blake closes his eyes again, gets back into the rhythm. Up, down, up, yank, jerk, et al.

"I was drunk, so I don't really remember."

"Spencer, shut up, I'm gonna come." Blake whispers.

Then he does, and so do I.

5. Sunday Morning
By Stefen Styrsky

JUST BEFORE SUNRISE, the three men fell asleep in Nathan's four-poster bed. The bed was a gift from his mother when he bought his first condo, as it had been a gift from her mother, and before that from her mother. The mahogany frame held the mattress much higher up than a usual bed, and when Nathan was young, he would sprawl about the pillows and imagine he sat atop a palanquin borne aloft by servants. Because it wasn't fashionable for a lady to climb upon a mattress the way a mountaineer grappled over a rock ledge, a stepstool, similarly decorated as the headboard with rosettes and scrolls, once accompanied the bed. The stool was lost years ago, stuffed into the corner of an attic and forgotten. If one accidentally rolled off the mattress, an outstretched leg would not touch the floor until another two feet, long past any hope of stopping the fall.

This being his first time in the bed, Drew turned into space, then thudded on the floorboards. The noise woke Christopher, and he looked over the edge. Drew lay naked and beautiful; his lithe frame and pale skin put Christopher in mind of a descended seraph. Somehow still asleep, Drew looked even younger than he had last night dancing shirtless and alone. Self-awareness gave him a maturity he lost when not posing.

Drew stood. "I'm all right. I'm all right."

Nathan sat up. "What? What happened?" He had heard someone talking. He thought it was Christopher telling him to turn off the alarm clock. By the time Nathan realized what had happened, the boy Drew was snuggled alongside Christopher. Seeing the two curl around each other, he felt deficient in some essential skill, the same feeling he had last night as he watched Christopher accomplish Drew's gradual seduction. That kind of courage was something he didn't have, and which many attempts proved he couldn't fake.

Drew felt Christopher's arm (that was his name, wasn't it? Christopher?) wrap around his waist when he was back under the sheets. At first he was flattered Christopher had slowly, but noticeably, worked his way across the dance floor toward him. A good-looking guy—a bit older—but still good-looking. Then the boyfriend showed up. A handsome guy also, not weight-lifter muscular like Christopher, more like someone who watched what he ate and exercised every now and then. Drew feared a boyfriend spat, the worst thing that could happen at a gay club; he thought "nasty, brutish and long" was a clever description. The surprise was that the boyfriend didn't mind Drew might come home with Christopher. In fact, the boyfriend (he couldn't remember the guy's name at all) was supposed to join the fun. When they finally got around to it, Drew gave the boyfriend attention enough, though he wasn't really attracted to him, before spending the rest of his time with Christopher.

As Nathan watched Drew fall asleep, he recalled what his friend Val occasionally said when he asked for advice about Christopher. "You can't control many things, least off your boyfriend." He and Christopher had lived together for nine years, and as far as he knew, never once had Christopher strayed. About two months ago, Christopher rented a porno movie, "A lark," he said, though Nathan knew Christopher was deliberate in all things.

One of the scenes was of three men. "I've always wondered what that would be like," Christopher said. Nathan admitted his own curiosity. Under the circumstances—three boys proportioned like ancient marble statues with the faces of gods—who wouldn't be curious?

But it was if the gates of inhibition had opened. Christopher brought it up the next afternoon, and again that weekend. Obviously, the idea had taken hold. Because after nine years together, there was nothing subtle between them, Nathan recognized Christopher's maneuvers. Nathan decided he would allow it once. Arguments only made Christopher more determined. Allowing Christopher the decisions, while sharing some of the mistakes, made Christopher realize how bad some of his ideas were, and avoided fights.

Drew was the second, but the first to fall out of bed.

Hunger awakened Nathan in the late morning, and he went downstairs. As he scrambled eggs and toasted bread, someone came up behind him and briefly pressed lips to his bare shoulder.

"Looks good," Drew said.

Nathan turned. When he was Drew's age, boxer shorts marked a straight man. One-syllable names did also. Another few months, and letting a stranger see your brown hair plastered straight up on the right, pillow marks curled around the same cheek, would also be something only the old guys cared about; out of fashion in the same way Nathan considered the men who wore leather vests and mustaches.

"Have some." Nathan prepared two plates and poured juice. They sat on the couch, and Drew bent over his plate without causing the ripples in his tummy that Nathan noticed on himself when he leaned forward. He'd once imagined he was beyond such cares—though his desire for that kind of tummy proved otherwise. He was thirty-three, he had other worries and goals besides a perfect midsection. Keeping his boyfriend—boyfriend? he meant husband—was one. Later today, perhaps tomorrow, or when the moment was right, and they were rested, he'd talk with Christopher about whether they had fallen into an open relationship. Until then, he was content to feed a young man whose only fault was that Christopher found him attractive.

"I'm sorry," Drew said, "but what's your name again?"

Nathan let himself not be insulted. Introductions had been shouted over music; they'd all been drinking. Names given like that were easily forgotten. He had done it himself.

"Nathan."

"Right. Thanks for breakfast, Nathan."

Nathan nodded. He went to the kitchen cabinet above the microwave and spilled out vitamin tablets for himself and Drew.

Drew stood before the painting above the mantel. "I know this one. *Hylas and the Nymphs*," he said.

"Yes." Had they dragged home an art student? An actual brain as well as a body?

"I used to be into the Pre-Raphaelites."

"I have a book of prints."

Drew went back to his eggs. Maybe because no one else had ever recognized the painting, Nathan felt compelled to show him the book. Usually it was on the shelf below the coffee table's top. This morning he found it in the study.

"Here it is."

"Cool." Drew laid his plate aside to page through the volume, obliviously half-naked in front of a stranger. Nathan wondered if at his age he might have carried off such a pose. He had a hard time remembering what it was like when all one had to do to look good was show up. These days he waxed his chest, plucked the stray hair or two from his back, skipped dessert, did push-ups, sit-ups, and jogged. He massaged creams into his skin every night, but still couldn't regain that pearly tinge of the young. There was a point at which he might give up, but not yet.

When Christopher finally came downstairs, he headed for the coffeemaker and turned on the machine he had filled with water and

French roast last night. Voices from the living room meant Drew was still here. This was the moment he dreaded, when he wasn't sure how much or how long he should talk, or how he might suggest the person could go home. Well, he had to admit, he wished this person would go home. Drew made a nice adornment, but he had things to do this afternoon, and he needed a little time alone before returning to work tomorrow. He certainly didn't want a houseguest all day.

Christopher waited until a cup's worth dripped out, and he had stirred in milk and sugar, before going to the living room.

"Good morning," he said and sat on the other couch opposite Nathan and Drew as Drew flipped through one of Nathan's art books, positioned so the covers rested on their adjacent legs.

Christopher was surprised at this intimacy. Drew actually appeared interested in the paintings; he knew their subjects and references, mentioned the few he had seen in museums. Christopher liked the prints Nathan chose for the house but lacked Nathan's appreciation for art. And Nathan seemed to be enjoying Drew's leg against his as much as he enjoyed discussing the prints with him. A flash of jealousy seized Christopher. But jealous of what? His sudden thoughts of Nathan running away with Drew were ridiculous. Not only was Nathan too committed for that, but practical Nathan would consider before any wild decision that they'd have to sell the house, rearrange finances, alter wills, change insurance forms. Reduced to paperwork, their relationship was solid.

"Good morning," Nathan said. He enjoyed Drew's leg against his as much as he enjoyed discussing the prints with him.

"Hi," Drew said and went back to the book. "*Circe Offering the Cup to Ulysses,*" he read a title aloud. "She knew."

"What?" Nathan said.

"Men are pigs."

In some other life, this would be a dream come true. A beautiful boy who knew his Greek myths. Ten years ago, Nathan would've immediately fallen in love and made himself sick with wanting. Now he can smile and imagine, hope the kid finds someone who appreciates him.

"You like art, Drew?" Christopher said.

"Studied it at Amherst."

Nathan straightened from hunching over the book. "What do you do now?"

"Graphic design."

Nathan looked over at Christopher and raised an eyebrow, his expression of curious surprise. "Well. I run Albedo Studio," he said.

Drew nodded, turned Nathan's way. "I've heard of you. I'm at the R&D Factory."

"You're the guys people use when they want to look cool."

"I just started. But I did help with the last Cherry Dance ads."

"That was good stuff."

Christopher felt he should contribute. "Present company excepted, of course." Drew and Nathan appeared confused, unsure what he meant. "That men are pigs." He sounded stupid, picking up a piece of the conversation long past, but he had to make sure they knew he was still in the room.

After the first threesome, he realized the desire for it wasn't because he was bored with Nathan, rather that the newness of his body to someone else was a sensation that exhilarated him. Nathan was the most satisfying partner he'd ever had, but he wished he could forget their lovemaking, so it was new each time. He liked being assured the effort spent making himself resemble a gymnast hadn't been wasted. He liked being appreciated. Nathan appreciated him, but not in the same way of wonder and newness that gave Christopher such a thrill. At least this way, if Nathan was there, it wasn't actual infidelity.

Drew realized sitting with Nathan (thank God he wasn't offended he'd forgotten his name) disturbed Christopher. Well, he had the attention last night; it was Nathan's turn.

And what luck. A graphic designer, somebody who might give him a job, though how that would go over with Christopher was suddenly a problem. Drew swore this would be his first and only threeway. Tension between two boys was bad enough. Three, forget it.

"What do you do?" he asked Christopher, a show that he was still interested.

"Market research."

Then he asked the question he should—"What does that entail?"—and regretted it. The description Christopher gave was long, detailed, and beyond what he wanted to know at this time in the morning. He nodded every so often, and at a pause picked up his plate to take to the kitchen.

"I'll take that," Christopher said, lifting the plate from Drew's hands.

He'd actually been content lolling around until just a second ago. He wished there was an easy way to leave. Of course, he could just walk out the door, though escape wouldn't be so easy because his clothes were upstairs. Should he give them his phone number? Offer his number and let them say yes or no? Ask for theirs? And did you say, "I'll call you?" (A lie, everyone knew; he winced thinking about it.) "See you around?" (Possible, at least not a lie, though most hoped it wouldn't happen.)

But the connection he'd make now was worth being uncomfortable. Graphic design was a shaky business. People got laid off as soon as contracts stopped coming.

"Are you hiring?" Drew asked, just as soon regretting the forward, even mercenary, question. He was smarter than that.

"Come by with your portfolio in a year."

Desperate to change the subject, Drew said, "Thanks for a wonderful time." And what the fuck was that? Asking for a job, then reminding Nathan that they had sex last night. He sounded like a whore. He wished he could slap himself.

"It was very nice."

"Coffee anyone?" Christopher said from the kitchen before Drew opened his mouth and uttered something else stupid.

"Sure," Drew said. He went into the kitchen. Without looking at him, Christopher poured a cup and asked if he wanted milk and sugar.

"Yes."

"Milk in the fridge. Sugar here." Christopher pointed to a bowl on the marble counter.

Drew had to go. He had blundered into a house full of two people and their lives. He hadn't a single idea of who they were, or what they thought, or the problems between them. These guys were old. Not geriatrics (hell, he wished he looked as good when he was their age), but old because there was this giant life behind them; fights, happy times, and just regular, everyday stuff. Experience he hadn't gathered, because he hadn't lived long enough. Their motives for last night were different than his. He wanted fun. They wanted a young guy, a last fling before they settled down; a bragging right; another notch in the bedpost. Who really knew? He was sure not even they did.

In his experience of clubgoing, the morning after was usually full of resolutions. Past ones included no more than four drinks; don't talk to strangers who share a cab ride with you; buy your pills from a friend rather than the dealer in the bathroom. Today was no different: Stay away from the Scylla and Charybdis of couples. (He couldn't wait to share that with someone.) Unlike the others, maybe he'd keep this resolution.

*   *   *

"I don't have any designs on Nathan," Drew said.

Christopher was embarrassed his fear had been so obvious. This boy was perceptive. "I'm not afraid of that."

"You seemed uncomfortable when Nathan and I were on the couch."

The shop talk had scared him. *He'll give the boy a job and fuck him at the office and lose interest in me and it will be my fault,* Christopher imagined in one tumbling thought. A third person wasn't supposed to be a frequent occurrence. In fact, Christopher considered it a phase, something they'd do maybe once or twice more. A way they could look back without regret, say they'd had their fun. He never saw this happening.

"Confronted with that waist, most men are powerless," Christopher said.

Drew looked afraid he might offend Christopher again if he said anything.

"This is my fault, Drew. You're not doing anything wrong."

Christopher sensed circumstance catching up with him. He tried sorting the details—not only of last night, but of life with Nathan. Nathan's passiveness bothered him, yet he used it when it suited his needs. When they had first met, Nathan was this successful design artist with his own studio, not the type to cede control in a relationship. Christopher often wondered what had changed, or why Nathan seemed content with whatever he decided about where they lived, the furniture, what they did on weekends and for vacations. He had hoped Nathan might forbid three-ways.

When Nathan heard voices go from normal volume to whispers, he went and stood near the doorway.

"I like both of you guys," Drew said.

He wasn't a spy. He stepped into the kitchen. Drew was biting his lower lip as if he waited for something from Christopher that might hurt.

"We like you, too," Christopher said. Drew smiled quickly and walked out of the kitchen.

"I don't understand." Nathan said.

"Drew realized I was jealous when you two were looking through that book."

Nathan barely held his thrill inside. Gloating wasn't right, though he had every justification. Why did Christopher demand these strange duels where each of them revealed vulnerabilities and demonstrated hidden strengths? Arguments never worked. Except—and this was now so clear, he almost fell over—they proved he loved Christopher. Was that it? Did Christopher need proof? Proof from a fight. A fight not to change someone's mind, but to demonstrate that he, Nathan, considered the partnership his as well.

"So what's the problem?" Nathan said.

Drew, though, was a spy, and listened from behind the corner. Briefly, he considered suggesting they play around again to show there were no hard feelings. He strode upstairs for his clothes. They were strewn alongside the bed that had earlier almost killed him. Never had he seen such a large bed; the posts were nearly tree trunks. He wasn't sure if he'd tell this story with the bed in it or not.

When Nathan first slept in his family's heirloom, his fear was of falling off. His first serious boyfriend also admitted it scared him, and they broke up soon after he tumbled out one evening. Nathan ascribed no connection to either event. Most people who have used the bed take time adjusting to its height. Not only can a fall be serious, but, stepping out in the middle of the night for a drink of water or a trip to the bathroom, one had to probe with a foot and slide down the mattress, difficult when semiconscious in the dark. Instead of a mountaineer, one was a spelunker looking for the bottom, searching for secure footing.

Nathan hardly ever slipped anymore.

6. All the Young Boys Love Alice

By David Pratt

DID YOU READ Alice Munro's story in *The New Yorker*—about how at sixteen she secretly dated the Salvation Army boy? The tale is touching, forgiving, wise, with poignant and subtle shades of feeling. I long to write the same way about my youth, and to be approved.

Young Alice is daring, trespassing on a strange woman's property to lie beneath a certain tree. She lies on her back and imagines that the trunk grows from her head. This girl will grow up to tell truths and touch souls and be loved.

As she escapes the woman's property, she sees the boy. He works for the woman, a sharp-tongued horse breeder who shouts a rebuke after Alice. Alice sees him again on a Saturday night in town, preaching and making music with his family in full Salvation Army regalia. They meet again in the countryside, riding bicycles. The boy turns out to be like Alice, thoughtful. He doesn't find it silly that she imagines a tree trunk growing from her head. They kiss, and she feels his erection against her.

But the boy belongs to a lower class, so Alice keeps him a secret. She accepts his family's invitation to dinner but lies about where she is going. How noble, the lies of sixteen. Memories I wish I had.

After dinner they set out for her home. He wants to detour by the

horse breeder's barn. Alice follows him inside. They kiss, then . . .
Well, I won't spoil it. You might read the story sometime. You
should. It's beautifully etched. (Or limned—whichever.) And the
prose is even lapidary. Alice evokes universal feelings, as though you
are there and know these people. I will take Alice's idea and fit it to
my own life at sixteen—it should be easy enough; it's universal—and
make the story I've always dreamed of, the one everyone will love.

So—it is summer 1974, and I am sixteen. With whom would I
have gone biking? Invited to my home for dinner, stolen into a barn
to kiss?

I dreamed of such a person, but there was none.

Instead, silently but with primal inevitability I longed for
Jeremy, a night manager at the diner where I washed dishes. Jeremy
was two years older than me. His taciturnity, his compact body and
mop of dirty blond hair, his quick little smile and slight swagger captured what I longed to be. I wasn't really male, not really human. To
Jeremy and to many others, I thought I was a soft, fumbling, impotent girl-boy, busing tables, mumbling confused answers to their
snappy questions. It filled me with despair, but thinking of Jeremy's
swagger obliterated the pain and confusion. Jeremy had what I
needed to make myself real and good, and I used it secretly.

Late, after he'd scrubbed down the grill (face flushed, shirt
clinging, the sweat and rippling forearms setting off his prettiness)
Jeremy ducked into the manager's office to change. I made up reasons
to pass the half-closed door, to see what I should be. He was too
modest to reveal much. He did sometimes emerge with the clean
shirt unbuttoned, chest smooth, cigarette hanging from red lips. He
slouched on a stool and spun, eyes narrowed, watching me as he blew
out smoke. Or he might come out still tucking in the shirt, jeans
unzipped an inch or two, and I'd see the elastic of his underpants,
snug against his hard belly.

Once a girl called Jeremy on the pay phone. I knocked on the manager's door, and he came out shirtless. As he murmured to her, I racked the last dishes and grill implements while attending to my life's true, secret work: glancing at his downy triceps, golden hair under his arms, the gap between his spine and the waistband of his jeans. How in his glory he was!

Once, when I was on during the day, he came to pick up his check. He wore a blue flowered shirt and had his arm around a girl. She was delicate like him, the kind of girl I wanted in my arms.

Maybe it was best I never investigated a barn with Jeremy. But I can't get an Alice Munro story out of him.

Nor could I get one out of Jeff, my fellow busboy.

He was more gregarious than Jeremy, but not as smart. Rangy, with a big grin, prominent Adam's apple and black curls, he grabbed pots one-handed, and veins stood out in his forearms. I couldn't dream of dreaming of Jeff. He liked motorcycles and, of course, girls. Every question he asked about what I done in my life or what I liked I just had to mutter, "No, sorry," or "Not really," and frown to discourage further questions. I couldn't tell Jeff that after work I stayed up late with *Moby-Dick*. Maybe I could have told Jeremy, so long as I added, "Yeah, I was bored . . . s'posed t'be some 'great classic . . .'" Jeremy would have understood what I couldn't say. But even Jeremy could go down that road only so far.

Or Mark, another night manager, like Jeremy. I felt relieved the nights Mark was on. Smart and bubbly and soft-voiced, he'd been one of my father's piano students. But in Wintonbury, Connecticut in 1974, no one talked about what smart and bubbly and soft-voiced and playing the piano might mean. Mark was my sanctuary, so long as I wasn't like him. Jeremy and Jeff were not sanctuaries, and I wasn't like them, either. I wasn't like anyone I knew. My struggle with life was a stain on the sheets, singular and disgusting.

One night Mark burst into the Rice Krispies song: "No-o-o mo-o-ore Rice Kri-i-ispie-e-es!" he sang in his thin tenor, eyes wide, rushing down the aisle at Jill, the waitress with whom I'd gone to Sunday school. "We've run out of Rice Kri-i-ispies!!!" He pulled little boxes of cold cereal from under the counter and sang, "But we do have Sugar Pops, Froot Loops, and Frosted Fla-a-akes . . ."

I grinned from the kitchen doorway. What happened the nights Mark was on with Jeff? He probably didn't sing. He probably barely spoke, except to Jill. Only thirty years later does it occur to me that, just as I felt safe the nights Mark was on, maybe he felt safe the nights I was on.

Jeff came for his check one night when Mark and I were on, and Mark spoke a few friendly words to him. Jeff spoke friendly words back—to someone he'd decided Mark was. I also recall chatter passing between Mark and Jeremy: Mark chirping, Jeremy nodding with narrowed eyes, reaching for his girl. I think I remember thinking: They . . . *share* something . . . *understand* one another . . . that's why he just nods. Except I didn't think it that specifically. I just stared and wanted more than ever to be Jeremy, to gather a girl to me and please my mom and dad as Jeremy must have pleased his. And the goodness of my longing fulfilled me, for a moment before it crashed.

Or maybe Jeremy listened to Mark to be polite, and later he told his girl, "Those types make me uncomfortable." Maybe, like many people in relation to many things, he didn't think anything. You never know what people are thinking, or why they do things, even when they tell you.

Nights Mark and I were on together were nights off to me. Nights off from fear—of how I looked, what someone might ask me, what they might say to me or behind my back, what they might expect me to do or say, nights off from my face, reflected in the stainless steel of the dishwasher. Usually the boy I saw was a shell—frightened and angry. Nights Mark was on, that boy, if I stopped to look at all, was whole, busy, unself-conscious, in motion as boys his age should be. No stack of dishes was too big; all was right with the world because nights with Mark belonged to a world more right than any "real" world of motorcycles and girlfriends.

I had no sexual interest in Mark. He shut the office door when changing, but I wouldn't have looked anyway. Not that he was bad-looking. But the bubbliness, the turn with the cereal boxes . . . People looked up from their burgers, rolled their eyes. . . . I didn't want to be like Mark. I just wished the whole world was like him, so I could breathe, go anywhere, do anything in peace. That's my grown-up rendering of the wish. What normal sixteen-year-old would expect the world to sing the Rice Krispies aria? Instead, I had to fit the world's requirements—somehow become strong, simple, decisive, in charge. And leave Mark behind.

But I couldn't.

I'm not doing well mimicking Alice here. The best fiction is predicated on hope. "Fiction" might be a synonym for "hope." But so far I haven't offered much.

Maybe if I stop and focus on the elements of Alice's story. So here's what I need: ache of youthful love; ennobling awareness as adulthood dawns; rebellion; the shock when the boy and the situation turn out not to be as innocent as one thought; the sadder-but-wiser ending.

The seduction I want to practice on you would come especially from the love and dawning awareness. So: Whom did I *love?* I felt a longing when I saw Jeremy with his shirt off, but I denied that longing thus:

> I. I didn't *love* him, I merely envied:
>> A. His easy, boyishly cool masculinity.
>> B. His trim body.
> II. So if I mastered that cool, if I could be trim and easy:
>> A. My envy would go away; and

B. My desire to masturbate after seeing Jeremy with
   his shirt open would go away; and
C. I could turn my attention to girls, who,
     i. if I mastered that cool; and
     ii. if I could be that trim and easy,
     iii. would turn their attention to me.

It was just envy, don't you see? It wasn't lust (certainly not *ho-mo-sex-u-al-i-ty*), just envy and resentment, on the part of a guy who hadn't made it. Yet.

But isn't it sad that, upon first feeling first love and desire, I had to call it envy and resentment just to survive it. My love was a tightly wrapped, mislabeled masterpiece, ignored in a museum basement for years. The desire/cancellation, desire/cancellation loaded me down with guilt, fear, hopelessness, a feeling I was shrinking. Love— Jeremy?? How? Why? For what?

Oh, lighten up! Adolescent boys have crushes all the time!

It wasn't a crush! Why exchange one lie—treating Jeremy like he meant nothing to me—for the lie of a "just a crush"?

Well, you could have made friends with him.

So we could—do what?—shoot hoops together? Go for beers? Sit close, give the occasional pat on the back, over before it began? Talk about girlfriends? Maybe if I, too, had had a girlfriend, Jeremy and I could have been closer. Yet, if I'd been like him, he could not have lived inside me in that way. O, Alice, help me!

So what about Mark?

I liked Mark, I felt safe with him, but I didn't want to be him. And if he and I did things together, *everyone* would suspect. And my family knew him. And no guarantee anything would happen, which with Mark I didn't want it to, I just wanted to be Jeremy in his flowered shirt with his arm—*my* arm—around a girl. . . .

We'll get this yet. Wasn't there a girl you did go out with?

Ellen, from school. We went for ice cream one afternoon, walked along River Street. I'd imagined a whole romance, but she reacted to me as a friend. And I felt relieved. I felt drained by expectations, leaving me no strength to leap the chasm. I felt no primal electricity; I had no idea who to be for her. Still, I had electricity for the idea of *someday* having a girl. Or I had impotent desperation.

But now I must be sage and forgiving. That's what puts the glow around Alice's stories. That and her loving detail. I've neglected to mention the scalding plumes of steam unfurling from the dishwasher as I pulled up the stainless-steel doors, jammed with grease. I haven't mentioned the bursting laughter of customers as I scurried with bus pans of dishes gummy with melted ice cream, smeared with ketchup. I haven't mentioned my somehow-favorite duty: cube and boil potatoes, frothy pot hubble-bubbling, for next morning's hash browns.

Maybe I should have been able to get a better job, in an office, where a nice boy in a tie . . .

But we exhaust ourselves thinking how a summer might have been different. Really set the scene, fill in the nice boy, script an encounter with him. Then the wish, the child of regret, will die. Its death rattle: "You were who you were." Stillborn wishes exhaust me, but in the womb they feel better than reality.

I should be telling you of first love, but I still can't find anyone I *loved* at sixteen. I thought I couldn't love, and stories exist only if someone loves.

Alice and I do share one motif: books. After the Salvation Army boy disappoints her, Alice retreats to a world of literary lovers: Rochester and Mr. Darcy. I didn't seek men to love in the books I read. Mr. Darcy wouldn't understand or even see me. There on my bed by the window overlooking the neighbor's unmown yard, not the characters but the books themselves became my lovers, their powers of resolution conferring on me purpose, worth, hope.

I didn't love Thoreau's *Cape Cod* for Thoreau, but because our family went to the Cape at Christmas. I had maps of the Cape on my walls. I tried to own the windswept dunes of Orleans and Truro. I'd be a naturalist-philosopher, tramping the dunes with my walking stick, sketching dune grass, describing waves. I'd meet a girl on the beach, someone soft I could love, who'd love me because by then I'd be different. I'd be strong and save her from the riptide. We'd have babies and live in a cottage looking out to sea.

I did like girls, but never enough or in the right way. I wanted to impress them as other guys did, but they scorned or didn't notice me. Girls I felt attracted to, like Ellen, slipped away—apparitions that other guys made real. Sex was a sheer rock-face, impossible to climb. But I desired those boys who clambered up it effortlessly, who were unconsciously born to climb. What turned me on about Jeremy's chest, glimpsed beyond the half-shut door of the manager's office? It was how his girl loved it, how he felt as she stroked it and whispered, "Oh, Cliff!" Jeff's veiny arms: if I had them, girls would want me. But I had been made too girly, too soft and timid, too fruity, my mind rotting with warped desire and fantasy.

Like all great artists, Alice is brave. If I liked girls, why didn't I ask one out? If I liked boys . . . ? But I just gazed over the beige dunes. How did love work for those like me? I didn't think to ask, because there were none like me. Yet people operate without evidence all the time. Brave people, like Alice.

My shift is almost over. No, I won't be like Alice. How you write is how you live, and I have not lived in a way worth reporting. Alice lives with vision and courage; she's earned her audience. I've hewed to fear and sought to diminish myself. I won't be writing an Alice Munro story, but can I tell you I'm frightened? Frightened that there can be no victory, that destruction rules the crippled house, frightened now, as then, that no effort can bridge the chasm between what I wish I wanted, and what daily life reveals me as wanting. Should I take a graceful bow and leave the stage?

I lock the back door, turn out the lights in the storeroom, kitchen, and bathrooms. On my way to the door, where Jeremy waits, I pass the cold, fluorescent aura at the fountain.

"All set," I say, emerging into humid night. A cigarette hangs from Jeremy's lips. He presses the door shut. He stands legs spread, denim cupping his bottom, his shoulders stretching his white shirt, stout forearm turning the key. He yanks the key out and tests the door. He turns to me half-grinning, gives the keys a little toss, snags them and clips them to a belt loop. An almost-full moon lights the parking lot.

"Headin' home?"

"I guess."

"Stay," he says. "Lemme finish my cig."

"'kay . . ."

He puffs, shoots me a look, jerks his head toward his rusty Camaro at the far edge of the lot. "C'mon!" I follow. Is that a light across the street in the Cymerys Funeral Home, or just a reflection? Jeremy unlocks the car door. "Drive ya home."

I get in.

Slouched close by him I watch his small, strong hand turn the radio dial. I lean forward, trying to pull out of the deep bucket seat. He stops turning and looks at me. "Relax," he says. "What groups you like?"

"The Rolling Stones," I lie, and he must know it's a lie because I didn't call them "The Stones."

"Cool," says Jeremy, as I try to recall titles: "Tumbling Dice," "Satisfaction" . . . Jeremy can only find Elton John: "Mongrels who ain't got a penny . . ."

"Your girlfriend didn't come tonight?" I ask. Sometimes she picks him up. He shakes his head. I wait for an explanation, but there is none.

"This car yours?"

"Kinda . . ." He blows smoke out the window. His gaze nails me, eyes narrowed. A smile curls the corner of his mouth. "So what you like to do?" He's slumped so the top of his shirt pulls open, revealing clear skin that is so much and nowhere near enough.

What do I like to do?"

He laughs, leans forward, pats my left knee twice, hard, then flops back again, shirt open, blue denim in a nice, tight V between his legs. I say, "That's a dumb question!" and we laugh. I think he's blushing. He shakes his head.

"God!" He regards his cigarette. "Gotta give up these things!"

"You should," I say, and realize that I really do think Jeremy should give them up, so he'll be more pleasing to me and won't die.

He squirms. "Make your blood race."

"Cigarettes? Make your blood race?"

"Yeah. Feel my heart. Go on!"

"Feel. . . ?"

"Feel my heart."

His hand circles my wrist and I let my palm open a little. He draws it to him and I open further and he places it on his shirt, but so my thumb rests on the exposed skin of his chest. I have never touched another boy's bare chest. My palm cups his left pectoral. My face is hot. I nod, like "Yup, sure is beating fast," though I can't feel his heart and have no idea how to find it. I can feel him breathing. My hand lingers a moment, then I take it away. Jeremy flicks his butt out the window and blows smoke. I glance at the funeral home and try to remember the perfect fit of his bare pectoral in my palm, the cloth of the shirt, moving as he flexed a muscle. He twists around, hunches up to the wheel, and turns the key. "Let's go," he says.

On the way up Granville Avenue, I keep my eyes front, but I know he's watching me. I ask, "So, you gonna give up cigarettes?"

"I should . . ."

"Yeah, your heart really was racing . . ."

The grin again, but he doesn't look at me. "Was it?"

"Yup."

In front of our dark house, I pull on the door handle but don't yet open the Camaro's door. "You on tomorrow night?" I ask, though I know he is. Is that the light over the kitchen sink, or just a reflection?

He nods. I nod. "Great," I say. His face is so still, so blue-shadowed, so pretty. Softly I add, "See you then."

"For sure," he says.

I heave myself out, shut the passenger door, then poke my head back into the fetid warmth. "I can"—I stop and clear my throat—"I can check your heart again."

He smiles. "Cool," he says. He nods a couple times more, then averts his eyes as he smiles. We wait, but nothing more will happen tonight. It will tomorrow, an age away. He gives me a last grin and shifts the Camaro into gear and I step back. My knees feel weak.

"Oh, it's you!" My mother stands in her blue-and-green–patterned housecoat and slippers once pink, now colorless.

"What're you doing up, Ma?"

"Oh . . . heard the car. You didn't walk?"

Suddenly I'm incredibly hungry. I want to get rid of her so I can raid the fridge. I need to sit and eat and think of the compact mound of muscle over Jeremy's heart.

"Got a ride."

"Oh. Who with?"

"Jeremy," I say, inching toward the fridge. "The night manager."

"Oh . . . Isn't he the one you like?"

"Ma! I don't 'like' him!"

"Oh . . . well . . . I saw the way you looked at him that time I picked you up from the day shift. I saw—"

"Mom!"

"You should invite him to dinner one night when you're both off. Your father and I can get to know him a little more."

"Maybe." I pull the fridge open, putting my back to her.

"You know, we don't want our son going around with just anyone!" She giggles.

"Mom! I told you: I'm not 'going around' with him. I don't even . . . Never mind . . ."

"Well, whatever you say. I just hope you'll invite him over and let us meet him."

"Yeah, well, maybe . . ."

I busy myself taking three slices of cheese and the mustard. When I turn around, she's gone.

The top of the house is hot. I smell the damp wood of the banister and mildew in the walls. In my room I start the thrum of the fan. I take off my clothes and stand in the shower.

I lie naked on top of the sheets, turn my face to the window screen, the dark vegetable-smelling night. The neighbor's yard is a black sea. I place my hand over my own left pectoral and feel the thud. I close my eyes and squeeze. I have a little breast. I have a heart. I think of Jeremy's red lips, his shirt open. The tip of my penis skips up the still-damp inside of my thigh. I think maybe Jeremy wanted me to notice his shirt open. How maybe he thinks I am beautiful and good and exciting. Me.

Life has begun. It stretches as far as I can see, a hundred times more to be revealed tomorrow. I am loved and nothing touches me— not parents or friends, not my job, not time, for I contain everything. If I yawn or scratch my shoulder, it is special. My fingernails are beautiful, and the pimple on my back. Angels envy me. Most of all, I am without fear. I'd jump out of an airplane to embrace the sky; I'd run into a burning building, strip my clothes off, and laugh as flames bubbled my skin.

Tomorrow evening, I'll keep asking Jeremy how his heart is. He'll let me feel quickly. After we close, he'll call me into the manager's office where he'll stand with his shirt unbuttoned all the way.

I'll put out my hand, and he'll say it's more accurate if I put my ear to his chest. I will, with my right hand on his back, where it narrows. Then I'll straighten up, and I'll bring that heart to mine, and we'll kiss, and he'll blush and tell me that, from the first night we were on together, he thought I was sexy, and I'll say, "Yeah, I thought the same about you."

I'll invite Jeremy to dinner. He'll be nervous and keep asking me what he should wear, and I will find it annoying, yet utterly adorable. The evening he comes to our house, he won't smoke. He'll wear his flowered shirt. He'll put on mitts to help my mother lift a dish from the oven. He'll call my father "sir" and tell him about his plans to study accounting, and I will watch my parents' faces; they're both teachers, and I fear they'll think accounting is not enough. But all during dinner my mother will give me little suppressed smiles.

Tonight, as I lie in the dark, unchanging breeze, I know none of this. I do not know that I'll walk him home (his brother will have the Camaro that night). I don't know that as we step out into the dark, my mom will catch my eye and she'll mouth, "He's very nice." I don't know that my dad will beam and nod and not say anything.

I don't know that Jeremy will take my hand on the empty streets of town, or that we'll detour past the darkened restaurant because he has the key. I don't know that we'll kiss passionately against the still-warm dishwasher. I don't know that suddenly we'll hear a noise, nor do I know that it will be Gary, the manager. He'll say, "Hey! Who is it? I've got a gun!"

Jeremy will shoo me out the back, promising to handle this and to call me tomorrow.

I don't know that I'll linger by the back door and hear "Just me, Gare."

"Oh, Jeez. Hey. What're you doing here?"

"I, um, left my jacket . . ."

"So you're alone?"

"Um, yeah . . ."

"You been out somewhere? You look good in that shirt."

A chuckle. "Yeah?"

"Yeah. I've told you that. I like that shirt."

A pause and another chuckle. "You doing anything now?"

"Uh, not really . . ."

"Want to go over to Winton House for a drink?"

I listen. I wait for Jeremy to spurn dopey Gary.

"Or we could stay here . . ." Gary says, and Jeremy says, "We could." I hear the little half-smile in his voice. It is my half-smile. Or was.

I see him toss the hair out of his eyes. "How about it?" says Gary. "You ever done it at work?"

I see Jeremy slowly shake his head.

"No?" Gary says hoarsely. "You never had a man fuck you up on the counter?" Silence. Then nothing more, except once I think I hear Gary sigh, "Yeah, that's right . . ."

Then I go home.

I'll go home and I'll bury myself in book after book, in *Jane Eyre* and *Pride and Prejudice*. I'll imagine Mr. Darcy half-dressed, gently moving my buttocks apart, saying, "I want to get inside you. . . ."

I'll find that next week I'm only on the nights that Mark is on.

And summer will end.

But tonight I know none of this. Tonight, pleasantly exhausted, naked with the fan going, I caress my chest and belly. I imagine a big house with lots of windows, and my parents' car pulling into the driveway on a Sunday afternoon, and I imagine, even before Jeremy and I emerge, that Jeremy Jr. charges out the door and across the lawn, his blond hair flashing in the sun, his little heart thudding faster than it ever will again.

7. Ofelia's Last Ride

By Jaime Cortez

DOWN THE BLOCK, I can see Flaco's bony grasshopper knees move up and down as he bikes over to us. The dirt is so hot it looks like he's riding over boiling water. Flaco waves at Doña Sara who is hosing down the dirt. He nods to Don Fosforo, who has like fifty thousand kids waiting for a *raspado*. He is shaving ice so hard you can see the little chunks of it jumping all over his arm. From here, I can see the bottles of flavors: yellow is mango, red is strawberry, and green is lemon. Brown is the best of all the flavors: *tamarindo*. It makes my mouth all watery just thinking about it.

Near the corner, Flaco shouts *"Ese mi Negro!"* Negro smiles and his shiny teeth look extra white and perfect because Negro is like thirteen years old, but he's been shining shoes on that hot corner since forever and he's burned to the color of his shoe polish, even the part of his arms under the sleeves. That's why he's "Negro," and no one even knows his real name no more.

Flaco stops and walks his bike to us at the clothesline and he keeps saying, "Big news, big news, big news." If he wasn't so skinny, they'd probably call him "El Periódico" because he always has the news. Of course we want to know, so Mami asks him, "What's the big news today, *mijo?*"

"Big news from Palma Street." He holds out his long fingers to show how big the news is.

"Is it Doña Ofelia? Is she sick?"

"No. Doña Ofelia is not sick. Big news is that she's dead." Mami is quiet, then Flaco says, "Patti the Parrot says they found her dead in bed, with beer bottles everywhere. Yesterday she served dinner right at six like always. Then she went to lie down. She doesn't do that usually, so later, Roberto the Sasquach went to check on her and found her dead. The wake is tomorrow from four o'clock on the porch, and the burial's the day after at noon. They asked me to tell you the news that you, Señora Dolores, are invited."

I never saw a dead person in person before, so I ask, "Mami, can I go with you to see her?"

"Mario, why do you want to go? You'll just get scared and have nightmares." She's probably right, but I wanna go see a dead body. Anyway, I hate it when Mami goes away. There is some mean people on this street. They call me all the fat names they can think of, then invent brand-new ones so I don't get used to it. Beto Jr. once threw a rock at my forehead just because. My forehead got cut open, but thank God my brains stayed in, so my dad smacked him across the face, grabbed him by the hair, and dragged him to his house, where his own dad smacked him till his nose bled. And still my dad was angry. He is a bad mother. Everyone's afraid to hit me now, but they still make fun of my Spanish and say how come I'm always with my mom, and do I do the dishes because I want to be a girl? Shit, even my grandma asks why I like to work in the kitchen, and Mami just says that I am her best helper. Yeah, it'd be way better going with a dead lady than staying here.

Mami says I can go, but if I get scared it is not her fault. The next morning, I wash my face, and fix my hair with Tres Flores oil the way Papi taught me. My hair gets shiny like Superboy's. I feel like maybe I look super sharp in my button shirt and I'm ready to see my first-ever dead body. Mami made *pozole* to take to Ofelia's wake. We don't even get to the corner when Flora calls to Mami.

"DOLOREEES!"

Damn, that woman's voice reminds me of those big ol' parrots they tell you not to pet in the pet shops.

"Felisitas, did you hear the news about Doña Ofelia?"

"Yes, I heard she left in her sleep last night."

"*Pobrecita*. Oh well, at least she's not suffering anymore, may she rest in peace." Flora is pretty full of shit because Doña Ofelia never suffered. She was mostly pretty drunk, and always laughing and laughing, with her big old mouth open and full of gold, like when you see the inside of the Vatican for Christmas mass on TV. She really doesn't have to rest in peace now, 'cuz that's all she did when she was alive. She'd sit on the porch under the mesquite with an ice bucket of Tecates. The big ones. She had a console stereo on the porch. One of the legs was missing so she used two bricks and a Bible, I swear to God, A BIBLE to hold it up. She'd sit and jam to the oldest Mexican songs in the world and talk to anyone on the street; her neighbors, little kids, and even men she didn't know.

I'd be kind of embarrassed if she was my mom, but those ugly sons of hers must've liked Doña Ofelia all right, because I heard that at the end of each week, they gave her their entire melon-picker paychecks, and she'd put them together and give them back some allowance. They're like big kids, except they use their allowances for beer and girls and cars instead of candy. When they bought the custom van with the little round windows on the side and the blue Firebird with the T-roof at the same time, everyone started saying they were taking marijuana across the border. They said Doña Ofelia was sleeping on a mattress full of drug money and betting thousands of dollars at the wrestling matches. Even buying gold rings and watches for El Puma. I know for a fact that El Puma would never let her or nobody look at his face under the mask, so she must have fallen in love with the way he looks in those little black underwears and boots, which I don't blame her for, 'cuz he gots all kinds of muscles on his arms and chest and even his caboose looks hard, like two turtles taking a nap. Personallly, it is my opinion that I think he looks good. Even my Papi, who loves to make fun of everybody and their dog, shoes, and haircuts, says El Puma looks good.

So we keep walking and on the corner, Negro says, "Hola, Señora Dolores. You want me to give Mario a shine?" Mami looks down at my shoes. I feel embarrassed that he saw they are all scratchy and dusty, but she's not sure about getting a shine.

"Seño," he says, "if you're going to Doña Ofelia's, his shoes should look nice. Gotta look nice if you're gonna pay respects, don't you think?" His smile is so nice, Mami has to think about getting me a shine. She touches the side of her neck with her handkerchief.

"Alright, *mijo*, but quickly, OK? It's hot out here." Negro tells me to put my foot up on his shoeshine box while he kneels in the dirt. He begins the shine and his hands just *go*. Voosh! Voosh! Voosh! He takes the dust off with his brush. He opens the wax and smears it on. He tells me how good it's gonna look and smiles. He rubs it in and pulls out the cleaning rag, and he snaps it so pretty and fast. Pah! Pah! Pah! and it's this dance with dirty hands and the dirty rag. Pah! Pah! Pah! and his shoulders and muscles move under his shirt with a wet spot on the back and I can't stop looking at how beautiful he makes a stupid shoeshine. Ptoo! He spits on my shoe and it gets even shinier and he tells me I look good and the girls are gonna love me in those shoes and I smile 'cuz I'm excited that he said that even though I don't like girls yet. One more time with the brush and then BOOM, the shoes look like fresh from the store window. He's done and he smiles.

He reaches up for his money, and through the hole of his sleeve I can see his underarm. There is a little black bush of hairs in it.

When I see his little hairs, I get this embarrassed feeling like I just saw him naked, and then I feel super sorry that he is so nice but he's stuck on this corner where the sun is going to burn him into a raisin and he'll still be poor. Mami pays him and then I put my hand into my pocket and all I have is American money, so I give him my special fifty cents with the beautiful dead President on it. Negro looks at the coin and he looks like it's Christmas. He smiles at me again. His eyes are *color cafe* with no milk.

"Thank you, seño," he says to Mami.

"Thank you, Isidro."

Isidro. Negro's real name is Isidro.

At Doña Ofelia's house, her family is all over the place. Even in the tree branches I can see their kids with their wrecked hair all wild and dusty like they been living in caves or something. When I see all the people I don't know, I wish I'd just stayed home reading comics or something. But it's too late, and now I gotta stay no matter what they say. Near the front gate, Doña Ofelia's sons, Los Sasquaches, are lined up, and shaking people's hands and sometimes hugging people. It's kinda mean to call them Sasquaches, but it's true. They're super tall with really big heads and bushy hair, and once the TV started showing *El Hombre Bionico* with Lee Majors fighting the Sasquach, well, that's what everyone called them.

When Mami shakes with each Sasquach, her hand looks like a pink baby hand.

"Ay, Roberto," she says, "your poor *madre*'s gone."

"Yeah," he says.

"I'm sorry, Roberto. The only good thing is that she didn't suffer. She went home in her sleep."

"True." Roberto looks at the ground.

I shake their hands, too. Tavo, the number-two Sasquach says "Are you Mario?"

"Yeah."

"Damn boy, you've grown." He looks me up and down. "And look how fat you've gotten." He grabs my stomach and says real loud to Roberto, "How many steaks you think we could get off this one?"

"Awww, he's just full of life," says Roberto. "He looks good, pretty like a pink piglet, not like those black bony monkey-boys of yours. This is a healthy boy. Señora Dolores!" he shouts to Mami, "what have you been feeding this boy? You trying to raise a wrestler?" Everyone looks at me and laughs because Roberto's pinching my cheeks, and mom just smiles and disappears into the house to join in the rosary. I want to follow, but he's got me trapped. Finally, I take my cheeks back and walk away. My face feels hot and it kind of hurts, then I kind of like it because he said I'm pretty, and then I don't like it because boys are supposed to be handsome, and he basically called me a pig. People in Mexico will say anything.

Whoa. The coffin is on the kitchen table under the porch. I walk to it, and I can smell her flowers. Her face looks puffy, but her makeup is more natural than usual. I touch my first dead hand and it feels almost normal, just a little cool and hard, like a muscle hand. It's weird because I am touching a dead hand and all around me the people are talking, eating, and drinking like it was a picnic. Under her back, they put this big satin pillow, and this is the creepy part, because the way she's sitting up, it looks like if she's trying to get outta the coffin. I'm glad it's not dark.

The bottom half of the coffin is closed and covered with all kinds of chrysanthemums and palm leaves. I know chrysanthemums because my Papi worked at Monterey Nurseries back in Watsonville, and he always brung them home. Even though chrysanthemums leave the water smelling like caca, they are very beautiful, especially the ones that are red on the top and yellowy underneath. All around the coffin they have these little stands with flowers. They have red carnations, white gladiolus, roses with baby's breath, and believe it or not, some Scrooge actually brought an empty mayonnaise jar full of pink and white oleander off some bush. They tried to make it all fancy an' shit by wrapping aluminum foil around it, but it didn't work.

The moms brung all kinds of food. There are beans, arroz, chile con carne, Mami's *pozole*, stuff to make tortas, Peñafiel sodas, hot coffee, and *Sponch!* cookies with marshmallow and coconut. This funeral is boss, man! When I look around, no one's crying. The Sasquaches just stand there all serious until people go past them, and then they just turn around and drink from their beers until someone new comes. The family and neighbors pass by Doña Ofelia's body and some of the visitors don't even *pretend* to be upset. They just look at her like they're at the store looking at pork chops or something.

Before anybody tells me to go play with the Sasquach kids, I look for Mami inside the house. It's dark and empty in the first room, but I follow the sound of praying. I see her and a bunch of women and a few old guys kneeling for the rosary. The curtains are shut tight, but there are lots of candles. It is seriously hot in this room. The old lady who is boss of the rosary has been doing it for a long time. She's really fast. The kneeling people can't hardly understand her, so sometimes they don't even realize they're supposed to do the response part. I find a perfect chair, jammed in a corner next to a big bureau. I join in on the part where they pray to Nuestra Señora de Guadalupe. It's an easy prayer, you just say "Pray for her" after each part, so I join in like a pro;

> *Holy Virgin of virgins.*
> Pray for her.
> Mother of Christ.
> Pray for her.
> Mother undefiled.
> Pray for her.

Queen of the patriarchs.
　　Pray for her.
Mirror of justice.
　　Pray for her.
Seat of wisdom.
　　Pray for her.
Tower of ivory.
　　Pray for her.
House of gold.
　　Pray for her.
Mystical rose.
　　Pray for her.

When I hear that, I stop praying. "Mystical Rose." That is the most beautiful thing I've ever heard, and I'm tripping out about how busy the Holy Mother must be if she has all those jobs, not just simple jobs like being mother of all the Mexicans and Catholics, but weird jobs like "Seat of wisdom." Then I just sit and listen. Kneeling in the corner, in the dark, I feel invisible and that makes me happy. Nobody is looking at me. Nobody is saying anything about me. I like it in this room with the women and the old guys and the mystical rose.

By the time we finish, some of the older people need help standing up. Mami finally gets to say hello to Patti the Parrot, her best friend of high school. Mami's eyes are all wet—but Patti seems pretty normal. I've heard since forever that Patti was the biggest talker ever, and I can see that it's the truth. She sits Mami down on the sofa and immediately starts talking. It is truly amazing. The words and the spit waterfall out of her mouth:

"It was so unexpected, the way Ofelia died, Dr. Maclobio saw her just last month, and he said she was overweight but healthy, and that she would dance the dance of the hot huarache all over our graves and would you believe what Maclobio did for his mother, which is so beautiful, he sent her on a trip to Rome and she got to see the first Easter mass of His Holiness the Pope John Paul II, may God keep him, and, as if that wasn't enough, she also got to go to the Holy Land, and she walked the twelve stations of the cross just like our Señor did, but she's always been a good walker, not like me, but I tried, you know Chavela and I started walking, but you can't do anything in this neighborhood without everyone trying to copy you, and pretty soon we had five or six *viejas* joining us every day for a walk. Hmmph. They even bought the same walking shoes as us. The only thing left was for the dogs to be wearing those same sneakers."

She stops and wipes the corners of her mouth. "Hmmph, and speaking of dogs, you should have seen Don Antonio cry when Chocolata died. He did not weep for his own wife half the tears he wept for that dog. I don't see what he was so upset about, poor creature had cataracts and was always farting, she must have been rotting from the inside. 'Don Antonio,' I'd say, 'Are you feeding this dog dead rats or what?' Always some kind of tragedy in the neighborhood, no? Did you hear about El Cerebro? You remember Rosita's baby, with the really big head? Can't remember his real name, but everyone called it El Cerebro, the poor thing. She had warned her old man about fixing the water boiler a thousand times, because it was making suspicious noises and shaking like Tongolele every time she got a cup of hot water, and of course, Mr. No-Good Drunk didn't fix it, and one day that rusty old boiler just *exploded* as the baby was passing by on his walker, and the poor thing got scalded on his big Martian head. To tell you the truth, I always thought that poor child was a bit retarded, and I'm sure this accident won't help. . . ."

I can tell Mami wants to add a word, but there's just no room for it. Patti describes the burns, which are pretty interesting, and Mami just kinda droops in her chair. I try to get her attention, and when she finally looks at me, I give her the "I wanna go home" look, but she just gives me the "There's nothing I can do" look.

I go back into the living room and sit on the sofa to watch TV. It's *Happy Days*, but it's not. It's in Spanish, and the voices are all weird. Mr. C. sounds really young, and the Fonz, to tell the truth, sounds like a pussy. I fall asleep and don't wake up till Mami shakes me. She looks kind of confused like she just got out of a car accident, but I can tell she's ready to leave, so we head out.

On the way home, I say "Your friend Patti really likes to talk, huh?"

"Yes."

The next morning, everyone is busy getting dressed for the burial. I take out my number two favorite shirt and put it on. Shit. I haven't worn it since Easter and now it fits really tight around my belly and my chest. The buttons look like they're trying to escape. I try to hold it in, but it doesn't help much, and besides, I can't hold it in all day. The only thing to do is wear a sweater vest, to cover up my poppin'-fresh shirt, which sucks because it's going to be hot. But I can't go in a plain T-shirt, so I put it on.

At Ofelia's house, everyone is waiting for the funeral car. Then it comes and I'm surprised. It's Roberto in a white flatbed Ford pickup. Four Sasquaches carry the coffin and then the flowers onto the back of the truck. The roses look all melted with their big red heads hanging down like sleepy winos. The gladiolus aren't looking very glad. Hah! The chrysanthemums are the worse of all. When Roberto loads them on the truck, they drop all kinds of petals. I guess the oleander in the mayonnaise jar were the best flowers after all. They look fresh like yesterday, except that the buds actually opened a little during the night.

The Sasquaches get into the white truck and we begin the trip to the cemetery.

In our Impala station wagon, we follow. Then I notice that we've passed the sports arena twice.

"Papi, are we lost?"

"No."

"Well, if we're not lost, how come we passed two times?"

"Because Ofelia loved going to the arena for wrestling matches, and she always said that when she died, we should take her around three times."

My sister and I look at each other real quick, and I look the other way, because I can tell we wanna have a laughing attack, and since it's a funeral, Papi will for sure slap us across the head.

After the third lap, we continue down Avenida Juarez, and then the white truck pulls over and everyone else does, too.

"Papi, why are we stopping here?" asks my sister.

"Remember Chon?"

"No."

"He was Ofelia's youngest son. The redhead."

"Ooh yeah, the crazy one."

"He wasn't crazy, *mija*, he was a *marijuano*."

"Now I remember him."

"Well, we've come to let him see Ofelia and say good-bye."

"They're taking Ofelia into jail?"

"No."

The guards bring Chon out. His hands are cuffed and his legs are chained together. Maybe his eyes are sad, but I don't know for sure from the sunglasses. His hair is cut super, super short. His droopy mustache looks like a big sad mouth. They open up the coffin for him and it's like he's looking at Medusa, because his face becomes stone. The wrinkles on his forehead. His jaw. It's all stone. With the back of one hand, he touches her face as if he doesn't wanna wake her up. The guards are really nice and they just stand there with their guns and don't say nothing. Finally he finishes and walks back. His jail pants are all saggy in the back. His chains drag on the floor. He walks up the steps and he doesn't look back.

The Centinela Cemetery is pretty far out from town. Most of the people have little wooden crosses painted white with plastic roses and daisies, but then you get to the good neighborhood of the cemetery, where people have big crosses made of cement or rock, with their names in it. One lady named Aurelia Pacheco even had a little window on her cross and behind the window was her picture. It was pretty fancy, except that inside her window, the glass was full of drops of water, like tiny, tiny tears.

People are already circled around the hole and it feels strange that even now, it feels like they're going to church or something normal. Tomorrow, they'll just keep doing what they always do except they won't see Doña Ofelia, and it probably won't make a big difference anyway.

The top of Father Santamaria's head is pink and sweaty. He keeps drinking from his water bottle as he does the eulogy. "Ofelia loved wrestling matches, mariachi music, swimming in the ocean at San Felipe, and cooking for family dinners. She was the mother of five children, fourteen grandchildren, and two great-grandchildren. For her, family was everything, and we should now rejoice that she has rejoined her own mother Elpidia and her father Salvador at the feet of God. Now, if you will join me in a moment of silence before the mariachis play the music she loved best."

Mariachi is the music of Papi drinking with his friends all night and playing the songs again and again and I usually hate it, but today it's different. The first mariachi lifts his trumpet, puts it on his mouth and it cries. I feel the beginning of *"Volver Volver"* cutting through my chest and I finally understand why the drunks scream like women when this song comes on. It feels like you'll never stop being sad, never stop wishing you weren't a loser, but you are. You lose things. You lose people and you can't get them back. It almost feels good to admit it and start bawling like a baby, which is what everyone's doing now. The Sasquaches finally get it. Tavo covers his face, and his chubby fingers look so sad. Roberto's crying face is twisted up like he's laughing, and he stares at the coffin. It's too late for anything but a sad song and a quick good-bye.

I look up at Mami. She has her eyes closed, and still the tears sneak out. Even though I don't love Doña Ofelia, I start crying, too. I move a little bit so the sleeve of my shirt touches Mami's arm. While I stand there with my sleeve touching her, the trumpets sing the last bit of the song, and a breeze carries it into the desert.

8. Yesterday's Nihilist
By Randy Romano

"What else should I say? Everyone is gay."

Listening to Kurt Cobain, I'm standing at the train station waiting for Gea. She's late again. I'm looking for the orange spiked hairdo and leather jacket with patches all over it, her uniform. My mother dropped me off at the diner across the street, and now I light a cigarette at the station. Hopefully, no one saw her drop me off. I hate that minivan she drives. It's big and slow and my little brother always has his toys cluttered inside. I told her I was meeting friends at the diner. I lied. That car is fat and ugly, just like my mother. She's perfect driving it.

Still with headphones on: *"We feed off of each other, we can share our endorphins."* Kurt reminds me of the time Gea called me up at 2:00 A.M. on a school night. She was at a pay phone in the city. I heard a piercing beeping ambulance, then Gea crying and sucking snot through her nose. She wasn't making sense. I tried to comfort her, but she hung up on me. Later I found out she had an abortion. It was when she was working at this dom house as a dominatrix assistant. She was fifteen then, and already on heroin for two years. Gea Genocide.

Someone taps me on the shoulder. I turn around and it's her. With her used skinny arm and bony fingers, she grabs my nuts. It hurts a little so I smack her hand away and then we hug. She kisses the side of my cheek. On her cheek she has given herself a sexy mole. I kiss it.

"When's the train coming?" she asks.

"Not for another twenty minutes."

"C'mon." She grabs me.

I follow her and we walk around the parking lot looking in car windows. Then she says, "Give me your key." She takes it out of my hand and starts keying all the cars that have a "W'04" sticker on them.

"Let's see how those fucking bastards like it when they get home and see a scratch on their car," she says. "Oh, this one! This one has to go. Is anyone looking?" she asks.

"Nope."

"Whip it out and piss in the gas tank."

I stare at her.

"You got a dick. Whip it out and piss in the fucking gas tank."

Gea has never seen my cock before. At seventeen, no one really has. I don't want to, but I don't want to seem like a coward either. I try to open the covering to the gas tank, but it's locked. I whip it out, but cover my dick with my hand. She's not looking anyway.

"You done yet?" she asks.

"The tank's locked."

"Then just piss on the car."

"I can't get started."

"Ugh, get out of the way, I'll do it."

She pulls down her tight Jean-Paul Gaultier pants, which she stole from Tokyo 7, and tries to piss the best a girl can standing up. She doesn't notice the gas tank is closed. Not wearing any underwear, she's pissing down the side of this guy's car. It gets all over her legs, and when she is done, she pulls up her pants without wiping. She has no problem getting naked in front of me. Why would she? She was in a magazine once. I have a copy at home. She lied and told the photographer she was over eighteen. With the money, she bought heroin.

We get on the LIRR and people are looking at us. The train is filled, but not overflowing. Everyone has a seat. Lots of black people, but they all get off at Jamaica Station. All the black guys are listening to rap music. It's so loud you can hear it off their headphones as they rap to themselves. The black women are mostly older and carrying too many bags. They look as if they have been working too hard and have more work to go home to. My mother never has this look, yet she goes on about how tired she is all the time. Not so many yuppies on the train because this is a reverse commute. And it's too early to get all the drunken-loud-white-Long Island bridge-and-tunnel trash.

The conductor comes and I pay for Gea's train ticket. This goes without saying. Gea has a cigarette in her mouth and the conductor tells her there is no smoking on the train. Gea sticks out her tongue in a way that is more funny than mocking. The conductor's name tag says "Eddie." Weird name for a woman, but still, she looks like an Eddie. Masculine, but not dyke-ish. White and big-boned. Dark blonde uncombed hair under a LIRR hat that is not flattering. Taller than me, but I'm only five-foot-six. The conductor leaves and Gea gives me a present.

"Here," she says.

"What is it?"

"A book, stupid. You should read it."

It's one of those Dover thrift editions they sell for a dollar on spinning racks in stores. Oscar Wilde. I've heard of him. I know he's some kind of fag, or something.

"Look inside," she says. There's an inscription. I read it aloud.

"We are all in the gutter, but some of us are looking at the stars." It's in a script I didn't know she was capable of writing. The ink is red and very sexy.

"That will be a good starting point for you," she says.

"What the hell does that mean?"

Of course she laughs. I get sort of offended, and we don't say anything. She is playing with her safety pins and looking out the window. I want to look out the window too, but I can't without seeing her, so I look down the aisle.

We ride to the city in silence. We get to Penn Station, take the subway downtown, and then walk over to Alphabet City.

"Where are we going?" I say.

"I gotta go see somebody, then we'll go get something to eat at Yaffa," says Gea.

She takes me to her squat on Avenue D. We walk past lots of garbage on the street and don't say much. You can see a couple of rats scatter, or hear them move around inside the garbage bags looking for food.

I feel like I need to say something.

"How's Alan?" I say. I know she's been dating this punk kid Alan. I'd met him a few times; he was a lot nicer than I thought he would be. He didn't do drugs and was about the only punk in the whole city who wasn't in some kind of band.

"Ugh, that fucking asshole."

"I guess maybe you guys broke up?" I realize I haven't talked to Gea in a while about him, about anything.

"He moved to Chicago to become a Goth. Dyed his hair black, mascara and everything. I should've taught him how to do makeup before he left. He's dumb; he'll never get it right. He'll just go buying the first black something he sees."

We get to the squat. It's alright I guess, if you don't have any place else to go. They have running water somehow, but they all shit in buckets. I guess they don't have toilets. The building has several floors, but this room is one large open space. There are old couches, graffiti, a Chrissie Hynde poster, people sleeping scattered. Surprisingly, I don't think it's so bad, although I could never live here. I need my own toilet. I hear two people arguing whether Billy Idol was a punk or a sellout.

Gea introduces me to Scum. He got his name from a movie that was made from some book that got banned. He is from the UK and has been in and out of reform homes like the character in the movie. That's how the name stuck. I have no idea how he got to New York, though. Gea told me all this.

"Hey, mate." He shakes my hand. There are a bunch of other kids standing around. Some punks, some junkies, some dykes, I think.

"I'll be right back," Gea says to me. She goes to another floor with Scum and I hear them laughing loudly as they are walking away.

I sit on an upside-down milk crate against the wall. I take out the book Gea gave me on the train and start flipping through the poem titles. I don't read any of the poems, just the titles. That's when I see Matt. I had met him once before, standing outside a punk show Gea took me to. We didn't go inside; we had missed the show. I think she just went there to cop.

Matt is a skinhead and a huge guy. He must weigh about three-fifty or three-sixty and is over six feet tall. Bald head, tattoos, military pants with the straps hanging out, white laced Docs, pale skin, red cheeks. I glance over at him and he is doing something manly. Playing with the other boys and girls, arm wrestling and winning, picking people up and tossing them easily; they are all joking and having a great time. I am thinking I'm just the fag in the corner.

The thing that turns me on most about him though, is not his masculinity or my daydreams of him protecting me. It's his fat chubby fingers. I have a thing for chubby fingers, as well as chubby boys, but I can't say anything about it. It would be like coming out twice.

There is this kid in my math class, Craig. He's a pale chubby boy and plays offensive line. He has this husky corn-fed look like he grew up in Indiana. I steal secretive glances at him when he is at football practice and I pass by the field, lighting a cigarette, walking home from detention.

Craig used to sit next to me before he moved to sit with his jock friends. He wasn't the smartest guy, but he tried to pay attention. We had a logic test. I knew my stuff, but looking at Craig, I could tell he was nervous. I moved my arm and exposed my answers. If he would copy my test, he would pass just fine. I was done with my test before him, so I put my head down and stared under his desk. He has those meaty thighs that rub together and generate lots of heat when he walks. The kind of thighs that always look ready to bust loose when he wears jeans. I bet they would keep my cheeks nice and warm while my face was down there under his fat belly.

Like Craig, Matt has chubby fingers, but they are tattooed. There is something sweaty and sincere, comforting and protective about them. I have never gotten close enough to see what they say. Doesn't matter really. I just picture myself in embarrassing naked positions, the chubby fingers telling me what to do. It would hurt at first if he stuck them in me, or I might have to open my mouth real wide to suck on them. I also imagine how large the imprint would be if he were to smack me hard on my butt or chest. He would get into that sort of thing, I bet; smacking my chest and back and butt while he makes masculine grunting noises, and I moan like a little brother. Big hands, chubby fingers.

Gea comes back into the room with Scum. Matt runs over and hugs her, squeezes her, roughly. She puts up her hands like she broke something, like when someone doesn't want you to touch their hair. He is joking and having fun; she doesn't want to be bothered. He says something loudly to her that I can hear, but I can't make out the actual words. She isn't angry, but she keeps walking toward me like a drunk, and flips him off with two fingers like they do in England. One time she told me about how she fucked this guy named Matt.

How he had a small penis, but smelled good like alcohol. It wasn't until I met him outside the punk show that I knew who she was talking about.

"C'mon let's go," she says to me. She grabs my hand and I rise off the milk crate. I take a last look over at Matt. I don't think he ever knew I was in the room. She puts her arm around my waist and I put mine around her shoulder, only because I am taller.

"That guy who grabbed me, that was Matt," she says.

"Oh."

"Next time, I'll introduce you two. He's an asshole, but a good guy. You know what I mean," she says.

What does she mean by "introduce"? She saw me eyeballing him? I didn't think I was being that obvious. She knows I like boys; she knew it before I did. She knows I wish I were her so I could've fucked Matt. She knows I wish I were her.

"Where we goin'?" I say.

"Avenue A. Gotta go see Gerry."

"Aren't we were going to Yaffa?" I say. She doesn't hear me.

We get up and go outside; climb through the chain-link fence and onto the next block. She is walking real slow and looks very heavy all of a sudden. Her eyes for sure. I know what she did, but it's not a big deal. At least she didn't shoot in front of me—it grosses me out. I wonder how many times she will puke. I know she won't be happy until she does; that's when the feeling gets good, she says.

Gerry's is where she cops from most of the time. I've never met Gerry or been inside his place, but I have stood outside. I know he does a lot of business. He buzzes us in. The door to his place is wooden and crackling. Gea doesn't seem to be so doped out anymore. She seems kind of excited.

We get inside and this Spanish guy comes up and hugs her.

"Hey, girl, what you got for me today?" says Gerry.

"I didn't bring CDs this time, I brought cash." She proudly displays

two twenty-dollar bills. Gea told me once how Gerry accepts DVDs
and CDs in exchange for drugs.

"Who's your friend?" pointing at me.

"Oh this? This is . . . Strawberry." Strawberry! I could've
fucking killed her!

"Hey, Strawberry, nice to meet you." He can't help but smirk as
he shakes my hand. He knows that isn't my real name.

"Hey, cool place you got here, man," I say.

"Thanks. Hey, Gea, come check out my new laptop. Have a seat,
Strawberry." Gerry takes Gea to the other end of the room and I start
checking out his place. I sit down on a black leather love seat. The
apartment is much nicer on the inside than the building let on. A flat-
screen TV with a DVD player and surround sound. The walls and
floor are lined with CD towers. Lots of DVDs, too.

There are two white boys sitting on the couch; they are hooked
into this movie, passing back and forth a blunt that makes the room
smell real funny. I don't know what they are smoking, but it's not pot;
maybe it has pot mixed in it. It's definitely more chemical than natural.

"Hey, what you guys watching?"

They don't say anything at first, as if they are studying. Then one
of them says, "This *film*"—he makes sure to stress the word *film*—"is
called *Pi*."

OK, so we're watching *Pi*.

Then they start talking this technical language, and I don't know
what the hell they are saying. Cinematography this, editing here, and
mise-en-scène. They must be NYU trash. I try and latch on to what
they are saying and then watch the movie. But after about ten minutes of horrible acting, it just looks like a shitty black-and-white student film.

Gea comes back over with Gerry. "Why are you watching this
shitty movie?" she says. The two boys shrug her off like she is a kid
and doesn't know what she just said. They don't know what I know

about her. That she knows about films and books and crap like that. Lots of knowledge about artists and whatever, and she's never even been to "art" school. They don't know that she used to steal books all the time, read them, and then give them away or trade them. They don't know that she hooked up with this Polish director one time, and now she has a small part in some documentary that is viewed in a foreign country. They don't know that she used to hang with Richard Kern and he took all kinds of pictures of her. They just think she is some punk junkie. I have a book now, one. It's Oscar Wilde.

"Let's get the fuck outta here," she says. "All this motherfucker has is coke."

Gerry comes over before we are out the door. "Don't forget these so you don't come calling me later." He hands her a few Valium. I guess she bought some coke after all. "And don't go speedballin'!"

"Yeah, yeah," she says and we walk out.

We start walking around. Gea keeps bumping coke. It's Friday night and the avenue is packed with all sorts of characters. We get to Tompkins Square Park and just kind of hang out by one of the railings. It's real dark over here at night. There are usually lots of cops around, but we just take a walk when we feel they are getting too close.

"Hey, are we gonna go to Yaffa now? I'm fucking hungry," I say.

No response from Gea. She is just standing there. Not nodding off, not talking, not sleeping, not crying.

"Want me to take you back?" I say. No response. The only thing I can think of is to take her back to the squat. I don't know where else she hangs out around here. I grab her hand and we start walking. She is following me now. We walk past all the people on the street, and I guess we look like a couple. I like this feeling.

One time when she was real fucked up and came to school, I cut fifth period and we went out for pizza. She was nodding off in the booth as I was eating, but I was hungry and used to seeing her like this, so I just kept eating. All the JAPs kept looking over at us. I didn't care; they know nothing of Gea's world, or mine. I had to help her out of the seat when I was done, and I held her by the arm as we walked back to school. Walking though the suburbs, she asked me why we hadn't fucked yet. I didn't answer her. She asked me if I wanted to fuck her. I said I would, but I wanted her to be my girl first. I lied. I had to make something up; I was on the spot.

Again, on Avenue A, we look like a couple, walking through the East Village. We get to her squat and she sits on a stained chair. No one is around really. I sit next to her on the floor, which is filled with magazines. The magazines make a crackling mushy sound like when you step on them, or throw them across the room.

"Will you be OK here?" I say. No response but she is breathing and awake. I look around and I see Matt. I didn't see him when we walked in because he is lying on his back behind a couch. I am thinking I should go over there. That's what Gea would do. He is chubbier and not as tall as Craig. I think about Craig for a minute, but I need to see some belly.

I look over at Gea and she is sitting there breathing with her eyes closed. She looks uncomfortable the way she is propped up but doesn't seem to mind. There are two other people in the room, and they are lying on the floor facing the wall. They have their leather jackets covering themselves, and they are fucking very slowly. I don't know if they are a man and a woman together, or what.

I walk over behind the couch. Matt looks like he is passed out from alcohol as opposed to being tired. I see an almost-empty bottle of Jägermeister. What if he catches me touching him and kicks the shit out of me? What if he doesn't catch me and I get to see his penis? He's so fucking out of it.

The best part though, is that he is wearing a tight shirt of this punk band The Adicts. He has passed out with his big fleshy arms over his head so the shirt is up, exposing his belly. It is large, fleshy. It is white and pale just like the chubby checks on his face. His pants are

tight. Even though he is lying flat, his belly is big enough that it over-
hangs the waistline. His belly button is a great big hole but not cavernous. Everything on him is big. I notice the scraggly dirty-blond
hairs around his belly button. The hairs are not very long, but bent,
and in all sorts of directions.

No one is around. I decide it's OK to lift up his shirt. I want to
bunch it up toward his neck. I do it slowly and his snoring is not
interrupted.

He has a huge chest but no man boobs. His chest is not saggy at
all; it is very taut for being so massive. He's got chest hair, though not
as much as on his stomach. It's patchy and swirly, like an undeveloped
crop circle, more strawberry red than dirty blond, thickest in between
his breasts. There's the beginning of a stripe that badly wants to connect with the top of the hair on the belly. I still don't know how old
he is. I'm thinking definitely not over twenty—he can't be that old.

I stare at his chest. I'm still wondering what Gea would do. So I
take a finger and put it in my mouth to wet it, and circle one of his
nipples. My heart is beating, but he doesn't wake up. I feel my cock
leaking in my underwear. His nipples are baby pink, bordering on
translucent.

I want to see the hair under his arms. I can see a few strands peeking
out. They're a reddish color, against the backdrop of his T-shirt.

He's still asleep. I lean down to lift his shirt higher around his
underarms. Then I hear a bottle break, and a gaggle of punks coming
in. I quickly pull down Matt's shirt. He stops snoring but doesn't wake
up. It sounds like they are right behind me, but no one is there. I run
over to sit on a pile of magazines next to Gea, my back bent and knees
hunched into my chest. There's enough time for me to close my eyes
before the first punk walks in. Punks are always asleep here and in
weird positions; I figure no one will mind how uncomfortable I look.

All the punks walk in, making lots of noise. I pretend to wake up
from a slumber and poke at Gea. She wakes up but does not open her

eyes. Instead she adjusts herself to the side of the chair I am leaning against. She takes off her leather jacket without opening her eyes and puts it over me as I huddle closer to the love seat. She nuzzles her head against the arm of the chair; our faces are close enough to feel each other's breath. I rise a little to my knees, kiss her cheek again where the mole is located, and move back to the side of the chair, underneath her.

9. Thirds
By Dan Taulapapa McMullin

THE HIGHWAY FROM Moscow Minnesota was wet with rain. The rain swept through the trees of the farms, and off the sides of Karl's truck. A photograph from a trip to Mexico was tucked into the window's sun visor of a smiling woman with dyed blonde hair and reddened eyes holding a gun in both hands by her face, as behind her a desert stretched toward low blue hills. The photograph was more than twenty years old and had been on the sun visor for those more than twenty years.

The pores on the backs of Karl's hands were black with motor oil from working on his truck's engine for the second time this trip at a rest stop outside Moscow, and the thick veins running from his fingers down his forearms were outlined black with motor oil, too, although he had scrubbed them pink at the rest-stop sink. As he crossed the state line into North Dakota, the engine began rattling again. "Fuck," he said out loud, running his hands on his short-cropped red hair, pulling at the vee neck of his white T-shirt.

Orange-and-white striped road signs blocked the highway ahead of him, with a painted Detour sign pointing south. "Why can't it say how far the detour goes?" he thought, slowing. Turning south on the side road, his 18-wheeler truck rattled among the endless cornfields golden in the late afternoon, as the rain ended and the sky turned pale as blue can, again.

"*La Feria de las Flores*" played on the radio tuned to the once-rare, now-common Midwest Spanish-language station. Karl sang the words of the song with only a slight gringo accent; "*Atravesé la montaña pa' venir a ver las flores. No hay cerro que se me empine . . .*"

And then the radio died, and the truck's engine ground to a halt. "Fuck!" Karl groaned, the road empty for miles ahead and behind him. Without a choice, he slowed to a stop on the side of the road. No cars moved by, there was just the slow movement of the leaves of corn bending to the late afternoon wind. In the middle of the cornfield was a painted metal scarecrow, and in the distance beyond it was the shadow of a house.

Climbing down from his truck cab, Karl slammed the door behind him and lifted the side hood of the engine to find it covered in motor oil. Something had blown, he thought; it was not a quick fix. With a truck container full of frozen meat and a faulty refrigeration unit, Karl stared at his cell phone which was giving him an outside-service-range message. In the quiet of the fields he heard the barking of dogs from the direction of the house.

There was a narrow utility road running into the cornfield, which Karl followed, in search of a telephone. As he passed the painted scarecrow, he saw that it was a flat metal cutout, of a naked man upside down, legs and arms being torn apart by cutout metal dogs, Russian wolfhounds, the group painted in a realistic if somewhat stylized manner like an icon, the painted man's eyes wide with pain, blood streaming from his limbs. Karl stopped and stared. It felt as if time stopped, as the field took on the shadows. And then time started again.

Karl continued walking toward the house, the sunset behind it. He could see it was a villa, three stories high, built to resemble an Eastern Orthodox church with onion domes at three of the corners of the building and a balcony at the fourth. Small double windows with ornate metalwork dotted the sides of the house, the walls painted a smooth yellow with white trim. Crossing a paved driveway, Karl entered an encircling rose garden when he was attacked.

Falling under their weight and teeth before he saw them coming, one took him at the thigh on the groin, another at the opposite arm near his armpit, and the third held him by the neck, Russian wolfhounds, tall and elegant with long gray-and-white mottled hair and long fangs. None of them had broken his skin, they simply pinned him down with steely wet jaws, the ground rumbling with their growls.

He heard a door open and quick steps, as laid out on the gray gravel pathway he stared at the long thorns of the rosebushes and the bulging eyes of the hounds. A young woman stood above him, dressed in black with a white apron and a black-and-white cloth hat, a very old-fashioned maid's uniform. Her hair was long, thick and curly, she had a beautiful long face and hands and dark brown skin. She spoke to the wolfhounds in a foreign language, shouting with a strong voice:

"Halu! Halu, Maile! Aue! Halu!"

The dogs had let go of him and had scattered as she approached. Karl sat up feeling his neck and limbs but there was no blood, his skin was only scratched.

"Fuck, I thought I was dead."

"Bad dogs. Very bad dogs. Are you alright, then?"

"Yeah, I think so. Damn your dogs . . . sorry. But I'm alright, I guess. I need to use a phone, if I can. My truck's broke down on the road."

"Yes, of course. Come inside."

Karl followed the maid to the service entrance, which led to a large white kitchen. She leaned against the counter by the stove and pointed to an alcove to a small table in front of a window, a white telephone on the table. Although shaken by his encounter with the

dogs—or because of it—Karl felt annoyed by the shining surroundings
and the maid's uniform. He picked up the phone, but as he began to
dial, he got a busy signal. Trying again, he got the same result.

"The phone isn't working."

"The phone doesn't work."

"Well, thank you." Karl began to leave.

"Stay until morning."

"What?"

"The dogs will follow you in the dark, but in the morning,
Countess will put them down to sleep."

"Thank you. However, I don't want to stay here overnight."

On the gravel walk the three hounds stared at him with jaws
hanging, saliva in strings to their feet. Looking at the distance to the
open road, he took a firm step forward. The lead dog's lips curled
against its fangs, as the other dogs followed suit. Karl took another
firm step forward. The lead dog's jaws circled his ankle.

"Halu!"

The dogs moved away as the maid put her hand on Karl's
shoulder. Her touch was surprisingly strong.

"I can't bring them in; only Countess puts them away. They're
her dogs. I would just as soon throw them in the pot; they annoy me.
Come inside."

Their faces only a hand's width apart, Karl could smell the red
wine on the maid's breath and suddenly realized he was looking in
the face of a young man with long hair.

"I'm Mahu," the maid said, a young man named Mahu, who
seemed to sense Karl's realization of his gender but couldn't be bothered to acknowledge it, and didn't change the softness of breath in his
or her voice. "You can call me Mahu. What is your name?"

"Karl."

"Karl, it's clear skies now, but it could rain again, and there's no
place you can walk to around here, not tonight."

Karl looked down at the young man's arms that held him. They were dark and sinewy, the veins like black stone, and a taut waist. He could see the muscles and veins of Mahu's belly through the thin black gauze of the uniform, where the the white string of the apron cinched tightly. Karl looked up into Mahu's eyes, which shone black and wide as coming night.

Alone in the white kitchen, Mahu stood staring at the hot oven door that she held slightly open. A short, pale woman in a black dress entered the kitchen. She was barefoot, a triple necklace of black pearls encircling her neck, her rough gray hair tied back at the neck.

"Mahu, has it happened yet?"

"No, nothing's happened yet. Takes time, Countess."

"What do you stare at?"

"His whiskers. But they're gone now."

"Close it!"

"Why? Besides, I can't."

"Close it!"

Mahu closed the oven door. "The king is dead, let's eat the king."

"A horrible thing to say; that's the adjective I'd use."

There was a whining behind the wall of a shower tap being turned off and then the banging of a shower door closing.

"What was that?"

"Unexpected company, a truck driver. His 18-wheeler broke down on the road."

"I'm going to be sick."

"He'll be gone in the morning."

"This is madness. Did we do the right thing, Mahu?"

"We did what we had to."

"What will I tell people at church on Sunday, when they ask for him?"

"Tell them he went flying."

The short woman rocked with suppressed laughter as she sat at the kitchen table by the window. Her pale face was sweaty with hysteria.

"He couldn't fly."

"Do they know that?"

Karl stood at the doorway of the warm kitchen, wearing a fresh T-shirt and jeans, his hair still wet, a muscular man with a rough pale face, in his forties, staring at Countess and Mahu both shaking with laughter.

They stopped to stare back at Karl.

"Your truck broke down on the road?"

"Yes. Your dogs stopped me from getting very far away."

"I have little control over them; they were my late husband's. But they'll go into the kennel for their morning feed, and I can lock them up at that time. You're very welcome to stay the night, I can drive you to a garage tomorrow. You see the phones don't work. My husband didn't like phones. He was an art collector, not, unfortunately for us, a businessman. Sorry for the inconvenience."

"That's alright, you've been kind to me."

"Mahu, what's for dinner?"

"A soufflé, Countess."

"Let's eat upstairs in the library. Please set a table for three, Mahu. 'Countess' is the nickname my husband gave me, and it's what I go by now."

"I appreciate the hospitality."

"You're welcome, it's no problem."

Countess left the kitchen.

"Did her husband die recently?"

"Yesterday."

"You're kidding. Sorry to hear it."

"He was in a coma for months, from a car accident last year. He died here at home."

To Karl, Mahu would at one moment seem like a handsome,

wiry young man in black, as if dressed like a priest, and another moment she could seem like any calm young woman, leaning in her chair on one hip, her chin on one shoulder. Karl looked around the immaculate white room.

"You keep a very clean kitchen, Mahu."

"Let's go upstairs to the balcony, Karl, I want to have a smoke. The stars will be out tonight, my friend."

Mahu led Karl out of the service area, up a hallway filled with paintings into the main foyer, which, like most of the house, was covered from floor to high ceiling in paintings. There was many a room, such as the library, where there were paintings on the ceiling itself. Through the third-floor library, they found the balcony, where there was a glass dining table, the lamps and heaters shut off in the warm August night, the Milky Way as bright as a highway in the sky.

"Do you smoke?"

"No . . . Do you mind wearing that uniform?"

"I don't look so bad in it."

"You make the dress look good; it's not the dress."

"Where are you from, the Midwest?"

"All over the Midwest and Southwest, too. Now I practically live in my truck. I have an apartment in Minneapolis."

"Karl, what would you say if I told you we are cannibals tonight?"

"I'd say you were trying to make yourself too interesting, Mahu, and you don't need to."

"I'm not the kind that has the sort of device one uses to engage in deceit. But I should see how dinner is coming."

Countess walked onto the balcony with a small dark object carried on the palms of her hands.

"I brought our box, Mahu."

"Kalofa e si ̧keige." Mahu left them.

"I told you my husband was an art collector. He lost all the money we ever had collecting art."

Karl stared at the small black object, which disturbed him for the reverence in which Countess seemed to be holding it, as if it had religious meaning.

"What's the box for?"

"This? Nothing."

"Strange."

"It's just a little box."

"What's in it?"

"I don't know."

"I want to put my hand in it. But I shouldn't."

"Tell me, why?"

"It reminds me of something; I can't say."

"Then it doesn't remind you of anything. My husband had a mania for art. You can do anything you want to my box. But don't touch me. It's supposed to be sublime."

"I think so."

"Go on."

Karl could see now under the rising moon that the little box glittered; it was made of polished ebony.

"It's beautiful."

"How does it make you feel?"

"Ugly."

"Then it is beautiful."

"I'd like to ruin it."

"If you put your ugly hand in, you would."

"Then it wouldn't be beautiful, and I couldn't want it."

Soon Mahu came back pushing a dinner table toward them. She had changed into a dark red dress.

* * *

After they'd eaten, Countess left the table. Mahu idly shoved her hand into the bole of a tree growing in a large ceramic pot. The relationship between Countess and Mahu had changed over dinner, as though the maid's uniform was a game they'd been playing that day, which Karl guessed it indeed was.

"What brought you here, Mahu?"

"Countess and her husband are—were—are my parents. They adopted me and I adopted them a few years ago, when they were visiting American Samoa."

Countess had left the small black box on the table.

"Why didn't you put your hand in it?"

"I can't while you're watching."

"But we can't leave you alone, that's how we feel."

"I love to play catch. I love to run back and forth."

Mahu accepted Karl's humor and then suddenly touched his face tenderly.

"There are attic rooms in the onion domes of this house, Karl. My bedroom is right over there in that one. Let's go there, now."

Countess had turned out all the lights. Mahu led them through the hallways of the third floor by flashlight, something she seemed used to doing in the big house. Paintings loomed around them, leaning over on hanging wires and strings. There was no pattern to the collection; abstracts from the 1950s hung next to photorealistic paintings, next to nineteenth-century American primitive works. Karl hardly noticed though. Mahu glanced back at him as she led him up a cast-iron spiral staircase to her bedroom and her bed.

"Sometimes I find myself walking through this house not remembering at all where I'm going until I get there, like sleepwalking."

"I was going to sleep in the cab of my truck. It's comfortable there, the way I've got it rigged now. Sorry about my boots; they're dirty. I've gotten dust on the fine carpets. You know, I wanted to pick up that little black box Countess was showing me, and throw it over the balcony into the cornfield!"

"I think that's what she wanted you to do. To erase . . ."

Karl leaned to Mahu and kissed him, dark lipstick easing the movement of their lips and tongues. Mahu took Karl's hand and guided it under her dress until he grasped the large erection and Karl leaned over Mahu taking in her sex while holding both Mahu's hands down, until Mahu came with a moan.

"Fuck me now, Karl."

"Fucking ruins the thing for me."

"What thing?"

"The sublime. Looking at this beautiful painting, above your bed."

"I'm better than a painting, although they last longer."

"Do you miss him?"

"No. We spent our grief this whole year. We have no more to spend. One of the last artworks he purchased was a conceptual performance piece. It consisted of instructions in pencil on an index card telling the buyer how to dispose of his body when he passed away. The index card was signed. I couldn't tell you what it cost. Performing the concept of the art piece was the last thing we could do for him."

"What was it?"

"I already told you, but you can't take it in. Take your clothes off, Karl. It's getting late."

In the circular room, Mahu was stretched out on the small bed that barely fit the two of them, wearing just traces of paint on her face, her body dark and muscular from growing up on the family plantation; she smelled faintly of coconut oil and sweat. Karl took off everything but his boxers, as Mahu curiously touched lines of scars that could be traced on either side of Karl's chest.

"What are these from?"

"When I was a little boy, my mother wanted me to be a girl, Mahu. I grew up as a girl as a small child. One night there was an electrical fire in our home, but I woke up by the smell of the smoke. I still don't understand how, but I found a handgun. I went downstairs carrying it, to where my mother used to sleep on the couch when my father's snoring kept her up. We escaped the fire, my mother and I, but my father died in it. Afterwards we took a trip to Mexico where, with the gun I'd found, my mother shot herself. From then on I grew up with other homeless kids on the streets of Tijuana and San Diego, living as Karl then, living as a hustler until I could buy a truck, the same one I have now, although it's on its third engine."

The moonlight had moved from the bed to shine on the painting over Mahu's bed, of Dionysos and Ariadne flying in the night. Mahu poured a small amount of coconut oil into her hands rubbing them together to warm them and massaged Karl's very pale but muscular body in the quiet dark, until he fell asleep.

Mahu left him there and went downstairs to make some hot cocoa as she did almost every night before sleeping and as usual Countess was sitting there waiting patiently for Mahu to make the hot milk and mix the chocolate in.

"He looks like your dad."

"He looks exactly like him, but I thought we wouldn't talk about it."

"He could be his brother."

"I don't think they were, but who knows?"

"And did you. . . ?"

"Unlike you, when I touch something, it becomes beautiful to me, or when I touch someone."

Countess held a large knife in her hand.

"I'm going upstairs."

"What are you doing?"

Countess dropped the knife and it clattered against the white stone floor. "I don't know, anymore."

"I'm not stopping you. Go ahead, Countess. Go ahead, Lisa, it's time."

Lisa picked up the butcher knife again. Its blade was a long triangle, thick at the base, the handle was thick, too, and white. Lisa went with the knife up to the third floor, Mahu following her. In the dark of the hallway, Lisa began cutting down the paintings from the walls. She went into a mania, staggering from room to room knocking down the images that had obsessed her late husband to the floor, creating a havoc, until she was exhausted her body wracked by sobbing, falling on the dark green carpet of the library.

Mahu had watched silently the whole time and now sat cross-legged on the floor beside Lisa, wondering at the woman whom she'd called "Mom" for the last few years, the widow of her shared lover, the man whom she'd called "Dad," who had brought her to North Dakota like a piece of art from the South Pacific. And for the first time in years, Mahu sighed, she sighed as though she could relax at last, out of love and anger into a sadness that was peacefully common and everyday.

A splash that in time settled into the mirroring surface of a pool of water, was Lisa, calm again. Finally she rolled onto her back, her face near the open French doors of the balcony, the moonlight making her pale, smooth forehead shine in the darkness almost like the moon herself. She stared up into her "daughter" Mahu's eyes.

"Why don't you go up to him?"

"He's for you."

"No. He's for you. That's why he's here."

"He's here for you." What Mahu couldn't say—what she could see—was that she was a third in America. And that is what she would always be in houses like the one the art collector had built, guarded by silent alarms, ornate unbreakable windows, and highly trained watchdogs. She was outside the sanctity of something the safe call "marriage," that another camp would call "monotheism," but she could leave unnamed. Her mother closed her eyes as Mahu's tears touched Lisa's cheeks.

In the circular bedroom Lisa slid out of her black dress, keeping on her necklace of black pearls, taking off her bra to reveal firm white breasts over a small waist. In black panties, Lisa was now lying down next to Karl, who had woken up when she entered the room.

Leaving the situation unquestioned, Karl merely stated it as he saw it: "I don't think Mahu can understand someone like me, not really."

"I understand both of you. My father was a Russian-American film producer in Hollywood, but my mother's parents were Chinese and Hawaiian, I grew up in Hawaii. My mother was a contract player for Paramount Studios in the forties. She was in all the South Seas movies of the time, but because she was really Polynesian, she couldn't actually play a Polynesian in the movies—at least, not a talking one. She was a stand-in while the set was being lit for Dorothy Lamour, or she would be in the wide shots, dodging falling coconut trees in the film *Hurricane*. When I was a teenager, my mother had my eyes altered; I wanted to have Bette Davis eyes, and now I do. My cheekbones and nose were changed, I've avoided the sun religiously; my skin's been treated. What's more, when I left home, I began to live as a woman, which was even more important to me. I wanted to be a White Russian countess, not a Chinese-Hawaiian *hapa mahu*. I'm a she-male, I got breasts when I married Mahu's dad, but I never made the full transition. My late husband wouldn't let me. He needed that part of me more than I did. I'm a she-male."

"I'm a butch bitch."

"You mean?"

Karl pulled off his boxers to show a red triangle of pubic hair, and parted his legs to reveal the clean pink mons of a vagina. Lisa's breath quickened as Karl pulled down her black lace panties to reveal her large red uncut penis, which hardened completely as he touched it. Lisa entered Karl kissing him openmouthed, Karl's hands on Lisa's breasts. They both closed their eyes as Lisa traced the thin scars on the sides of Karl's chest.

Mahu, wearing blue jeans and cowboy boots, a white V-neck T-shirt, her hair tied in a thick ponytail, and with only a trace of mascara on her face, walked past the sleeping wolfhounds in the rose garden, and down the utility side road past the painted metal scarecrow to the main road. At Karl's truck, Mahu tried the door, which was unlocked. The key was still in the ignition. Climbing into the trucker's seat, Mahu slammed the cab door shut. At first try, the starter merely clicked. Mahu tried again, and on the third try the engine coughed, hesitated and, as she gave it more gas, rumbled into first gear, Karl had mistaken the truck's stalling for a complete breakdown. Negotiating the truck's difficult gearbox, Mahu turned and headed back toward the highway, where turning she drove the 18-wheeler toward the rising sun. *"La Feria de las Flores"* was playing again on the recorded broadcast. In an hour, Mahu was flying east passing Moscow, Minnesota, farther from her home back in the Samoan Islands than she ever dreamt she'd go.

10. Jax City Limits
By Michael Carroll

TOM AND I wouldn't start fighting until halfway through, but fighting's what comes to my mind first when I remember us together. Two high school kids fighting in the parboiling summer, the warm fall, the hot rainy spring, or the winter that could be unexpectedly cold in the morning, sunny and cool by noon, and hot and sticky again in the late afternoon. Three seasons in a day.

I'm in Arizona now, trying to put this together. Arizonans are superior and say, "Oh it's not the heat in Florida, it's that damn humidity! You couldn't pay me to live there." But they're mostly retirees here and they could use a little moisture themselves. God knows I miss the rain.

I saw Tom's book in a bookstore today, picked it up, saw his author photo (older, still handsome, even more so), and now I can't help thinking about north Florida.

We've been out of high school forever. It really only seems like recent history—not half a life ago—when we met in tenth grade, in world history.

When you're a kid, the most ridiculous, insincere, or unintended gestures can become the most serious acts of devotion.

He was tender, if not always affectionate. He was trusting. He was sweet if he wanted to be. He was a mama's boy. He liked things. He didn't tear them down, or he didn't until he felt crushed. He revolted a lot. He was always in a huff about something. I'd say something one of my parents would say, like "Don't get yourself in a lather," and he'd laugh hysterically. That would just kill him. "A *lather?* Is that what people in Pittsburgh say?"

My family had moved to Florida from Pennsylvania the year before, and he was always amused by my "Yankee" way of talking, my "proper" air, and my Catholicism, which I'd just as soon have gotten rid of.

I used to wear a tweed jacket my mother had given me, a hand-me-down my grandmother had always worn to church with a matching skirt before passing it on to my mother. Mom let me have it when we moved to Florida, I think, because it was too hot for her to wear it down there, and giving it to me was her signaling defeat and saying she'd never get out of Florida. Otherwise she mocked melodrama. Her parents were stoic, determined English Catholics who'd only ever known rural Maryland, before my grandfather's business expanded into Pittsburgh and brought them to Sewickley Heights. Mom always thought she'd stay there forever in that wholesome, self-satisfied environment. She couldn't figure out what had gone wrong or why my father was transferred to Jacksonville. She'd always done everything right.

After it started between Tom and me, she told me no matter what, I should try and make it work with Tom. He was a keeper. He was going places. She was just as in love with him as I was. I'm already getting ahead of myself. Usually the Zoloft helps me organize my thoughts.

Anyway, I'd pin my New Wave buttons to my wool lapels and wait for cool weather. The Police. Flock of Seagulls. Duran Duran. I sat in my room listening to that stuff, not doing my homework, just reading history and biographies of monarchs. Novels about nobility.

I could tell you the names of all of Henry VIII's wives and their daughters, but I couldn't concentrate on my schoolwork.

I used to set the needle on Side One of *Rio,* open *Anna Karenina,* and read a chapter for every song. ("Hungry Like the Wolf"—Prince Oblonsky's wife finds out he's having an affair.) After a while, in my dreamy loneliness, I couldn't separate literature from a series of three-and-a-half-minute pop masterpieces. It was like private transportation for a sixteen-year-old girl who had her driver's license but, until she met a guy in world history, had nowhere to go.

There was my neighbor Natalie, a primrose of a transplant from Ohio. Cincinnati, I think. Presbyterian, too, and didn't we all know it. That was the thing down there. You always knew everybody's faith. She went to Sunday school and church every week with her parents and brat of a little sister. I'd be sitting in the breakfast nook that looked out on the street with a southern exposure, and I'd see them all dressed up and getting in their Pontiac Bonneville. I'd be drinking chocolate milk. Natalie would be in her hat with the beaded veil and lace gloves—in that heat.

It was the same window, too, I was sitting at drinking Nestea whenever Tom would pull up in his father's Pinto wagon with fake paneling, beaming out with his big, straight smile (he'd gotten his braces off the year before). It was Natalie I was with when the whole thing started.

At the Baskin-Robbins. Tom worked there afternoons. He was the first guy in tenth grade we knew who had a job. We were all in world history together, Jack and Tom and Natalie and me. And one night Natalie and I went to see *Altered States* together at the Expressway Mall shopping strip, where the Baskin-Robbins was. In history that morning, Natalie had gone right up to Tom and asked if he was working that evening. Some shy and demure Presbyterian. She had two things in her sights, one of which was William and Mary. The other thing, she was going to work on Jack through Tom.

After the movie, as I was contemplating the sexiness of William Hurt in his wireframe glasses, she said, "All right, now let's go get us some big cones."

"You think?"

"Heck yes, we've gotta get you a man, girl!"

That was her way of saying she had to get herself one. She was nuts about Tom's best friend Jack. The grungiest blond-haired blue-eyed boy she could find; the sacred young gentile gone wrong, in need of some after-school evangelism. She couldn't stop talking about him, she was fascinated, repelled and smitten all at the same time. He didn't wear buttons, but he had T-shirts for every concert occasion. Ozzy Osbourne. Black Sabbath. AC/DC. He was very opinionated about all of them—like Tom was about books. Movies were where they connected, Tom and Jack, the shaded-in area where two circles overlapped. They were interesting together, those two, and this put double-dating into Natalie's mind.

We'd already gotten a lot of getting-to-know-you time in in world history. But it wasn't quality time, the time Natalie needed to get close to Jack. The lessons were usually over before the period was, and the teacher had severe headaches. Just Jack or Tom making some smart-ass comment about ancient civilization could send her into one: "And Mrs. Cash, this guy homo erectus—wasn't *he* the first man to learn how to use his tool? I mean properly."

"Believe it or not," she'd say wearily, "I've heard them all. I've been up here long enough to've heard them all. I know they're coming at me before you can even *think* of 'em."

And she'd proceed through the lesson as quickly as she could, dodging the barbs and zingers they flung her way, and be done with it. Then touch her fingertips lightly to her temples and make a tiny sound and announce, "Okay, quiet study time."

It would start off quiet enough, but then note-passing would turn to talking and laughing, and before long I was noticing every-thing wonderful about this guy, and he was smiling at me.

He looked silly in his uniform—ugly brown pants and a shirt of pink and brown and white stripes. A long girlish neck poking up out of the chocolate collar. Dark eyes and sandy-brown hair to match. You could see the handsomeness he would come into out of the awk-wardness one day. Outside of the classroom, he looked more vulner-able, and we weren't so smooth and glib together. The humor fell away, or should've. Natalie had suddenly gotten in the way without trying. She wanted him to be funny, the way he and Jack were together. She wanted Jack there with us.

I could see Tom watching me, trying to connect, making eye con-tact. He said he'd give us our ice cream free. The owner was an Iranian who'd gotten out of Tehran with his family, his life, and his Swiss bank book and started his business over here—where it was just as hot and just as backward. That was a joke, and Natalie laughed, but at the same time it wasn't a joke. It was the kind of ironic twisted-up dou-bling-back humor I realized he had and Natalie didn't (she *loved* crazy religious Florida, so Reaganish, so churchgoing!). I hadn't seen it behind the Plexiglass wall of sophomoric pranksterism he'd hidden behind playing straight man to Jack in the classroom.

Natalie babbled, wanting to know how Jack was, how long he and Tom had known each other, what they did together when they were alone. Vaguely Christian questions, come to think of it, and Tom could see her mind working behind her heavily mascaraed eye-lashes and lipsticky smile.

Tom dealt with it politely. He leaned against the glass door of the ice cream case—an act which he said if the owner saw it would get him fired, not that he cared. He was already looking for another job. He crossed his arms and rested his chin on his wrist. He said to me, "You care if I take you to a rehearsal?"

"A rehearsal? What rehearsal?"

"A band I'm photographer for. You haven't heard of them. They haven't broken yet."

"What are they called?"

"Swamp Honey."

I must have let out the hintiest bit of a knowing titter before I could control it. He smiled, nodding ironically, as if to say *I know, I know,* but went for it: "They're kind of Southern rock."

Now I really had to work to hold it in. Around there you were supposed to show your reverence for the local headliners who'd made it nationally. Some of them died in motorcycle crashes or been killed when their planes went down in some backwoods pine flats. They turned into redneck martyrs. But that wasn't the point. A rehearsal was something to do, something ominous and even maybe a little dangerous that gave the likes of Natalie a pause.

"Where?" I said.

"Out in the singer's dad's garage in Neptune Beach."

"That sounds interesting. Why do you have to be at rehearsal?" I asked.

"They want pictures of everything, the whole rise from starting-out to the record deal they're waiting for. They're opening for .38 Special at the Jacksonville Beach Flag Pavilion."

"When's that?"

"Soon. Thirty-eight Special want to do a thanks-Jacksonville concert for helping them make it, even though the big guys who've made it all live in Atlanta and L.A. now."

There's one concert I wasn't dying to attend.

"They want to give some of the other local boys a chance," he said. "I have this camera."

"It sounds like fun," I said.

"Great. I'm off in half an hour." He looked at Natalie.

She said, "I have to get up early for a canoe trip to Ichetucknee with my youth group in the morning. But, is Jack gonna be there?"

" 'Fraid not. He's more into the Clash and stuff like that."

That satisfied her, though she took it and tried to look like she didn't know what to do with it—as if she needed things like rock rehearsals and church youth group trips to tell her what to do with her time, how to make her decisions. But the worst of it was, I had to talk to Natalie and beg her to do something I knew she wouldn't want to. I had to ask her to lie—to deceive.

I took her aside and asked, "Can you please, please not let me drive you home tonight?"

"But why?"

"Because if they see me dropping you off my parents'll wonder where I went afterwards. They'll ask a million questions and won't like my answers."

"Well, what do you think, silly? They care about you. I can't just lie and say I was with you the whole time."

"You won't have to, if you go home the back way. It's not far, through the parking lot and down across the ditch behind here, then up to the back of your house."

Natalie made a face. "I don't know about doing it alone. Maybe if Tom comes with me, just till after the ditch."

"I don't mind," he said.

"That way I'd feel safer." Then she made another funny, wrinkly face. "But I just don't feel comfortable about the lying."

"It's not lying, it's avoiding the truth," offered Tom. "It's not the same thing."

It took a while, but we convinced her in the end, because she knew he still had to mop the floor and close the place. She left with a sarcastic smile, her voice in a theatrically higher pitch: "Okay! I just hope I don't get *raped.*"

We laughed about that and imitated her in the car all the way out to Neptune Beach.

It was just as awful as we expected. Loud and out of tune, redneck preening and rock star posturing. The singer was obnoxious, a pretty boy with a Simon LeBon shag haircut petrified with mousse. But we had a great time. We laughed a lot and ate a cheeseburger at Denny's, then Tom got me back into town by midnight. I told him how strict my father was with me, how he liked knowing I was with Natalie because she was the next best thing to me being with a nun and he couldn't afford to put me in Catholic school. Tom thought Catholicism was exotic. I got my first kiss from him in the parking lot, before I got back into my mother's car and drove home.

"I want to keep seeing you," he said.

"That sounds exotic," I said. We laughed. "Around my house at least."

It was helpful that my father was out of town a lot on business, setting up shop for his dairy company in Orlando and the rest of the state. My mother loved Tom and let him in the house at all hours. We had dinner and watched TV. We went to the movies. Even after meeting him and being pleasantly surprised, my father didn't realize just how safe I was in Tom's hands. Neither did I.

"Your dad doesn't want me to let you out on school nights," Mom said. "That's why I want you to go out and do exactly what you want tonight. Have fun!"

At the Ludlows', we spent a lot of time in his room listening to records—and listening to Tom talk about himself and his big plans for the future. He was constantly mentioning his body, asking for my opinions and suggestions: Was he "hippy"? Was he dangerously close to getting a big butt again?

"You had a big butt?" I said. "When?"

"Well I got close in junior high. I wasn't getting my growth spurts on time, in the right proportions. I looked like a pear, to be frank."

In my family (fat-policed to within a hair's breadth of our lives), having extra flesh or love handles was a capital crime. If any evidence showed itself in any unflattering positions—bending over, laughing heartily, or shaking to reveal my cellulite—my father wasted no time pointing it out and said I was lazy, I slept too much, ate too much, I had no discipline. (He was the paragon of discipline with his beer flab and football couch and cigar-smoking.) I was constantly beating back the rising tide of water retention that came with my menstrual cycle, bloating like an ocean swell at full moon, eating grapefruit, taking my mother's diuretics and flushing my system with a flood of the heavily chlorinated water flowing from our tap. But Tom didn't care what I looked like—and I should've taken this as a first sign. For the first time in my life I got out of myself and stopped being so self-conscious. Tom made me feel like it was great for me to just be me. There was always an adventure to be had with Tom, and he managed to make me feel something people in my family had never made me feel: vital, worthy, intelligent, needed.

I went everywhere with him, holding his camera bag as he took Swamp Honey's photos. In eleventh grade we joined yearbook together and I became an editor—I joked that I would be his editor when he became a writer—and he was assistant photographer. Anything to be together.

At one of Swamp Honey's barroom gigs, where we got in as the press despite the fact we were underage, Tom turned to me in the middle of all the banging and screeching of their good ol' boy metal and said, "Let's go to New York!"

"What?" I almost dropped one of his lenses.

"Let's drop out and move to New York!"

"Now? We're only in high school!"

"Screw that! We don't need school, we have our imaginations! We have our brains and our talents!"

In those days everything was coming on so fast, MTV and block-buster movies, new books we loved and kept up with and skipped school to check out from the library. And Tom was winning county contests for the essays and stories he wrote. He was drunk on the idea of telling a story. He sat at his typewriter for hours at night after dropping me off at my house. He'd call me at midnight and say, "A thousand words in two hours—that's a record for me!"

We were talking about marriage. We were reading all of John Irving and Tom said he could be happy just staying at home, being a househusband and writing his books. I said, "What am I going to do?"

He waved away the question. "Oh you'll think of something." All I could conceive of was reading. That's the only thing that felt like work that I was sure I was capable of. I flattered myself with the fantasy of myself as an editor in New York and supporting him while he stayed at home in our tiny cramped apartment and typed for hours on end.

The trouble, the arguments, began toward the end of eleventh grade, around the time of Mr. Ugly. And this is something I'm constantly going back to with Marinka, my therapist—an Austrian concentra-tion camp survivor who has this amazing lucidity, and can laser in and detect the finest shades of thinking a mixed-up girl was going through in Jacksonville, Florida back in the early Eighties. She says it was a simple case of denial on my part, and that Mr. Ugly would have been the perfect sign-post for me to have read if I hadn't been such a "narcissistically felicitous enabler."

Mr. Ugly was a drag show at our school, Terry Parker. Weird that a public high school in a Baptist-run town should sponsor a talent contest that featured boys in dresses prancing around on stage in front of their classmates, seducing the audience and drawing on their hidden feminine moves and instincts? Maybe not if you consider that the contestants were all athletic stars and club darlings, lip-synching to our favorite songs. Most guys didn't bat an eyelash at an offer to be a part of the silliness and camp. I just assumed that Tom, who when he was with Jack acted like he didn't care what people thought, would jump at the chance, too.

"Yearbook doesn't have anybody," I told Tom one day in the yearbook office.

"Yearbook can find somebody else," he said. He was working on a stack of backlogged photo cropping and acting as if instead he were going over plans for a nuclear reactor.

"It's always a lot of fun," I said. At first I actually thought I could talk him into it.

"I'd rather watch. And take pictures."

"But you heard Jack's going to be the one for Honor Society."

"He's the only one in that whole stiff bunch of jerks who'd do it, too. Don't bug me."

Lately he was starting to get irritable with me over the smallest exchanges.

I didn't realize they'd practically stopped hanging out together. I didn't know what the problem was, but Natalie—who had her ears to the ground for war drums, and her reasons—had fielded the intelligence. "Did you know that something happened between them?" she said one day in my kitchen.

"I didn't. What is it?"

"I don't know."

"Well, it's obviously private."

"Obviously."

"What do you think it is?"

She shrugged, evidently excited I was pursuing it, grinning victoriously.

"They're close pals," I said. "Things like that are bound to happen."

"Oh really? You and Tom are close. Has anything like that happened to the two of you?" I knew she wasn't getting anywhere with
the elusive, moody Jack, and she was digging around for explanations.

Natalie was president of Honor Society, so this was her big
chance. She offered to help Jack work up a really great number,
something New Wave with lots of balloons. There was a cute song
out on MTV, "Happy Birthday," and she wanted him to skip around
in a short velvet Shirley Temple skirt with ruffles underneath, which
she'd design and make, and a wig of sausage curls—and jump out of
a huge prettily wrapped giftbox when the curtain went up. Naturally
Jack wanted to go to the opposite extreme. He was working up a Led
Zeppelin number.

"Led Zeppelin?" I can hear her now. "Led Zeppelin?"

Natalie didn't approve of Led Zeppelin. She'd heard they were
Satan's helpers on earth or something Young Life-ish like that.

Then one day she suddenly announced, "I'm glad to report that
Tom and Jack seem to be making up."

"Tom said."

"And Jack's doing this weirdo number. Whatever, but Led Zeppelin? I mean, aren't they kind of in the past to start with?" Just a
couple years before the drummer for Led Zeppelin had asphyxiated
in his own vomit after an all-night drunk.

I got regular reports because Natalie was officially in charge of
the act and let him rehearse in her garage. What she'd said to me earlier was on the money: Tom and I had been fighting. He was stressed
out about something I didn't get and asked that we didn't see each
other for a while, though our lives were so closely entangled now with
school and yearbook I didn't know how we'd manage to swing that.

I had my own set of problems. My parents were fighting about
money and my father's frequent absences on "business trips," and I
needed someone to talk to about it. Without Tom I was high and dry.
I let him have his way, but at the same time we were supposed to be

going to the junior prom together, a week before Mr. Ugly. In the yearbook room and in class he'd ignore me, sitting doing his work, trying to look as if nothing bothered him. I didn't dare touch him, but I was saying my private prayers. One day I came toward him to talk to him about some captions and he tisked his tongue and turned away venomously.

"What is your problem?" I said, but he wouldn't talk or even acknowledge me. He stared away as if I were a fly or a bad smell he was waiting to go away.

So I waited. I bought my dress. I resisted the urge to call him at home and ask him coquettishly, "Wanna go with me to look at dresses? I'm a new woman, I can go to the prom alone if I have to. There's no obligation . . ."

I pouted and huffed around the house. My mother knew everything, but my father was confused. "I don't understand why you don't know if the two of you are going or not," he said.

"Because neither of us knows."

My father backed out of it. He was starting to give up easily on things now, I noticed. If my mother started an argument, he got flustered and threw up his hands.

"This is weird," he said, tisking his tongue.

"Men," my mother said over her shoulder, with a dry wink at me.

We went. Tom wanted to see all his friends, including Jack, who himself had had a hard time deciding. I guess you only get to attend senior prom as a junior once. At the last minute, I scoured Jacksonville for a dress, even the parts you weren't supposed to go to, and found one.

The event was going to be held at a downtown hotel overlooking the St. Johns called the Timucua—which had just been downgraded from a Sheraton. Other schools booked the Osceola Room in the Pelican across the river, elegant and just what you want. We got fluorescent lighting and no windows. But Tom didn't seem to notice. He was suddenly in one of his mysteriously sweet phases—and in the yearbook room the day before he said it was going to be beautiful, the night of his life, and he was glad to be sharing it with me.

He showed up in his new-used tomato-red Rabbit, which his father had bought him from a windfall. We sped off to the Rialto section of San Marco, the Art Deco district near the river—to a fancy meal without wine. He was restless, but effusive. I was pretty in lemon-pie taffeta, with my hair grown longer and curled at the ends. He was adorable in his black satin tux with the notched velour collar and a tennis tan and just-cut sandy hair. The waiters and other customers said we looked cute together and I wanted to cry. Then, strangely, his mood shifted south again and we got to the prom somber and serious about dancing. But we milled. We caught up with Natalie, the hopeful, conquering Amazon who'd briefly tamed a grateful, or a cowed, Jack, who right now was off in the men's room. When he came out, he was awfully mellow. I let Tom go over and spend some time with him before I said hello.

From across the room at the punch bowl Natalie and I watched them. Tom grinned and joked, Jack nodded slowly, looking trashed. Natalie was getting impatient. It was time to dance. When Tom came back I said, "Is Jack all right?"

"He's on 'ludes," he said, shaking his head disapprovingly. "I'm worried about him."

"Don't worry too much," I said.

He glowered at me. "Don't tell me what to do."

"Sorry."

"Seriously. He's my friend."

"I know."

He kept glowering. "Bitch."

Well, that sullied the mood. When the recorded music came on, it was this year's second biggest school theme, "All My Love," Led Zeppelin's power ballad with synthesizers squealing and drums hammering and bass and guitar coming in for the old reliable finish. Really romantic. But Tom was in heaven. Jack danced hectically with Natalie, whose boobs were coming out of her emerald strapless and projecting up at his greedy eyes. Each time he got his hands around her curves she giggled, but whenever he tried to move them up toward her breasts or down behind her full exuberant posterior, she snatched them away and gave him a flirty, but firm, grimace.

Sullenly Tom and I danced too. Then he offered to dance with other girls and let me dance with somebody else, which got me riled just as it was supposed to. "Do what you want, with whoever you want," he said.

"What's that supposed to mean?"

"Nothing. I'm going to go talk to Jack."

And off he went. The hens repaired to the punch and cookie table.

We watched as the guys slipped out of the main ballroom. "Where are they going?" said Natalie.

"To give you a rest and me a start," I said.

"Oh? Trouble in paradise?"

"Kiss off."

"Hey, what's that all about?"

"Nothing. Have some punch. I feel like eating this entire tray of pecan sandies."

"Nuh-uh, sister. We have to watch the back-forty, keep it trim."

"I noticed it didn't stop Jack."

Our friendship had always teetered, but now I didn't care. If I lost Tom I might as well lose my neighbor—that's really all she was to me, anyway. Not even a friend but a geographical accident, a circumstance, a convenience.

When Tom came back he had liquor on his breath, and that defined the rest of the evening. He got distant, but grabby. I settled for grabby. Cut to us in the car, speeding toward the beach down a deserted extension that was waiting to be connected to a bridge that wasn't yet built—all in anticipation of growth that could only happen if the deserted byways were opened.

We didn't talk. He'd stopped touching me. He just drove and sulked. We ended up at a Swamp Honey rehearsal.

When we walked into the garage in our prom clothes, without a camera, the lead singer sucked in his gut and lit a cigarette. "Look at that, y'all! Coupla young lovers, dressed to the *nines!* Hey remember the prom, guys?"

"No."

They were working on a song that didn't have a title yet, because the last line of the refrain, usually the goldmine for your title, didn't make sense to the rest of the band. The singer had written it. The theme was boy and girl doing what boy and girl apparently do best— drinking and carrying on and participating in this group figment called partying. Everyone just accepted the idea that lovers could get closer if there was booze and pot and your boyfriend's best buds were around to enhance the macho element smoothing the way for love— meaning sex. They had gotten it all wrong, and not just because the song had horrible lyrics.

"Well all right!" he screamed into the mike, to the accompaniment of a guitar flourish. "Hold on tight! Let's get it on! Let's all night!"

"The shit is that supposed to mean?" said the bassist, stopping the music. "That last part about 'let's all night'? Let's all night *what?*"

"Maybe it's a verb, Bobby," said the drummer, holding back a chuckle.

"Kiss my ass," said the singer, puffing on a voice-roughening, character-building Winston.

"Maybe the verb's missing," said the lead guitarist. "You know, like, let's do *blank* all night. Fill in the *blank.*"

"Yeah," said the bassist, "let the people listening to the album do all the work."

"It's a think piece," the drummer offered.

"First of all," said the singer, "fuck y'all. Secondly, we've got to pull together on this. It's not doing any of us any good to criticize and make fun of it. Now we need a song, y'all—a fucking good singalong-type song. We need something sounds like a hit."

"This ain't it," the guitarist said into his sleeve, wiping his nose on it.

"That's a real good attitude," the singer said, and Tom and I left, repeating parts of the conversation for laughs, doing their tired hard-times drawl, and making it up some. We went out to the beach and walked in the darkness and salty wind getting our faces sticky. We went back to the car and necked awhile with the gearshift between us. We kissed and tears came to my eyes. I reached down and felt his thigh, testing him. I moved my hand a little further up, and— nothing. No erection. He smiled and played with my hair. "I'm—I'm in love with Jack," he said.

The news relaxed things between Tom and me and let us talk. I learned everything I didn't already know about him in the next two weeks. What Tom didn't tell me fell into place like puzzle pieces.

We had to get through Mr. Ugly. The whole thing seemed to make him a lot more nervous than it did Jack.

He said he was in love with Jack. He could tell Jack that and Jack didn't mind hearing it, so long as Tom didn't make passes at him or want too much. They went way back. They had survived a boating accident together in junior high.

Now I kept a distance but on one occasion Natalie, as if forgetting how rude I'd been to her at the prom, invited me across the street for one of the final rehearsals. Perhaps she sensed imminent triumph over the recalcitrant Jack and wanted me to witness it, learn something.

Jack was in the outfit Tom helped him put together and Natalie had only tolerated. He'd gotten blade-thin in his latest growth spurts, and looked tall and forbidding in black suede boots, black catsuit, leopard-print gloves and matching scarf. The shock effect was topped off by a pair of wraparound shades which as he gazed at you through them, with his face made up, his lips cherried, put a chill in me. It was like looking into the face of my own irrelevance. How could I hope to compete with that?

The steps had been reluctantly worked out by Natalie—who'd taken Jazz dancing on top of all the other lessons she'd ever been able to round herself out with. Tom was following along in some of it, trying to make Jack more "pliable," but Jack didn't look like he needed much help. He had a mean, sexy determination and a red, red mouth that never opened. "Make the hip go out there," Tom would say. "Make it undulate. *More slowly.*" Then Jack would insinuate a hip-throw so smooth and controlled it took Tom's breath away. His stare went soft and placid. He was all but ignoring me and so I left before they got too far into the act.

It was all so surreal, this school-sanctioned perversity that was meant to be fun but that drew students and the contestants' families out by the hordes each year. It was a night of bracketed machismo. I don't know *what* it was but it wasn't what the church and community leaders had in mind for St. John's—the most conservative and whitest suburb in Jacksonville.

Tom was covering it for the yearbook, but he'd bought plenty of extra film to get Jack's every move. He told me that Jack hadn't told his father about being in the show. It was all very hush-hush, and for once Jack seemed nervous about something. His father was apparently very conventional and worried about Jack's nerdy taste for J. R. R. Tolkien and Dungeons and Dragons, as if somehow this was all an unhealthy sign of effeminacy and deviance.

So much expectation went into the show every year that tickets were sold out weeks in advance and people lined up for general admission seating a couple of hours before it started.

There were a lot of the usual acts—girly-girl parodies primping in front of cardboard vanities to *South Pacific* or Marilyn Monroe records. One head-scratcher was the moment two or three numbers in when a linebacker from the Braves (who'd finished "strong" but lost at the conference) came onstage in a wedding dress. His name was Fatboy and though he'd lost a lot of weight last year, he was regaining some of his sophomore year's heft in the off-season. He did Blondie's meandering and wan "Rapture," and with the wedding dress and his flatfootedness it got old fast; that song is five and a half minutes long. The audience loved it, though. It was one of the moments they'd waited for: seeing one of the BMOCs cutting up and showing us all what a good sport he was. That even though he was a cool guy, he still had heart and personality too.

But Jack wasn't a star. He wasn't a big man on campus. He was kind of a stoner and misfit and although people knew his face around school, they didn't know what to make of him. He did things his way. He'd gotten into a few fights. He'd never been busted but there was an unsavory air of screw-you settling in his vapor trail when he passed by. Mr. Ugly really wasn't a good venue for him. Maybe that's why he was here.

He came on with a few bars of "Whole Lotta Love." Just to establish a motif. Instantly there was a weirdness to somebody pantomiming a girl with a male singer's high-screaming but undeniably macho voice. And you didn't mess with the holy Zep or try anything funny.

The hip-tweaking bars faded and, with the help of Tom's brother who'd done the editing on his stereo at home, the coarse groaning chords of the scorching "Heartbreaker" broke through the darkness. The lights came up. He was standing with his back to the audience, his head down, one hand on his hip: "Hey fellas, have you heard the news?" filled the Terry Parker auditorium.

Sitting near the front row, I looked up at Tom, at the foot of the stage. He winked at me. But I was uneasy. I'd already started hearing reactions rumbling and rippling through the crowd. I felt heat coursing around my head and through my hair. My ears itched. My roots prickled.

It got a lot worse. Jack's was easily the best act—the best-choreographed, most together and professional number all evening—which must have scared the rednecks. He was all over the stage, breaking the rules and stinking up the joint with his hip-throws and kicks and whole-body snakey undulations. He didn't lip-synch: that was too corny. He moved and tossed his head to Robert Plant's blues-howling phrases—a slut in tune to the harsh judgments of her man.

The barroom-brawl music banged and ground toward an unknown payoff, but Jack kept on burning up the stage and shaking and pumping his legs and ass and windmilling his arms with far eastern hand movements flashing his red nails. It was like watching a cat without a mate burn itself out in heat.

"Faggot! Homo!"

It started in the back and moved like sheet lightning forward. The more they protested the harder Jack ground. Tom had all but stopped taking pictures, and he looked back and took a survey of the auditorium's reactions. I saw him give Jack an unsure warning look, but Jack didn't register more than a wink back to Tom.

The guitar cycled back over and over through its repetitive notes, and Jack slid sideways in his heels. The protests died down for now, and besides Jack had edited the song to go right into "Living Loving Maid," the funk-hop tune that got them swaying in their seats. Then out came Natalie—onto the stage in a midthigh babydoll dress of thin pale pink cotton, her hair up in pigtails, her expression a satire of kewpie innocence. Then a seduction dance began and the two war-ring forces, girlish innocence and womanly experience, had it out on stage, with Jack as the butch softening and needling and prying the prissy Natalie loose. The crowd loved it—or rather, the same guys who'd been quick to condemn his uncomfortably studied display of vampishness fell silent, then melted into hoots and hollers of appreciation when he gave them a fantasy scene of lesbian sex. The rest of the crowd—parents, teachers, and advisors—were visibly startled and uneasy. They stared, they turned to each other, they gasped and they groaned, and when it was all over, they'd had their way with the judges—and Jack came in second, on a technicality. He'd violated the one inviolable rule: there weren't supposed to be any *real* girls in Mr. Ugly.

He was angry, but Tom was satisfied. He was amazed that it got even that far. "They've never seen anything like this!" Tom said backstage.

"Fuck the judges," Jack said. "And fuck those redneck-ass hypocrites! We've gotta get out of this shitty city."

"That's what I've been trying to tell you all along," Tom said. "Let's go man! Let's get through the next year, graduate and go! Just you and me."

"Just fucking fly."

Natalie was taking off his makeup and stripping the catsuit from him. I looked over and she gave me a look, sighing. I knew she knew something. "Didn't you like *my* part, Tom?" she simpered.

"Yeah," he said, but in a lackluster voice. "It was cool."

"Cool?" said Jack. "It was dykey deluxe. *Blew* 'em away. Freaked 'em out!"

"Jack, will you stand still? I'm trying to peel this vinyl off your thighs."

"Ouch."

"But it was great," Tom said. "You had me scared there for a sec."

"*You* were scared? I thought they were going to come up on stage and kick my ass! I was ready, too. I wanted to kick some bubba butt, some queer jock ass . . ."

In the confusion of people thronging through getting at their loved ones I caught a look from Tom. But Jack didn't amend what he'd said. Natalie had a pleased look on her face. She was finally getting, in some form or another, exactly what she'd been working toward all along.

Tom and I drove to the river. An ungodly odor of pulp and acid drizzle floated in the air. The straggled lights of the Northside dotted the far bank to our right. The hubris and gaudiness of downtown shone in the towers and the arches of the bridges to the left.

One more year here. One more year of waiting for the final death blow to my parents' marriage. One more year of uneasy shelter—but shelter all the same.

I go back to this scene, over and over. I know I'll get it right in my head someday, but for now it still confounds me. The desperation. The denial. Everybody's denial. And, eventually, everybody's sudden, hands-thrown-up acceptance. It seems the whole identity movement since then has gotten it all muddled—and that somehow back then we'd gotten it all clumsily right.

Tom scooted over to the middle and gently nuzzled his hip against the gearshift. He took me in his arms and kissed me, holding me and caressing me and brushing, this time, only one tear from my eye. I can still taste the bitter firmness and feel the gliding warmth of his tongue.

11. The Oryx
By Lawrence Rinder

1

GRANT DROVE GINGERLY down the dusty washboard track, both hands gripping the leather-covered steering wheel.

"C'mon, Grandma, if you drive faster it won't bump so much," Dale scolded, slouching on the passenger's side of the rented Lexus SUV.

"It's so beautiful here," Grant answered. "What's the rush?"

The sky in front of them was radiant in the way that only Western skies can be, brimming with light even as the moon, full as a glass of milk, rose above the purple-dark ridge of the Anascopus Mountains. As they rounded a bend, the SUV's headlights cut across the desert, suddenly illuminating a herd of elk, eyes shining like demons, that stood on the opposite side of a broad arroyo. The car shivered over a ridge, bringing into view a valley enclosed by rocky mesas. A nearly dry creek wound across the valley floor, through fields of gray green alfalfa, and emptied into a small lake abutting the low-slung adobe once called Fort Chance and now known as the Fort Chance Inn.

"Looks like there's no one else here," Grant observed as their car swung into the gravel lot and crunched to a dusty halt. The inn presented a sullen face to the darkening valley: high walls of chocolate brown adobe broken only by widely spaced gun portals, round watchtowers, and several ancient wooden doors. They pulled their bags from the car and stopped to marvel at the silence, a silence broken only by the rhythmic shushing of swallows' wings.

A pair of dogs came bounding from the inn, tumbling over one another as they scampered through a portal and across the lot, wagging as they came, not merely their tails, but each entire dog wriggling and twisting in a corkscrew of obsequiousness and joy.

Grant crouched down. "Oh, yes, what fine animals!" he burbled as they lapped at his face.

"That's a blue pointer," Dale noted. "Best shooting dog money can buy."

"Really." Grant had detected a distinctly fecal odor to the dogs' breath. He stood up and made a mental note to wash his face at the first possible moment.

"The other one is just a stupid retriever," Dale added.

The dogs were already bounding back toward a glowing doorway in the dark-walled inn.

Dale and Grant lifted their bags and followed. Passing through the portal, easily as thick as it was high, they found themselves in a peaceful inner courtyard where small lanterns, arranged in regular intervals along the flagstone walkways, cast warm light onto the walls and into the drooping branches of several ancient pepper trees. At the center of the courtyard, a small fountain splashed; a discreet sign toward the far end indicated the location of the office.

"Good evening, how're y'all tonight?" Dale held out his hand across the office desk. "I'm Dale Rogers and this is my friend, Grant Atkins."

"Hi, I'm Sally-Ann," said the woman behind the desk. "And this is my husband, Fraser." She gestured toward the man entering the door behind them. The couple looked to Grant more like pastel-and-khaki Martha's Vineyard types than true Texans.

Fraser shook their hands firmly. "Welcome. Did you have a nice drive out?"

"It was spectacular," Grant replied. "Who knew Texas was so beautiful? The moon came up and we saw some elk at the head of the valley. They looked kind of shaggy for a desert climate."

"They're not indigenous to the area," explained Sally-Ann. "The owner keeps them here. He's got loads of species. Did you see the oryx?"

"No." Grant tried to conjure an image of an oryx. "We must have missed that."

"Maybe you'll see him tomorrow, if you're lucky. Have you been to the inn before?"

"I have," said Dale. "With my wife and boys, about a year ago. We were here with the Museum of Modern Art group."

"We've been seeing lots of museum folks here," Fraser noted. "They come for the art foundation down in Marfa. I never would have guessed that place would be so popular. Bunch of metal cubes stuck out in the desert. Go figure."

"Who else comes here?" Grant asked. "It looks like we're the only guests tonight."

"Oh, we get all sorts of folks," said Sally-Ann. "Mostly oil people from Houston. Sometimes L.A."

"I can't wait to look around," said Grant enthusiastically.

"That would take a while," said Fraser with a quick laugh. "We have thirty thousand acres. Thirty miles from one end of the ranch to the other. You're going to love riding here. The terrain is stunning. Classic West Texas."

"Unfortunately, we have to leave early tomorrow morning," said Dale. "No time for a ride."

Sally-Ann cast them a sympathetic look.

"Unless maybe we can go now," offered Grant. "The moon is pretty bright."

"We need at least two hours' notice to saddle up," said Fraser. "And anyway, Pete, our wrangler, has gone back into town."

"Maybe we can take a walk, at least, before dinner," Dale said. "We can bring the dogs."

"They'd love that," Sally-Ann assured. "Especially Juana."

Hearing her name, the blue pointer, now settled by the door, raised her eyelids.

"She's a great dog," said Dale.

Juana's tail thumped knowingly.

"Yes," said Sally-Ann with a proud, motherly look. "Let me show you to your room."

Dale and Grant retrieved their bags and followed Sally-Ann across the courtyard and down a broad wooden veranda. Stepping through a set of tall French doors they entered a large hall that smelled of leather and mesquite, with a high ceiling supported by at least a dozen enormous wooden beams showing traces of having been festively painted long, long ago. At the far end was a cavernous fireplace above which the whitewashed wall was streaked with soot.

"This is our formal dining room," said Sally-Ann as they traveled the length of a massive table lined with more than two dozen high-backed, intricately carved Spanish Colonial chairs. On the walls hung ancient canvases, gloomy black rectangles in which Grant could discern the pale shadows of long-departed *patróns*. "The furniture and most of the paintings are original to the place. Some of them are seventeenth century," she said over her shoulder.

They passed into an equally spacious but less-formal room, where leather sofas and overstuffed chairs were arranged into several sitting areas. "The bar's over there," said Sally-Ann. "Help yourselves to anything. If you like to read we have a wonderful library." She gestured to an area filled with the distinctive russet, magenta, and golden hues of fine antique editions. "We have satellite TV and a collection of over three hundred DVDs, on the other side of the courtyard near the weight room and spa."

Passing through a swinging door, they entered a large kitchen where a casually dressed woman was busy scooping out avocados.

"This is Graciella, your cook," said Sally-Ann.

"Pleased to meet you," Dale said. "Looks like you're fixin' up some amazing guacamole there. That's good, because I'm starving! What time's dinner?"

"*A que hora está la cena?*" translated Sally-Ann.

"*Eso depende de lo que ellos quieren el pez o la carne.*"

"Would you like fish—it's fresh sea bass—or elk steaks from our own herd?"

"Elk!" exclaimed Dale. "I bet you cook a mean elk, Graciella!"

"I'll take the fish," said Grant despite his chagrin at consuming something he'd heard was on the endangered-species list. He couldn't bring himself to eat one of those exquisite animals he'd admired just minutes before.

"*Uno de cada uno,*" Sally-Ann explained.

"*Bueno, la cena está a las siete y treinta.*"

"Got that, boys? Dinner will be right out here." Sally-Ann led the way onto a broad terrace overlooking the lake they had seen from the drive. A table was already set for two, complete with a pair of elegant candles and a bottle of champagne chilling in a silver ice bucket nearby. I guess they know what the deal is, Grant thought, relieved that it didn't seem to matter.

Sally-Ann continued down an enclosed walkway, pointing out old photographs of the fort and ranch that hung along the walls. "This place was settled before Jamestown," she told them. "Oldest site inhabited by Europeans in the United States. Spanish for three hundred years, Mexican for fifteen, and Texan for the rest. The present fort was built in 1740 to guard the pass between the Rio Grande and the Rio Verde against the Apaches. Indians took it six or seven times but never could hold it for long. During the War Between the States we actually kept a garrison out here. After that, without any wars to fight, the place fell into disrepair. When Warner Brothers bought it in 1930, it was more or less a ruin. Didn't have to do much fixin' up to use it as a location for Westerns. Then, in 1955, when they filmed *Giant* up in Marfa, Fort Chance was given a real Hollywood makeover so the stars would have a suitable place. James Dean, Rock Hudson, Sal Mineo—they all stayed here. Liz Taylor, too. What a wild time they must have had! In fact, Rock Hudson stayed in your room. Here we are."

Sally-Ann opened heavy double wooden doors and turned on the lights. "We've tried to keep it pretty much as it was in the studio days, just added a few modern amenities. You've got five hundred channels on the TV. A Jacuzzi. The sound system is great—Bose— and you'll find tons of CDs in that cabinet. Feel free to light a fire. And the lake is heated—it's really a big pool—so even though it's chilly tonight, you might enjoy a swim. There are extra blankets in the armoire, for whoever is sleeping on the couch, or I could switch you to the room next door, which is just as nice but with two beds."

"That's OK," Dale said. "My wife always makes me sleep on the couch. I'm used to it. I know this is the only room with a Jacuzzi."

Sally-Ann laughed. "Not many people come to Fort Chance to sleep on the couch, but suit yourself. I'll be in the office until seven if you need anything. Have a nice walk." She pulled the doors closed behind her.

"Nosy bitch," said Dale.

"You didn't tell me you came here with your *wife*."

"What difference does it make?" Dale pulled the curtains shut and peered into the night to make sure Sally-Ann was gone. He walked over to the bed where Grant was sitting and unzipped his pants. "Want it?" he asked.

Grant stroked the inside of Dale's thigh and massaged his balls and stiffening dick. He loved the way men were impossibly soft in their most masculine part; it was something secret and anomalous about them. He thought about James Dean and pulled Dale onto the bed.

After changing clothes they set off in the direction indicated by Fraser. Grant called out, "Juana! Juana!" As they were leaving the compound through the animal-proof fence, she came speeding across the grass, followed by the slower Labrador.

"Look at that lazy shit," said Dale.

"She's fine, just a bit old," said Grant, giving the Lab a pat on the head.

"Like someone else I know," Dale smirked.

Grant punched Dale lightly in the arm. They followed an irrigation ditch lined with ancient cottonwoods until they came to another fence, beyond which the road curved onto a rocky hill.

"Let's go," Dale said and clambered over the gate.

The dogs wriggled underneath, then tore around the bend. Grant was tired and wanted nothing more than to settle in front of a fire with a nice glass of wine, but he scaled the fence and followed twenty paces behind Dale, ascending the steep road.

Dale was lighting a joint when Grant caught up with him. He inhaled deeply and passed the joint to Grant.

"No, thanks," said Grant. Pot didn't agree with him.

Dale sat on a boulder and took a few more hits before pinching out the joint with his fingers. "Awesome weed," he said.

"Investment bankers are not allowed to say 'awesome weed,'" noted Grant.

"Fuck you."

Juana tore by, emitting a despairing, plaintive wail.

"She's on to something," Dale said. "My blue sounded like that when she found a brace of doves."

"You hunted?"

"You betcha. Don't tell me you think it's wrong to hunt. I've seen you eat meat. It's a lot more honest to kill your own food than to buy it all wrapped up neat in a store."

"You eat doves?"

"Sure. Hell, we'd feed half the county when we went shooting at the King Ranch. Those Mexicans would pour into the fields after we were done. What's wrong with feeding the people?"

"I think it's revolting," Grant said. "I can't fathom how anyone could get pleasure from taking the life of another living thing."

Dale shrugged. "Let's go see what she found." He stood up and walked in the direction of where Juana was baying eerily.

They hadn't gone far along the road when Grant noticed tracks in the sandy soil, big tracks. "Check this out," he said.

Dale crouched down. "That's a puma," he said. "Not something I'd like to mess with at night without a gun, even with dogs around. Let's get out of here."

"Juana! Come!" called Grant.

They headed back the way they had come.

2

Dinner was not quite ready, but Graciella had set out the guacamole, chips, and salsa, and lit the candles on their table. The champagne bottle was coated with a glaze of dew.

"I wonder what she thinks of us," Grant whispered.

"It doesn't matter, as long as no one says the word," Dale answered. "Deny, deny, deny. Champers?"

Dale poured, then raised his glass.

"Deny, deny, deny," Grant toasted.

Fraser came through the kitchen door. "I thought you boys might like to know that we're going to have a couple more guests. A fellow from Houston and his son are flying in later tonight."

"To El Paso?" asked Grant. "They'll have a three-hour drive from there."

"No, they're landing here, a couple miles away, on our airstrip. He has a G4."

"Great plane," said Dale. "I had a G3, but the G4 is much handsomer. Great style."

"Absolutely," Fraser agreed. "That's the one I'd want. Makes those old Gulfstreams seem like a public bus."

Dale laughed. "Yeah, steerage."

Sally-Ann joined them. "Dinner's almost ready. Can I get you a cocktail?"

"Champagne's good for now," Grant replied.

"I wouldn't mind a martini, dry, no olive," Dale said.

"Coming right up," Sally-Ann said and made for the bar.

"Where y'all from?" asked Fraser.

"Birmingham," said Dale. "But this one's a Yankee. New Yawk City."

Fraser smiled and raised his glass as if to toast Grant and his arrival on Confederate soil.

"I'm from Gulfport. Met Sally-Ann there, though she's originally from Tuscaloosa. We used to be in real estate but got tired of the grind and moved out here."

"What kind of real estate?" Dale asked.

"Mostly condo development, Mississippi Gulf Coast, area around De Buys."

"I know it well," said Dale. "Used to spend my summers there when I was a kid. That coast was the most beautiful in America, miles of perfect white-sand beaches and nothing but a few funky towns. It's incredible what's happened to it."

"I know, we grew up there, too. It's kind of sad, but what can you do? There's nothing but high-rises now from De Buys to Beauvoir. And the traffic!"

Sally-Ann returned with Dale's martini and one for herself. "That was a good idea," she said. She'd put on a Johnny Cash CD; his melancholy voice floated gently from the inner room.

"He knows De Buys," Fraser said to Sally-Ann. "Spent his summers there."

"Isn't it wonderful?" she gushed. "I miss it."

"You certainly were in real estate there at the right time," Dale noted. "Must have cleaned up pretty well, especially if you were involved in the oil-boom days. Those Texans went wild."

"Alabamans, too," said Fraser. "Folks from Mobile, Houston, as far as Midland, come down, pay about anything for a piece of that pie."

"What's a place on the beach go for now?" asked Dale.

"Condo with an ocean view run you close to a million, depending on the location."

"Imagine that!" Dale shook his head. "My grandma's place must be worth a fortune."

"Where's that?" Sally-Ann asked.

"She owns Belevedere Island. And she's never even there. Lives down in Naples now."

"Lucy Chartres? She's your grandma?" Sally-Ann exclaimed.

"Yep," said Dale.

Graciella pushed backward through the door, carrying a tray with two plates of salad and a basket of steaming fresh corn muffins.

"Thank God!" Dale said. "I thought you'd died or something."

"This looks great!" Grant spread a napkin on his lap and filled his glass with red wine, a 1996 Chateau Lafite.

"That's the *white*-wine glass, dear," Dale said.

"We'll leave you to enjoy your dinner." Fraser took Sally-Ann by the arm.

"*Bon appétit,*" chirped Sally-Ann.

Grant poured his wine into the larger glass and filled Dale's. "You *do* want red, yes?"

"Sure." Dale toasted, "To a night of hot sex."

"To a good night's sleep," Grant returned.

"You're such an old lady!" Dale dug his fork into the pile of spinach, mesclun, and chard.

"I'm just kidding," said Grant.

Dale *did* look hot in the candlelight. At thirty-three, he was just outgrowing his baby fat and could sometimes look a bit bloated. Unshaven for two days and out of his Paul Smith suit, he had acquired a handsome, rugged look that matched his brazen personality.

"Did you take that Quaalude yet?" Dale asked.

"No."

"What are you waiting for? I want you loosened up after dinner."

Grant fiddled in his pocket until he found the pill. "Are you sure this is a Quaalude?" he asked.

His friend Mindy had made Grant promise that Dale was not going to kill him on their little desert adventure. She was highly suspicious of Grant's rich new lover from the South. "He's an asshole," she said when Dale got up from their table at Da Silvano to pee.

"It's great sex, that's all," Grant assured her.

"Eeeeuw!" she squealed, so loudly that diners at the adjoining tables glared.

"Yes, I'm sure. I told you, my cousin gave it to me. He's the king of pharmaceutical joy."

Grant swallowed the pill with a mouthful of Bordeaux.

"That's my boy," said Dale. "Would you look at that dog? Is that not the most beautiful dog you have ever seen?"

Grant turned to see Juana perched on a divan across the terrace, watching them with disconcerting alertness. The Lab was asleep next to her, his paws hanging comically off the edge of the cushion. Grant turned back.

"Sounds like Sally-Ann knows your grandma."

"I can assure you, that woman does not know my grandma. She may know who she is, but she doesn't know her."

"Still, don't you think you should be careful about telling them who you are? They already know you were here with your wife."

"Relax."

Graciella came in to clear the salad plates.

"Mucho gusto," said Grant, embarrassed that Dale had barely touched his food. Graciella smiled. She returned shortly with their main courses.

Grant's fish was perfect, flaky and dripping with buttery béchamel. Dale found his steak too rare; he asked Graciella to put it on the grill for another minute. As he quaffed the last of his second glass of wine, Grant felt the familiar floating sensation of the Quaalude kicking in.

Sally-Ann reappeared at the kitchen door holding a framed photo. "This should amuse you," she chirped, handing it to Dale. "That's my grandma and your grandma. They were in college together. Same sorority. Kappa Delta Tau at Ole Miss. I remember hearing stories about her when I was a kid. My grandma thought she was so exotic, always going off to Africa or some crazy place."

"Public education, the salvation of our democracy," Dale pronounced, handing back the photo.

"We saw panther tracks on our hike," Grant said.

"Puma," Dale corrected.

"Did you hear that, Fraser?" Sally-Ann asked. "They saw puma tracks."

Fraser had just come onto the terrace, carrying a fresh martini for his wife and another for himself. "Where? By your room?"

"No," replied Grant. "Up on the ridge, where you sent us for our walk. They were huge." He held his hands in an oval to indicate the size. "Juana had it cornered, but we didn't want to stick around."

"That's good. She's got the scent," said Fraser. "Better go see if the oryx is OK. Come on, Juana." He put down his martini and hurried off.

"What's an oryx?" Grant asked.

"It's a magnificent animal," Sally-Ann explained. "Very rare. African. Two long white horns. The coat is incredibly soft. You should be able to see it tomorrow morning, depending on what time that guy and his son get up."

"What's it doing here?" Grant asked.

"The owner likes to keep all sorts of animals. It's good for business."

"Who is the owner?" Dale asked.

"His name is Delaroche. Michael Delaroche."

"You don't like him, do you?" Dale said.

Sally-Ann smiled. "What makes you say that?"

"The way you say his name. Hard boss?"

"Little bit. He's very . . ."

"Fussy?" Dale offered.

"I guess you could call it that."

"You can tell," Dale said. "This place is too . . . I don't know. I mean, is this a ranch or a country club? All these fancy antiques. I bet he's single, right?"

"Right," Sally-Ann agreed.

"'Nuff said," concluded Dale.

Sally-Ann turned to Grant. "Are you married?"

"Not at present," he confessed.

Sally-Ann sighed. She checked her watch. "My goodness, it's almost time for *Angels in America*. Fraser and I watched Part One last week. He fell asleep, but I cried all through the last hour and a half."

"I saw it on Broadway," Grant said brightly. He was about to add how much he'd adored it, when Dale kicked him under the table.

"Did you?" Sally-Ann put her hand on his shoulder. "Well, if you boys would like to come see Part Two with us, please feel free. We'll be watching on the large screen in the main room since we have to hang around for those guys from Houston. I hope they're not too obnoxious. Sometimes hunters can be a real drag. I wish all our guests were as civilized as you two. It's one problem, living here: Not all the company is as liberal as we are."

"What makes you think we're liberal?" teased Dale.

"I don't mean politically," she clarified. "I don't care how you vote. I'm a George Bush man—woman—myself, even though Fraser can't stand him. Liberal socially. You know what I mean?"

"Not really," said Dale. "What *do* you mean?"

Graciella entered with dessert, a homemade rhubarb pie. *"Quieres café?"* she asked.

"Sí," Grant responded. *"Gracias."*

"OK," Dale said. "Cream and no sugar."

"Sí, señor," she said.

"How was your dinner?" Sally-Ann paused at the doorway.

"The salad was inedible and the steak was raw," Dale answered. "Let's see about this pie." He put a forkful in his mouth. "Hm-hm, that's a good rhubarb pie. Graciella is redeemed."

"I'm going to fix myself another cocktail," said Sally-Ann. "Want one?"

"Now, you hold on there," Dale protested. "Let me do the honors." He put his napkin onto the unfinished pie and got up. "Martini?"

"That would be nice," she replied silkily.

"You?" Dale said, looking over at Grant, who was watching the melting ice cream fill his plate with beautiful white and brown eddies.

"I'm fine for now," said Grant.

"Wimp," said Dale, winking at Sally-Ann as he walked past her into the next room. "I'm sick of this shit," they heard him say as Johnny Cash's crooning came to an abrupt end.

"Fun guy," Sally-Ann commented.

Grant could only grunt his assent. He found himself unable to lift his arms, which made finishing dessert—let alone tasting it—out of the question. Still, as long as nothing else was expected of him, he felt he'd be able to maintain his composure for a while longer.

A thumping hip-hop bass line pounded into the quiet night air. Dale reemerged, holding two filled-to-the-brim martinis, singing along with Missy Elliott. Sally-Ann seemed momentarily taken aback; her face twitched as if she'd been stung by something.

"Don't tell me you don't know how to have a good time," Dale said. "I know you Alabama girls!"

He took her hand and without much effort had Sally-Ann swaying back and forth to the music. He favored a bump-and-grind style that she resisted initially, but halfway through her martini— which Dale assisted her in drinking by holding the glass indulgently to her lips and pouring—she had become a more-than-willing accomplice.

Graciella came to clear the table. Seeing Dale's desecrated plate and Grant's untouched pie marooned in a puddle of silt-colored muck, she gave Grant a weak smile and shook her head, as if to say, "You didn't like it?"

Grant felt tears well in his eyes; his upper body started to quiver. Graciella sat down in Dale's chair and took hold of Grant's hand, hanging limply at his side, and held it to her breast, in the warm place above her dark cleavage. With her free hand she stroked Grant's face, wiping away tears that flowed uncontrollably now, down his cheeks.

"Dios mío," she said, shaking her head. *"Que sucedió con los jovenes pobres? Que sucedió?"*

Grant had no idea why he was crying. In fact, he found the whole scene quite amusing and was trying to remember as much as possible, so he could tell Mindy all about it when he got back to New York.

Dale had Sally-Ann bent over the divan that formerly held the queen of dogs, Juana, and was making rhythmic thrusting movements toward her rear, when Fraser appeared in the doorway with a shotgun in his hand.

Grant saw him—Dale and Sally-Ann could not—and tried to speak. Only meaningless syllables emerged. He watched helplessly as Fraser crossed the terrace behind them and vanished into the main room. The music stopped. Fraser reappeared, holding the shotgun by his side as carelessly as if he were carrying a shopping bag.

"Sally-Ann, let's let these boys enjoy themselves," he said wearily.

Sally-Ann stood up. She looked at Dale incredulously. Suddenly she slapped him hard across the face. "I ain't no Alabama ho!" she spat.

Graciella uttered something in Spanish and hurried into the kitchen.

"Come on, baby, time for bed," Fraser pleaded.

Sally-Ann snorted and marched toward her husband. As they were about to exit, Fraser turned and said flatly, "By the way, that cat you mentioned? He's in the back of my truck, if you want to take a look."

3

When Grant woke the following morning, he couldn't recall how he had gotten from the terrace into the bed. For that matter, he could not recall anything that had happened after the abrupt departure of Fraser and Sally-Ann. He turned over and saw that Dale was already up and doing e-mail. "What happened?" he asked, his voice cracked and gravelly.

"Better get a move on, baby-doll," Dale said. "We gots a plane to catch."

"Oh, fuck!" Grant disentangled himself from the sheets and shuffled to the bathroom. He could see that Dale, or perhaps both of them, had used the Jacuzzi the night before. The tattered remains of a dozen candles lined its marble edges, their drippings trailing like

miniature volcano flows into the tub; a torn condom wrapper lay on
the tile floor, and a towel with what appeared to be blood on it had
been tossed into a corner.

Grant stepped into the shower and adjusted the water to the
right degree of bite. He reached around to wash his tender asshole.
The Quaalude had not entirely worn off; he had to steady himself
with one hand on the side of the shower. This had not been a very
dignified holiday, he thought. He toweled off, shaved, and applied his
various morning creams. When he got back to the bedroom, Dale
was already carrying his luggage out the door.

"Hang on a second," Grant said.

"OK, but hurry up." Dale stood in the open doorway, letting in
a draught of frigid morning air.

Grant slipped on his jeans and a shirt and stuffed everything
else into his suitcase. He put on his shoes and coat, then followed
Dale along the walkway by the lake and through a side door to the
parking lot.

"Don't we have to check out? Did you pay?"

"It's all taken care of," Dale said. He opened the back of the SUV
and threw their bags inside.

They climbed in. Dale started the car and gunned the engine,
turning on the wipers to remove a pattern of frost from the windshield. As he backed the car into position to turn out of the lot, Juana
and the Lab came bounding from the doorway where they'd first
appeared when Dale and Grant arrived at the inn.

"Careful," said Grant.

"Don't worry. Dogs know how to stay out of the way."

They started down the dirt drive.

"What happened last night?" Grant asked. "I must have
blacked out."

"Let's just say you weren't the life of the party."

"What happened?"

"Well, Fraser must have forgotten about the other guests, because he left with his wife without waiting for them to arrive. I was trying to get you to stand up so I could walk you back to our room when Graciella came onto the terrace and said someone was there. I went with her to the front and met them, a really hot guy, probably forty-five or so, and his seventeen-year-old son, also stunning."

"Really?" said Grant. "Like how?"

"The older one: Viggo Mortenson. The son: Ashton Kutcher."

"Hm," said Grant. "Go on."

"I explained the situation and they said not to worry, they'd been here many times before and knew the place. I offered to make them some drinks. While they carried their stuff inside, I mixed martinis. The older guy, Brian I think his name was, got on the phone with that wrangler, Pete, the one Fraser said had gone to town. Graciella's husband. I heard him offer the guy a thousand bucks if he'd come up to the fort. We settled down and chatted a bit. Found out that he's a hedge-fund manager from Houston. The Carlyle Fund. My sister is invested with him. The kid is in boarding school in Virginia; Brian flew him out for the weekend. Likes to shoot."

"So they are hunters."

"Sort of. Anyway, after we finished our drinks, I asked if they'd help me carry you to the room. The three of us lifted you and lugged you to the bed. It was fun stripping off your pants in front of them—kind of tested the waters. The kid noticed lights in the driveway, so we headed back to the main house. Pete was waiting for us. Brian talked to him for a few minutes, and then he and his kid got their stuff and we piled into Pete's truck and headed out—this way, in fact. We drove for about ten miles, until we got to a corral. Pulled up next to a platform structure that overlooked the enclosure. They unloaded their things from the truck bed and carried them onto the platform. Down below, in the corral, was the most amazing animal I've ever seen—big as a horse and solid white, with two enormous horns, straight and sharp like two ivory spears, must have been four feet each. The moon was so bright, the animal cast a shadow like in midday. It was weird. The thing just stood there, looking up at us."

"The oryx," Grant moaned.

"The oryx. It didn't take them long to set up their equipment. High-powered automatic guns, probably designed to shoot holes in armored vehicles or something like that."

"This didn't happen," Grant moaned.

"Wait," said Dale, "I haven't gotten to the good part. The shooting lasted just a minute or so, although it seemed like a lot longer. It was certainly longer than necessary. There wasn't much left of that animal after the first couple of seconds. Then they repacked and we piled into the truck again. I guess that's what they do here."

Grant wanted to grab Dale by the throat and smash his head against the window, but forced himself to stay composed, to gaze straight ahead at the brown landscape of nameless ridges and ravines.

"Pete drove us back to the fort. The shooting had gotten the guys all worked up. Brian said something jokingly about wanting to check out my Jacuzzi. Of course I took him at his word and invited them over. Pete said he needed to get home or Graciella would worry, but Brian wouldn't take no for an answer. Finally said he'd make it worth Pete's while. That did it. Before you knew it, we were all in there. It was un-fucking-believable. Pete took it every way you can imagine."

"I *don't* believe you," Grant said. "You're a damn liar! You put me to bed, fucked me in the ass, took a bath, and fell asleep. Where was their car this morning?"

"Gone, I guess."

"Liar."

"There's the corral, look for yourself."

Ahead to the right, down a short slope, was a round wooden corral that looked like the kind used decades ago for rounding up sheep. Grant saw a platform beside it, just as Dale had described, then caught sight of something distinctive and incontrovertible shining in the morning sun. Blood. Splattered across the dirt in a wide arc, spreading well beyond the corral and mixing with the desert soil into something pink and indescribable.

"She said you'd see it in the morning," Dale said. "If you were lucky."

12. Cotton Candy
By Alistar McCartney

FOR A WHILE it seemed as if everything was going the way it was meant to go. Every day he wore the same thing, a simple dress of thin blue-and-white gingham that ended just above the knee. Although it was unusual for a boy to wear a dress, and although the dress, due to overuse, was beginning to smell like trash left out in the height of summer heat, a dress was what he was supposed to wear. He wore his warm auburn hair in two pigtails, plump as cinnamon twists. He lived on a farm somewhere in Kansas, with his Aunt Emmy and Uncle—what was his name?

There it was already beginning.

And although it was somewhat sad to be an orphan, his aunt and uncle were extremely kind, and farms are peaceful places, perfect places to grow up on, and he was on very good terms with all of the farmhands, and more importantly, that was how it had been scripted, and that was how it was, so that was good.

He had a constant companion in his yapping, sharp-toothed terrier Toto. The dog was daily subjected to death threats from—now, what was her name? You know, the woman on the bicycle, who rode very upright, who when placed under Technicolor light becomes a green witch?

And again here, it is already beginning.

Well, you know the woman I mean, and her threats, though they were upsetting, were impeccably stitched into the story, so they could be tolerated.

He spent an inordinate amount of time moping around the farm, dragging the heels of his pumps in the dust, tangled in webs of thoughts, lost in daydreams. He was fixated on rainbows: all that they concealed, all that lay beyond those pretty warps of water and shattered light. He positively thirsted for those brief arcs of colored water. You would not be wrong in saying that he was obsessed with them, but his thing for rainbows was the part that everyone loved the best, so its eccentricities could be ignored or forgotten.

The story only really begins t/here in the forgetting, in the lapse, in the unraveling. Now we have forgotten we can begin. We must begin.

In fact, the rainbow and the naïveté were placed there, as bright blinding decoys, to divert everyone from what really needed to be concealed: his secret taste for amphetamines, ground down into a fine white powder, then shot deep into the veins. Makes him grin a wide rind of a grin; makes him certain there's a rainbow rushing through his bloodstream. Bends him. His skin breaks out in red and blue and mauve and yellow bruises like his skin's the rainbow, blotting out the oh so much that is beyond him. Makes him for a moment forget the nagging grief and gnawing doubt curled tight within his heart, his core.

In blackout is how the story begins. With the song-and-dance resulting in amnesia. With his dancing on the fence bordering the pigsty; the fall into muck, and the bump upon the head. In blackout. No, that's not how it happens; it happens later, as he's looking out the window at the view. The view is flat and stark, and the force of the wind is so strong, the window is flung from its hinges the wind it tears the window flies out of the wall. The frame hits him hard on the head. Suddenly the view has disappeared; you can't have a view without a window. Or can you? What-

ever, he's out. Only now can the story begin. In the blackout and the sudden shift from stark to color. Everything was bare and barren, now it is a gaudy overflowing. That's the story. Is that the story? But we are leaping ahead.

His taste for speed was taxing, no question about it; not only that, it was a desperately kept secret the whole world knew about. The whole world was in on this habit acquired to curb his despair. That was slightly embarrassing, but it was all according to plan, so it could be borne.

Potentially worse were the premonitions. These visions came to him at all times, but especially while he was performing, singing and resinging *that* song he had come to dread, in concert halls all over the country, to auditoriums full of rouged men with flouncy hair and brittle wrists, men wearing silk blouses and brooches; slim-hipped men in tight wool trousers.

These visions varied, but there was one that was particularly persistent: it was an image of his own burial, even down to the date; June 28, 1969. In it, he saw his corpse sealed in a glossy black lacquered coffin with gold handles. This was terrible, but even more disquieting was the strange scene that ensued as his coffin was lowered into the ground, as the dirt and rose petals were shoveled onto the lid of the coffin. The men who had attended his concerts were all present at his funeral, dressed soberly in black frocks and black veils, balancing on black spiked heels. He could see faint traces of eel-silver and electric blue mascara peeking out through the scrim of their veils, a discreet concession to the dazzle that ruled their lives. Oddly enough, although they had loved the boy more than they loved themselves, loved him to the point of worship, in this grim reverie not one of them were crying. Their mascara was intact; their initialed handkerchiefs were dry.

Rather, to show their grief, they were stooping over, exposing their frilly knickers and girdles, picking up rocks and bottles, loosening their stiletto heels. The minute the last scoop of soil had covered the coffin, and the boy had fully disappeared, the mourners turned their attentions to the ink-blue rows of cops observing the funeral. They began hurling the rocks at the cops' stocky beer-barrel bodies, grinding the ends of the broken-off glass into the officer's bulldog baby faces, gouging out their bloodshot eyes with the sleek spikes of their stilettos. Some of the boy's mourners were overpowering the officers, pushing them facedown into the dirt, pulling down their trousers, lifting up their own skirts, and making a forced, violent love to them.

But we are leaping ahead. And the story begins, not in the blackout, but just before, and just after, with the whirl of the trees, their uprooting from the ground. In the spin of the cow and the bicycle and the kitchen table and the wooden chair and the china vase and the brass bed and the boy's body in the house and then the house. Torn from the foundations. In the tearing. In the uprooting, that's how the story begins. When things are set spinning.

This recurring omen of his own dying, and the odd, angry mourning that followed, made the boy dizzy.

When things are set spinning.

It affected his vocal performance: One night the black veils of the mourners were hovering there so close and clear it was as if he could touch them; in fact, he reached out his hand to pull back one of those black lace screens. Of course there was no real veil to touch, and losing his footing, he fell off the obstinate lip of the stage, and sprained his left ankle. Reporting the incident the next day, all the papers put it down to the boy's heavy intake of scotch and junk and speed. What with the daily delirium, and the bad press, the boy had a constant migraine. He was miserable, but there was a structure to his misery that had been mapped out for him, so the boy could not complain.

One day, back on the farm, a tornado came. This could have been highly alarming, for if you have seen the recent footage on TV,

you would know that tornadoes are devastating deeds. But the boy
was not overly concerned, for he had watched TV, and he knew that
this was how his life was meant to unfold. With the dog under his
arm, he stepped calmly into the giddy spool of the tornado.

But there was something about this tornado that deviated from
the one he had expected to come sweep him up in its twist and turn.
This tornado was pink and sticky, as if spun from cotton candy. In its
wake, it left not only acres of flattened silence, but also a sinister cloud
of sugared dust. It spun him and Toto right up out of Kansas and, as
arranged, delivered them somewhere else, far away. To be suddenly
so far away was disorienting, but at the same time it wasn't a surprise.
What was surprising was the taste and shade of the tornado. As he
alighted out of it, he looked down at his skin: it was coated in soft
crooked lines that glittered in the light, lines like the trails left by the
tide, yet not white and salty, but pink and exceedingly sweet. The boy
was taken aback slightly but thought that perhaps he had not read the
script carefully, and had missed this part.

He looked around him, and as he had anticipated, he was in a
new and very strange place. The grass and the buildings and the
flowers, everything looked plastic and fake in the bubbly air, bathed
in a soda-pop light. The place seemed so strange that it felt familiar,
and this pleased the boy.

He wandered around, soaking up the strangeness of everything.
For a time, this was enough, but soon he grew bored, and in his
boredom, he began to notice that a great number of things that he had
been informed would be there, were missing. Where, for instance,
were the very short compact folk with the shrill voices? Where was
the curved road of canary yellow brick? And what about the Wicked
Witch of the West—where was she, with that dry skin of hers, like
green crepe paper? What of the man constructed from tin, and the
other guy, formed out of straw? The lion in the forest and the coma
in the poppies and the malevolent monkeys with the wings?

The boy searched everywhere, but not one of these features was to be found. Well, he thought, the story can't proceed, without them there is no story.

In the beginning.

And I've seen everything there is to see here; perhaps it's time to go home. He glanced down at his feet, hoping that by chance he might be wearing those red sequined homing slippers he had heard so much about. But of course he was not, and his hunt for the crushed body of the famed shoes' original owner, the Wicked Witch of the East, the witch he was meant to have murdered, proved fruitless.

So he waited for that surge of homesickness to hit him, readied himself for the arrival of that swell of yearning, a force of feeling on which, he reasoned, he could simply coast his way home. He waited and he waited, like a farmer waits for rain, but it did not come. He missed home—there was no question about that. Most days, as foretold, he was little more than a strung-out parcel of loss and longing. But although he was overly preoccupied with the past, he had no real desire to go back there, and moreover, he could not clearly remember that place from which he had been thrown so suddenly.

Why would you want to return to a beginning you can barely remember? In the beginning.

Of home he remembered only the tiniest slivers: traipsing through the sawdust of the county fair, holding his aunt's hand, getting his aunt's hand all covered in cotton candy.

Back where he came from, they called it "Fairy Floss."

Hurrying home with his uncle, clutching his uncle's hand, the tornado was coming, they were hurrying to get back home, grit of sand searing the empty spaces round the lacing of their grip.

It was not a tornado, he corrects himself, but a cyclone. Where he grew up, they did not have tornadoes. And he does not actually recall ever walking with his uncle hand in hand.

To jolt his memory, the boy called home. On the first try, he got his uncle, but the boy was taken aback, and all he could do was listen to the crackle of long distance for a few seconds, and then hang up.

He rang a second time, and his aunt picked up. They had a brief conversation, if you could call it that, his shy silence and the aunt's difficult-to-breathe breaths, punctuated by a few stray words. But soon it became obvious there was little to say, and long distance is so expensive.

The boy clicked the receiver back into its silver place. Only a fool would think it an urgent matter to find his way back to such a thread-bare past, a past that was little more than an abbreviation. The boy was still dazed, but he was no fool. In the beginning, having forgotten almost everything, he was in no hurry to get home. And all the absent elements of this queer new life no longer bothered him. He sat himself down on a patch of shiny green Astroturf beside the phone booth, tracing the prints of his fingers again and again, over the comforting precision of those blue-and-white checks on his only dress.

13. Psychic Rosemary
By John Mancuso

WHEN LONELY, VAN searches through the scraps onto which he has held—bits of envelopes, holiday napkins, torn labels from cleaning products, frayed pieces of phone books—precious fragments he returns to again and again. Overflowing out of drawers in a kitchen cabinet, each piece of paper contains a number, maybe two or three—sequences of digits that work like passwords—the codes to everything else beyond the eight blocks where he has spent his whole life.

Like many of life's most intricate subplots, this one began simply: when Van found a health insurance brochure poised over the wastepaper basket, with the numbers to the HealthInfo® line at Little Rhody Regional Hospital. He raised the three-paneled pamphlet to his face and discovered the menu of topics the recordings addressed, everything from heart disease to low self-esteem. Over and over, he listened to the prerecorded messages, memorizing the aberrations in the narrator's flat, unwavering diction. He grinned when she sighed at the end of "Kidneys Know No Holidays" and coughed and excused herself in "Million-Dollar Smiles." But save for those few irregularities, she was all business. And this gave Van the feeling that he knew nothing about her. When he listened to her detached, stoic presentation of "Being a Good Friend," he wondered what her friends looked like and if she followed her own advice about sending them thank-you notes.

During one long, snow-choked Saturday of debilitating monotony, he finally heard something magical. Just when he thought he'd experienced every diversion the tapes offered, he detected a faint voice in the background of "Good-for-You Goodies," saying, "Betty, mike one." Overjoyed by this hint of potential intimacy, he began a lengthy campaign to find Betty.

From that afternoon and into the weeks that followed, he called the hospital and demanded to speak to all of the Bettys, Beths, and Elizabeths on the staff. Intimidated by Van's persistence, the three women who answered the phones remained patient during this difficult time, wishing Van luck in his search and offering the optimistic caveat that the hospital employed twenty-four hours of interns and temporary contract employees who might not have listed extensions. Finally, they lost patience with his constant haranguing and insistence that they were purposely withholding information about Betty's identity. They left memos and Post-its with devil-faced doodles, and even filled a huge dry erase board with things they wanted to say to him.

As luck would have it, Van called on a day when Helen from administrative support was covering the phones. She transferred Van to a diffident temporary in medical records. The unfortunately named Betty Grable received his call right after lunch on her second day at the hospital. Instead of asking her supervisor how to handle Van's request, she spent the better part of the afternoon following a phone trail of tenuous leads handed down from the hospital bureaucracy, sacrificing her assigned duties. She managed to learn that the tapes were made for a consortium of hospitals and medical educators, by a voice-over and industrial-production company headquartered in Schaumburg, Illinois. When she called the company, the human resources assistant told her that legally she could not reveal the narrator's whereabouts but could confirm that she had freelanced for the company as recently as the current tax year. When Betty said plaintively, "Is that all you can tell me?" the woman's professionalism evaporated.

"Yeah, everybody knows how to find Betty. She leaves flyers all over the office about the highfalutin plays she does in Chicago. I guess that makes it public information. In fact, I just read today that she's playing Lady Macbeth."

At nearly five o'clock, Van got the call with the information he wanted: the whereabouts of *his* Betty—with the authoritative manner and no-nonsense delivery, the mystery woman who knows everything. His parents had warned him about long-distance numbers, but Van made the sign of the cross and dialed anyway.

"Theatre Schmeerter. How can I help you?"

"Yes, is a . . . Betty there?"

"Hold on. She might be in the dressing room."

After seconds of suspense, the soothing voice of life's instruction saturated the line.

"This is Betty."

"Hello. It is you! It really is . . . uh . . . your voice. I am a big fan of yours. You know so much and deliver it so well. I have to tell you, though, that you did make one major error: In '101 Groovy Hints and Tips for Teens,' you say to take vitamin C in the fall to ward off winter colds. Now, I read in a lot of places that your body doesn't store vitamin C. Did you mean to say . . ."

"Who the hell is this? And, more importantly, how on God's green earth did you find me?"

"Betty Grable told me."

"Betty Grable is dead."

"No, she's working in medical records at the hospital you used to work at."

"Listen, I don't have time for this. Why don't you call Dial-a-Prayer if you want someone to talk to? I've got a show to do tonight."

She hung up before Van could ask her the name of the guy who said "Betty, mike one" on "Good-for-You Goodies," and whether allergies or a dry throat made her cough during "Million-Dollar Smiles."

He reached for the phone book.

Van replaced pretaped voices with live ones. He found every possible Dial-a-Teen, Dial-a-Prayer, Dial-a-Nurse, and Suicide Crisis Line that required only a local call. He learned all of the employees' and volunteers' names and schedules and demanded to know their days off in advance. He wanted descriptions of the rooms in which they sat, what they wore, and whether or not they loved doing the things he did: smoking cigarettes, eating doughnuts, and drinking coffee. But he couldn't keep them off course for too long; invariably, they ended up saying, "What's wrong with you?" or "How can I help you?" After this, there would be a long silence, with Van unable to speak. Even the most unflappable and well-intentioned volunteers eventually said they had to assist the other people holding in queue and disconnected Van.

When Starla, a prayer counselor from Ocean State Ministries, said, "I know Jesus will save you, but I can't," he started to get their point. He tried to feign voices but was unsuccessful. They always recognized his Benny Hill—butchered with Van's particular Rhode Island regionalisms. Instead of reprimanding him, they put Van on speaker phone and laughed at his pitiful attempts to conceal his identity.

Van spends his time off the phone working as the morning custodian at the Beacon School and Residential Treatment Facility. Many years ago, the same buildings had housed Saint Mary's School, which Van attended from kindergarten through high school. Originally, he worked full-time at Beacon and was a fixture in the community, handing out prizes at staff holiday parties and running lights and sound for the drama productions. People picking up children after school yelled "Hello, Van" from their cars, and the parents of the permanent residents gave him cookies and slices of birthday cake when they came to visit. These perks had ended five years ago, when his manager caught him in the supply closet with one of the residents.

Reactions were mixed. Like Van, much of the administrative staff had walked the building's gray corridors as youths. They'd known his parents. Many of their extended families had intermarried with his. They didn't believe the allegations or refused to consider them. So management, who'd rejected Van years ago for being sickly, thin, earnest, and slow, smiled and waved away a messy scandal and put Van on the 6:00 A.M. to 1:00 P.M. shift, when most of the residents were either sleeping or in classes with the day students.

Now Van never enters the residents' rooms. Instead, he lingers in the boys' room in the wing that houses the most severely retarded and nonverbal patients, who are too disturbed to get him into trouble. When kids come in, he can expect a handshake, a pat on the back, or maybe to run his fingers through their hair. On an average day, Van will give at least one "great big bear hug"; maybe once a month, he gets to assist a kid with his business. When the kids leave, or if they never come, he lights cigarettes and stands at the scratched windows, looking through the lens of marred glass at the rusty metal jungle gym and monkey bars from his school days. It is there that he often conjures up montages of cold asphalt and winter dimness: himself in a shrunken circle of boys waiting for the suspense to break, watching the circle get pared down until only he remains, the final loser a team is forced to accept.

One day, Van spies a pair of legs in a stall. It has been a long time. He stops in his tracks, confused. Usually, he observes the kids as they enter the boys' room. He paces, crouches down to see if he can recognize the shoes. He approaches the stall and looks though the space between the door and the partition. He can only ascertain that it's a person much taller than most of the residents. He jumps back, suspecting a trap, an adult planted there to catch him. Words involuntarily escape his mouth, a combination of panic and reflex.

"Is everything OK in there?"

"I'm OK. You can leave me alone."

It's the voice of someone young and unknown.

"Wanna let me in there? C'mon. I'm here to help you."

"I can take care of myself."

Resistance from another human being, the most familiar obstacle in Van's life, sends him into spirited pursuit. He pushes against the door. No luck. He jumps into the next stall, stands on the toilet, and looks down. The kid is curled up on the seat.

Van hesitates, then mumbles, "Look up, I'm right here. Right up here. Look up at me, please."

No response.

"Just look up for a minute. I . . . I . . . want to know who you are, to see if you're all right."

The boy tightens his grip on himself.

Van jumps down and out and then kicks the stall. He wipes his brow. He fishes through a pile of broken tools in his maintenance cart, walks back to the stall, and jams a ruler in the space created by the hinges, trying to flip the latch that locks the kid's door. Something keeps the latch from freeing itself.

Van hurls the ruler at the window, drops his body to the floor, and crawls under the partition. He feels the cold hardness of the worn tile, takes a deep breath, and looks up into the face of the crouched-over boy.

Monster.

Van squirms backward, out of the stall, springs to his feet, runs from the bathroom and down the hall to the custodial room. He slams the door and suppresses a dry heave. He stares at the floor and sits on a trash can, concentrating deeply. A few drops of water express themselves from his eyes.

He looks at the clock: twelve-thirty. He has to go back and get his cart, so he can be out on time; since the incident, they sometimes enforce his one o'clock departure.

He walks down the hall toward the bathroom, smelling the customary smells, waving to familiar faces, listening to the radiators pump out heat. Maybe he imagined what he saw.

Van reaches the bathroom door and stares at the hard block letters that comprise the word BOYS, focusing on the smudges that cover the black paint.

Things to clean everywhere.

He pulls out a rag and tries to wipe away the iridescent layer of oil from years of fingers on the door. The marks won't budge. His body begins to shake and get hot. Opening the door a crack, he hears nothing. Clasping the handle, he crouches down. The coast is clear.

"Hello! Hello! Anybody there?"

Van lets go of the door and grabs his cart. Suddenly, a stall whips open and the boy jumps down from the toilet.

Van chokes on a scream. His lungs expand and contract.

In silence, Van studies the boy. The skin on his face looks like peanut butter smeared on bread. Some patches are smooth, others are bulbous and craggy. Brown and red strips cut through bleachy white areas, tiny pocks cover much of the cheeks. His eyes appear to be different sizes. Only the nose and mouth are unscathed.

"Where did you come from?"

"Way deep inside this cinder-blocked labyrinth. They like to keep me out of sight, confined with the really bad ones."

The boy walks over to the window and turns to face Van.

"I came from the bin in Syracuse. It burnt down. I was trapped in the fire. But I lived. So they placed me in a box, put a third-class stamp on it, and shipped me here."

Van backs up slowly, his heart pounding, reaches for the sink behind him. His wet palms squeeze the hard basin.

"My aunt and uncle live in Providence," the monster continues, "and their rich, liberal, white guilt deluded them into thinking they wanted me close by. They visit once in a while, but the whole thing is really more a big fuck-you to my trashy parents who didn't handle their responsibilities and forgot about me. You know, *they're* together enough to clean up everybody's messes."

Van notices little stubs of fingers growing out of the boy's knuckles, winces. The boy waves his hands.

"Oh, these. I had these before the fire."

Van can't reconcile the monster's physical hideousness and his refined speech and mannerisms.

"Are you a student?"

"I guess so. I've read thousands more books than any teacher I have ever had—especially this bunch of philistines! I bet I could have fucking gotten a GED in seventh grade."

"Why are you here?"

Van pushes the cart toward the door.

"My parents thought I'd freak out all of the *normal* kids; so they put me away before I could friggin' walk. But now, *Van,* I work for them, the people that run the bins. I catch perverted freaks like you who take advantage of poor, innocent kids."

Van looks down at his name, emblazoned in gray cursive on the right side of his chest.

Van always starts his days with doughnuts and coffee in the school's little gym, where the peaceful light of dawn shines through narrow windows. One morning, he hears, "Hello, pervert!" He looks up; the yellowing felt banners still display the names of athletes from Saint Mary's. His glance shifts across to the old clock, the fracture in the glass running between 11 and 12. The voice echoes again.

"And what are you doing cleaning up after retards at your age?"

Van drops his cup and the coffee scalds him. He rubs his ankles, dancing in pain from the burning liquid.

"Please leave me alone," he pleads toward the rows of empty bleachers. "If I promise never to go near you or look at you, will you leave me alone, please?"

The boy jumps out from behind the wooden seats and approaches Van.

"Listen to me, shit-for-brains. In case you haven't figured it out, I was not hired by the administration to spy on you. I'm forced to live here and have my fate dictated by losers like you who have no control over your own."

Van takes off his socks and begins to cry.

"I will be nice to you if you listen to me. I'm so glad you didn't repress your instincts, because now I can get what I want from you. I never met anybody more stupid than I am ugly."

The boy reaches for one of Van's cigarettes and puts it behind his ear.

"The reason you haven't heard from me is because I have been doing some research. Because I am only seventeen, I have to get an adult to sign me out to leave this hellhole."

He moves closer to Van, who stretches his arms out in fear.

"I told my aunt and uncle I was becoming good friends with a certain staff member who wants to take me places. Do you understand?"

The boy extends his hand, an offer to help Van up. Van looks away.

"You want me to take you out? Where? Where do you want to go?"

The boy pulls a powdered sugar doughnut from the bag Van dropped. He takes a huge bite.

"Yum, they don't feed us these. Stop crying. You really are annoying."

Van watches the stumpy fingers.

"Anyfuckingwhere. How would you feel being forced to live in a world where you don't belong, where you can't relate to anybody because they're not on your level? I'm not fucking retarded. But hey, don't think I'm a bigot. Some of my best friends are retarded."

The monster laughs and white powder sprays from his mouth. He throws the rest of the doughnut across the gym, then brings the cigarette from his ear to his nose, sniffs deeply, and asks Van for a light.

"A bowling alley, the movies, a place where you can get pizza by the slice—somewhere normal people go."

Van remains hunched over.

"C'mon Van, I'll show you my pee-pee if you stop crying."

Van looks up, astounded. The monster grabs the matches out of Van's shirt pocket and clumsily tries to light the cigarette. Minutes pass.

"You've got to breathe in when you hold the match to it," Van says, wiping his face.

The monster tries again but chokes.

"I'm new at this smoking thing."

Van lights a cigarette and hands it over. The monster holds it in front of his face and watches the glowing ember burn. He waves his arm and makes circles, then spells his name in cursive, calling out each letter before the smoke vanishes.

He laughs and runs around the gym, holding the cigarette over his head, laughing harder and harder.

"Take me anywhere, anywhere but the confines of Dickens's London or Conrad's darkness."

Van stays up at night, sitting on the couch and staring into the television, or at nothing, cataloging the monster's threats and deformities. When he feels like he will explode, he pulls out his drawer of numbers.

Every call sounds the same. He explains why he hasn't been in touch, then tells them about the monster who haunts him. At the same point in each call, he realizes he cannot tell them why he feels blackmailed. He then pauses, backtracks, trips over his speech, and contradicts previous details. He notices a lack of sympathy; sometimes his friends even hang up before he says good-bye. He believes that somehow they have figured out everything he has tried to hide.

He begins to tell them that the monster comes from his nightmares and never really existed.

Your final deadline will be reached tonight at five P.M.. If you don't come to get me, I tell. You need to update your emergency contact information. Your mother is dead. Lovies, Me

Van calls in sick, something he hasn't done in five years. He spends the morning with his head in the toilet bowl, vomiting. Between upheavals, he stares at the words "American Standard" on the upturned seat and imagines the aunt and uncle watching him walk up and down the boulevard with the monster. It seems impossible that people will perceive their companionship as charitable, an inevitable duty for someone in Van's occupation. If it came down to the two of them, would his bosses really believe the monster? The neighborhood would come to his rescue, wouldn't they?

After many hours at the toilet, Van has nothing left to purge. He reflects on the one thing that has stayed with him from his years of religious instruction: "God will never give me too much to bear." Repeating this over and over, he feels compelled to open the boxes from the house in which he grew up.

The hallway to the back door appears to be littered with unorganized rubble, but Van knows where everything rests. He puts on the old 78s: Jerry Vale, Louis Prima, Rosemary Clooney, and Dean Martin—songs from the endless string of rainy Sunday afternoons when houses busted with bowls of pasta, baskets of fruit, and the spirited exclamations of aunts, uncles, and cousins. Searching through the flimsy boxes, he finds the candles, statues, and madonnas from the altar his mother created in their old basement. He sets Mary and Jesus on his kitchen counter, gets on his knees, and prays. Palm crosses, new Easter outfits. Catechism, church, First

Communion and confirmation with the neighborhood kids. And, of course, Saint Mary's Catholic School, where he spent thirteen years of his life, in the same building to which he must return tonight.

His mother's votive candles provide him with comfort while the early November darkness enters the apartment. In the orange halo of light, he dresses in his one good suit, something he formerly referred to as his Sunday best, now worn only to attend the funerals that continue to mark the decline of his parents' generation. In one fluid motion, Van blows out the candles, puts on an overcoat, shuts the door, and leaves.

From the sidewalk that borders the school's fire lane, he sees the monster's craggy skin in the waiting room's fluorescent glare. Filled with nausea, Van stops in front of the double-paned glass. His finger presses the buzzer. A nurse looks up from a magazine and buzzes back. Through a slot in a window, the nurse passes a card and release form to Van. The monster waits behind the second series of double-paned glass doors. Another buzzer: Van nods to the monster and turns around. Another buzzer: The nurse returns to her magazine.

They walk from the building and stand outside.

In a tone that sounds to Van as sincere as a priest's, the boy thanks him. Van wonders if this whole thing will wind up easier than he thought. They walk toward the street. Before they reach the end of the school driveway, Van stops in a patch of darkness and pulls out a cigarette.

"Where do you want to go?"

Looking up at the stars, the boy says, "Like I said, anywhere. Anywhere but a bookstore or pharmacy; *they* take me there."

"Let me finish this cigarette."

Van peers at the lit-up street in the distance and estimates how many steps it will take for them to get there. The monster sits on the curb and looks around him.

"Wow, it really smells like fall out here. I love the smell of dead leaves. It reminds me of Halloween. Something you can't get from a book."

Van wants to say something mean (like "You have the scariest costume for it") and then run into the path of a speeding car. Instead, he takes a deep drag.

Wind gusts; a blizzard of leaves falls from a nearby tree. The boy dashes into the middle of it, picks up already-fallen leaves and tosses them in the air, then jumps until he catches hold of a thick branch.

Van extinguishes his cigarette, lights another. "I didn't know you could do that," he mumbles.

"You sound just like those motherfuckers in there. They say they care. They tell me they want me to get better, but every time I do something that exceeds their expectations, everybody gets uncomfortable and tries to push me down again. Even my parents did that."

He pauses.

"Does it bother you that I can do things?"

The boy reaches for another branch, screams, "I told you, there's nothing wrong with me." He jumps down, plays an air guitar. "Just too physically aberrant to be mainstreamed. *Ahhhhh!*"

Van watches the smoke travel from his mouth into the dark, reviewing the small list of places he could take the monster.

"Let's go to the playground. I like it there."

"Come *on,* Van. I've been patient. You might even say I've waited years for this. I want to go to a place where you can order off of a menu. An arcade. The movies. My aunt and uncle just take me to their house, and if I'm lucky we go to the drive-through, where they keep me hidden in the backseat."

"We will. I promise. Let's just go over there for a few minutes."

Van looks at the sky and wonders if God and his parents watch him. He weakly makes the sign of the cross. He thinks about time bombs: vessels that sit in warehouses until they explode and ravage things to the point that they can never exist as they originally did.

The boy collapses into a small pile of leaves.

They hop over the playground fence and Van lights another cigarette. He sees the dark, scratched glass through which he looks during the day. He takes a deep breath, says, "I love it here," thinking that each lie gives him more control. The boy climbs all over the jungle gym.

"It's OK. Anything's better than what I would be doing in there."

He looks at his watch.

"It's Psychic Rosemary time."

Van freezes.

"You listen to her? So do I. She's been on that same station for my whole life."

"She's from Providence, you know, right near here."

"No way."

"Of course. You can't tell by her accent?"

Van doesn't know what the monster means by a Providence "accent." He's heard that people in Boston, like the Kennedys, have accents, but he doesn't know what they are, either.

Van exhales.

"I knew that, yeah. I was just seeing if you did."

The monster climbs the stairs to the big slide.

"I know a lot about her. My aunt's best friend went to school with her. Her whole name is Rosemary Abruzzi and she had to drop out during her sophomore year to get a job. Apparently, everybody teased her because she was fat and her parents spoke no English."

That sounds like people Van knew growing up. Such valid evidence of the monster's story ruffles Van. "I've been on her show many times," he boasts. "The last time she had me on for four or five minutes."

The monster remains poised at the top of the slide.

"I've talked to her, too," he responds. "When I told her my story, she gave me her private home number and we talked for hours. She said my intelligence will make me transcend my physical limitations."

Van finishes his cigarette and reaches for another. Although uncertain about what Psychic Rosemary meant by that, he knows it stands for something good. He looks at the boy, who is now yelling the names of the signs he can read, laughing at his own jokes.

"Narragansett Beer! Never fear! Blanchdale Shoe Repair! For a scuff or even a tear!"

They ignore each other.

Van thinks about how even during blocks of prerecorded programming, human beings run the studios. After years of listening to talk radio, Van figured out how to find them. With much practice, he decoded the methods of bypassing the computerized welcome greetings, tape loops, and hold queues. Press three here, pound sign there, wait for the beep. No matter what time, from the dull grays of stubborn late winter to the balmy windblown midnights of July, he always made a connection. He starts to tell the monster about this feat, but stops abruptly when he realizes how much better the boy's story is.

"Maria's Pastry! Bet her cannolis are tasty!"

As the match strikes, Van interrupts the boy.

"What else do you know about her? I want to see if it goes with what I know."

The boy turns around.

"She's too old to drive and gets a car service to the radio station. She's not much unlike me, isolated and lonely. We both know I'm gonna end up doing something with my life, even if it means working in a place where nobody has to see me. She'll always be a real-live Miss Havisham."

The boy runs down the slide.

"Maybe one day we can call a taxi there—Red Cab, that's who she has an account with. I've looked on a map; it's only up I-95 a few miles, in Central Falls. I'll tell her about you."

Van remembers what Rosemary once told him: "Find your inner strength or you will always be the village idiot."

"What does Maria's look like?" says the boy. "Have you ever had her pastries? What about Henry's Diner? Is it good? Is it nice? Is it Greek? Oh! What about baklava? I have a recipe for that in my scrapbook. I've always wanted to make that!" He hops the fence and heads for the street.

"I've never been to those places."

Van drops his cigarette and tries to jump the fence but cannot get over this time. The boy runs back and grabs Van by the arm.

"C'mon! Let's go see! Even if we just peek through the window. C'mon!"

Van recoils.

"Don't touch me! Don't ever touch me!"

He makes it over the fence.

The monster looks stunned.

"I've given you so many chances! You pervert!"

He runs away. Van follows.

"Go! Just go! You're the one who knows everything around here! Go to Central Falls on the highway! You know how to get there! Call the taxi. I don't know any of the numbers, but you do."

The boy reaches the street. He turns around to Van, now right behind him.

"Do you know how fucking hard it is to always be aware of how much they're staring at you? You must, or you wouldn't make us sit in the dark!"

Van shifts his focus between the street and the brick of the school building, his head jerking back and forth. "Go!" he shouts over the noise of the traffic. "Go see your friend Rosemary—someone I used to listen to with my mother when I was too young for school—because *you* know more about her than I do. Go! *Go!* Where am I going to take you that you don't already know about, Mr. Big Shot? Just go!"

The boy stops. Cars race past them.

"You don't want to see things and go anywhere? That's not my fucking fault. I want to see things. My eyes are open. I'm scared but I am *going!*"

The boy stares at the light, waiting for it to change. Van steps closer to the curb.

"Why don't you hold your arm up in the air, so the cabdrivers can see you? C'mon, big shot! Let everybody see you!"

The roar of engines absorbs most of Van's words.

The sign changes to WALK; at once, the noise ceases. Cars halt. A path clears.

The monster takes a few steps. Van watches him move ahead, into an arc of streetlight. It illuminates the monster's face, his shoulders, his entire body.

Van runs and grabs him, pulls him off the street, through the open gate, back to an unlit portion of the schoolyard. He wraps his arm around the monster's neck and holds him tightly. The traffic waits to resume its flow.

Through heavy breaths, Van strengthens his grip, waiting for DON'T to appear above the blinking WALK.

14. A Separate Reality
By Robert Marshall

I STEPPED A few inches to the left. Didn't feel any different. A few inches back. Maybe *something?* No. I hadn't really thought, though, that, during PE, I'd be able to find my place of power.

I'd started reading Carlos Castaneda a few months before—at the end of sixth grade—my art teacher, Anna, had introduced me to him. Anna had taught me a lot of things. I'd learned about Taoism; I'd shown her my poems; she'd tried to show me how to throw on the wheel. She's my mentor, I thought. Don Juan was Carlos's. He'd taught him to talk to coyotes. Once, they'd flown over a canyon. He was trying to teach Carlos how to *see*.

I stepped a few inches back. Silly, I thought; much too hot. People don't believe that in Phoenix it's still hot in October, but it is! Far away, I could hear the boys shout. As long as our team was winning, there was nothing for me and Douggy, the other fullback, to do.

Nothing but think. I wondered if I could explain Castaneda to Dr. Kurtz. Maybe he already knew. Castaneda's an anthropologist, I imagined saying. His books are nonfiction. But even with all of Castaneda's Western knowledge, he is Don Juan's student—and not always a good one! He's *always* intellectualizing, I imagined telling

Kurtz. Don Juan tries to teach him *not doing*. Tries to show him the
invisible world.

I probably won't get far, I thought, explaining this stuff to Kurtz.
I have to work on my patience. Often when I saw Dr. Kurtz, we
didn't end up talking about the stuff I'd intended to bring up.
Because of this, there was still a lot he didn't know about me. He
didn't understand about Anna. Perhaps he never would. I looked
over at Douggy, lost in his own world.

To my left, the field was lined with a row of pale paloverdes
through which "American Pie" could be heard from a senior's car
parked on Montecito. Behind me the goalpost's double white crucifix.
Beyond them, if I turned my head, I could see the power lines leading
past South Mountain to the desert. Power lines, *lines of power,* the
lines of the world. Don Juan said you could feel them in your hand,
these imperceptible white fluorescent fibers crisscrossing the air.
Sometimes, standing on the dead grass field, in the heat and the afternoon glare, I felt I could.

A hundred miles to Mexico. I could follow the power lines, I
could turn and start walking. I imagined the TV movie they'd make,
the point in the afternoon when someone would notice. I wouldn't
get to see the movie, I'd die in the heat; even Don Juan's friend, Don
Genaro, couldn't find Ixtlan on a map.

I'd almost finished *A Separate Reality*, Castaneda's second book.
Next: *Journey to Ixtlan. A Separate Reality* was hard to put down; I'd
stay up reading late into the night. I'd *always* been a big reader, my
parents had encouraged it. Still, my father had begun to worry that I
spent too much time in my room with books. If I was outdoors more,
he reasoned, I'd have more friends. If I just gave sports a chance. I *do*
give them a chance, I'd argued. "Just *try* to be open-minded, Mark,"
he'd insist. "You might enjoy it." I *am* open-minded, I thought. I'm
making the best of the situation. Sometimes he made it sound as if I
purposely didn't want to have friends. But it wasn't my fault Tim

Goldner had moved to Wisconsin. And I do have new friends, sort of. Even if they're older. Sometimes I thought Dr. Kurtz understood my position. Sometimes I thought he was taking Dad's side.

In the distance, I heard the shouting. A crow flew overhead. It was unfair of Dad, I thought, to accuse me of not-being-open-minded. Why couldn't I just let go of these thoughts? Let them float off? Useless to be angry. Before introducing me to Castaneda, Anna had told me about Lao Tsu. His teachings weren't incompatible with Don Juan's, I told myself. There *were* differences. But a lot of overlap! *Yield and Overcome*, said *The Tao Te Ching*. I tried this approach at school, and sometimes it worked. Don Juan was always telling Carlos he was too impatient. My problem, too. Too impatient with myself, with others. Too impatient to have a vision. Anna had had visions, when she'd gone hiking in the canyons. I'd come close, I thought. But it would take time.

Sometimes wanting something too much stood in the way of it happening.

I looked over at Douggy. We were at the two far ends of the body's bell curve, me thin, him fat, always the last two chosen. "Crush, kill, destroy," he muttered lethargically, from his side of the field. I hoped he wasn't getting started: sometimes when in a bad mood, he'd be the sheriff and arrest me. He'd drag me out to the dry wash, where, while I practiced *not doing*, he'd sit on me next to an anthill. He'd sit until I confessed; this didn't usually take long. *Yield and Overcome*. I knew it wasn't anything personal. He was on automatic. Sometimes he and Tim Ratter would pants me, throwing my shorts into the weeds at the edge of the field.

A ball came whizzing toward us. A cloud of boys rushed in pursuit. I tried to stop it but didn't have *the gait of power*. I ran like a girl. "Get it, big guy," Dan Baltz, the blond-haired center, shouted. An affectionate sort of joke: "big guy." Dan was popular and he was nice to me—or at least decent. I knew it was part of the personality he'd chosen. But sometimes I wished he would ignore me the way most boys did. His "you can do it" made it worse when, in a gawky display, I missed.

Douggy missed, too. Their team scored. John Mazur, who used to hide under the bleachers with me in fifth grade, rushed by without looking in my direction. John, who wasn't much bigger than me, had gone out for football the year before. He'd transformed himself. I hadn't. Occasionally, he was still friendly. Dan Baltz was always friendly—no risk to him. Dan, trotting past, slapped me on the shoulder. The game again became a far-off thing.

After PE, I walked up to Anna's room, but she wasn't there. On the way to my locker, I passed the teachers' parking lot and saw her truck.

Her light green pickup. I planned to drive a pickup, too, someday. I couldn't imagine what other car I would drive. I wanted to be able to think of some other car besides one just like hers, I wanted to be a *little* different, but I couldn't think of another car that would have the same magic.

The other cars, Mr. Lewis's Buick, Mrs. Binder's Ford, were just cars.

Anna's pickup had a bumper sticker: "I love trout." I knew my parents would never have a sticker that said "I love trout." Ours were for the UJA and the Sierra Club.

Dr. Kurtz leaned back, a bemused expression on his salt-and-pepper bearded face. On his desk, three kachina dolls, a large black notebook, a box of Kleenex, an ashtray. Above him, diplomas from the University of Indiana and the Menninger Institute.

"I'm wondering why you changed the subject," he remarked.

"I thought we were *done* with that." We'd been talking about my problems with my peers. Peers: We'd circled like crows around the meaning of that word. Peers in what sense? I didn't want to say I was better than anyone, but I kept getting cornered into it. Maybe I *had* changed the topic because I was angry. I didn't know what I felt. Should I still be going to Dr. Kurtz? Maybe I've outgrown him. I'll talk with Mom, I thought.

"Why don't we try something," he suggested. "You don't have to. . . ."

"OK," I replied, trying to sound upbeat and open-minded.

"Think of someone you want to be better friends with."

"OK." Dan Baltz. John Mazur. I didn't know who I was supposed to think of.

"Imagine some activity you might ask them to do."

"OK."

"Have you imagined something?"

"Yes."

"What would it be?"

"Go bowling."

"So now can you picture asking this person to—"

"I don't think it would work."

"Why?"

"It would just make things worse."

"How?"

"It would be like . . . it could be humiliating."

Baltz would never go bowling with me. And it would be a *major* mistake to ask him. "Mark, I wonder whether you sometimes make things complicated as a way of defeating yourself. You're always able to come up with reasons to *not* do things."

"I am not," I whispered, pulling into myself, wondering if he was right.

He hesitated, then continued. "How would it be humiliating?"

I'd tried to explain this before. Things were OK in school as long as I didn't push too hard. If I stayed in my place, Baltz and at least *some* other people would be friendly. Baltz wouldn't want to *do* anything with me. Being realistic was important.

Birds chirped in the atrium. Anna corresponded with a poet in San Francisco. A woman she knew was building her own house in New Mexico. Why couldn't I have friends like these? Why did I have to be friends with people I had *nothing* in common with?

Anna had had me to her house several times. She lived with her husband Karl, a woodworker, in a house on the west side. She'd shown me her ceramic sculptures. A group of older students met there once a month. They read poetry and smoked pot. I hung out with them in the art room, and, I thought, I was starting to be friends with them. Although none of them liked me as much as Anna did, still, I had a lot more in common with *them* than with the kids in my grade. But Dr. Kurtz, I knew, wouldn't take me seriously if I said so. He was only interested in *peers*.

Being in the same grade doesn't matter, I thought. That's seeing things superficially. *"After all these years of learning you should know better,"* said Don Juan. *"Yesterday you stopped the world and you might even have seen. A magical being told you something and your body was capable of understanding it because the words had collapsed."*

"What was the thing that stopped in me?"

"What stopped in you yesterday was what people have been telling you the world is like."

Should I start the next chapter? I lay on my bed in my room, beneath my Simon and Garfunkel poster. Lilly, my mouse, went round in her wheel. Sometimes I didn't like to start something when I knew I was just going to be interrupted. And I will be, I thought, any minute. The late-afternoon light cast shutter patterns on the wall. I wished I could be more like Lilly. Centered and simple. Less thoughts.

I heard the knock on the door. I closed the book and went down the hall to dinner.

Mom had made spaghetti. I was glad because, unlike Carlos, I didn't eat meat. Although I'd agreed with my parents that I would *sometimes*. Anna ate it sometimes, too. The sauce was delicious. It had artichoke hearts. Mom and Dad talked about the problems we'd been having with the irrigator. He didn't come when he was supposed to. Dad thought he was a drunk. I drank my sun tea. My older sister Sharon looked bored. My younger brother Jason looked bored. Parts of the lawn were dying, Dad said.

"You're too weak," he said, "you hurry when you should wait but you wait when you should hurry."

"How lovely are thy tabernacles, O Lord of Hosts."

"You think too much. Now you think that there is no time to waste."

"What can I do, Don Juan? I'm very impatient."

"I had rather stand at the threshold of the house of God than to dwell in the tents of wickedness."

"Live like a warrior! You failed with the guardian because of your thoughts."

Mom looked and saw I wasn't reading the Union Prayer Book. She might have thought this clever. Once, years ago, I'd read *Newsweek* during one of Rabbi Horowitz's sermons. Everyone had laughed about it afterwards. My parents hadn't liked Rabbi Horowitz. But he'd been fired, and now we had Rabbi Berger. Beth Shalom had hired him out of retirement in Fort Lauderdale; my parents liked him. Mom thinks I've been disrespectful, I thought. Even though I was certain Rabbi Berger couldn't have seen the book, I felt ashamed. I put Carlos on the floor under the folding chair and returned to the responsive reading.

I still hadn't talked to her about quitting Kurtz. I'd *almost*— but then felt unsure. Kurtz said that a lot of the time, when you wanted to stop therapy, it was because there were things you were scared to deal with. Things in your unconscious mind. Both he and Castaneda believed in unseen worlds. Maybe I would talk to Mom tomorrow.

After the service, during the Oneg Shabbat, I stood next to my parents while they talked with the Nachmanns. They were discussing Watergate, which was interesting, but then Mr. Nachmann brought up the membership committee, which was not. I walked over to join Sharon, who was talking seriously with Dr. Wagner. Jason stood next to them, eating sugar cubes from the silver bowl by the coffee machine. I took a few and put them in my mouth. Once, at Bob's Big Boy, some tourists had been given LSD that way. They hadn't known what was happening so they'd had a bad trip.

Dr. Wagner turned to me. "How are you doing, Mark?"

"Oh, fine."

He didn't have anything to ask and I didn't have anything to say. The sugar dissolved in my mouth. Dr. Wagner asked Jason about Little League. Jason, looking down, answered quietly. I slipped out the glass doors into the dark.

The lights glimmered from the houses on the other side of Quail Run Drive. I'm ready, I thought; ready to quit Kurtz. I'd been going for five years. I'd first been sent in second grade; I'd told everyone at school that I wanted to be a girl; Mrs. Ross had called my parents, and they'd called Dr. Kurtz.

I'd grown more realistic over time.

I wandered away from the building. I've changed in *many* ways, I thought. Weird that people lived in such different worlds. My parents couldn't imagine Anna's. They didn't realize that I didn't care, any longer, about temple. Not much. I used to care *more*, I thought, though never in the way Sharon does. I kicked a twig down the sidewalk. Although I like some parts of the Bible, I thought—Ecclesiastes, Micah, the Song of Songs—I'd never known why the God of the Jews meant so much to her. Maybe, I told myself, she'd seen something in Youth Group. I'd tried to make him powerful in my head the way Don Juan was—it hadn't worked. I walked toward the darkness and the creosote smell. To her, I thought, he was wondrous. To me he'd always seemed like someone I'd grown up with, a friend of the family, an uncle perhaps. He did say some interesting things. And he had a mysterious side. But so does Mr. Nachmann. So does Dr. Wagner.

Squishing tiny sky-black fruit into the concrete, I walked slowly down a path lined with olive trees, tracing my fingers along the cool, dusty surfaces of the cars. I headed toward the empty unpaved section of the parking lot. The light and noise of the building grew distant and the dark seemed to grow more full and alive. I felt alert in the blackness; I should try to find my place of power. But once I'd thought this, I couldn't feel anything. I tried to let my thoughts go. But the trying, I knew, was standing in the way. I had to be patient. This was always Carlos's problem; and I had to accept that it was mine, too. I shouldn't be so conceited. It often took years to become a warrior. Sometimes it was happening even when you didn't *know* it. There were so many contradictions.

Still nothing. I knew the dark was full of invisible fibers. The lines of the world. To the north, the Phoenix mountains. To the south, on the horizon, aureoles of light, white, yellow, red. There were radio towers and, in the distance, the tiny Papago buttes. Somewhere, Mexico. Something moved in the creosote. A jackrabbit? *Jackrabbit*, I thought, was just the name we gave it. I had to let the words collapse. Perhaps the *jackrabbit* was really my guardian. Perhaps it was a sign. But I shouldn't want it to be. Anna said that in poetry you had to *let* things happen. Let them come to you. Not force them. If I *wanted* it to be a sign, it wouldn't be. Let your thoughts go, I thought, knowing this was a thought, trying to let it go.

Practice *not doing*. The clouds above the mountains were mysteriously white, white as day-clouds, milk spilled on a dark cloth. I began to feel *something*. But it was as subtle as the breeze rustling the leaves of the olive trees. I tried to pay attention to it, as if I were listening to an almost-silent pulse, which seemed to disappear and then return.

I moved very slowly, letting it lead me. I walked toward an acacia tree next to the chain link fence at the desert-facing edge of the lot.

I wondered if I should touch the tree. I stood there in the darkness for a while. In the car, on the way home, my parents discussed how Beth Shalom could get more members. A lot of people had quit during Horowitz. They had to be persuaded to come back.

"Why was Horowitz so terrible?" Jason asked.

Why is he asking? We all know what Dad will say: Because Jason's the youngest, he doesn't remember how upset everyone had been by the weekends of couples counseling in the mountains near Payson. He doesn't remember how Rabbi Horowitz had been rude and evasive when Dad and Mr. Nachmann had questioned him about getting the board's authorization to use the van. Dad had never seen why a temple needed a van in the first place. Now they'd gotten rid of it—Rabbi Berger couldn't even drive.

"He wasn't so bad when he started," Dad said calmly (not in my head, but from the front seat). "But then I suppose he got carried away. Started to think he was some kind of prophet."

"Rabbis played many roles in the Talmud," Sharon replied. She'd liked Horowitz more than my parents.

This is *so* boring, I thought. They're going to ask me what I think. I don't think anything. But if I don't participate, Dad will say I have an attitude problem. I wondered what Anna was doing. I wondered if she would invite me to one of the poetry readings. I wondered if I would smoke pot. I still wanted, in some ways, to be part of the discussion in the car. But in more ways, I did not.

"That may have been so in the Talmud, but we're not living in the Talmud," Dad commented.

"She wasn't saying we were," Mom said, mediating.

"Anyway, Jason," Dad continued, "to answer your question, *as* I was going to do *before* I was interrupted, he did things he wasn't authorized to do. A rabbi is a teacher. But a teacher of psychology?

And if he's going to teach psychology, why gestalt? Why not Freud or something that's been proven?"

Sharon sighed again. I wondered what Dad would think if I quit Kurtz. I still wasn't sure what to do.

"The point is, Jason, a rabbi works for the community. That's what the van business was about. He should have gotten our permission. Otherwise, what's the purpose of a board?"

The question hung in the car as it moved down Glendale Road, past the Frontier Bank's lit fountain, past the school, past Texaco. Above, the stars were chromosomes of light. I pressed my face against the window, trying to get back the feeling I'd had in the parking lot. I could, somewhat.

15. Sucker
By Wayne Hoffman

"IN NEW YORK, you can have everything delivered," Moe Pearlman liked to say. "Even cock."

Hooking up with guys he met online meant that Moe didn't have to leave the comfort of his West Village studio. And since Moe, like most New Yorkers, was essentially lazy, this suited him perfectly. Some people found Internet cruising too reductive, unable to sum up their complex sexuality in a fifty-word profile. Not Moe. After writing "best cocksucker in town," he still had forty-six words to spare.

Incidentally, this description was absolutely accurate. Potential sex partners might have found Moe, a twenty-six-year-old grad student, too young or too old. Some might have deemed him, with some justification, too flabby or too hairy or too Semitic-looking to be "hot." But nobody could dispute his cocksucking talents. His list of buddies on Men Online included 146 regulars who kept coming back for more. And the list kept growing.

When he picked up someone online, the scene was usually the same. Moe would be in the rocking chair under a reading lamp in the corner, a buddy would walk into the apartment, come over and sit on the dingy brown couch in front of the TV, where a porno movie would already be playing. Without a word, Moe would unzip his pants, blow him, and then wait for him to zip up and leave. Sometimes it took five minutes, sometimes forty-five. Either way, the scene was reliably good, efficient, and left everyone happy.

If Moe was single-minded in his desires, however, he still needed to find ways to keep this standard routine fresh. Lately, he'd been trying to find creative ways to interact with his repeat customers. He'd get a few of them over at the same time—without telling them, of course, so they'd be surprised at the scene. He'd organize parties where he'd suck off four or five or six men in a row. He'd blindfold himself or handcuff his partner or take a guy onto his roof to breathe new excitement into a regular visitor's latest session. He'd change the porno tape—try a straight movie for a change of pace. On the one hand, everyone knew what they were going to get when they visited Moe; the scene remained essentially the same. On the other hand, there was always some new element, something to keep it interesting.

With the buddies he liked the most, the ones where he could sense an unspoken tenderness beneath the surface, he'd recently begun to change the scene into one he had never discussed or described in his online profile. Instead of sitting in the chair, fully clothed, Moe would leave the door open and climb into bed in his boxers. If the visitor was uncomfortable with the new scenario when he arrived, he'd sit on the couch as usual and Moe would get out of bed and revert to the standard script. But nine times out of ten—Moe was an oustanding judge of character—the man would climb into bed with Moe.

The sex itself was largely the same either way. Whether on a couch or under the covers, Moe serviced his buddies with unparalleled selflessness, never asking for reciprocation. But if sex itself was the same in bed, what followed was vastly different from the couch scenario. Instead of sitting up and waiting for the man to leave as soon as he came, Moe would pull up the covers, nestle into the man's arms, and rest his head on his chest. He'd close his eyes as he felt the man's arm around him, the man's hands rubbing Moe's shoulder drowsily and pulling him closer. Moe would imagine that this man was his lover—this man whose name he often did not know for certain, whose professional talents, musical tastes, and political leanings were unknown to him, who more often than not had a lover waiting for him at home. Sometimes the man would kiss Moe on the forehead or on the lips. Sometimes the man would whisper in Moe's ear and tug on a nipple as Moe jerked himself off. Sometimes—this was Moe's deepest desire, his favorite outcome—the man would drift off to sleep. And sometimes he would not wake up until morning.

Moe always remembered which guys would spend the night. He kept excellent notes.

But there was one buddy who stood out from the rest, one man Moe couldn't quite figure out.

Ever since he moved to the Village, Moe had seen him at least three nights a week, sitting on the same orange vinyl seat in the same booth at the Sheridan Square Diner up the street. He was always alone under the faux-Tiffany lamp, always working intently, looking utterly serious. Moe had never worked up the nerve to approach him. Whenever Moe saw him, he found himself at a total loss for words—which was something very rare.

He was the stuff of Moe's fantasies. Somewhere in his forties, with dark brown hair and a goatee. He clearly spent most of his free time working out, and the rest of his time showing off the results. Every time Moe saw him, he wore the same clothes: tight Levi's and a skintight ribbed tank top—not some trendy Raymond Dragon tank top, but the kind that straight men wear as undershirts. Even in winter, he just threw a leather jacket on over the tank top, which was cut low enough to show off his chest hair and a thin gold chain. Moe wasn't the type who jerked off thinking about guys he'd seen on the street, but this man had visited Moe in his imagination dozens of times.

After two years, though, Moe's fantasy had become a reality, ever since he met his dream man online. He had a name: Max Milano. And Max had quickly come to appreciate what 145 others knew so well. In the two months since that first wordless blowjob, Max had become one of Moe's regulars, and his visits to Moe's apartment had developed into a familiar pattern.

Tuesday night was fairly typical. When he got home, Moe (HotLipsNYC) logged onto Men Online and checked to see if Max (DownTheHatch) was there. Max was indeed online. He sent Moe a message immediately:

> DownTheHatch: You home?
> HotLipsNYC: Yup.
> DownTheHatch: 5 minutes?
> HotLipsNYC: Yup.

OK, so Max wasn't much of a conversationalist. In fact, they'd never had a chat, online or in person, that lasted more than fifteen seconds. Max's online profile specifically said he didn't want any "chatty queens." Moe didn't care. He wasn't looking for a discussion about Proust or the Mideast peace process. Besides, he didn't like to talk with his mouth full.

Moe turned on the TV, rewound the porno tape, dimmed the lights, and waited. When Max rang, Moe buzzed him up, opened the door, pressed the play button, and went to wait in his chair.

And it was the same as usual with Max: sex in three rounds.

Max came in, hung his leather jacket over the doorknob, and walked over to Moe. Without sitting down, he opened his fly and took out his uncut dick. Moe, still seated in the chair, blew him. This first round took four minutes—Moe could tell by the timer on the VCR. For Max, this was just warming up.

For round two, Max peeled off all his clothes, revealing the body that Moe longed to worship. He sat on the couch, legs apart, and watched the movie silently while Moe knelt before him and started again. He was slower this time, pulling out some of his patented tricks that he used to drive men crazy. It took Max seventeen minutes to climax this time.

But if Max seemed spent after shooting twice, the scene wasn't over yet. He moved to the bed for round three, lying on his back with his hands behind his head. Here, Max finally relaxed into the moment—the first two orgasms apparently lessened the edge a bit—and Moe could do almost anything he wanted. He spent half an hour nuzzling Max's balls, licking his armpits, chewing his nipples, and sucking his toes. Whatever it took to get Max hard yet again. Max just lay there, accepting the pleasure without comment. When he was ready, he flipped Moe over onto his back, straddled his face, and popped his cock back into Moe's mouth. As Moe worked to get load number three out of Max, he looked up at him. Max rarely made eye contact in return, but that only gave Moe a greater opportunity to ogle him.

What turned Moe on the most, though, wasn't Max's rock-hard stomach, or his dense goatee, or the pelt of dark hair covering his chest. The thing that pushed Moe's buttons the most was the crucifix Max wore on his neck chain. He never took it off, and every time Moe looked up when he was blowing Max, he'd see the cross resting between Max's pecs.

He isn't just a goy, Moe said to himself, looking up from between Max's thighs. He *advertises*. With that thought in his mind, Moe pushed Max's cock deeper into his throat, and sent Max right over the edge.

But there was something more than sex going through Moe's mind when Max wasn't around. Moe was obsessed. He even did a bit of digging into Max's background, finding out about Max's personal life and his professional history as an acclaimed theater director. This only made Moe, a freelance theater critic, more intrigued. Maybe they actually *could* have a conversation—if not about Proust, then about the wit of Stephen Sondheim, or Sam Shepard's oeuvre, or the relative merits of the Roundabout Theatre. Maybe he could become more to Max than an online buddy, cloaking himself in a pseudonym and using his mouth for just one thing.

"I've never seen you so worked up over a trick," said Gene, Moe's friend and former lover, who had heard stories—sometimes amusing, sometimes shocking, but never particularly intimate—about dozens or even hundreds of Moe's sexual partners. "Normally, when they're out the door, they're off your mind."

But Max was unlike anyone Moe had ever met over the Internet. Moe thought about him every day and logged on to Men Online every night hoping to find him there, eager to see more of him, taste him again, connect on a deeper level.

Moe had even started turning away many of his other regulars to make more time for Max. This was definitely serious.

The following Wednesday, Moe was busy all evening, but as soon as he was free, he logged onto Men Online and found Max waiting for him. Max made the first move:

> DownTheHatch: Finally!
> HotLipsNYC: Waiting for me?
> DownTheHatch: All night. 5 minutes?
> HotLipsNYC: See you then.

Moe logged off without even replying to two other guys who'd sent him messages. He didn't feel like talking to anyone else.

Moe had on nothing but a pair of boxers, so he opened his closet to get out his 501s and a T-shirt. But as he stood there, he started to think: How would Max react if I changed the scene?

Not that he didn't like the usual three-round session. On the contrary, he dreamed about it. It was perfect every time.

Max had never even hinted that he might be interested in anything else. He hadn't ever kissed Moe, held him, or stayed more than a few seconds after his third and final orgasm. He had been in Moe's bed, but he had always stayed above the covers.

It's bound to be a mistake to push anything with Max, Moe thought, looking at himself in the bathroom mirror as he brushed his teeth. He can't possibly be attracted to me—I mean, look at his body and then look at mine. "He lifts weights every day," Moe had explained to Gene, "and I don't look like I've lifted anything besides a pint of Häagen-Dazs."

Max could have sex with anyone he wanted, Moe told himself; he just comes over here because it's convenient and reliable. He doesn't even look at me when we have sex. He watches the porn on the TV.

Still, Moe thought, he *does* come back pretty often. He must find something appealing about me. Even if it's just my mouth, that's still something, right? And I'm sure he'd enjoy a little more. I mean, who doesn't like affection? I'm sure he wouldn't turn down the offer. He wouldn't even have to *do* anything.

Moe often imagined what it would be like to rest his head on Max's hairy chest, to take in his scent, to rub his stomach softly. Even more, he dreamed what it would be like to lie in Max's arms, his back to Max's chest, Max's arms wrapped around him, with Max tickling the back of Moe's neck with his goatee and breathing warm sleepy air in his ear. In this fantasy, they talked while intertwined—about theater, politics, New York, their families—and Max realized with sudden tenderness that Moe was more than a hot mouth.

This fantasy alone was enough to make Moe want to push their sexual relationship to another level. But he knew there was a great risk. If Max wasn't interested, he might well leave forever, figuring Moe was some starry-eyed kid who'd grown too attached. Moe might ruin what he had sought for two solid years—hot sex with his fantasy man. He'd gotten his wish at last, and so much more, too. He wasn't eager to fuck that up.

Max rang from downstairs. Moe buzzed him up, turned on the VCR, and opened the door. Only one minute to make a decision. Put on the jeans and get in the chair like he usually did, or leave the jeans off and climb into bed?

Figuring that his first dream had already come true, Moe decided to pursue the next one. He left the jeans on his desk chair and climbed into bed.

When Max walked in, he stopped to evaluate the situation. The TV was playing the usual porn, and the apartment was dark as usual, but Moe wasn't in his usual spot. He was in bed. Max seemed unsure what to do.

He approached the bed and stood beside Moe's head. He unbuttoned his jeans and pulled out his cock, already half-hard, and said simply, "Suck it."

Moe did. He's not getting it, Moe thought. This is just the same thing in a different part of the room. He's just going to stand here while I blow him, same as always. Although he didn't tell me to get back in the chair. And he didn't turn around and leave. That's a step.

Five minutes later, Max came for the first time. He stripped off his clothes for round two. But this time, instead of taking a seat on the couch, he pulled back the covers, motioned for Moe to scoot over, and got into bed beside him. This is it, Moe thought, the part where everything changes.

But Max didn't turn and take Moe in his arms, or kiss his forehead, or ask how his day was. He pushed Moe's head down under the covers to blow him. Moe obliged. And, once again, Max was watching the video while Moe was doing the work. Moe was thinking that perhaps this was a mistake.

Nineteen minutes later, Max had shot a second load, and he let Max up from underneath the blanket. Moe was ready to start working on the third when Max said, "Come here," and motioned to his chest. Moe looked up and met Max's eyes.

Max put his arm under Moe's neck and rubbed his back with his hand. Moe rested his cheek on Max's hairy chest and reached up to take Max's crucifix in his fingers. Max bent down and kissed the top of Moe's head, and said, "This was a nice surprise."

Moe was speechless. What could he say? "Thank you"? "Anytime"? "No problem"? He just nodded into Max's chest hair.

"How do you turn this thing off?" Max asked, reaching for the remote control on the nightstand. Moe took the clicker and shut off the porn. They were together in the dark, without any distractions.

Moe was overcome by this good fortune. He thought, Dare I push it even further?

He rolled over onto his side, facing away from Max. It was a test. And Max passed.

Immediately after Moe rolled onto his side, Max rolled over, too, enveloping him in his arms and spooning right behind him. Moe reached down and took Max's hands in his own, pulling his arms tighter around his waist. Within a few short minutes, and after only two orgasms, Max was asleep in Moe's bed. He stayed the whole night.

As for Moe, he didn't sleep much. He didn't want to miss a thing.

16. Difference

By Rakesh Satyal

NEIL WAKES UP and feels that there is nothing covering him. In his sleep, or what he calls sleep these days, the bedsheet has worked itself around his right leg, twisted from ankle to groin, making one last curve over his big toe before falling off the right side of the bed. His arms have opted for the left side, his right arm flailed across his chest, its hand meeting the veins in his left wrist as if, in the wee hours of the morning, Neil suddenly felt the urge to check his pulse. Or if he had one.

The blinds are drawn, but the flecks of silver poking out from behind them reveal that it is a sunny day outside. It is a sunny day that has appeared out of nowhere in these last days of October, amidst a week otherwise cloaked in brooding clouds and increasingly thinning air. Despite the light, however, Neil is pessimistic, for he knows that New York autumns bring days that are bright in pallor but cold in touch. The copious hairs on his arms and legs lift—reminding him that no cover is on him now, so he returns to the thought of his sheet-entangled leg, how its wrap spills onto the hardwood floor. Neil has slept naked, as usual, and the whiteness of the sheet has found a true opposite in the brown—as if dirty—of his skin, made all the darker by the fuzz of his black leg hairs.

He untangles the sheet, alternating lifts of fabric and leg. Once this is done, he swings his legs onto the throw rug. He refuses to look behind him, to the left side of the bed, because that's where Stephen used to lie. If Stephen were still here, he would feign sleep, which is to say he would feign indifference. Indifference to whether or not Neil turned around and curled into the crook of his out-stretched arm. Put his dark lips to Stephen's fuzz-covered cheek, slid them over to his mouth, which would remain immobile, receiving Neil's kisses limply until Neil, in one swift but gentle motion, touched Stephen's bare chest. At which point Stephen would cup Neil's head to his. It had been too late before Neil real-ized that Stephen cared about him mostly for these bursts of pleasure. Not for the way in which Neil would gaze with genuine care upon the white length of Stephen's body.

Neil is not used to getting up without Stephen. His underwear is still in the drawer. "His toothbrush is still in the vanity," Neil realizes out loud in his studio apartment's bathroom after opening the mir-rored door and taking out his own brush. Neil has yet to clear his head so that Stephen does not come with every thought. His mind has always been overactive, associating loved ones with everyday activi-ties. The sound of rustling newspaper instantly conjures up his father. The whir of a stove fan is his mother, flipping roti on the stove. But what triggers thoughts of Stephen is a virtual fanfare of sounds.

Neil once tried to explain this connection.

"I think of you all the time," Neil said just three days before Stephen made his Grand Exit. They were strolling down Central Park West after an outdoor performance of *Twelfth Night*. The sound of wind through the trees also triggers Stephen now. "I never shake the thought of you. I keep thinking of that Dionne Warwick song. *'The moment I wake up / Before I put on my makeup, / I say a little prayer for you. . . .'* You know?"

Stephen laughed, which sounded like a cough. "I'm glad that in your mind Dionne Warwick and I are like *this*"—he jabbed a crossed-finger salute into the air.

"Oh, just play along. I'm trying to convey a thought. *'I run for the bus, dear / And I think of us, dear. . . .'*"

"The thought being . . . ?"

"The thought being that you've become a continual part of my psyche. You're my default."

"You know what song I love? 'What a Diff'rence a Day Makes.' You know that song? *'What a difference a day makes / And the differ- ence is you. . . .'*"

As they passed the Museum of Natural History, Stephen, sensing that he hadn't made a lasting impression—not sensing that this had really nothing to do with the matter at hand—decided to sing through the whole song. Surprisingly, he was not such a bad singer; at least he had a sense of pitch. And the inherent sibilance of his gay speech gave the song a silky jazziness.

Neil gets into the shower and barely dries himself off afterwards because he loves the way the air cools him as he reenters the bedroom. Sundays afford him the luxury of taking as much time as he wants to dress, and so he pulls out a smart set of clothes—a black wool sweater, gray wool slacks, and a brown tweed blazer.

STEPHEN: Why are you getting all dressed up on a *Sunday?*

NEIL *(sliding one arm into his blazer)*: I like looking nice. Some of us have to work at it, you know. *(Now the other arm.)*

STEPHEN *(yawning)*: Hey, where do you have to go, anyway? It's Sunday.

NEIL: I have to get some editing done. Don't you have some briefs to write or . . . old ladies to swindle or something?

STEPHEN: Hysterical. I see you have a firm grasp on the legal profession. You look nice.

NEIL: Thanks. (*Neil throws on a scarf and picks up his bag.*)

STEPHEN (*sotto voce*): Now take all of that off and get back into bed.

These little rooms we inhabit, Neil thinks, suddenly aware that his life—or anyone's life—consists of moving a pile of bones and flesh from compartment to compartment, that life is simply a series of entering and not being, but rather being *in*. This bedroom. Neil thinks of his bedroom and how its title lives up to its name. In here, everything centers totally around the bed: the TV, the nightstand, the dresser. But not just objects. Neil's whole life, or at least his recent life (which is to say his whole life), has centered around that slab. What he has thought of as affection or confidence has involved that bed and lying supine with Stephen. The whole world has become a labyrinth of bedrooms, and the bed and its memories unfurl their sheets as Neil walks out the apartment's door, goes down in the elevator, and strolls down Broadway and into a busy Starbucks.

At the end of the day, Neil thinks as he sits down with his cup of mocha, the paper cup snug in its ridged brown holder, *you have only yourself*. You can reminisce all you want, think of the times the two of you spent together: the time the two of you walked along the Chelsea Piers and looked across the Hudson at Jersey, pointing out its vying church spires, how they made the Garden State the most sacred of places, as much Christian mysticism curled in it as in Flannery O'Connor's South (a comment Neil dropped to Stephen as a damsel would drop her handkerchief); the time the two of you ran through the rain and bought a cheap bottle of port and evaded kisses in Tompkins Square Park, intoxicated on the too-sweet drink and the fact that you were actually sitting in the rain with a bottle of port; the time you argued art over Italian food on Mulberry Street, where you whisked each other away after seeing the *Metamorphoses*. You can think of all the times you performed these attempts at romance, and how they involved the two of you, but now, once it's over, it's only you and *your* memories, *your* efforts toward him, that exist. You have no certainty that he thinks or is thinking of you. You have no assurance, as you sit here with your cup of coffee, as you open up your bag and pull out your afternoon's work, that there is anyone else out there. It is you and you alone, and you are alone.

Neil pulls out his little red editing pencil and a small sharpener that he fits between his thumb and forefinger. He sharpens the pencil slowly, intently, loving how the wood shavings, rimmed in red, curl down to the small, round tabletop and form a neat pile, which he sweeps into a napkin. The action of sharpening calms Neil, and once he poises his newly shorn tip to the page, he feels as if he could do mountains of work.

For an hour, Neil is truly industrious. The object of his scrutiny today is a book on Indian mysticism in the Upanishads, something about which he knows very little despite his ethnic background. The project was passed to him, he knows, because he is Indian and because his boss thinks him the logical person to handle it. So for an hour, Neil edits like a ninja assassin, attacking sentences and besting them with his power. For an hour, Neil is what he has wanted to be, a professional working like mad in New York City, earning his keep, using his twenty-seven-year-old intelligence to impressive yet pragmatic effect. For an hour, he feels as if he's done justice to the intelligence and know-how that others attribute to him, and nothing can ruin such a thought.

Nothing, that is, until his pencil has moved in one nonstop thirty-second movement of repunctuation, placing periods and commas in a fluid, insistent manner, and then Neil looks at the handiwork he has imparted to page 54 and sees a pattern reminiscent of the moles that adorned Stephen's white back. *That* adorn *Stephen's white back.* All at once, the page has become a body, and even though Neil shakes his head and bends to his work with renewed determination, he sees his lover's back, the way it would glow in the morning bed as Stephen lay turned away from him, brandishing it nonchalantly. So nonchalantly, so unaware of the possibilities Neil saw in its mole-speckled surface. *Possibilities of what?* Neil asks himself—*No, edit, Neil*—oh, who cares, just *possibilities.* Neil looks at the next sentence in the manuscript and sees the white perfection of his lover's arm. He tries to read another page and sees nothing but his lover's thin leg hair. He can try all he wants, but all Neil will see, over and over again, is a collage of his lover's body—mole-speckled back, white pecs punctured by auburn chest hair, lips as taut as a grape's skin. Neil can try to concentrate on his manuscript, on dharma and nirvana, on the secrets of the most knowledgeable maharishis, but it is his lover's limbs that will enlighten him.

Neil snaps his pencil down and wonders for a split second if he is not the only one hallucinating limbs, if there are people all over this café conjuring up the bodies of their lost lovers. He scrutinizes the two dozen people trying to be studious in this Starbucks. There is a skater in the corner with her headphones on—the kind that hugs the back of her head, lest they cross over its top and smash her purposefully tousled hair. She nods to a beat that only she can hear while scratching furiously in a velvet-jacketed notebook, writing poetry that no one else will ever read but that dozens will be made to hear. And probably hate. There is a man in a gray pinstripe suit, partitioning his espresso into a series of twenty, maybe thirty sips, reading his *Times,* which is folded in half to accommodate the one column he is reading. Neil thinks of Complication, of reading the newspaper—folding, jumping from page to page, tracking the evolution of a long article from A1 to A14 to B736 and on and on. Like a cartographer on some fucking expedition. Such a hassle.

It's the flaw that Stephen saw most in Neil, this impatience. It's what Stephen hated most in him, even though Stephen never came right out and said it. But Neil knew that one February night, the night when they walked across Manhattan, all the way from Astor Place, where the sculpture of an enormous black cube stood on one point, a crew of rag-festooned Goths keeping vigil under its many shadows, to the Empire State, then passing the old New York Public Library, stone lions guarding its front, passing Rockefeller Center, where a crowd was pouring out of the back of Radio City, up to the Plaza, light caressing its facade as if it had been created just to do so; Stephen leaning over and whispering that maybe they should just sneak right up to the concierge and get a room for four hundred dollars that night. Neil knew that this one night marked the end of their seamless interaction, revealed the sloppy stitching that held their memories together in one important—if casual—piece of work:

Neil had been anxious to find them a cab so that they could escape the increasing cold and go cuddle in his warm apartment. But there were no empty cabs, and Neil had begun to obsess about this, sticking out his arm with true frustration, sneering at the passing, full hacks as if they should have been ashamed of themselves. The Upper East Side was aglow with the fare of overzealous window dressers, and the Roberto Cavalli store shone with exceptional fervor, its five mannequins frozen in the act of thrusting their hips. But Neil could not tear himself away from the curb. More occupied cabs shot by, and he hated everyone in them, because it was just so cold.

"Just relax, Neil," Stephen said, peering wonderfully at a cream-colored dress that hugged one of the mannequins' silver frames, a burst of diamonds at the hip, casting stars across her bosom and legs. "Look how beautiful this dress is."

Neil turned and looked, not because he was interested—even though he was—but because, according to his last glance down Fifth Avenue, not a single cab was within sight. Neil walked over to the window and looked at the dress that Stephen loved, then sighed because he wished he could concur. Neil knew how annoying he was being in his undying search and wished he could have offered Stephen a hearty concurrence as compensation. But the truth of the matter was that he did not like the gaudy diamond burst, and he had decided that he was through feigning agreement just to please Stephen.

All the same, as he voiced his opinion, he felt a twinge of regret.

"I just don't think it's very graceful."

Now it was Stephen's turn to sigh, Stephen's turn to stroll to the curb and hail them a cab. It was time to end the walk. But a cab didn't come for ten more minutes, and both Neil and Stephen felt in that time that they were nowhere. They were nowhere together.

Considering everything, how dare Neil criticize these other Starbucks inhabitants? They probably possess a passion that he will never be able to express honestly. They possess the secret that could have kept Stephen by his side, that could have made Neil tear himself away from those *fucking* cabs and see in diamond glows.

It's a question of authenticity.

Neil is aware, as he gathers up his things, throws his stuff into his bag, wipes the surface of his table clean, picks up his still-full cup of mocha and tosses it out and his scarf on, that he has learned something about authenticity in this shrine to manufactured life. He has learned that we create our authenticity, that it is up to us to express passion *and realize passion in others*, and he knows, as he pushes open the chilled door and passes out of this bedroom and into the bedroom of the outside, where leaves could be crackling into precious pieces, where cars could be beeping songs, that he has not added such life to his surroundings.

"There's a rainbow before me." There was that song again.

He wants, suddenly, to rush back into the Starbucks and kiss the skater girl fully on her shiny magenta mouth, wants to take off her headphones and flick his index finger along the ringlets puncturing the white ridges of her ears, and tell her, "There is a boy out there who would appreciate your authenticity! And I didn't. I didn't appreciate it—and now I walk from room to room and contribute nothing but bad energy and a mind full of dueling limbs." But he doesn't run to her. He folds his arms tightly across his chest as the wind blows him into Lincoln Center Plaza.

When it's not a grand evening at the opera, Lincoln Center is silently austere, its stone like the unfeeling white of a hospital's walls. Behind the tall glass windows, the grand staircase of the Met, darkened in its midday desertion, looks like the enormous skeleton of a museum tyrannosaurus. The fountain lies dormant, its basin covered in a layer of sad frost. Neil is shocked by the somber atmosphere this morning—or is it afternoon? He checks his watch and sees that it is already one-thirty. It should be bustling around here—shouldn't it, at least with tourists?—but no one else has opted to traverse this plaza right now. Neil sits on the rim of the fountain and feels, for the first time in a long time, the sudden urge to light a cigarette. Neil doesn't smoke and rather hates the habit, in truth. But, like so many other things, he had taken to it once in a while to please Stephen.

As if on cue, a sallow-looking girl carrying a large cello case passes by, a half-smoked cigarette hanging from her pale lips.

"Excuse me," Neil says, realizing that, aside from talking to himself in the bathroom mirror and ordering a drink at the coffee shop, this is the first he has spoken today. His voice sounds tinny and nasal.

The cellist turns to him as if she expected his question. She walks to him, sets her case down, and reaches into the bag slung over her shoulder to fish out the cigarettes. Her hair, Neil sees from upclose, has gone through several dyes, so that the dark brown of her roots morphs into maroon and then the orange of an old hardwood floor. It is also the orange of her bag, a flea-market creation with red and blue pom-poms decorating its contour. The cellist pulls out from the bag a crumpled box of Marlboro Lights and offers a smoke to Neil.

Neil's scant experience makes him respond with too much effort, so it looks more like he is selecting the perfect rose than pulling out a cigarette. His companion giggles, which Neil returns with a shake of his head, joking at his own inexperience. This simple gesture immediately gives the two of them a sense of comfortable intimacy as the cellist holds her hot-pink lighter to the end of Neil's rose.

To his surprise, the cellist sits down next to him on the fountain's rim.

"Where is everyone?" she says, taking a long drag and looking out toward Broadway. From their position in this plaza, raised up from the passing traffic, they could be the king and queen of some vast urban realm.

"I don't know," Neil replies, realizing only after he has spoken why the cello girl is here in the first place. He assumed her to be a Juilliard student, but no, this girl is no student; she has come to peddle her musical wares to a crowd that has not shown up.

The cellist takes a long drag. She bears a conflict of auras: her tennis shoes and cool flea-market bag make her look altogether juvenile, but the adult way in which she sucks on her cigarette and the unraveling of a thread in her old navy peacoat make her a true sage. Neil looks at her peacoat again. It was once nice, and not so long ago. Perhaps this girl is the rogue child of some Upper East Side royalty. That's probably what she is. How else could she afford a cello?

"If you stare at me any harder, you'll bore a hole right through my face."

Neil snaps out of his critical daze.

"You think about things too much, don't you?" she continues. She takes another drag, and during that moment, the noise of the cars on the street seems louder. "I'll tell you what I told my ex-boyfriend: Breakups suck. But breakups happen all of the time. Move on. Get used to it or you'll rot."

Neil is dumbfounded. This is not something that happens; we

don't meet strange people like this who say something life-changing to us. At least not something that seems life-changing as they say it. Life-changing comments take time and effort and build-up; they need to gestate before our moment of epiphany.

"Wanna hear a song?" the cellist asks, clamping the cigarette between her lips and opening her case. Neil looks down to see the cherry wood of the cello, but it is not a cello. It's a guitar. This girl is not a cellist, but a guitarist. Neil does not know if this cheapens or enriches the situation.

She cradles the large instrument on her lap and strums a few chords. The sound is small in the plaza. It doesn't even disturb the pigeons. How could Neil mistake a guitar for a cello?

He warms to the music; the girl plays very well. He believes that one can assess a musician's skill by the way in which she warms up. If what the musician considers mere warm-up is impressive in and of itself, then the musician belongs to a higher pedigree, one of talent and not acquired skill.

"Talent is not acquired, it is innate."

Stephen said that the night they went to see a friend of his play a violin recital at the Brooklyn Academy of Music. He said it at the reception after the recital and did not mean it as favorable for his friend. She was not truly talented, he asserted; she was doomed for the acquisition-of-skill route. And it was in that moment, when Stephen made the comment, that Neil wondered if there was loyalty in any of Stephen's friendships and, more frighteningly, in any of his relationships. What things did Stephen say about Neil behind his back? Perhaps at the same reception, just before Stephen summed up his friend's playing, he had mentioned to someone—perhaps the violinist herself—in an equally nonchalant tone, his blue eyes calm with pride, "Grace is not acquired, it is innate" and motioned negatively, with his hand bearing a glass of cabernet, to Neil, who was on the other end of the lobby, active in conversation with a colleague.

"My yesterday was blue, dear . . ." Neil couldn't remember the next lyrics.

"Hey! Do you want to hear something or not?"

The guitarist has frozen, her hands ready to strum whichever tune Neil wants. She has clamped the cigarette between her lips again and speaks through it like a Marx Brother griping through a stogie.

"What songs do you know?" Neil asks and takes a puff of his cigarette.

"Everything," she says, then returns Neil's elegant exhalation with a luxurious flourish of her own, blowing smoke onto Neil's forehead. Her eyes seem to boast Arlo Guthrie, Janis Joplin, and Radiohead with equal fervor. Neil imagines stacks of CDs in her home (he has almost fully decided on Upper East Side brat by now, can imagine her throwing the new Prada bag her mother gave her onto the pink carpeted floor of her bedroom to take up her whimsical pom-pom sack), CD cases all over the place, scratched and cracked, one tower of them bearing Coltrane, Philip Glass, and Jeff Buckley, a mess covering the bay window with the fare of Etta James, Bach, and Beck.

"Do you know 'What a Diff'rence a Day Makes?'"

The wisdom behind the girl's eyes dissipates, and her face scrunches as if to say that Neil is the cruelest being alive.

"Who's it by?"

Who's it by? Who's it *by*? She's never even *heard* of "What a Diff'rence a Day Makes"?

"You know, 'What a Diff'rence a Day Makes' . . . ?" Neil tries a few weak bars: *"'What a diff'rence a day makes / Twenty-four little hours . . .'"* He continues on a hum, forgetting the rest of the words in his disbelief that someone could not have even *heard* of the song.

"Who's it by?" she asks again, and she sticks out her chin defiantly. In this moment, Neil sees that she can't be more than eighteen. His respect for her is dwindling.

But she poses a good question: Who *did* sing this song originally, anyway? Neil seems to recall seeing Esther Phillips sing it on some really old episode of *Saturday Night Live,* her violent vibrato transforming the song from a nice little ditty into a listening effort. But who sang that original? Neil can't remember the exact timbre of the voice, but it was brighter, he knows, than Esther's. *Not Ella Fitzgerald. . . .*

"I can't remember," Neil surrenders. A fist of regret fills the emptiness of his stomach. Neil can feel another series of digressions coming in his mind; he feels helpless to it; and although he offers a semi-encouraging sigh as the girl breaks into Joni Mitchell's "Blue," he has become one huge whimper all over.

Neil wonders if songs are like us—or better, we're like songs—passed on from person to person, each one singing us differently, adding his own embellishments, twisting us around to sound the way he wants. After all, from the moment Neil met Stephen at a crowded bar in Chelsea—Neil ending up in Stephen's bed that night—Stephen was playing Neil. Stephen was all types of musicians: He played Neil with the reckless cruelty of a rocker; with the somber touch of a torch-song pianist; with the grandiloquence of Mozart or the jubilation of a gospel great. Neil never knew what to expect except that he would find himself ready and willing to offer himself to Stephen's adept fingers, to his drawl, which sounded like the voice of an English actor trying on an American accent, so overly elegant and studied, yet so casual.

The sense of worthlessness and inferiority that comes over Neil now as the guitarist finishes her Joni is that Stephen's versatility has made Neil so many things that whatever Neil is, Stephen is still playing him, always and unfailing.

The guitarist's alto peters out after the guitar has stopped. The sound is once again small in the plaza, and not much has seemed to change after it.

Without a word, the girl starts into a song that Neil does not know, something folksy and weepy. No, he thinks. *No.* He didn't ask to be sung to. He was the first one here, damn it. The words come strangely out of this girl's mouth, her pale little mouth. She sounds Romanian. Can't she just pronounce the words? Can't she just sing "What a Diff'rence a Day Makes"?

Couldn't Stephen just have stayed?

Oh, God, Neil wishes such a question wouldn't pop into his head, that he could banish Stephen from his life and, if not that, then at least from this plaza, this one part of his day. But Stephen will win, Neil knows—he can feel the impatience flooding through himself once more.

He gets up abruptly, bumping the girl's arm and ruining her chord. "Whoa. What the fuck?"

Neil grabs his bag and whips it around himself, just missing the girl's face. He hasn't even asked her name.

"What the fuck is the matter with you?" she asks, still strumming.

"What the fuck is the matter with *you?*" Neil is surprised to hear himself reply as he walks away from the fountain, away from Lincoln Center. There it is. So soon after he thought of the benefits of patience and grace, so soon after he wanted to run back into that Starbucks and kiss the poet, he has spurned yet another person. He may tell himself from time to time that his essence is good-hearted and well-meaning, but his *habit* is another thing. Stephen was right. Stephen was always right, the consummate maestro.

He looked good no matter what. Although many of Neil's friends warned Neil to watch himself, that Stephen was nothing to fuss over. Certainly nothing to take Neil out of their social circle for long periods at a time, periods he spent shuttling from Manhattan to Brooklyn, to Stephen's breezy, wood-painted-white apartment on Eastern Parkway, across from the Brooklyn Museum. Neil felt a bodily frenzy, as if cocaine-laced—the sense that his little body was deteriorating from the stress of catering to whims. His eating became even more irregular than that of the usual stressed corporate worker;

he felt himself getting thinner, such as when he put his watch on and felt his wrist's shrinking circumference, or when he could buckle his belt another notch up.

Stephen noticed the difference.

"You're looking very thin," he said over coffee one morning, in Brooklyn. It was August, and the two of them had already begun to sweat after their showers. There was a big nick on the rim of Stephen's mug that he kept burrowing into with his index finger.

"I'm a thin boy," Neil replied with a smile, then sipped his coffee.

Neil looked so thin because, yes, he had been running all over two boroughs, but also because he had to borrow yet another of Stephen's shirts, which were too big for him.

"You don't take care of yourself," Stephen said. He set his mug down and clasped his hands on the table as if about to tell Neil about the birds and the bees. "You don't eat right. If at all."

"Jesus, I eat," Neil said. Stephen always berated him for an anorexia he simply did not have. "I am not starving myself, Stephen. Maybe if you came up to my apartment once in a while, I would look a little better." Neil knew that this statement sounded stupid and nonsensical; it was missing a logical step in the argument. He should have said, "I am losing weight because I shuttle all around the city for you." But he hadn't, and knowing he sounded incoherent, Neil got up as if to do something. But he had nothing to do.

"What? What does *that* mean?"

"Oh, you know what it means." But no, he doesn't. *You haven't articulated yourself clearly. Try again.* "I come here all of the time. You never come to visit me. And it takes a lot to run all over New York to hang out with you. I'm not good to myself because—because I'm so good to *you*. So I wouldn't complain if I were you."

"Neil, I'm not the one complaining."

And it was true. Who was complaining? The one who always complained.

To see in diamond glows. If only to see in diamond glows.

"Neil, I'm not the one complaining. I just want you to be healthy. You're being ridiculous."

"You're being so ridiculous," Stephen repeated, getting up and putting his arms around Neil's thinning waist, and kissed him. "My ridiculous little Neil."

"Shut up," Neil said, kissing back. "I hate that word." Kiss. "Almost as much as I hate you."

"I know." Kiss. "I hate you, too."

Sex.

Lying in bed afterwards, in the midday sun, Stephen asleep, back displayed again, Neil felt absolutely content. He was aware that there is quite a difference between being happy and being content—or, more accurate, *contented*. But he always rationalized the difference by thinking that he was lucky simply to have someone in his life. There could be a million differences everywhere if he wanted there to be. Why measure the difference between happy and happier?

Neil got up in that midday indolence and went to the bathroom. He stared at his reflection in the mirror. He *was* thinner. There were defined bags under his eyes. His collarbones protruded, as if eager to be snapped.

Snapped like the twigs under Neil's feet, which he notices only now, once he has walked deep into Central Park and is surrounded by a murkiness of brown trees and grass. Clouds have quilted the sky, and now whatever crowds might have taken to the park on a Sunday have dispersed.

He feels himself gravitating toward Bethesda Terrace, which marks the center of the park. Gray stone steps open onto a plaza of red brick, the tall fountain at the center asleep like the one at Lincoln Center. A winged woman, the angel Bethesda, sprouts from its top, her hands open to pour water from their fingers. But there is no water, so she seems instead like a *madonna*. Frost has gathered under her eyes and forms her tears.

A couple sits near the end of the terrace that lets onto the lake. The couple—a tiny man and a tiny woman, he in a gray hooded sweatshirt, she in a green one—turns and looks at Neil for a second, together, then returns to gazing across the brown water. Only once they look away does Neil feel justified in entering their realm, seating himself on a stone ledge under a line of bare trees. The stone is hard, but somehow comforting in the firm chill it sends up his spine. It was here that it all ended—here, where Neil always comes, the very place that Stephen told him, "I respect you. You are my best friend. But I cannot love you the way you expect," and then walked away, stopping to scuff his cigarette into the brick.

"Neil?" says a female voice.

Neil looks up and sees Gwen, an acquaintance of Stephen's. Her smile is polite and reserved, partly because she has recognized Neil's daze as half-crazy behavior, partly because she has not seen Neil since he and Stephen broke up. *Not so long ago.* The last time they saw each other was at a bar in the East Village, the night before Stephen left, and Neil recalls now that Gwen was truly plastered, her blonde hair obscuring her face. He can even see some recognition behind Gwen's eyes, can see that she remembers the shininess of the cigarette-and-martini-strewn table of the bar in front of her and her blonde locks falling in front of her eyes.

"How are you, Neil?" She stretches out her arms and Neil gets up, setting down his bag and then hugging her limply. She smells of vanilla; the scent is all over her long black overcoat and her hair, which she now wears in a bun.

"I'm doing great, actually. Just enjoying a little stroll. You?"

"I actually just had brunch with some coworkers at The Boathouse." She points across the water to the restaurant. Of course; she was here for a brunch. With friends. Neil hasn't called any of his own friends today, not because he doesn't want to see them but because the thought of being gregarious hasn't really lured him today.

But Gwen has a legitimate reason to be wandering the park. As opposed to Neil. Idleness drenched in loneliness is hardly a legitimate reason for anything.

"Nice," Neil says, sensing that the conversation has already reached a Stephen-necessary point. So he doesn't proffer anything.

"So . . . How is everything?" Gwen tries.

"Great. Really, really good."

"Working on anything great right now? You're still editing, right?"

"Right. Yes. Nothing huge. Well, I was working on this book today on Indian mysticism."

"Right up your alley, huh?" Gwen squeezes Neil's forearm encouragingly.

It's a question of authenticity.

"That's right," Neil lies, and he thinks once more to the page of punctuation, then to Stephen's moled back, then to Stephen's moled back covered in a powder blue oxford shirt, walking away from him on this terrace, stopping as Stephen stepped out his cigarette.

"So, how long has it been since I saw you?" Gwen asks, and both of them realize as she asks this that it is really an indirect question as to how long it has been since Stephen left. Neil thinks of the days since he left, thinks of one day in truth, as they have all passed like each other, all of them—

"Wow—has it been that long?" Gwen thinks out loud, answering her own question. "The last I saw you was that crazy night we had in Alphabet City, remember? That must have been last year. Last summer! Wow! Just over a year? I haven't seen you in a *year!* How is that possible? The days just zoom by, don't they?"

Neil doesn't really pay attention for the rest of the conversation. Gwen must take the hint, because she embraces him suddenly, squeezes too tightly, and then disappears with her high heels making a horse's clop across the brick walkway. Neil has been caught at his own game. He can no longer keep up his charade. The grace period passed a long time ago. It has been over a year since Stephen left, and it is no longer sane or acceptable for him to be going on like this. It is acceptable only for him to leave this terrace and never come back. But Neil knows he will be back.

Neil stays on the terrace for a long while. The sweatshirted couple gets up and leaves, and the sun begins its early winter descent. The red brick of the terrace turns gray as the light fades. Neil wishes that the clear skies from earlier would return; at least then the sun would give the dusk some hint of color. But the sky is still cloudy, and the effect of this dark ceiling is to transform everything beneath it to gray stone—the water, the trees, even Neil himself, who feels as if he has become part of the ledge on which he sits.

When Neil finally gets up, it is to wander through the darkening park, despite the danger in doing so. He continues north from the terrace, only partially out of a desire to return home to the Upper West Side; he wants instead to walk on the new wooden bridge that crosses the lake—a squat, solid arc of light pine. Neil's feet thud as he walks across the bridge. He senses the mad ramblings of a derelict somewhere on the other end. Still, Neil knows that he himself casts an imposing picture right now: here he stands, a tiny, brooding Indian man, dressed in a style of professional beatnik grandeur, his arms wrapped tightly around himself, gazing over the stony water toward the apartment complexes of the Upper West Side, careless to the dangers that must be around him. It is likely that the homeless man finds Neil scarier than Neil finds him.

As the sun disappears and the lights come on in the apartment buildings, the pinpoints of white like sequins on a ballroom dancer's dress, Neil thinks back to last summer, when he and Stephen lay sprawled together on a reclining lawn chair on Stephen's Brooklyn roof, a perfect view of Manhattan before them. It was one of those views of New York that served as undeniable proof that the Big

Apple was the greatest city in the world—the Empire State, far across the East River, stood proudly, almost patriotically, and when its lights clicked off as usual at midnight, it seemed that it was winking at Stephen and Neil, urging them toward romance. Neil, tingling with the glasses of pinot grigio he had just downed, lay in Stephen's arms, and then Stephen spoke, his voice whirring.

"I love you, Neil," he said, and it took Neil by total surprise, because even in their first year together, neither of them had said it. It had never occurred to him that Stephen would actually say it. And say it first. Neil pulled himself up and faced Stephen in that darkness, and the look that passed between them was the one that Neil had always wanted: when you are with someone and look at him and the two of you know that you are actively working to make each other better, that you want to go out of your way to make each other happy and spend time together and speak words of love freely and eloquently. It was the Stephen that Neil loved, but didn't know how much he loved until that moment, and he was so overcome with love that he didn't even think to return Stephen's words. Instead, Neil kissed him.

So how can Neil berate himself for falling in love and staying that way for so long?

Because, Neil tells himself, it was not three days afterward that he and Stephen were back on that same roof, Stephen having arranged a little nighttime get-together, and Stephen was flirting with another guy, a petite Russian. Neil knew what was going on. Still, Neil clung to that lawn chair night before the Manhattan lights, clung to the fact that Stephen had professed love first. It never occurred to him that Stephen would say such words even though he didn't mean them entirely, or because it was not Stephen but the pinot grigio talking. He had earned an *I love you*, after all. There could be a million differences if I wanted there to be. Why measure the difference between trust and trysts?

Suddenly something hits Neil:

"*I* made it love," Neil says out loud, stopping right next to the stone steps of the Museum of Natural History. "*I* made it love," he says again, realizing that the person he should really be blaming is himself. Despite all of his attempts to see every angle of his relationship, he has not until now seen his foolishness in all its plainness: *He* turned the relationship into love, not Stephen. Yes, Stephen said *I love you*, but it was Neil's fault not to test whether the statement was true.

"*'My lonely nights are through, dear,/Since you said you were mine,'*" Neil sings in the elevator of his building, as it carries him languidly up to his apartment. "My lonely nights are through," he says, chortling this time. He says this just as the doors open and a girl from several floors beneath his enters. Neil does not finish speaking until it is too late, so he is destined to be thought a madman for the rest of the ride. When the elevator finally stops at his floor, he exits quickly and rushes into his apartment, to escape the many humiliations he has brought on himself today.

He throws his bag onto the couch in the sitting room, then goes into the kitchen to get a glass of water. He then fixes himself a ham sandwich, which he eats at the counter. As he walks into the bedroom—*the bedroom*—he is reminded, the way a veteran made lame must remember his affliction with delayed reaction after waking in the morning, that Stephen will never be his.

It is now eight o'clock, and Neil is already tired. He turns on the TV, flips through channels for about an hour, then turns off the TV and listens instead to the traffic passing noisily outside. He knows that if he stays up much later, he will think of new ways to reflect on his loneliness, and so he readies himself for bed. It is when he sees Stephen's toothbrush on the vanity that his heart breaks yet again.

I made it love . . .

But don't we all make things love? Isn't that the point of life?

Isn't the best thing we can do to take the things we have in our life and love them as honestly and fully as we can?

And Neil realizes that there is a catch. In real life, "things" do not exist. Objects carry the spirits of the people that use them; places carry the spirits of the people who move through them; even other people carry the spirits of the people who meet them. Places and objects may maintain their shape. But they have been changed forever, and it is foolish for him to want them immutable. People are not quantities; people are not just words or measurements of time. People are measurements of love, of emotion, of forces without boundaries, and therefore the most dangerous—yet dearest—things.

People talk of "the day I met you"; "the day you told me you loved me"; "the day you kissed me." *The day he broke my heart.* But it's not the day that matters; the person makes the day important, makes the day different. *The difference is you*, is Stephen, is this ghost that follows Neil from room to room. And once you've opened yourself to the difference, accepted the change it has brought on you, you open yourself to one irreversible fact: You have not accepted just a difference, but a living, breathing human being, one that used to lie next to you and brandish his mole-bejeweled back; one that used to wink at you naughtily because he cared and knew you cared and knew it was more than a wink; one that turned your stomach into a swarm whenever you saw him; one that was, in truth, despite your current sadness, a shimmering, marvelous man, smart and eloquent, truly worthy of being loved. The living, breathing human being exists continually, and so you can meet him over and over, relive his confessions of love again and again, feel each kiss now and *now,* and your heart can break a countless number of times. Your heart can shatter every day, every moment, and you can find yourself undressing for bed, determined to reset yourself, struggling to reorganize your life. Or at least this moment.

Neil will have at least this moment. He gets into bed and lies cleanly snug on his back, the way people do in mattress commercials. He has this moment, when he can dream of tomorrow, when everything is new again, when all the bitterness can be replaced with motivation and resilience. No, not even "resilience"—"resilience" implies recovering from a dealt blow, and it is better to have no memory of the blow.

It is just Neil and his giving heart. For now, he is his beating, liberated heart, which pulsates through him one, two, three, eight, fifteen times. . . .

And this is enough. This is promising.

A breeze blows outside, and somewhere below, there is a swish of falling leaves.

I love you, Neil.

Neil's leg shifts, and the bedsheet, since Stephen's body is not there, goes with it.

17. The Lost Coast

By Ted Gideonse

1

WE HAD MET them the night before.

Paul and I were camping our way up Route 1, one night at Point Reyes, one in Mendocino, all the way to the Olympic Peninsula. We were planning on taking a month to get from San Francisco to Seattle, where I was starting a new job, where Paul hoped to find one. But when we found Usal Beach, in the Lost Coast, those fifty miles of untouched California oceanfront not traced by the Pacific Coast Highway, we decided to hang out for a while. I found the place calming: Something about the combination of the black sand and the gray fog and the albino Roosevelt elk that lumbered and wandered through the fields and forest. Paul didn't seem to mind the delay; he just read. We'd been alone there for three days when a couple of kids and their baby arrived in a dusty little Mazda hatchback.

"Some drive, hunh?" I called out from my lawn chair when a man—a boy, really—got out of the car and stretched.

"No shit." He shook his head. "Fuckin' treacherous."

"And in that little thing."

"No shit, man. No shit." He looked eighteen, talked eighteen, like an eighteen-year-old skater you'd see in Venice Beach: shaggy brown hair, baggy jeans, stubble covering baby soft skin. Paul would love him, I thought.

I heard a baby crying.

The boy looked in the car and said, "You need some help?"

I heard a muffled "no" and then the other door opened and a woman (girl, really) emerged with a crying baby in her arms. The girl was doing that jumping-rocking thing that is supposed to calm down babies. She looked a little like her boyfriend, except her hair was longer and underneath an orange bandanna. And no stubble. The boy watched the girl as she walked around the campsite, jumping and rocking and patting her baby while whispering something, maybe humming. The girl looked terrified.

"I think the ride down the mountain scared Harry," he said. It scared the girl more, I thought.

"Well, that car of yours isn't one for these roads," I said. It wasn't, either. I've got an old Suburban, four-wheel drive and a cab two feet off the ground, and I was still nervous about the road, that I'd get stuck in one of the holes, break an axle.

"When I figured that out, it was too late."

"Always the way," I said.

His girlfriend had walked to the edge of the cliff our campsite sat on and was watching the waves below, the baby's head on her shoulder. He'd stopped crying. She looked like she was relaxing; her shoulders weren't scrunched up anymore. The boy saw her soften, and he started to unload the car. I offered to help. I was bored—Paul had gone for a hike, and he took long hikes—and if I hadn't asked, it would have been tacky of me to sit and watch him labor over setting up a tent. The kid was friendly, the kind of person who goes into a 7-Eleven and asks how business is and actually cares about the answer. His name was Jim; his wife was Dawn. From the strange collection of personal items in the backseat—a framed photograph of a family, too much clothing, an old teddy bear—I figured out that they were living out of their car. I let Jim think I didn't know, because he seemed to be embarrassed. Who wouldn't be? Especially a man with a baby and a wife.

After we got them set up, I offered them beers. I had a huge cooler of Sierra Nevadas. Dawn declined. She took one of Paul's V8s, though. She cradled little Harry while Jim and I talked. She was a little skittish, looking at me from the side, wondering if I could be trusted, doing that shy-girl thing. They had that introvert/extrovert kind of relationship, just like Paul and I did.

Around seven, Paul came up from the beach. He always came home in time for dinner. He saw that I'd made friends, but being the introverted one, he avoided introducing himself for a while. He put on a sweatshirt, changed his socks, got a beer, and then came over and in a rare extroverted moment, kissed me on the forehead. Jim ignored the kiss, as he should. Dawn looked at Harry, embarrassed. I introduced everyone.

"How was your hike?" Jim asked.

"Good. Nippy," Paul said. He sat on the grass because Dawn was in his lawn chair. We must have looked strange to these kids. We're Laurel and Hardy, in a way. I'm not that fat and he's not that skinny and we're not abusive at all, but it's the closest analogy. And we were "Laurel and Hardy Goes Camping," dirty and oily and stained and alone together a little too long. It was probably obvious that I wanted to talk to somebody, anybody. Paul can be quiet; he can hide behind a book or a hike or a mood. It never bothered me when we were just friends, because if he wasn't in the mood to go out to a bar, he just wouldn't go. But one night he did, and our quiet ten-year mutual crush became kind of loud after a few too many beers. We hooked up, and then I realized what it was like to live with his demons or problems or whatever you want to call them. But we'd fallen in love, or whatever you want to call it. And now we were a strange-looking couple.

We all shot the shit for a long time and then Paul and Jim started making dinner: our chicken breasts and veggies and their ramen noodles. As predicted, I caught Paul checking out the little bit of chest exposed by the V in Jim's shirt. I smirked to myself and then asked Dawn if she wanted me to hold Harry for a bit.

She froze, stared, and sucked in cheeks. I might have asked if she needed to borrow some Preparation H. She must have taught herself how to stop her bristling, because she softened quicker than I expected.

"I'm OK." She looked over at Jim, who was lost in a cloud of steam.

"You sure? My sister used to cramp when she held my niece for too long."

She looked back at me and I smiled. She smiled but held tight.

"I'm a bit, um . . ."

"It's OK. I probably wouldn't want to let go either."

"Yeah." A bit embarrassed, she looked down.

"He's the definition of towheaded," I said, following her gaze to his swirl of blond wisps.

"Yeah," she said, nodding. I don't think she knew what I meant by "towheaded." But from my tone, she could probably tell it wasn't bad.

"Where you kids off to next?" I asked.

"Oregon," she said.

"That's where my sister is, in Salem. Whereabouts you going?"

"I think Eugene. We have some friends there."

"Where you coming from?"

"Bakersfield," she said.

"Not surprised you left."

"Yeah, it's a shit hole."

"Grow up there?"

"Yeah."

She stared off into the dusk. Something made me think of Meg Tilly. Maybe it was her small eyes. Harry: God, he was adorable.

"My parents wanted us to put Harry up for adoption," she said.

"Right."

"Jim's parents?"

"They hate me."

"What are you going to do up in Eugene?"

"I have no idea."

"And Jim?"

"Oh, he knows construction. I mean, he can do that. He did that last summer."

"Great. And you can take care of Harry."

"Yeah, like my mom didn't do."

She mumbled something about a hat and went over to the Mazda. I heard Paul laugh, Jim chuckle, and then Dawn was back with a little pink cap on Harry's head. She and I smiled at each other.

"You'll be OK," I said.

Dinner was great, even though the noodles were overcooked and the veggies underdone. Paul's not a great cook and I doubt Jim had ever made anything more complex than mac and cheese. But the pine smoke and salty fog made the food much better than it should've been, and we liked these kids. Jim had the charisma of someone self-possessed from an early age, a boy who has always been handsome, graceful, and charming. And responsible, too, taking on a wife, a baby, and a career trajectory clearly outside of his parents' imagination. They had no idea what they were in for. It made me happy.

Because Paul and I knew what *we* were in for: Another twenty years of work, twenty more of retirement, doctors, and assisted living. Maybe Paul's poetry will find an audience; probably not. I'll help some drug addicts; more will shrug off my advice. Maybe I'll be sad and cynical, giving advice to social workers right out of school. At some point I'll forget my friends who died, I'll watch my niece get married, I'll buy some new furniture. Paul will hate the couch—he'll cover it with an Indian throw—and I'll forget to water his plants.

Paul will stray, I will stray, we'll probably stay together, but we might not. Probably not. And that will be it. I don't know if we'll be content, if we'll be pleased with what we've become, if we'll even know what we've become.

"I'm worried about them," I said to Paul later, in the tent, in the dark. I didn't want to say I was jealous; worried is what I would be, what I should be.

"I think he's gay."

"Paul," I sighed.

"OK, fine." He giggled. "He's just cute."

"Yes."

"And you're right. They're worrisome. But only in that they're-young-and-it's-going-to-be-hard way. Don't worry, honey. It'll be all right."

Paul said the word "honey" with sarcasm. Honey coated in salt. And he said it as he caressed my chest, Jim in his mind and his hands. I responded, because I wanted to be Jim, to have what he would. To be wanted that way, sure, but to have nothing, too, to have the void in front of him and Dawn and little Harry.

2

The kids wanted to leave the next morning, to get on with it. Jim had said that: "Get on with it." But I convinced them to stay until the afternoon. The sun had come out and the fog had gone back out to sea, and suddenly it was hot on the campground. No wind at all. I told Jim and Dawn that they had to take a swim. The water was so calm there. When we'd first arrived and Paul and I polar-beared, my lips turned blue. But now it was really hot, so the water was soothing. Paul and I dove in and out of the surf like pink dolphins. Then I floated on my back and let the sun dry the salt on my chest. Paul bobbed next to me, humming a tune of his own devising. Then I sat with Harry while Jim and Dawn waded into the water. We were all content, pleased with ourselves, like children on Christmas afternoon. The kids left before we did, and I suddenly felt lonely. Maybe it was just the sadness from packing up the campsite—it felt like moving, which we'd just done a week before, and it was a bright, fresh wound.

The drive up wasn't as awful as the drive down. We weren't going back the way we came in, we were continuing north, so there wasn't anything we'd already seen, felt, and rolled over. But it seemed to have been driven over much more often; fewer rocks, shallower holes. I was pretending like I was OK with the road. I kept quiet and slowly breathed through my nose. Paul, however, gripped the dashboard and pushed his feet into the floor, as if there was a brake pedal on the passenger side. I could hear his breathing; dramatic sighs and grunts. He was scared.

"Let's take a break," I said.

"Hunh?" A slight whine.

"We'll just stop up there," I said, pointing to where the road turned with the curve of the mountain. "Take a breather, see what the view's like."

"OK."

I patted his arm. He was moist, sweaty. The hair on his forearm was matted.

I pulled the Suburban over. The road left about ten feet for someone to get by. But no one was coming, so it didn't really matter. I climbed out and stretched. The pine was stronger here, the salt air fainter, but the sun was filtered more, through the needles and much farther from the water. I walked to the side of the road and looked out at the mountain, the ocean below, and the ribbon of the road. It was, well, magnificent; I couldn't believe we were in California. It was Borneo or Madagascar, an island off Australia. I saw gulls, hawks, green everywhere. The sun was so bright.

"What's that?" Paul was standing next to me, pointing at the side of the mountain. Sunlight was bouncing off a piece of metal hidden by the thick trees that held up the road.

I held up my hand, blocking the beam. I could see now. It was a big piece of metal.

"It's a car," I said. "It fell off the road."

"Jesus!"

Usually, Paul would tell me to shush, stop jumping to conclusions. But it was a car. It was blue. I started running up the road. It looked like it was a quarter mile to where the car was, but it seemed to be much farther as I ran and ran and ran. I could hear Paul's feet behind me. He wasn't speaking, or yelling. He was running, too. I know he was because when I tripped and fell, he was right on me. In seconds.

"Baby!"

I looked at my hands. I'd scratched them up; they were dirty. My knee hurt. My elbow was bleeding a little.

"Baby!"

"I'm OK."

"That's their car!"

"I know."

"Call 911."

My cell phone had no reception.

"We can't," I said.

I got up and we ran to where they must have fallen off the road, where part of the road had washed away and a boulder was taking up too much space. We would be able to get around it, or over it, but there was no way Jim's Mazda could have. I started skidding down the mountain, and Paul was behind me. We were in our sneakers. It was ridiculous. We just slid down the dirt and leaves, pebbles and sticks, seashells dropped by gulls. We had no traction, just gravity and aim. Ridiculous.

The Mazda was fucked up, on its side, broken glass, twisted fender, missing wheel. It had rolled. We were facing the top of the car, the concave roof, the windshield shattered but in one piece—spiderwebbed, I think they call it. There was steam or smoke. Which it was, I couldn't tell—or smell, with all that dust in my nose and lungs. I didn't hear anything but the wind. And those weren't hawks. My heart was back in 1983, when I was on coke all the time. It was like a sense memory, but it was inside my body, an overplayed tape. I just stared and breathed and felt the sweat drip down my face.

But Paul kept moving. He went to the windshield and looked inside, peered through the web. He was shaking. He said something, but again, I couldn't hear. He looked at me and said it again. Finally he shrieked at me. I heard that—the shrieking, not the words. I walked toward him, and then my ears cleared, or my head did, whichever.

"Harry's crying!"

I nodded. I looked through the webbed glass. I couldn't see Harry in the backseat. Jim and Dawn were in the front, broken, red, mussed, unmoving. Then I heard the wails, tired and tinny.

"God," I said.

"We have to get him out!" Paul said.

"I know."

I guess the Lord made hatchbacks for a reason. It was the only way we could get to Harry. Paul and I pried the thing open, ripped out the barrier between the trunk and the backseat, and then Paul crawled in. No way would I have fit. He crawled past Harry, over the seats, talking soothingly the whole time. But his voice was shaking.

"Hold on, Harry. I'm coming. Gonna check on your parents first, check on Mom and Dad. Hold on, Harry. We'll get you out in a minute."

I heard him talking to Jim and Dawn, saw him touch their necks. To make sure.

Then to me: "I'm gonna take him out of the car seat."

"Right," I said.

"We should move him, right?"

"We have to!" I said.

"He looks OK," Paul said. "Are you OK?" he asked Harry.

Then I had Harry in my arms. He was perfect; angry and red
with tears, but no cuts, not even bruises. I was bloodier than he was.
But what did I know? I took CPR ten years ago, and I always killed
those dummies when I was doing chest compressions on them. I
always pushed too hard. I didn't know shit about medicine, and we'd
just removed a baby from a wrecked car, pulled him out like it was
lifting him from a crib.

"We have to get Harry to a hospital," I said. "I mean, he could
be hurt."

Paul was rummaging through the trunk. He retrieved the baby
bag, a padded pink sack full of diapers and bottles and implements of
infancy. Why was it pink? It must have been a hand-me-down, from
one of Dawn's friends who'd had a similarly unfortunate pregnancy.

"Paul."

"Yeah."

"We have to get him to a hospital," I said.

"I know we do!" he said.

"Are they. . . ?"

"Yeah."

I didn't look back into the car, didn't watch Paul. I turned my
head, looked out to the Pacific, and stroked Harry's downy head.
He was just whimpering now, and he was kneading my shirt with
his tiny fingers. His head was on my left breast, his little legs rested
on my belly. He quieted, gurgled a bit. And then, as I followed Paul
up the hill, Harry fell asleep and dreamt. He smelled like dust and
baby powder.

3

Shelter Cove was not created for people like me. (Or, for that matter, for Harry's parents.) The town was created for the rich folks in Pacific Heights and Sausalito, for their overflow. It was a trappers' town way back, then a logging camp, then the highway was built out of the way and made Shelter Cove way out of the way, and the village went ghost. Then that made the place valuable—near impossible to reach, near impossible to spoil with motels and the vacationing poor. Now there are fifty pricey houses, a tiny private airstrip, and prying eyes. We stuck out: Laurel and Hardy and a Little Rascal, arriving by car, and from the impassable south, too. Of course, these folks aren't the evil rich, or the ones we met at the general store weren't. We used their cell-phone tower free of charge, and a couple of the bored bankers, eager to break some sort of sweat, took their SUVs to meet the rangers at the crash site. A horsey lady, gray and lined, showed up, told us she was a nurse, and ordered us to a little clinic endowed by her late husband, a cardiologist who counted heartbeats before managed care.

"Give me that child," she said to me when we were in the spare little white house across the street from the post office.

I balked. I'd been holding Harry for over an hour. I'd made Paul drive; I wouldn't give Harry to him. I was being protective, but I was also feeling needed, the gentle, warm breath on my neck, the kneading hands. I stared at the nurse as if I hadn't heard her.

"Sam," Paul said.

"What do you think I'm gonna do? Poison the little guy?"

"No." But I didn't move.

"Look: You pulled him out of a car wreck. I need to take a look."

"Sam."

When I moved to give Harry to the nurse, I felt a cramp in my biceps, and my arm jerked in pain. Harry woke up and started crying. Not screaming, just that "Why'd you wake me up?" bawling. I moved slowly, and the nurse took Harry from my hands, his little head in her wrinkled, spotted fingers.

I hovered over the nurse as she examined Harry, whom she'd laid on the cushioned table. She took off his flannel jumpsuit (blue, covered in teddy bears) and gently poked and prodded him, stared into his penlight-lit eyes, scrutinized his diaper, and finally gooed at him as she buttoned him up again. She'd been a mother.

"You changed his diaper?" She didn't look at me.

"Yeah," I said.

"Did it look normal? The feces? No blood in it or anything?"

"No," I said. "Nothing like that."

"Well, good."

I glanced at Paul, who'd found a chair by a window. His chin rested in his hand, and he slumped. He looked bored. But he'd looked bored at his mother's funeral, and just like now, his creased forehead hid thoughts of more exciting places to be, to hide.

"Now it's time for an X Ray." She picked up Harry and glided through a swinging door.

I went over the couch next to Paul's chair. He smiled at me. His teeth were perfect, like dentures, so straight and white. Luckily, his nose was crooked. Otherwise, he would have been too handsome.

"What now?"

"We wait to see if he's broken anything," I said, a little perturbed by the obviousness of the question.

"I know that. He's going to be fine, though."

"Probably." I stared at the swinging door and the little line of light emanating from the room it closed off.

"No. What happens after that?"

"I don't know." But I wanted to take Harry with us. Paul figured as much, I think. He also seemed to think that I wanted to abscond with Harry just as I wanted to steal our more wealthy friends' houses or to never return from our vacation to Costa Rica. He was wrong: Harry and his watery green eyes, expectant and fearful and wanting and hungry and bright like Christmas-trees lights—they'd burrowed into me and become something permanently attached, embedded. And this was not evil symbiosis, like with an insect or a microbe or a drug. It was a bizarrely wonderful exchange, like the song you always whistle when you're happy or when you need to be happy, the place you always imagine when you're tired and you want to go home, the home of your oldest dreams, your first, true home, a place that is home because you are there.

When I woke up, Harry was asleep on my chest, and someone had covered us with a blanket. The light was dimmer; the sun was setting. Across the room, the nurse was writing at her desk, her hands illuminated by a reading lamp, the rest of her darkened by the dusk.

"Your friend's down at the store," she said after I shifted my weight. "The rangers are back."

"Oh, OK."

"Are you, um, together?"

"Yes," I said.

"Kids?"

"No, none. Did you and the doctor?"

"Yes, three. But they're your age now."

"Impossible," I said.

"Ha! Someone raised you right to say something like that."

I chuckled. "No one raised me right. I learned my manners from old movies."

She was quiet for a moment as she twiddled her pen.

"Someone gave you a television," she said.

"That's not much." I was surprised by her defensiveness.

"No, I guess not. Julian and I gave our kids everything. But they don't call me."

I didn't say anything. I don't call my parents. Not more than the obligatory holiday greeting. They only get that for giving me a television.

The nurse walked over to me and opened her arms for Harry. I handed him to her, and I sat up. I looked out the window. I could've sold that sunset to tourists, to the California Visitors Bureau.

I stood, my knees cracking.

"He's a beautiful boy, isn't he?" she said. Harry was awake, and he was playing with the nurse's gray curls.

"His parents were beautiful, too."

"At least they've left this little legacy." She was peering into his eyes.

"It's one way of looking at it," I said. This woman was very strange, I thought. Hard and brittle like old wood. "Can I have him back? I'm going to go find Paul."

She looked at me with a cocked head and a raised eyebrow. It was an odd request, I'll now admit.

"He'll be fine with me. It's getting kind of cold out there."

"Right."

I got my jacket from the Suburban and walked down the lane to the store. The fog was seeping into the town irregularly, thick here, thin there, and the now lowly sunlight was catching the vapor at its edges, lining it with red and yellow. I could barely make out the two police cars parked in front of the store, but their muted lights spun into these fancy weather-beaten houses, bouncing off the pebbles in the road. They were angry fireflies. Then Paul came through the fog, walking toward me and carrying a white paper bag.

"I got you a sandwich and some coffee," he said.

"Thanks," I said. "What did the cops say?"

"They called Jim's parents."

"Oh."

"Let's go over to the rocks." Paul pointed toward the sunset.

We found a wide, flat stone perch and sat with our legs dangling over lapping water and a few bored seagulls. The sky was purple, the sun under water. In another world, this would have been a romantic moment.

"The troopers are flying Jim's dad up here tomorrow morning. After the fog burns off."

"Really." I sipped the coffee. Starbucks. I hate that I loved its taste. "Jesus!"

"We couldn't have taken Harry," Paul said quietly. I could barely hear him over the wind. "We have no right to him."

It would have been pathetic of me to cry. I'm sure I would have been forgiven for my fatigue, emotional and physical. Paul didn't hold my fragility against me; if he had, he never would've moved with me to Seattle. I think he liked feeling protected by my size, my voice, my presence; but he also liked being the stronger one. He liked that he was stronger; I needed him for it. He was right to think that Harry would have fouled it all up, would have left me open to the elements, cold and bloody.

I looked into the southern sky, between the fog bank and the high clouds, and decided, yes, that's where the plane will fly from. It will be a small plane, a four-seater, and the pilot will be irritated by the little, unkempt runway. But he'll land just fine. And then Jim's father will climb down, queasy and terrified, and he will wonder how this happened, how he could let this happen. I wouldn't tell him because he didn't deserve my answer. I'd just let him wonder.

18. My First Story
By Seth Rudetsky

I FEEL LIKE I'd better write this whole thing down and mail it to myself with a beeswax seal so people will know it's true. That's how writers copyrighted (yes, that's the past tense . . . not copywrote) material in the old days. They would write their book or song or whatever on ye olde parchment paper and then mail it to themselves with a beeswax seal. They'd keep the seal intact so the date on the envelope could prove later when they'd written it in case someone down the line claimed they'd come up with the exact same song/book/idea and tried to pull a Vanilla Ice and steal it from them. (Remember? He stole that "Under Pressure" riff and used it in "Ice Ice Baby.")

Wait. I just realized: Mailing this to myself doesn't prove anything about the veracity of what I've written. All it actually proves is that I wrote something on this particular day and that the mail system works. Well, let me just say for the record that this whole story actually happened and it's not like one of my mother's "true" stories. When she tells a story, essentially every element is added for effect and/or conglomerated from other events in her life. She loves telling people about how I started playing piano when I was three (I was five), and how I would sit down and play "Here Comes the Sun" by ear (that was my sister Pam), and then how I'd finish off by running around the living room like a ballet dancer with arms above my head (that was Maggie from *A Chorus Line*).

It all began after my late-night shower.

Actually, it began because Whitney went out of town to that luxury eco-resort in Belize.

OK, let me start from the actual beginning.

I was on the phone with my agent. No, not acting agent. I'm one of the few gay New Yorkers who isn't an actor. My literary agent. I'm a writer. Hmm . . . can you call yourself something if you've never been paid for it? All right, if I have to be literal, I'm a dog walker. I make enough to afford my studio, food, and the occasional 900 number.

Anyway, it was yesterday afternoon and I was talking to Stan on my cell while walking a cocker spaniel mix and a high-strung Jack Russell.

"Jamie, I just got off the phone with Biblio Books," he chewed. He was obviously eating his signature onion bagel with lox *and* lox spread. Why the overkill? Why don't I invent a sandwich sandwich? A turkey sandwich *on* a turkey sandwich. Oh, wait. That actually does exist. It's called a club sandwich. The point is, he had the nerve to chew while I was waiting to hear about the life and death of my book.

He swallowed.

Speed it the fuck up!

"Unfortunately," he said, while half-burping, "they're passing."

"Wait a minute," I said, as I bent down, plastic bag in hand, to scoop up some Jack Russell poop. "Did you say Biblio Books?"

"Yeah. They're a small publishing house in upstate New York."

"I know. But when I first gave you the book fourteen months ago, didn't you say, 'We'll start with the good houses and if worse comes to worst, we'll go to Biblio Books'?"

"Right . . ." He trailed off.

My voice rose. "That means worse *did* come to worst, and it actually got even *worse!*" I threw the poop bag into a garbage can on the corner of 73rd and Broadway.

"Exactly, buddy. Listen, there's really nowhere else to go. People just don't seem to be interested in your one-hundred-year comparative series."

I've been trying to get a book deal for a project in which I do an academic comparison of two different years spaced a century apart. For the first book, the focus is on 1870 versus 1970. I've spent two years researching the differences in dress, politics and food all the way to hairstyles and popular music.

"What about my chapter on laces? Did you send it to them?" I sounded slightly panicked. "My writers in the gay nonfiction collective couldn't believe that shoelaces have varied only two and a half inches over a hundred-year span."

He sighed . . . or yawned . . . or a devastating combination of both. "Yeah, Jamie, they saw it. The consensus is your work is dry. Why don't you lighten it up? You know, in the 1970s section, why don't you try a chapter on *Bewitched?*"

"Sure," I said sarcastically, "I can investigate the mystery of why there were two different Darrens *and* two Mrs. Kravitzes."

"There were?" He sounded thrilled. "That's fascinating. Do it!"

"How is *that* academic?" I sputtered. "I might as well do a treatise on why Alice Ghostley's line readings are identical to Paul Lynde's."

"You should! That's funny!"

I glared at the receiver, wishing it were a videophone. "That's not the kind of writer I am. Would Noam Chomsky write about Uncle Arthur?"

"Noam Chomsky wasn't rejected by ten different publishing houses," he said flatly.

"Eleven," I corrected him.

I always had to be right, even if I was the punch line.

The Jack Russell began barking obsessively at a squirrel scurrying up a tree. "Champ!" I pulled him back. "Stop bothering that rabies spreader!"

"Listen, Jamie," he said tentatively, "maybe we should talk about self-publishing."

"Self-publishing? Doesn't that make you go blind?"

He chuckled. "Again, funny." He perked up. "Hey! What about a chapter on masturbation?"

Before I could respond to his idiocy, I heard the intrusive beep of call-waiting. I removed the phone from my ear and saw the name "Chad" flashing.

Great. My thrice-published/stunning ex-boyfriend whom I've been trying to woo back now for close to ten years. Yes, I said ten years. I'm no quitter. I mean, I've dated other people, but I've always been ready to drop them like a ton of bricks any time Chad would call to get a quick bite or borrow my cell phone because his minutes ran out.

We met in college when I was a sophomore and Chad was a senior. Our first encounter was at a lecture by an angry lesbian PhD candidate whose thesis was *Medea Pro and Con: Feminist Pro(se) or Feminist Con (Artist)?*

Chad went because he was a classics major. I went because I saw him walk by while I was in the mailroom, fell in love, and followed him without locking my mailbox. After a month of flirting, I decided to change my major from undecided to classics, based partly on his urging, and we dated for one delicious year. After pulling an all-nighter to finish a lengthy paper on early Greek drama, I discovered that I enjoyed writing, and I've set my goal on being a published author ever since.

Chad also found out he enjoyed writing and had three books published before he was twenty-five.

I don't really know why we broke up. Well, him saying, "I want to break up" certainly clinched the deal, but I mean he never actually gave me a reason. I haven't really asked, and I've always assumed that he felt his success put him in a different echelon from mine. He'd be more comfortable with someone who could know what it felt like to worry that their *New York Times* book review was 'too good' and might cheapen the book's scholarly appeal. Besides my love of writing, getting my book published could be the entree back into his Crate & Barrel walnut-veneered bed.

I was planning on seeing Chad tonight and thought we'd "celebrate" my book finally being published starting with a friendly hug that would linger too long and end in an awkward yet phenomenally satisfying position.

Bibilo-fucking-Books! How dare they ruin the last shred of my writing career *and* my love life!

I was torn about the call-waiting. I didn't want to tell Chad my latest devastating rejection, yet didn't feel strong enough to pass up a chance to hear his voice.

"Look," I said to Stan, finally deciding. "I've got another call."

"OK, but think about it, Jamie," he said enticingly. "Alice Ghostley . . . Paul Lynde . . . masturbation."

Ow! Three things that should never be heard in the same sentence. I clicked over.

"Hello?" I said quizzically, feigning I didn't have Chad's number preprogrammed into my phone.

"Hey, Jamie. It's Chad. Are we still on for tonight?" he asked.

Ugh! I *hate* when people make plans and then ask if they're still on. I'm not talking about vague plans like "Let's go out next weekend" and then a check-in phone on Friday to confirm. I'm talking about definite plans with time and locations set and then the passive/aggressive "Are we still on?" right before places. Why *wouldn't* we be on? ? ? ? The actual making of the plans was the confirmation!

"We're totally on! I'm psyched!" I certainly didn't want to show Chad how annoyed I was. I decided I can hate the sin and desperately want to have sex with the sinner.

"Excellent. I have the new scholar-approved Ancient Greek dictionary." Chad and I had made plans to listen to Homer's *Iliad* read by Chad's PhD adviser. It was a limited release on the "Books on Tape" subsidiary, "Tomes on Tape." The series is actually *more* boring than it sounds. Last year Chad lent me the tapes of *The Odyssey* and I was asleep before Homer's first ten miles were logged.

"I had all eight audio tapes FedExed to me overnight," he said. "Why don't we just split it?"

That was my karma for manipulating the situation. Yesterday, when he mentioned he was interested in the tapes, I essentially started panting like a dog, implying how eager I was to listen to them, too. Of course, I was eager only for the alone time it would grant us and the panting was from imagining the athletic sex we'd engage in between tapes five and six. I had assumed Chad would pay for mailing. I was on a dog-walker's salary and Chad was still reaping profits from his first three books. Recently, he'd been "forced" by his accountant to buy a country house to lower his taxable income. But I respected Chad's refusal to view me as a poor relation. He was obviously trying to treat me as an equal.

"Cash or check?" I asked.

"How about a check made out to 'Cash?'"

I was now walking through Riverside Park with the dogs. I bent down for a drink from the water fountain near the boat basin, but reconsidered when I thought about the many times the local color must have used it as a bidet.

"Oh, no!" Chad said suddenly. "I have to meet my publisher for dinner at Le Cirque. I totally forgot."

Wah! I really needed something to look forward to since my latest rejection. And I refused to think I strapped on those ankle weights to do fifty extra walking squats at the gym that morning for nothing.

"Why don't I come over after?" I asked, forcing my desperation down.

"I won't be home till eleven . . . Le Cirque is all the way on the East Side."

"Perfect! It will be more historically accurate." I started babbling. "I read on Odyssey.com that Homer did most of his writing well into the early hours of the morning. We'll be hearing it as he first heard it in his head!" As far as I knew, there is no Odyssey.com but I spoke of it with assurance and fervor. Employing the Nazi Big Lie technique was my only hope.

"But don't you have to take care of Whitney's dog out in Brooklyn?"

Shit! I forgot about that. Whitney was going out of town and had hired me to walk her dog. Her place was so far into Brooklyn, she said I could just stay over at her loft rather than travel back and forth. I hired someone to walk my regular dogs since Whitney said she'd pay me what I was losing.

"Yes, I am at Whitney's," I said slowly, thinking it through, "but I can give Madison his night walk around 10:00 and make it to your place by midnight. He doesn't have to be walked again till the next morning, so . . ." I trailed off, not daring to hope.

"Great! So you might as well sleep over," he said.

EXCELLENT!

"I got a new pull-out sofa at Macy's," he continued.

SHIT!

"You're gonna love it," he bragged. "It has a mattress that actually molds to the curvature of your spine."

Does it mold to the curvature of my middle finger?

I was in a rage at the universe. Can't anything go right?

I decided it could if I changed tactics. Maybe my stealthy way of trying to win him back had been too subtle.

"Chad, when I see you tonight," I said seriously, "I think we should have a talk." I lowered my voice an octave. "About personal stuff."

Did I go too far?

"OK, baby, I'll see you tonight," he said and hung up.

He called me "baby"! I knew there was hope! I looked out over the river and saw the skyline of New Jersey. It sounds tacky, but it's actually beautiful. It inspired me.

"Enough!" I thought, clearing my mind of those two words that, when said separately, are benign, but when linked are evil: Biblio and Books. My writing career may be going down the toilet, I decided, but I'm kick-starting the romance part. No matter what, sex with someone I've been in love with ten years is happening tonight!

Unfortunately, I not only thought that last sentence but also spoke it aloud as evidenced by the glare I got from an old lady and her nurse.

I arrived at my friend Whitney's place in Brooklyn at 9:00 P.M. Whitney was a trust-fund bisexual I'd met at the Gay Community Center's Writing Workshop. She was independently wealthy, so she was able to dabble in artistic things until she got bored and then she'd jet off to some crazy five-star resort in a country I never heard of.

Her biggest artistic talent was buying real estate in bizarre areas right before they became cool, renovating everything, and selling the property at a huge profit. Her latest "find" was a two-floor ware-house in an area that was surrounded by deserted warehouses. After a grueling thirty-minute walk from the subway, during which I noticed two ominous gangs of youths, I thought Ms. Goldfinger had finally made a bad choice. I was a little creeped out standing in front of her building because I noticed all the lights were out upstairs and I felt very alone. There were two entrances whose doors hadn't been replaced yet and were covered in graffiti informing me repeatedly that Mario indeed loved Suzi. One of the doors led to the upstairs space, and Whitney warned me that my key wouldn't work in it. Of course, I tried it just to be contrary, but she was right. I let myself into the downstairs space and immediately saw why she bought it.

The place was essentially a vast space she'd broken up into several smaller spaces with partial walls so everything seemed open and airy. I recognized the style of furniture from those trendy design stores in Soho where the only things not minimalistic were the prices. There were windows everywhere and I thought the space upstairs was probably even more stunning because you'd get a better view of the river from it. Whitney had told me she'd recently rented it out and was about to vacate the downstairs so the upstairs guy could buy the whole thing. Even though the neighborhood was deserted, I was sure it would soon be thriving because all the other warehouses held the same possibilities.

I turned on the enormous overhead light and really got the scope of the place. I put my coat on the low-backed soft leather couch and immediately picked up Madison's favorite ball. The length of the room was perfect for playing fetch, and after a half hour Madison was tired out. I was looking forward to a long bath to wash the rejection grime off my body so I'd feel refreshed for my night of winning Chad back. But first, I had business to do. I went to get Whitney's mail from the makeshift mailbox outside the entrance and noticed there was another box next to hers. I looked at the name. . . . A. M. Shomwitts.

I freaked out! My best friend/massive crush during freshman year in college was named Aidan Shomwitts! The M was his creation. He was so annoyed at his Jewish parents for naming him Waspy Aidan *and* changing their last name, Shlomowitz, to Shomwitts, that he legally added Moishe as his middle name on the day he turned eighteen. We met in French class and became inseparable after he saw my hidden checklist of how many times I could

make the teacher say "poussez" (poo-say) per class. I know it's immature but I felt such pleasure in setting up a sixty-year-old woman to
say what sounded like a highfalutin way of saying "pussy." I'd purposely get it wrong when called on.

"Madame Derringer, I'm confused about conjugating 'pousser,'"
I'd confess, feigning unsureness. "Let me quickly try it. Nous pous-
sons, vous poussoir . . ."

"Non!" she'd yell. "We went over zis yesterday! Poussez!
Poussez!"

"Pousah?" I'd say feebly.

"POU-SSEZ!"

Hilarious!

Aidan told me the middle-name story the night before summer
break as we drank beer after beer in his room. We had been having
almost every meal together since the middle of first semester, and by
February we were usually ending the night by chatting in each other's
dorm room. His roommate's high-school sweetheart lived in the same
dorm, so lots of times I wound up sleeping in the empty bed in
Aidan's room. Once, when his roommate came back in the middle of
the night, I didn't feel like walking back to my dorm, so I got into
Aidan's bed. When I woke up, his arm was around me. I didn't know
if it was on purpose or sleep-induced, but *I loved it!*

Essentially, we had one of those "we're both gay and we know it,
but we're too afraid to mention it" relationships you have when
you're young. Or at least that's what I thought that night before
break. I knew I'd be sleeping over because his roommate wanted
"one last uninterrupted bang" with his girlfriend before the summer,
and I thought Aidan and I would finally confess our mutual attraction/
gayness while we drunkenly got ready for bed and be all over each
other in seconds. Well, the only part of my fantasy that was accurate
was drunkenly getting ready for bed. The rest consisted of me
passing out on the floor and Aidan throwing up in the bathroom.

Apparently, he didn't have the energy to walk back to his room because, the next morning, as I staggered out of his room to go pee, I noticed him curled up in the hallway, using his shirt for a pillow. I was horrified at how degenerate he looked, yet impressed by his flat stomach and hairy chest.

We rushed off to catch our respective flights home and later sent each other a few random postcards when we had time. I didn't mind being separated from him all summer because I was convinced we'd finally consummate our relationship in September.

Well, we hardly saw each other the first week we were back at school. Our respective dorms were too far away from each other, and my phone hadn't been set up yet. By week two, I saw him in the dining hall, where he introduced me to his new girlfriend.

I couldn't believe I had misread all the signs. Devastated, I immediately got involved with a TA who always had a crush on me. We lasted until I met Chad.

As for Aidan, he wound up transferring at the end of sophomore year and we lost touch completely. It was only recently that I'd heard he'd become a successful environmental lawyer living in New York.

I thought of how bizarre it would be if I saw him again. I didn't think I'd feel any attraction for him because I was never into chasing straight guys. I figure that there are enough gay guys who'll reject me, I don't need to add to the till. I wondered whether we could resume our friendship if the sexual tension weren't there on my part. I decided we could because we always made each other laugh and I remember how much I loved when we'd talk liberal politics or the ol' "Do you think there is life in outer space?" and "What if we were born fifty years earlier?" conversations. I assumed he was probably married, which made me sad. Of course, *he* could sustain a relationship; meanwhile I was still chasing after the guy who broke up with me ten years ago.

I took Whitney's mail into the loft and saw Madison comfortably curled up on the enormous couch. He looked so cute, I lay down next to him and he stretched out to better accommodate getting a full body petting. I've read that petting a dog can lower one's blood pressure, and I totally believe it. Sometimes a quick cuddle with one of the dogs I walk puts me in a great mood for hours.

My cell phone rang.

"Hello?"

"Jamie? It's Chad."

I felt groggy, but annoyed.

"Yes, Chad, we're 'still on' for tonight," I said, referencing his penchant for confirming what need not be confirmed.

"Are you nearby?" he asked.

"No . . . why?"

"It's after 11:30." He was clearly annoyed,

Shit! The damn dog lowered my blood pressure till I fell asleep. Damn his snuggliness!

"Don't worry, Chad, I'm almost there," I said, completely contradicting myself. I was terrified he would decide it's too late and cancel.

"OK, pick up some ice cream before you get here. I skipped dessert at Le Cirque."

"No prob. See you in a snap."

I put my coat on, grabbed my bag, and was out the door when I remembered Madison. Shit! I had to walk him before I left. I leashed him and once outside, the only light was from the moon. Creepy. It was a warm night and, like an idiot, I had on my heavy coat, a remnant from my childhood when, no matter how far into the 90s the temperature went, my mother would force me to wear a coat because "the nights always get chilly."

By the time I got back to the warehouse, I was sweating like a pig. I checked my watch. 12:10. I couldn't go over there smelling up a storm, so I stripped quickly and jumped in the shower. I left the living room a mess with my sweaty clothes all over the floor and my suitcase spilled out from searching for another outfit.

I washed, shampooed, conditioned, deep-conditioned (because it was there), and got out of the shower. I put on a cute pair of 2(X)ist underwear and immediately realized from my difficulty breathing that they must have shrunk up a storm in the wash. I hoped that the other pair in my overnight case wouldn't cause so much major stomach overhang.

Then I heard it. Clack clack clack . . . What the hell was that? A mini tap dancer?

Holy shit! It was a remnant from the days when the warehouse was deserted. A *huge* waterbug (like a cockroach, but thirty times the size) clacking quickly along the bathroom tile. I screamed (yes, like a girl) and it suddenly made a beeline to the living area *and* all my strewn-about clothes, which were ripe for burrowing in. I picked up my sneaker that was lying in the doorway and gave chase. As the waterbug neared my suitcase, I made a swipe at it and it ran under the front door. I know you think I should have been glad it was finally outside, but I've lived in New York for a long time and knew that as easily as it crawled out under the door, it could just as easily crawl back in. *And* with me gone for the night, it would be able to make itself a delicious bed in my suitcase and finally give birth to the thousands of water-bug eggs it had been carrying. I had no idea whether it was a female, or if water bugs actually give birth, but I didn't feel like Googling it. I just wanted to smash it with my sneaker and get the hell over to Chad's.

I ran right out the door after the water bug not caring that I was wearing just my way-too-tighty whities because nobody was around and it was so warm out. I chased him for around thirty feet 'til I saw him scurry into a bug's best friend, an abandoned drainpipe that was lying in the street. Motherfucker! I put the sneaker on I had been brandishing just to kick the pipe in anger. No response. It refused to acknowledge me. The wearing of one sneaker and one bare foot gave me a slight limp and I loped back to the warehouse hoping the waterbug would forget where he began the evening.

I had an awful feeling as I approached the door, and turning the doorknob confirmed it. I was locked out. Locked out of a warehouse/apartment in a deserted neighborhood wearing underwear two sizes too small and one sneaker. What the fuck was I going to do? My keys were inside the apartment with my clothes, my wallet, and my cell phone. It wasn't as if this freaky part of town had any pay phones on the street so I could call a car service. I thought about somehow getting to the subway, but even if I could make it past the roaming gangs unscathed, how would I get on the subway? I had no money. I guess I could jump a turnstile, but then how could I take a whole subway trip to Manhattan in this getup? I'd be booted off the train for indecent and unattractive exposure.

Gangs, abandoned warehouses, jumping turnstiles, . . . When did my life become a real-life version of *Grand Theft Auto?* I figured my best bet was to run fast enough to the subway so a gang couldn't catch me, hail a cab, take it to Chad's, and ask him to spot me the money.

Right at that moment, I saw headlights in the distance. Do gangs drive cars? It got closer. A cab! How lucky was I? But the light on top indicated someone was in it. Who the hell lived over here, anyway? It stopped right in front of me and out stepped a man holding an overnight bag.

Aidan!

He looked the same as I remembered but cuter. Stocky, tousled black hair, jeans with a button-down Banana Republic linen shirt, untied tie, and sparkling blue eyes, widened to imply horrified-ness.

The cab drove off.

We stared at each other.

"Jamie?" he asked warily, not believing what he saw.

I nodded.

He started laughing hysterically.

What was I gonna do? I started laughing hysterically along with him, trying to keep my stomach from shaking too much.

"You look crazy!" He was still laughing.

"At least I'm not passed out in the hall, using my Human League shirt as a pillow."

"Oh my God! How dare you!" He gave me a scout's honor. "That was the only time I've ever gotten that drunk."

"Drunk is right, Motherfucker. I had to *poussez* you down that hallway to your room so you could get dressed to catch your flight home."

He pointed and said, "You have no right to bust me for anything wearing that old whore outfit." I laughed, admitting defeat.

I explained the whole dumb story to him while he led me upstairs to his place. He flipped on the lights and I looked around. I was right. It was even more beautiful than downstairs.

He told me to go to his bedroom and look for some clothes. I threw on some comfortable sweatpants and a Brown University T-shirt. I looked at the night table full of photos. Tons of rain forest shots but where were the pictures of his wife? Hmm . . . maybe he traveled too much to have time to get married. I was just glad he hadn't married that girl from college. She was a French major and thought it was hilarious to thank people by saying "Mercy buckets."

Aidan and I sat on his vegan imitation leather couch. He said had just gotten back from a trip to the Amazon. Where was I headed, he asked. Pathetically, I told him all about the Chad saga, realizing halfway through that I had outed myself in the process. I thought he'd be taken aback but realized that he probably remembered the 10x20 poster I had of Xanadu in my dorm room next to my unicorn jumping through a rainbow painting. No doubt he realized 2+2=gay many years ago.

"Isn't ten years a long time to hold out?" he asked. "Wouldn't you be happier moving on?"

My friends have been asking me that question for so long, it's lost its meaning. My answer usually is, I've seen all that's out there, and, even though he has faults, Chad is the best of the bunch. Actually, the more I thought about it, it seemed like the pursuit of him had become my favorite hobby. I could always keep my mind occupied cooking up schemes to see how I could snag him.

Aidan must have sensed my discomfort because he changed the subject. "Tell me about your book." He repositioned himself to sit cross-legged.

I described it and as I did I couldn't quite muster the enthusiasm I usually have.

"A scholarly book?" He looked miffed. "You've always been so funny . . ." he trailed off.

"Yeah, but Chad says humor is an excuse for someone stupid to sound smart."

He looked annoyed. "It sounds like *that's* an excuse for someone unfunny to sound like a dick."

Aidan grimaced. "What is that smell?" He sniffed the front of his shirt.

He got up from the couch. "Do you mind if I take a shower?"

I was so hoping to hear a "care to join me?" yet embarrassed that I'd entertain such thoughts about a straight man mixed with feeling guilty about Chad that I quickly said, "I just took a bath, so . . ." Uh-oh! What was I saying?

Aidan cocked his head. "So . . . what?" he asked, confused.

I was mortified. "So . . . I'm obviously procleanliness," I chirped. He was silent.

I changed the subject. "Can I use your laptop?" I asked, as I briskly walked over to his Pottery Barn computer table, not making eye contact.

"No prob," he said, obviously relieved. He showed me how to log on and ducked into his bedroom.

I realized my laptop question wasn't just a diversionary tactic. I needed to tell Whitney what had happened. She was a night owl, and I knew she'd freak out if she tried to call the apartment and/or my cell phone and got no answer till tomorrow. I was glad Aidan was taking one of his signature lengthy showers because Whitney is the type of person who needs all details spelled out in a story or else she'll obsess. I knew I had to write out everything starting from the phone call with my agent. I actually was looking forward to it. Even though writing to Whitney took hours out of my week, I always enjoyed it. It was certainly more fun than my chapter on shoelaces.

When I was around three-quarters of the way through, I realized that Aidan was reading over my shoulder. He smelled like he did in college. I could never forget that delicious Body Shop shampoo he always used. I resisted the urge to turn around and take a thirty-second inhalation and said, "I'm sorry this is taking so long." I went to sign off.

"No, keep typing. I'm enjoying it!"

He really did seem excited to keep reading, so I started up again. Every once in a while, Aidan would laugh. I loved it, even though it was so quiet in the apartment that his outbursts scared me every time. I got to the part about him letting me into his apartment and wrapped it up. As soon as I pressed *send,* Aidan swiveled my chair around so I could face him.

He was beaming.

"Jamie, that e-mail was hilarious."

"Thanks." I said, flattered that he stood there reading for so long.

He grabbed both of my hands. "Why don't you actually write stuff like that?"

I was confused. "I *do* write stuff like that. You just read it."

"Duh! I know." He pointed to the screen. "I loved it. I would buy it!"

Did he mean on eBay? "Aidan, I don't think people buy and sell old e-mails."

He spoke slowly. "Right. But what about funny stories?" He looked at me expectantly. Did he mean I could make money at this? I always thought work was supposed to feel like work. You know, awful and tedious. I never thought I could enjoy something *and* have it be profitable. Chad said that the only way he knew that a chapter was good was if he hated writing it. Only then was he sure that he had pushed himself to the extreme.

Come to think of it, how does a scholar "push himself"? By thinking extra-hard? What kind of sweat do you break? A brain sweat?

Oh, no! Chad! I hadn't called him since I said I was "almost there." "Can I use your phone?" I asked, getting up from the couch.

He pointed toward the bedroom. I dialed Chad's number.

"Jamie!" He sounded relieved. "I've been so worried. I've called your cell a hundred times!"

I told him the whole story, omitting the stomach-hanging-over-the-underwear description.

"Oh, thank God you're all right. Look, it's 2:00 A.M. but we can still be hearing the tapes when the sun comes up. What time do you think you can get here?"

I thought about all the times I'd dropped everything to run to him. All those tricks I've used to try to win him back, always adding up to nothing.

Finally I spoke. "Chad, I don't think I can come over tonight."

"You . . . you can't?" He sounded shocked.

"I, uh, don't really like sofa beds," I said feebly.

"Well," he said, with a hint of sexuality, "if the sofa bed's uncomfortable, maybe you can sleep in my bed."

I didn't say anything. This is what I had been waiting for all these years. . . .

Suddenly I thought, what if my e-mail got lost in cyberspace? I wanted to make sure I had a hard copy so I could show it to my agent.

"Chad, I'll call you tomorrow!" I said quickly, as I hung up.

I ran out of the bedroom, logged on, and printed out the whole letter. I breathed a big, relieved sigh, walked over to the couch, and flopped down next to Aidan.

"Do you have to go?" Aidan asked.

"No . . ." I said, thinking through what had just happened. "Actually, I just told Chad I'm not coming over," I said proudly.

Aidan beamed. "Good for you!"

Suddenly I realized how me-centric the last few hours had been. "Aidan, I'm sorry we've spent the whole night with you Dr. Phil-ing me. Tell me everything."

Aidan told me about his job and all the traveling he did for it. At least, I think he did. I couldn't really concentrate because when I had first sat down on the couch, my leg touched his and I spent the whole time he was talking obsessing on the fact that he *didn't move his leg.*

I came out of my fog and told myself to numb my body and to concentrate on what he was saying and then, when ten minutes had passed, I would be allowed to return feeling to my lower extremities and see if his leg moved.

He told me about Kenya, Chile, disenfranchised people.

Ten minutes passed.

I allowed feeling to enter my quad/hamstring area.

His leg hadn't moved!

I couldn't take it anymore.

"So" I adopted a breezy tone infused with incredible tension—"are you involved?"

"No." He shook his head. "My partner and I broke up a year ago."

I froze. He looked away.

I dared to ask. "Partner, like in 'we weren't married, but were going to start making plans as soon as her career was set,' or partner, like in we used to say 'lover' in the 70s, then 'longtime companion' but the only moniker he accepted was 'partner'?"

Aidan spoke. "Jamie, I'm gay."

Aha! Vindication! I hadn't read those signals wrong during freshman year!

He shook his head regretfully. "I had this big crush on you the whole time we were friends, but I was too young to know what to do." He looked somewhere into the distance. "That whole night before summer break I was hoping we'd do something, but I freaked out and kept drinking to loosen myself up and . . . you saw the result of that."

"What about the next semester?"

"I spent that whole summer trying to talk myself out of being gay, and I thought a girlfriend would end those feelings. She didn't. Then I thought it was just you. So I transferred schools to get away, but the feelings came with me."

I tsk-tsked. "Wherever you go, there you are," I added solemnly.

He looked stricken. "Please don't tell me you've ever said that cliché before."

"Of course not!" I said, insulted. "I just wanted to see how it felt. There was such a Lifetime Channel movie quality to this conversation that I thought it was the perfect line to say before the commercial break."

We both laughed.

"Actually"—he moved closer—"there's something more perfect that should happen before the commercial."

He leaned in and we kissed. I mean, *really* kissed. We'd been storing up these feelings since freshman year.

It's around 5:00 A.M. and I'm lying in bed with Aidan, adding the recent developments to the e-mail hard copy. I just got to the big kiss, put down my pencil, and smiled. I realized that if I didn't get this story published, maybe I could get work as a psychic. After all, I predicted I would have sex tonight with someone I've been in love with for ten years.

Hmm . . . I should tell that old lady and her nurse in the park that my prediction has come true.

Twice so far, and the night isn't over

19. A Bright, Shining Place
By James Grissom

I SHOULD BE happy to be here, Jess told himself, as the priest held a large silver chalice above his head and recited Scripture. I must be happy, he reminded himself, yes, happy, and proud, standing here with his black lover, Wayne, and his six-year-old son Bobby, who is celebrating his First Communion.

Jess was ashamed that at several points in the service Wayne had had to lean over and ask if he was alright. Each time Jess had replied that he was fine, but he was not. The church was small and hot, and his arms were sticking to the pew railings and the arms of the sweet-smelling woman sitting next to him. He could tell that she did not approve of the fact that two men, obviously lovers, were presenting a young boy into the Church, and occasionally she would make a clucking sound that enraged Jess. What with the heat and his general discomfort and anger, he was sighing often, and Wayne kept squeezing his arm, offering support and the unspoken thought, This will be over soon.

Jess hated that he could not enjoy this moment. He and Bobby had been preparing for this day for months now, memorizing Scripture, searching fabric shops for the perfect material for his robe. "It must be resplendently white," the boy had said, and Jess and Wayne had laughed: Where had he heard that word? Throughout the shops of the city, he repeated the demand, and the clerks laughed and pulled out madras, cotton, silk, polyester blends, acetates, all in the hopes that the boy would be pleased. Eventually, he found the proper fabric, and he watched every moment as Jess sewed, creating the garment. Bobby's vision of the robe was so exact and demanding that he often cried out at Jess as he cut and pinned; and at times Jess lost his patience, but he held his tongue. Instead, he took his anger out on Wayne, who would come home from work and listen to Bobby's excited progress reports on his studies, then have dinner with Jess, who fumed and scowled.

"What's wrong now?" Wayne would always ask, and Jess would admit that he was lucky to have such an understanding lover.

"I hate my life," Jess had replied once, which he knew was a cruel rejoinder. Wayne and Bobby *were* his life, and Jess hated the impact of his statement the moment he made it. Wayne had cleared the dishes from the table, then gone into his room, and closed the door.

And yet Jess did hate his life, and love it, too. In conversations with his parents, he often spoke of the happy days, those delirious times when he felt as if on some new, exotic drug, his heart racing with joy as shopped for groceries with Bobby, or cleaned the house, or made a dinner he knew Wayne would especially enjoy. He had days when he was proud of himself for choosing a black lover, proof that he had overcome any of his inbred Southern bigotry; then others when he asked himself why he had purposely placed himself in an untenable situation, loving a man with a young son and the memory of a wife who was killed in an automobile accident, but who had known she would never be the object of her husband's desires.

"When Clarice died," Wayne had told Jess once, "I went looking for what had been missing and I found you, and I know she would approve."

Jess nodded at the statement, and his eyes clouded at the many mentions of her name and during the visits with Clarice's parents, two rock-solid, taciturn people who simply had no idea people like Jess existed, and therefore had nothing to say. Wayne wanted Bobby to grow up with a sense of family, but Jess could barely tolerate the family reunions, dinners, and impromptu visits that came with being in this household. Phone calls or announcements were unheard of, and Jess dreaded the sound of wheels on the gravel driveway, which meant he had to throw on clothes, act friendly, pray that he had gotten groceries that would somehow satisfy the palates of these people.

They often arrived in packs of ten or twelve, all jovial and happy to see Bobby. They brought gifts, and the women tried to talk to Jess about "wifely" things: good cuts of meat, television programs, the exhausting regimen of keeping a house with men in it. The men avoided Jess completely; they were polite, but they couldn't make eye contact. Among themselves, they agreed he was good to Wayne and Bobby, but he might as well have been from Mars. A white man, twenty-nine, wants to be a writer, takes up with a black man in Louisiana, breaks with his family, active in the church, but clearly queer. It didn't compute, and on those long visits, everyone crowded in the hot, small living room, Jess also realized it didn't compute, and he took to asking himself why he was there.

Lately, he had spent the length of the visits in the kitchen making pots of coffee, putting out plates of fudge, pound cakes, fruit. The bills at the grocery store had piled up, but Wayne never complained, and Jess had told him if all else failed, he would put his disability checks entirely toward food. Wayne had refused, reminding Jess that he took care of his own household. The relatives loved the new bounty that awaited them, and Bobby welcomed the opportunity to eat the sugary foods that were normally off-limits.

"Tell me," Anna, one of the more severe aunts, had said at the last visit, "will you be standing up with Bobby and Wayne at the church on Sunday?"

"I assumed as much," Jess had replied, realizing he sounded arch, and fully aware that everyone knew he had been planning his portion of the ceremony for weeks.

"Have you spoken to Father Mervin about this?" she continued, and suddenly Jess hated her. She was Clarice's oldest sister, and although Clarice was certifiably dead, she viewed this white man as the interloper, the man who stole her brother-in-law and nephew, and she didn't approve of this relationship being recognized in a church.

"Father Mervin has met with us several times," Wayne said in that deep voice he adopted when he wanted any nonsense to come to a conclusion. "All is settled for communion." Then Bobby, who recognized a tense situation (and he had many opportunities to witness them) stood and began the recitation of Scripture and a description of the resplendently white robe Jess was making for him. Jess took the opportunity to sneak into the kitchen, where he made another pot of coffee and slowly, methodically, ate an entire pecan ring, licking his fingers of caramel and syrup and pecan shavings.

Father Mervin was a verbose priest, and Jess was growing hotter and more anxious as the ceremony crawled on. The piece of paper in his hand was growing wet and rumpled, and he feared he would be unable to read from it, and he could not remember, despite the many rehearsals, what was written on it. He wished now that he had allowed his parents to attend the ceremony. Wayne had been all for it, and Bobby wanted to see them again, but Jess had ultimately said no. Now the lone white face in this church, he longed for another white face to gaze upon, even if one of them would be the painted one that belonged to his mother, who simply didn't understand this latest turn of events, but who would support them if they meant happiness for her son. Jess felt so much enmity in the church that he felt his head was actually expanding from the evil thought being transmitted toward him. Earlier in his life he had studied Christian Science, and he tried now to recall the prayers to ward off malicious animal magnetism, but they failed to come forward.

Although he hated people who did such things, Jess turned around in the pew and searched the rest of the church for Bobby. Bobby loved him, he reasoned, and if he saw his face, he might relax. But Bobby was far into the foyer of the church, and out of sight. Instead of Bobby's trusting face, Jess was met with hundreds of glaring black eyes, people who didn't hate him so much as see him as something inappropriate, the advent of the unwelcome. Father Mervin had called a special meeting of the church members to discuss the admission of Jess into the church, and the comments had been harsh and swift. Most of the parishioners were against it, seeing homosexuality as a sin punishable by death, while admitting that Jess was a nice man who was good to Bobby and a solid volunteer around the church. Finally, Father Mervin had overruled his flock and decided to welcome Jess into the church. Only Wayne, Bobby, and Jess's mother had attended the baptism and confirmation, and even that small sanctuary had seemed immense, all those empty, shiny pews stretching out into a judgment. As Jess had sat in the front pew, fully confirmed, St. Francis de Sales his patron, and Wayne pumping his hand for support, he had fought back a laugh when Father Mervin reminded the small audience of the obligation to God and the Church. "Remember," his voice thundered, "by your fruits you shall be known."

At that moment, Jess had learned that blacks could blush.

Although Catholic in name, St. Peter's Church was not austere in the usual sense. Situated in Brusly, a small town across the Mississippi River from Baton Rouge, it had all the trappings of a Catholic church—altar, statues, fillips of design—but the spirit of a gospel Baptist congregation. When Mary Bernard got up to sing a solo, meant to welcome the new members of Heaven, Jess knew he would begin feeling better. Mary, a large, happy-faced singer with a voice that could raise the dead, tore into "Softly and Tenderly, Jesus Is Calling," and Jess felt his blood pressure plummet, the sweat cease to pump out of his body. The entire congregation relaxed, and Jess suddenly remembered why he was here. His many journeys within churches had led him here, full of the Spirit and leading another to Heaven. Something to that effect was written on the piece of paper in his hands, but he didn't want to stop and reread it; he wanted to close his eyes and listen to Mary Bernard tear that hymn apart. Listening to her sing made his heart hurt, and he wished one day to be able to evoke that feeling through his writing, but so far his works consisted of aborted paragraphs, sentences parsed to perfection but never leading to a second, good intentions leading to bad short stories. All of his promise seemed years away—the scholarships, the encouraging words of teachers, even his youth. Can you be a wunderkind as you approach thirty?

He had always known that whatever good had happened to him had been in a church. His parents had taken him to church twice a week all his life, and those early years were structured around those activities. He had been a good boy if he had remembered the Beatitudes, a perfect boy when he recited the Ten Commandments and the Sermon on the Mount before the congregation, receiving from Cleta Sue Cunningham a large, anemic sugar cookie for his efforts. "You are full of the Spirit," Cleta had told him the day before he was baptized, dressed in white, about to enter a room seven feet deep and full of water, to be fully immersed, coming up a clean person, reformed, ready for Heaven. He had felt the redemption then, but over the years he felt it had worn off, like a cheap paint job, and so he had asked Father Mervin to rebaptize him, to hose him down, so to speak, make him clean and new again.

"Are you sure?" Father Mervin had asked. "You know, we accept the Baptist version, too? It's acceptable."

"Not to me, not to God," Jess had answered, and so Father Mervin had arranged for a new life to begin.

How many churches had he sat in before he met Wayne? How many bars had he sat in before he realized that nothing would happen for him? First he had toyed with Christian Science because it seemed the farthest in doctrine from his Baptist upbringing; it didn't escape his notice that it would enrage his mother, who was a nurse. And so, for two years, he denied the material aspects of humanity, denying sin, disease, and death, fervently reciting passages from the works of Mary Baker Eddy and remaining terrified that his spiritual weakness would result in a tumor or instant death. He had somehow rationalized sleeping with men while going to the church, and even after he was admitted to the congregation, he went to the bars where he had once seen a fellow member, who grew bright red and ran away. Human contact, he told himself, and anyone who would listen, was a human need, and nowhere in Mrs. Eddy's writings did he find a condemnation of homosexuality. "My feelings for men are pure," he told friends.

Once one of them asked, "Pure? With two a night?"

Well, Jess had rationalized, even Mrs. Eddy was against numbering the people. Quality versus quantity.

Only when the purity of the Mind of God had failed to heal him of a social disease did Jess break his vow with the church and seek medical attention. Which led him to Lutheranism, Presbyterianism, Unitarianism, Religious Science, and the myriad nondenominational churches that sprout up everywhere. He loved the affection and attention that came in those first days in a church. Everyone reaching out to the fallen one searching for salvation, hungry for answers. Free Bibles, dinner invitations, conferences in offices smelling of Murphy's Oil and verbena, long, silent prayers. And then admission, and then that slow dissatisfaction that always set in. He would stand in the church and announce that he would be moving soon, but thank everyone wholeheartedly for their concern, their understanding, their setting him on the right track. And then there would be the farewell parties, the good-bye gifts, the promises that he would write, the gardenia-scented notes stuffed in his hands bearing cash and the addresses of well-wishers. He always cried and slept for two days after he absconded from the churches. Then he knew he would have to avoid that part of town or that particular city, for now he was in Boston or Hartford or Bennington or New York or Madison. He wondered if they ever saw him as he drove through the city, if they ever wondered why he never wrote. He wondered if they knew that had moved to a small house in Brusly across the river and took to visiting a black Catholic church during its off-hours so he could pray alone.

It was on one of those days, a mild February day, that he walked through St. Peter's, making the Stations of the Cross, when he met Wayne, who later told him he had come into the church at his wit's end, depressed, miserable. They had stared at each other for a full minute, neither knowing what to do, but Jess had remembered that the glances had been gay-bar glances, sizings up, and he was attracted to the roughly attractive man. Wayne had never seen someone so white, and so seemingly pure, making the stations in the middle of the day with no witnesses. Wayne had invited him for coffee, but instead they had walked on the levee, watching the boats move down the muddy Mississippi, and people throwing sticks into the rapidly moving water. They had walked for nearly two miles, all the while talking about what religion meant to them, when Jess asked Wayne if he would kiss him. It was a passionate, desperate kiss; lonely, fearful, a kiss that wouldn't end. Wayne was crying when he pulled away, but before Jess could ask what was wrong, Wayne began tearing off his clothes and Jess did the same. With no protection, no foreplay, and no words, they had sex on the levee, unaware and unconcerned that they might have been seen. No one had ever made love to Jess so fully, as if it were the last great fuck of the world. When it was over, they dressed quietly, and Jess invited Wayne over to his house for dinner.

"Can I bring my son?" Wayne had asked.

"Oh, shit!" Jess had muttered. "Why not?"

A son? Jess laughed out loud, and the laugh rang out like a car backfiring. Wayne looked over at him with concern and not a little warning. Father Mervin looked his way, a look on his face that seemed to display his fear that he and Wayne would some somehow provoke a scene during these ceremonies.

He remembered the day that he took Wayne back to his house after they had made love. First they had walked back to the church, for their cars. The talk had been clumsy. What do you say after such an outburst of passion? After such a raw fucking on a grass levee, with boats passing by? Jess had driven him to his house, a small two-room frame house that the previous owners had painted a bright turquoise, and which Jess had highlighted by placing pink flamingos in the yard, along a birdbath, a Blessed Mother painted fuchsia, and an enormous swing with a canopy that would have looked at home at Tara. Wayne missed the facetiousness of the design and instead focused on the statue of Mary. "You *are* religious," he had said, and his observation was not changed when he saw the groaning bookcases in Jess's house, which housed mostly religious titles.

"Did you ever study? Religion, I mean?" Wayne had inquired.

"I studied, but I never intended to be a priest or preacher, no."

"Why not?"

"Do you think that was the first time I ever fucked a man I'd just met?"

The reply came with such fury that Jess was sure that Wayne would leave. Instead, he laughed and agreed to stay for coffee.

"It's not the first time I ever fucked a man, either," Wayne admitted.

"So where did the son come from? Don't tell me a man, or we'll have a true miracle on our hands."

"No," Wayne said, with gravity and slowness. "My son came from a woman. Lovely woman. Her name was Clarice. She was killed three years ago. Car accident. She died instantly."

"I'm sorry."

"I am, too," Wayne said quickly, rubbing his hands on his pants, as if wiping away the memory of that moment. "But it was unraveling. I mean, I'm gay, she knew it, and the marriage was ending, and we had a three-year-old son. It wasn't good."

"How did she know?"

"Oh, I told her. I told her not long after we were married. I said, 'Look, I've been with men before. I thought it was over, but these thoughts—God, these thoughts keep coming. I can't stop thinking about being inside a man.'"

"How long, before today, had it been since you were with a man?" Jess asked, although he knew the answer.

"Jesus, years. Four years," Wayne had said, looking at Jess for either applause or censure.

That explained the passion, the urge to get at something that had been denied for so long, the sense of anger in the lovemaking, retrieving what had been absent.

"Did you have a good time today, Wayne?"

"Yes. Did you?"

"Very much. I don't even mind that I never finished the stations." They laughed together, then kissed until their stubble began to chafe their faces. Wayne left to pick up Bobby from school, and later that night they spoke on the phone until three in the morning.

"How can we be good people, good Christians, and still do what we do?" Wayne had asked him.

"What is it that we do?" Jess had needled him.

"We fuck on levees; we make out on front porches. You're white, I'm black. And still we go to church and call ourselves good."

"We *are* good, Wayne, and what happened today was not normal. We needed each other. Maybe it was ordained that we meet."

"You think so?"

"Well, I'm going to rationalize it that way." They had ended their conversation with promises to meet again—alone—the next night for dinner, in a proper, upstanding restaurant. When they met, Wayne had told him that one of his sisters wanted to know who the woman was: she could see her brother was smitten.

"What did you tell her." Jess asked.

"I told her a pretty white thing."

They giggled through dinner like teeenagers and then went to Jess's and sat on the ridiculous swing until past midnight.

"Would you like to move in with me?" Wayne asked.

Jess was surprised by the sudden desire from this seemingly balanced, thoughtful man.

But perhaps he was as needy as Jess was; as desperate to fill some of the voids in his life.

"I think I would," Jess replied. Perhaps, he thought, Wayne was the final piece in the puzzle that was now haphazardly spread about, but which would soon be complete, tightly constructed, a minor but whole piece of art.

"If you *do* move in with me, promise me one thing."

"Anything."

"When you come, don't bring this fruity swing."

"It's a deal," Jess said, and the next day he prepared the dinner in which Bobby was invited to meet his father's new friend.

*   *   *

Bobby was walking down the aisle of St. Peter's now, and Jess turned in his seat to see him. Bobby smiled at him, an open, sincere smile, and Jess felt his heart swell. Despite all the doubts about Wayne and their relationship, he did love this boy, looked forward to the endless questions, his open outlook on everything. Watching Bobby ascend the stairs to the altar, Jess didn't care about anyone else in the church, what they might be feeling. He only loved Bobby and wanted him happy. Reading his mind, Wayne reached over and squeezed Jess's hand.

How many times had Wayne squeezed his hand? In their relationship of six months, how many comforting, reassuring taps and squeezes had been visited upon him? Frail and terribly white, he must have seemed infinitely delicate to Wayne, who was tall and husky, never ill or tired, always ready to make a living, solve a problem, end a dispute, go to a party. If Jess's life was all about getting ready for something, Wayne's was all about looking forward to something. While Jess fretted over clothes and his hair and whether he looked right, Wayne could stand in a shower for two minutes, dry off, then throw on anything, and look healthy and handsome. When didn't he show any discomfort in their relationship? Why did Jess seem to bear the complete burden?

"I don't sweat the small stuff," Wayne had said. "I have a great son. I have a wonderful lover. I love you, I have you. Fuck anyone else."

Jess wished he could feel the same way, but he didn't. When he had announced his intention to move in with a forty-one-year-old black man in Brusly, his parents were horrified and had refused to speak to him for several weeks. Eventually, after a number of chilly standoffs, his mother had invited Jess and Wayne for dinner. It was formal and as uncomfortable as a dinner could get, but Jess tried to love his parents for the effort, their attempt to meet and understand Wayne, to understand how their son had wound up in love with him. During dinner, when Wayne had reached over and begun to caress

Jess's hand, Jess's father had started to sweat and his lips to shake; he looked as if he was ready to cry. Surely they had known that their son was queer, Jess reasoned. But taking a black lover was the last straw, the ultimate indignity in this town, this region.

"They seemed nice," Wayne had remarked on their drive from Baton Rouge to Brusly.

"They can be," Jess had answered, fingering the gift-wrapped package his mother had given him as they were saying good-bye. When their car reached the Mississippi Bridge, Jess threw the package over the railing, hoping he would hear it hit water.

"Why did you do that." Wayne had asked, mystified.

"I didn't need it," Jess replied.

"But you didn't even fucking know what it was!"

"It was a Bible," Jess answered him tensely. "It's always a Bible."

Jess had moved all of his things out of the blue house in a mad rush of excitement and determination. He feared that, as with all good things, the invitation to be Wayne's lover came with an expiration date or a clause that he would be unable to fill if he failed to show the correct amount of industry. Everything in the house that he pinpointed as unnecessary he put for sale in the front yard. Bobby helped him with price tags, and he loved asking people if they needed assistance as they wandered among the furniture, books, pictures, and the enormous swing, which an elderly couple bought for a hundred dollars. As they stuffed it into the back of a pickup truck, Jess taunted Wayne, "I got that swing for five hundred dollars from Smith & Hawken."

"You got screwed, darling."

Jess made over seven hundred dollars from the yard sale, and he gave one hundred to Bobby. Wayne insisted that he put it in the bank, as a savings account. Bobby was ecstatic as he sat in the bank and received a passbook and was told how much money he would have in twenty, thirty, forty years.

"How about we keep adding to it?" Jess had asked.

"I want him to earn it," Wayne had said, and Jess could feel the judgment. He felt brackish fluid rising in his throat. Unlike me, he thought, who has had fancy colleges and handouts from home, and now disability from depression.

"You know what I mean?" Wayne asked, after an uncomfortable silence.

"Sure," Jess said, a little too brightly. "He should know the value of a dollar, but he should also know that we love him and want him to have money for the future."

"OK, but let's balance it. OK?"

"Sure, you're always right."

After disagreements like these—small but irritating—they always made love. They would send Bobby out to play; then they would begin to kiss. As erotic as the encounters with Wayne were, Jess never felt as if they were passionate or in pursuit of sexual pleasure. In the past, sex had been furtive, forbidden. With Wayne it was expected, sweet, slow. Jess liked that feeling of belonging to someone, but he found himself asking Wayne to do new, different things.

"I don't want to do that, "Wayne had said, bristling at a certain suggestion.

"Why? It *is* done, you know."

"Not by me," Wayne replied, reminding Jess that he was no career fag, and that sex, like everything else in his life, needed to follow a particular pattern, fill a precise need.

"What does that mean?" Jess had yelled back at him.

"You *know* what it means," Wayne had said in a voice that ended the conversation.

After that conversation Jess knew never to discuss their pasts again. Wayne felt that Jess had been promiscuous, fervent, clinging, and Jess knew that Wayne felt cheated of his sexual truth, having only had, outside of Jess, brief, guilt-ridden attachments. When they had agreed to be tested for STDs at the Public Health Center in New Orleans (far, far away from any of their friends or acquaintances), Wayne had been honestly mortified as Jess told the counselor of his past partners and practices. Jess could count eighty or more; Wayne, five. They had both tested negative for everything, but Wayne admitted was surprised that Jess had *nothing*.

"My God," Wayne had said, in front of the counselor, "can't you say no?"

The counselor had begun playing with his pencils, clearly unsure of how to handle this situation. Partners were usually far more familiar with each other—and their sex lives—before coming in for testing, but Jess and Wayne seemed determined to meet some self-imposed, and daunting, deadline.

When they got back to Brusly, Wayne had let Jess out at the driveway, then driven off. Inside the house that Wayne and Clarice had built together, Jess wondered if this was the end, if Wayne would return and ask him to remove his things and get out of his life. Jess looked at the surroundings, the paneled walls covered with photos of black faces, the books that Wayne studied to improve his life, his vocabulary, his standing at his job as a security guard, and he realized he could leave it. He could find another home, another city, another man, another church. When Bobby came home from school, Jess helped him with his homework, let him fix his dinner, and then, as they ate together, talked more about the upcoming First Communion.

Wayne came into the house as they were finishing. Jess avoided his eyes, quickly cleaning the kitchen, eavesdropping as Bobby repeated, almost verbatim, the conversation that had accompanied dinner. Jess heard Wayne send Bobby to bed and then heard him approaching the kitchen. Silently, Wayne pulled Jess's shirt up over his head and clamped his mouth over a nipple and pulled greedily. Soon they were naked and making love on the kitchen floor, Jess's viewpoint revealing dust bunnies beneath the refrigerator and a lone french fry under the microwave cart. Wayne's lovemaking was more passionate than usual, but painful, predictable, the only unnerving aspect when he reached down and grabbed Jess's hips in his hands and said in a guttural voice, "This is mine, you hear. *Mine*."

"Oh, you black men," Jess had said, laughing, and they had both laughed, at themselves and their location.

"And now, they come to God," Father Mervin was saying, and Jess's head snapped up. He had begun dreaming during Mary's solo, and only now was coming awake, for he heard his cue. Soon he would be going up to the altar and reading with Wayne and Bobby. Jess looked at the piece of paper in his hand; it was perfectly illegible. He nudged Wayne and showed it to him. Now they would have to wing it, hope for the best, pray that memories didn't fail them. Jess felt a pang of guilt. After all those hours of preparation, would it now end in embarrassment? Wasn't everyone staring at them anyway, searching for any justification to remove them from the church. Jess began to sweat again, his heart raced, and even the woman next to him—someone he was sure hated him—handed him a small paper fan.

"They come seeking directions to a bright, shining place." Father Mervin continued, and suddenly the youngsters were marching down the aisle, their faces happy and nervous. Bobby searched for and found Wayne and Jess and broke form and waved. Jess smiled back, a bit weakly, but he smiled. Jess suddenly felt weak and humiliated, a faker. What was he doing here, anyway? A white man in a church of blacks? Raising a black boy? Staying with a man who clings and has moods and doesn't understand that people move at different speeds. A man who doesn't understand that Jess's life is not rooted to Brusly, but may take him to faraway places.

Jess stood upright in his place, and the people of the church, and

Father Mervin, looked at him as if he were about to speak. The procession of young people stopped dead, confused by this unrehearsed bit of business. Jess said, to no one in particular, "I want to find that bright, shining place." And then he moved swiftly up the aisle, moving the youngsters aside, including a confused Bobby, whose gaze followed Jess as he left the church. Wayne stayed in his seat, turning his head toward Bobby and nodding assent. Yes, his eyes communicated, the ceremony will continue.

Outside the church, Jess took in deep gulps of air, and he leaned against an oak tree and felt his aching ribs. He felt as if he had run for miles and his mouth was as parched as his face was wet with sweat. He looked longingly at the small man-made lake on the church property and remembered his own baptism in such a lake so many years ago. He thought of his mother and father, sitting in their own church across the river wondering how this ceremony was going. He refused to cry, but that is what he felt like doing. He fought a sob and instead called out to the overcast sky, "God, please forgive me my ways. Please cleanse me now." He didn't care if those inside the church heard him or not. He suddenly had a heavy heart that needed to be unburdened and he proceeded to list all of his sins: His hatred for Anna and the other relatives, their bad manners and evil thoughts. Wayne and his possessiveness, leaving him to feel like a prisoner in that small, tacky house with its endless chores and touch-ups. Wayne's anger and rough affection, as if he were branding Jess like a runaway calf each time Jess possessed an emotion that ran counter to Wayne's own simplicity. Feeling as if all these black, malignant faces were judging him.

A deacon of the church had come to the front door of the church and lit a cigarette. His mien displayed the fact that he had no time for nonsense and could easily handle whatever Jess had in mind. Jess decided to give him the show he wanted; the show he would enjoy describing to the curious parishioners inside.

Jess headed for the lake, then plunged in headfirst. It was a mistake, he knew that the minute his face hit the dirty, foul-smelling water, but he was determined to go through with it. "In the name of the Father, the Son, and the Holy Ghost, I cleanse myself of my sins," he yelled, plunging himself beneath the water three times, each time coming up with a sound like sin leaving the stratosphere. "I do not pledge to stand here as a guide for life to this child," he yelled, a direct contradiction to the words he had rehearsed with Bobby for weeks. "I do not pledge, I do not pledge. . . ." Each time he uttered the words, he slapped the surface of the lake for emphasis. He suddenly stopped yelling and it grew quiet. Jess could smell the cigarette of the deacon and knew he was still there, watching. He had lost a contact lens in the lake, and his white shirt clung to him, revealing chest hair; his pants were full of water. As he climbed out of the lake, the water rushed from his clothes as if in a silent-comedy film. The deacon uttered a sound that was a complete dismissal, as well as a confirmation of all he had believed about Jess from the beginning. With his one good eye, Jess could see a black face in each window of the church, watching him as he stood, wet and vacant, not knowing what to do next.

Jess looked at the deacon, who stomped out his cigarette on the ground, imagining, Jess thought, that the butt were Jess's head. "I'm clean now, Deacon," Jess said, and the deacon's reply was to enter the church, slamming the door behind him. With the slamming, all the faces left the windows and Jess was alone, with no audience.

He began running, first in the wrong direction, then toward the house he shared with Wayne and Bobby. He knew that he could pick up his manuscripts and his few books and throw them in the car and be on his way, heading toward a better life. He ran faster, determined to find out what lay in store for him.

"I'm free!" Jess yelled at the air as he ran down the street. "I'm free of sin and all obligations."

Once again, he felt elated to be alive. He felt a purpose.

20. Last Summer
By L. Steve Schmersal

1

I AM NOT dead, he thought, lying in his bed, I am not dead. It came to him almost mantra-like, though Johnny wasn't the type ever to chant a mantra, over and over in a far-off way, a kind of white noise behind the other thoughts that performed in front of it, actors before a background, or rather film images projected onto a screen, and the screen was this mantra, I am not dead, I am not dead, I am not dead, I am not dead.

It had been almost a year since Scott died, and although Johnny's gut had finally relinquished the tight, tightening anxiety that had writhed there during the last year that Scott lived—or rather during that year while Scott died slowly—the writhing that had only intensified after Scott finally did die—although the anxiousness had sloughed out of him, Johnny felt its possibility still, a hovering trace, like being in love.

Spring was coming, or nearly, and Johnny had opened his window some to let the air in, to let it wash over him in the pale early light. It felt like water, he thought. Cool, not brisk, with currents, as water has, flowing through the shimmering long-and-narrow rectangle of the slightly opened window—not even troubling the window shade—and over him; and the cool flow of air reminded Johnny of the river upstate, the house, and always—therefore never far behind—Scott. Johnny would have to go up there soon and begin preparing the house for the summer: mow the lawn, plant creeping vines, get the garden ready by himself since these chores had always been the ones he and Scott had done together. Lying in bed, Johnny looked forward to the coming green, the dogwood blooming in Easter-white crosses, the gaudy forsythia and rhododendron, the wisteria in the gazebo, honeysuckle weighting the air, and the huge bank of lilacs along the drive, whose scent always left him stranded in childhood.

Last summer, after five unbearable months tiptoeing around his apartment, Johnny had spent last summer abroad in the arms of strangers, trying to bury himself, he thought now, running away to be very sure. Running and running from the snake coiling inside his belly, rushing away from old friends he was realizing he'd never liked anyway, through London to Paris to Strasbourg into Germany, and then down through Switzerland into Italy. He'd stopped briefly, stupidly, in Lucerne for two far-too-long days, and the sight of the Alps, their hugeness, made him wonder how people could live under all that weight all their lives. The mountains baffled him, made him feel as though proportion were all, somehow, wrong—had always been wrong—the way they hovered over the lakeshores behind him, always over the opera house in front of him, and over the stores. And it became so that the mountains unnerved Johnny to the point where he couldn't bear to look at them; he felt he was going crazy under their shadow. Somehow they were too real.

He'd expected his return to the city to change him, or he'd expected to learn that he'd changed, or to find himself somewhere in the haze between the two. Everything reminded him of something else. When he was traveling, even while he was fucking his way through Italy, he kept missing Scott, kept thinking Scott were traveling with him, that he would be at the hotel taking a nap when he returned from a stroll; or he would actually see Scott, rounding a bend away from him in Florence, stepping into a car in Rome, with a tour group in Venice. With increasing regularity, he would see Scott's back, or his eyes, catch his stance, his gait, in distant silhouette, or see the back of Scott's head in a line, or hear Scott's intonation in some tourist's voice, catch sight of his hand clumsily attached to a waiter's wrist, catch his scent (from the old days, before he got sick) on someone's skin, see his eyes, hear his voice, see his back, catch his stance, his glance, his gait, his eyes, his back, his hair, his eyes, his voice, his back, his eyes, his eyes, his eyes, always tacked on to strangers. Each time, these sightings—were they citings?—tightened Johnny's gut around a nausea, a nauseating emptiness. And each new town made him feel like he was running from these shadows only to find them waiting for him around the next bend, in the next tour group, in the next little shop whose mirrors, still giddy from Scott's reflection, gave back with a jolt Johnny's gloomy face instead. Back home in the city, the pattern continued, though Johnny had finally stopped seeing his dead lover everywhere. Now strangers or smells reminded him of his trip, of people he'd spoken with, places he'd stayed, and though the first reminding wasn't of Scott, behind it, wearing the first as a mask, was some memory-Scott. It seemed that Johnny was slowly replacing memories of Scott with memories of memories of him; and part of Johnny hoped this meant that these recollections too would soon be lost under other associations, and that eventually Scott would be buried deep and deeper under the accumulating sediment of Johnny's living.

The night before, Johnny had picked up a man at the bar across the street. Johnny had taken an interest in a burly Italian-looking man and was about to make his move when another man arrived by the first man's side. The interloper was slender, tall, with blond hair he constantly swept to the side of his forehead. Johnny waited nearby where he could cruise the big Italian speaking to the man Johnny imagined with amusement to be his "rival," a campy note suggesting melodrama, suggesting Italians. The rival seemed to be doing most of the talking, and Sal or Jake or Nick only listened and nodded, as straight boys do. Soon Sal-Jake-Nick noticed Johnny watching him and began looking back, his eyes full of something like sullen humor—a Labrador's sad brown eyes.

The blond went to get a beer and Johnny strode forward, his eyes locked on those other eyes, and introduced himself. Not Nick, but Mark was the man's name. He spoke with a Brooklyn accent, but not for very long as he lapsed into silence when the blond reappeared to stand next to Johnny. They looked at one another, the blond with a bemused smile, Mark with his unchanging mournful eyes, Johnny amused and hoping his rival would soon lose interest and leave. Alas, it was Mark who excused himself ("Haveta take a piss"), leaving the blond and Johnny to glance about the room, anywhere but at each other. When Johnny finally looked over, the blond was smiling at him, and Johnny's lips jumped involuntarily into an echo. The man shrugged and extended his hand.

"I'm Josh."

"Johnny."

They shook hands; Johnny noticed some blond strands of Josh's bangs stuck to his forehead with sweat.

"What's your name?" Josh asked. "Your last name?"

"Mattran."

"Johnny Mattran," Josh said. "Sounds like—"

"Like a porn star's name, I know." They both paused. Johnny looked directly into Josh's eyes. "You, uh, you wanna get naked?"

"Right here?"

"I live across the street."

In his bed, Johnny lay still as Josh's lips, teeth, tongue, and stubble worked him, his skin, the muscles underneath, eventually settling, as though finding the focal point, on Johnny's asshole. The feeling was a pleasurable version of being turned inside out, and just as alarming for Johnny, who had never experienced these sensations before. Scott hadn't been into rimming; like most couples, their sex had settled into a routine and, to be sure, Johnny's butt hadn't figured much in their fucking.

"I need to tell you something." Johnny put his hand on Josh's thigh.

Josh's face was wet with spit. "Are you positive?"

Johnny braced himself for the usual awkward silliness that followed. "Well . . . yeah."

"It's cool," Josh said, returning his tongue even farther into Johnny's ass. Johnny lay there, unsure what he was feeling, aware only of his anus and the sensations emanating from the tongue and mouth of this man into his body, inside his body, up from Johnny's guts into his throat.

"I wish you could fuck me."

"I can." Josh grinned.

Johnny shook his head. "No condoms." The wrinkling latex would be unpleasant. "I don't think I could do it with a condom, anyway. . . ."

Josh had hooked Johnny's knees into his elbows and was sliding the length of his penis back and forth over Johnny's asshole. Johnny felt the room tilt suddenly, he felt, he felt . . . he didn't know what he was feeling.

"I don't need a condom," Josh said.

"Man . . . I haven't fucked without one in fifteen years—"

The weight of Josh's warm body against him and the smooth stroking over his ass stopped Johnny's words; and then, just then, the head of Josh's cock caught itself on the edge of Johnny's asshole. Johnny relaxed instinctively and Josh's penis slid in, all the way in, easily, till it was buried to the balls up Johnny's ass.

"You want me to stop?" Josh said.

Johnny reached around to pull Josh farther inside him. Delirium washed over him; he wanted all of Josh in his ass, to somehow feel the whole man inside him. He moaned at the sensation. Josh's mouth covered Johnny's, dissolving the sound, his tongue teasing Johnny's tongue as his cock began sliding slowly out and then back in Johnny's hole. *This is what it's like to lose control,* Johnny thought.

Josh began to pump faster. Their bodies became slick and wet; sweat from Josh's brow fell into Johnny's face, into his mouth, which he could not seem to close, could no more close than say anything with it, and through this frenzy something surfaced: *Tastes like tears*—and for a moment Johnny thought he was crying.

Johnny woke up with Josh's head lying on his chest. They'd fallen asleep talking in the dark, exhausted and wet with sweat and semen, and Josh's open mouth had drooled saliva onto Johnny's chest. In Italy, a beautiful dark-haired man had fallen asleep with his head on Johnny's meaty pecs, his spit pooling in the smooth groove of Johnny's sternum, his dark curls almost tickling Johnny's lip as he slept, outside the pensione window the sounds of the restaurant, people eating and speaking an Italian Johnny didn't understand. The beautiful tan Italian had reminded Johnny of Scott, who had slept with his head on Johnny's chest in those last months, as he was dying. Most nights, they'd begun like this: Johnny read, Scott slept, snored, and drooled onto Johnny's chest; this was hilarious to both of them, one of the few bits of comic relief from that time. As his dying loomed nearer, Scott, who'd always said he was unafraid of dying, would hold Johnny's hand, stroke his hair, lay a hand on Johnny's leg or arm, beginning sleep in their bed, in this bed, with his head lying across Johnny's chest, and snoring. Now Scott's snoring became Josh's snoring, for the sound was in the same key.

Johnny felt itching lines of heat slide down his temples into his hair, his vision blurring into a crosshatch of tree limbs against a night sky, and wept. He did not touch the tears—not because he didn't want to wake Josh, but because wiping them away would diminish the tribute they paid. He let the stinging tears well in his eyes and slide down his face, tracing its surface, weeping in short little grunts for the memories flooding him now, too late.

Josh awoke. "Sorry, man, didn't mean to fall asleep," he muttered. He got up and started dressing. "I should get home; gotta be up tomorrow. Sorry, man. Sorry." In the darkness, in his hurry, he didn't notice Johnny wiping his eyes.

2

Kathryn found packing excruciating. True, in comparison to *un*packing, throwing some things in a suitcase or two seemed easy. Unpacking was always an exercise in lost chances, missed opportunities, all the things presupposed, as she pulled each unused item from the suitcase: the perfume she never wore, the suntan lotion she never spread across her arms, the earrings she'd packed for a dinner out they never took: each item a reproach. Sometimes she had the feeling she was planning her regret, not her trip, when packing; but that was crazy, since she would only realize that she'd fallen short of her expectations, fallen behind, when she was unpacking.

Each time she unpacked, she brought the summer another week closer to autumn, another flurry of activity into and out of her suitcases—in her mind, clothes, magazines, tampons, sunglasses collected in and emptied from the suitcases on her bed, as though a wind were filling them with sand, then blowing them empty, only to fill them again. Then the final insult at the end of the summer, when she'd bring home all the things she'd kept at the house for the season. All the shorts, skirts, and dresses she'd decided she'd never wear in the city, all the well-reasoned books for reading on the lawn by the river, so many things she had never thought of using while at the house, had forgotten she'd brought—until they were closing the house and she found herself remanding her expectations back to the city.

Kathryn never felt that way during the weeks and weekends at the house, of course; it was only in the unpacking and in the packing. *This is the book I'll never read,* she thought as she placed it in her bag, *this is the dress I'll never wear,* knowing full well she certainly would put on this light, loose dress, of all dresses, unless the nights were cool and breezy, which they might be, making this the dress she would never wear. When you pack, you plan, you seek exigencies and prepare for them, you imagine an intersection between the future and now; when you unpack, you learn how little you know yourself.

How like at the end of a love affair, when Kathryn would think back to the things she'd never said or gotten to say, the flowers she'd never bring, the poem she should have written when she had the urge. Did regrets always resolve themselves into pop-song clichés?

> *All of the flowers I'll never bring*
> *All of the poems I'll never write*

Perhaps . . . but sometimes love affairs are unusual, are unexpected, not eroticized Hollywood elegies where the accent is on The Affair. Other sorts of stories harbor other kinds of love, and packing her suitcase now made Kathryn think of Scott, and how much more absent he'd seem this summer with Johnny back at the house. It was easy to mistake her lack of sadness last summer for callousness, as she had done for a time herself. The house, the whole summer, had felt strange without Scott and Johnny, but as they were both gone she'd found it easy to avoid the subject; she'd imagined them sometimes as taking a vacation abroad that season, pictured them laughing together on an Italian beach. Having been such a loving couple, such an in-love couple, the kind of couple others envied (a couple she had envied), it was easy to place them only in relation to each other, to think of them as present or absent as a unit. Had Johnny been at the house last summer instead of in Europe, Kathryn would have been unmoored in her grief, she believed; Johnny, alone, would have represented the loss, to all of them, of Scott. Somehow he'd be half of Johnny. Instead of grief, she'd felt last summer such wonderful melting relief, felt glad that it was over, that Scott was no longer hurting, that she didn't have to witness his dying any longer, that it was over. As the witness, she had found it unbearable finally to be around Johnny, who was strong in the face of Scott's dying, strong as blue metal—he'd worn it, or borne it rather, in his shoulders, even when he was smiling. Unbearable. All last summer she was amazed that, except for the occasional postcard from Johnny ("Hi from Switzerland!"), she'd rarely thought of him or Scott. When that postcard came, she would freeze, as though it were bad news, then relax as she read Johnny's latest glib missive ("In Italy. Stop. Sun and men hot. Stop").

Last summer, she'd initially had to force herself to enjoy the house, had to find a way to enjoy herself. She and Jess would stay up there as long as possible, waiting to catch every sunset as it came, earlier and earlier. She'd worked hard in the yard, growing new herbs in Scott's herb garden, mowing the lawn, making preserves, working on her French for the first time in years, having sex with Jess in the gazebo. She hadn't even read the newspaper. And in this way, she'd moved outside of the great sickroom the world had become. Slowly, of course, and without noticing. Later she would refer to it in smaller and smaller descriptions that utterly belied the experience of watching one person die and another person live. Someday, perhaps, her comments would reel out in an offhand manner about "that time," the way, Kathryn supposed, novels enshroud a whole drama of love, loss, and pain, of war, with "Time passed," with "A war began and ended," with "They lived together for many years." How silly. Ellipses, nothing more, each black dot a tiny, silent world.

The approach to the house always excited Johnny—after the heat and rush of the expressway and the progressively smaller, sleepier, dustier country roads turning into back roads shrouded with trees, the air stirred by the frenetic swirl of the tree frogs (which aren't frogs at all)—to see the drive, amble up it, round the bend, and see the house. It was like coming home when he was a child, a sleepy, pajamaed kid in the back with watchful dad in the front. It always made Johnny giddy. His arm rested, dad-like, on the open car window now, the damp air freighted with honeysuckle. "Smell that?" he said to Sam, who was sitting in the passenger seat. When he and Scott had first come here, Johnny, who had lived only in the city for a decade, falling asleep to traffic sounds and ambulances, would lie awake at night, wide-eyed with the incessant racket of crickets.

Johnny enjoyed the house in the country, but Scott loved it. He'd acted like a kid when they were preparing for each summer. Suddenly, the calendar would become annotated, numbered, as it counted down to the appointed day when Johnny and Scott packed the car and drove up, the map in Scott's lap the whole way. Calendars, maps, and lists of things to do were Scott's talismans, but what had made all that ordering more than just charming to Johnny, who was considerably less organized, was how much Scott enjoyed his lists and notes. He was not anally warding off disorder by being careful—as some of their friends accused—it was that Scott enjoyed the details so very much. Johnny had surrendered himself to the scribbles on Scott's calendar—which, Leonardo-like, only Scott could decipher—because in so doing he could enjoy, along with Scott, not only the arrival but the preparation for the journey, the journey there, and the journey back. Scott was always getting there because there was no there there.

"It's awesome," Sam said as they stood in front of the house, a dark mass looming in the pale blue twilight. Johnny smiled and, grabbing Sam's hand, tugged him up the stairs.

"Let me get a bag," Sam said, pulling in the other direction.

"Nah, we'll do that later."

Turning lights on as they went, Johnny showed Sam through the house. He appeared nonchalant as they went, but to any sensitive eye it would have been clear that Johnny was showing off for Sam, was proud of the house he, Kathryn, Jess, and Scott had renovated for the past eight years. He showed Sam where they kept the food, the room in which he'd be sleeping, which bathroom to use, the embroidery Kathryn had hung over the liquor cabinet, the liquor cabinet itself, the whiskey inside, which they began downing like frat boys on a weekend home without parents, taking only the bottle with them out to the gazebo. Johnny, Scott, and Jess had built it three summers ago. Wisteria covered it now, so much so that Johnny had been shocked when he first saw it; having been gone last summer, he'd missed a whole year's growth, the haphazard twisting and creeping, the delicate looping infiltration of the supports and latticework. The image alarmed him; he'd remarked to Kathryn the week before that they should cut it back before the gazebo was choked with it. Yet at night, lit with candles, the leafy wisteria conjured a magical effect, like a cave, and the gazebo became a favorite place to eat dinner that summer.

Johnny leaned over Sam to light a candle. Sam reached up and slid his hand along the groove where the quadriceps of Johnny's right leg smoothed into his inner thigh. Candlelit, Johnny straddled Sam on the deck chair. "Pretty cool, huh?" he said, indicating around him with his arms.

"Thanks for bringing me up here," Sam said, reaching up and pulling Johnny's head down and Johnny's mouth into his. Whiskey on Johnny's tongue came burning back to life on contact with Sam's tongue. Johnny loved this, loved tasting someone's breath in his own mouth, loved the sensation of his lips against someone else's, loved the taste of whiskey, warm everywhere, warming his gut first, then his hands, his eyes, his face, his groin. He could feel the heat from Sam as well, amped up suddenly, whiskey-warmed, Sam's crotch grinding insistently up into him as they kissed.

It was sex that had come between Johnny and Scott at first. Not right away, but they'd discovered within the first few months of knowing each other that Johnny liked to fuck around and that Scott didn't. Johnny would pick up someone, maybe on the street or at the gym, have quick sex somewhere; then he and Scott would have a date later, make love, candles, long talk, blow out the candles grown low. But Scott knew of Johnny's other lovers; he could taste them on Johnny's body, he said, on Johnny's lips, his breath tasted of someone else's, Johnny's cock felt worked over and raw. He always knew, he said. So it came down, as it does for many, to the choice between one or more than one. It was Johnny's choice. Scott explained to Johnny that he had tried the other ways. He'd tried to have both a lover and others on the side, had had a lover who didn't want to be monogamous, had tried several arrangements. But he couldn't play the score just any way; it turned out that it mattered very much to Scott which instruments played which notes.

Johnny, who was in love, was torn and had opted for Scott and never looked back. He'd thought at the time, and thought back to it sometimes, that this was how you choose love, and that at some point, even if it chooses you, as love is said to, that you must still make that choice. In turn, he had exacted a price from Scott, who was nothing less than a stoner of many years' standing: He'd asked Scott to quit smoking weed. And Scott, who was also in love, had kicked the one habit for the other.

Johnny wasn't thinking of Scott now, he was thinking only of Sam's body, hard under him, he was only thinking of Sam's smooth pecs and abs, his brown nipples, rising under his shirt with the heat of alcohol and arousal. A body as far from Scott's as could be, Scott who had never had muscle on him but was always unremarkable physically, unremarkably slender, with a slight paunch sometimes, always unremarkable, especially next to Johnny's beefed-out frame. Unremarkable, except for the fact that Johnny had loved Scott's body, that Johnny had loved Scott, loved the moles and large soft-brown birthmark on his inner thigh, even the irregular, asymmetrically placed patches of hair on Scott's back. In that remaking alchemy which is loving, these dross, pathetic, pale features, places on Scott that Johnny had tried at first to ignore or tried to imagine didn't exist, became those spots on Scott's body that Johnny loved best.

Kathryn arrived much later than she'd meant to. She'd left the city late and gotten into traffic at the bridge—an accident, it seemed. As with so many traffic jams, the cause was simply absent, or in a past that hadn't worked itself out of the present, which swirled around it the way a whirlpool circles a hole, a nothing. The resulting extra cars that clogged the expressway past the bridge irritated her, and on top of everything, Jesse had a client to see and wasn't coming up till the next day.

It had been a long journey of red taillights mapping the way ahead, the harsh glare of headlights chasing her from behind. She often felt that way on these journeys—chased from the city. She focused on the red lights ribboning their way through the dark ahead with the tense calm of an evacuation. This weekend escape was demanded: If you chose to live in the city, you must choose to leave it; the alternative was overstimulation and a sort of psychosis. Thus each inhabitant fled the city as a way of fleeing her own madness, led out by a sort of pillar of fire. So biblical.

Perhaps this was how Noah's animals had behaved when the ark finally landed after the forty days and nights of rain—they fled in the orderly way they had come, anxiously escaping one another. And all that water, all that dying, to punish one animal, really. How typical of that vengeful desert deity to overdo it, like a fucked-up child with his toys: global drowning, burning cities on the plain, Egyptian exile, Babylonian exile, crucified offspring, millennial guilt trips. How warm. And, just as the kinder and gentler teachings of the Essene Jesus disclosing the Day of Judgment are only the beautiful beginning of the terrible End (in the same way that the comforting red glow of votive candles in church prefigure the fire next time), the warm trail of taillights are a premonition of the bright flashing of ambulances and flares at an accident site. But typically, the accident scene never emerges, only the effects of one, perhaps only the rumor of one, the fear of one, which, as the punishment that strikes even the creature who never sinned, who can't sin, casts its wave over believer and nonbeliever alike.

With these thoughts, Kathryn eased herself toward her weekend home. Eventually the cars thinned out, and soon she was on the back roads, which she always found disconcerting in the dark, no matter how many summers she drove them. Scott and Johnny, especially Scott, had always made merciless fun of her for it. She was tired after the past three hours of irritability; it was exhausting to be annoyed for so long. By the time her car was rolling up the drive to the house, all she could think about was lying down for a bit, or perhaps going to bed early. In the morning, out in the gazebo, she would meditate for an hour and do yoga, and thus leave behind with finality the city that had pursued at her heels almost to the doorstep of her house. Jesse would arrive on the noon train and, along with Johnny, the three of them would have drinks in the gazebo, watch the sun set over the wide hills, make a large elaborate dinner, and speak, but not too often or too long, about Scott. He was finally being missed at the house in the country, and it only sometimes made Johnny snappish. (He'd confessed to Kathryn one night while they were chopping vegetables for dinner that he was sick of missing Scott.)

Lights glowed inside the house, in deeper rooms away from the windows, like a lantern turned low. A breeze stirred the wind chimes on the back porch, insisting that she walk around to hear them closer; the air was warm, and she was glad that Johnny was already home. The lights, his car in the drive, the wind chimes, and the scent of honeysuckle surrounded the annoyance of the trip, soothing it the way a mother calms a child, through touch. She picked up her suitcase and strolled around the house to the porch off the kitchen. Through the screen door she could see Johnny and some other man, tall, broad-shouldered, dark hair clipped short, his shirt off, his torso smooth and powerful-looking, like that of an overdeveloped dancer. She paused, taking in the scene as though it were a religious diorama from her childhood: the man sitting on their kitchen table, Johnny rubbing his feet and looking up at him—searchingly, it seemed—from his chair, the conversation paused for a moment and the moment frozen. It was a diorama, after all, but instead of "The Magdalene Washes the Feet of Jesus," this was titled, as she realized with a start that the scene included herself, "The Interruption." (What was a diorama without dramatic irony?) And then, absurdly, she knocked on her own screen door.

The next morning, Johnny woke early and walked barefoot out to the gazebo, the dew on the grass shockingly cold on his feet and sparkling just like, yes, a carpet of diamonds, as the story, in some far-off memory, prescribed. The morning was not quite cool, and mist rose from the river and was erased as quickly as it left the water's surface by the sun's insistent light. The image left him feeling hollow as he watched the mist gather, rise, and die; yet, from where he sat, on the gazebo step facing the water, he couldn't take his eyes away from it.

Sam snored upstairs, a late sleeper, but for Johnny the utter silence of the mornings out here always woke him early. This allowed him to watch the qualities of light changing as they played over the house, the water, the trees. He liked this. When Johnny was a kid among the yawning, treeless lawns of the suburbs, the only time he saw the white sun of midmorning was Sundays, before and after church. Unable to sleep late, even after a night of getting drunk with Scott and Kathryn, Johnny had always felt he was living a string of Sundays up here, each day white-hot and burning with whatever they wanted to do, full of possibility and space, but always with Monday looming near; the heat of the morning, the day, burning hot, burning out to reemerge miraculously as another Sunday. Johnny had never understood if Sunday was the last day of the week or the first; did it mean ending or beginning? Somehow always both, somehow always in danger of turning into something else, the sensation of every day in the country house being a Sunday made him both grateful and anxious, which is not at all the same thing as sorry-grateful.

Sam snored. Johnny hadn't known that. Drunk, they had walked up the back stairs together, silently, and simply sauntered into Johnny's room as though it were expected. Simply undressed and got into bed naked, practically with their eyes closed, and clung to each other under the cool white sheet, and fell asleep. They had been fuck buddies on several occasions, but this was their first time together in bed where they hadn't fucked. And the first time they'd slept together.

Johnny had not expected—had not wanted to expect—that Sam would sleep in his bed. He'd invited Sam to the house as a guest, intending to formalize the weekend, intending maybe to visit Sam in the guestroom in the morning. The whole college-boys'-weekend-at-home feeling that had colored their arrival only served to stage his intentions for him. But to sleep together. To Johnny, sleeping with someone, listening to his breathing deepen into sleep, change within sleeping, to see his face in repose or set in an expression conjured by a dream was to see him at his most private, as he was when he was not responding to you, persuading you, to see him perhaps for the first time, and, inevitably, in all these ways, also to be seen. Seen in ways you didn't know yourself. For Johnny, sleeping with someone was more intimate than sex, more intimate than kissing.

At the gym one day, Sam had asked Johnny to spot him on the bench. Later, in the shower, he'd eyed Johnny more carefully while they toweled off near each other. They'd continued checking each other out as they got dressed, then walked out together, had a quick dinner, a quick drink, and long, long sex back at Johnny's apartment. When it came time for Sam to leave, Johnny had walked him home. They'd kissed for a few moments in front of Sam's building, and then Sam had gathered Johnny into his arms, holding him fast, and Johnny had felt a loosening within himself, like an echo.

Since then, they had met twice for sex, gone to a movie once (sex) and dinner once (no sex). Even though their dinner evening was short due to Sam's schedule, it had felt more serious to Johnny than their other nights together, since this was the first time they had not met to fuck. It was during that dinner that Johnny had asked Sam to the country house and, as he'd heard himself talking, without even meaning to, found himself formulating other weekends away with this man, trips upstate to go hiking in the fall, road trips to Chicago or Atlantic City, and the inevitable weekends in the country.

The lawn was blinding in the morning light; Johnny lay back onto the sun-warmed wood of the gazebo floor. He felt the heat of the sun on his skin, on his chest, his belly, and one patch of light shining through the opening in his boxers, directly onto his penis.

So silent.

Light is silent.

Johnny felt a presence near him.

"How are you?" Kathryn sat gently down on the step next to Johnny.

"I'm fine." Johnny didn't open his eyes or move his head as he spoke. "The sunlight has a pressure, doesn't it? It feels like heat, but it's pressure."

Kathryn squinted out at the lawn and the river, its water brilliantly streaked and sparkling, sparking. The sun heated her face, and mostly her dark hair. Her hands. Her arms. "Yes," she said. She placed a hand on Johnny's warm belly, which felt almost feverish. "How are you?"

"I'm fine." He looked at her briefly and put his hand on hers. They sat like that for a while, not speaking, just feeling the silence of the sun on them.

"I thought we'd have breakfast out here today," Kathryn said. "How does that sound, baby?"

"That sounds wonderful." He squeezed her hand resting in his own and smiled into the warm rectangle of light painted over his mouth. "Maybe I'll go wake Sam."

"Let him sleep late if he wants," Kathryn said. "People should relax when they're up here."

There was a pause, and Kathryn went to say something, perhaps something like "Sam seems nice," but Johnny overlapped her, "I'm being selfish."

"'Cause you're hungry?"

"'Cause I'm horny." He laughed and got up. "I'll come down soon and get breakfast started." He blew her a kiss as he walked toward the house.

Kathryn hoped Sam and Johnny would take their time having sex so she could sit in the sun, watch the water, and write a little. Sam did seem nice, though Kathryn wasn't sure what to make of his smiling self-assurance. In other men she'd known who'd shone with a similar cockiness, she'd found little behind the smile. It was a distinctly American malady: The confidence man supplements your lack of confidence with his own surplus. Sometimes, when you look into the void, the void smiles back, but it sees nothing at all.

Maybe she was being hasty; maybe she was being nasty. Last night, after they had been drinking and talking for a while, the three of them had ended up in the living room looking in the albums for a certain photograph of the famous gazebo-building project. Soon Sam had found a whole series of pictures of Scott and Johnny, which led to a series from Scott's last summer at the house, the summer before that, and the summer before that. In each image Scott and Johnny glowed; smiling or not, caught in the gaze of the camera, they were so fucking happy together, and you could see it. They were the only couple Kathryn had known to be that way for so long. For years. Sam had stared at the photographs as Johnny and Kathryn laughingly recounted some story—strange that she couldn't remember which story—and, when they'd finished, Sam had looked up from the pictures at Johnny, his face fixed oddly (almost as though he'd been struck in the face, Kathryn thought). "You look so in love," he'd said.

Johnny had grinned and said, "Everyone loved Scott. He had that effect on people."

Kathryn had stood there, also smiling, watching—she didn't remember which story they'd been telling because she'd been observing Sam's absorption in the photographs. To the point of cliché, Scott and Johnny had been inseparable, which is not to say indistinguishable, for they were very different from each other. But they'd worked off each other; one caught the rays off the other to gleam with his own brightness, as the moon does the sun's light, yet seems its own source. Which man had been the moon and which the sun was the question, though Johnny and Scott had seemed to switch roles so effortlessly, it was the pleasure of earthbound observers to watch and marvel at the mystery of how and when it happened. At the end, Scott had reflected back light from Johnny, which was to be expected, she supposed; he'd lived for it, because of it, was it. But then, sometimes it had seemed that Scott was keeping Johnny alive. The more their relationship had simplified itself as it moved slowly toward dying, the more the long-standing nuances had tightened, were cast into deeper and higher relief, the more the terrain was itself, was clarified—and the more it was therefore alien to her. Kathryn had felt lost in this intimacy, lost in her own relation to this death. Nothing felt familiar; they were making it up as they went.

During that last summer, Scott frequently had stayed in bed, too weak to move around. One morning, Johnny was writing Scott's infamous list of things to do, ticking off the leftover items from the day before, while Scott named newer tasks, their banality so touching to Kathryn. This ritual of theirs had been installed at different times when Scott had been ill, and ended when he'd gotten better, but as the summer days grew shorter so had Scott's, and he'd retired to the guestroom with its hospital bed and light-filled corners. "Get a card for your mother's birthday," Scott had said and paused for a long time, thinking. Johnny wrote it down.

"Did we weed the garden behind the shed?"

"No," Johnny replied, writing.

"Let's mow the side yard." (Later that day, Scott would watch from his window.)

"I'd like to go for a ride at sunset." Pause.

"Let's have *caprese* at dinner, since the basil's come in so well." (The tomatoes would prove upsetting to his stomach, and he wouldn't eat them.)

Kathryn would always remember the *caprese,* never forget that list. The next morning, she'd sat with them during this time of recording Scott's list, stitching needlepoint by the window. The light was dazzling in the room, the sunlight glancing off the sheets over Scott's legs and throwing itself against the ceiling.

"What will we do today?" Johnny had said.

After the usual pause, Scott said, "Today? . . . Dying would be nice, today."

And Johnny wrote it down. Then Johnny had gotten into bed with Scott and lain alongside him, his heavy arm thrown over Scott's midsection, and Kathryn had left the room to be with Jesse.

Scott had not seemed, had never seemed depressed to Kathryn, but from then on the only item on his list was always the same. After two months of these single-item lists—and days would pass when Johnny avoided their ritual—after they had moved back to the city, there came a day in autumn when Johnny called her from the hospital. By the time she'd got there—urging the cabdriver, "My friend is dying. Do you understand?"—Scott was no longer dying. Johnny stood at the window, staring out. Kathryn came in, touched his shoulder. He sat her down next to the bed, put Scott's hand in hers, and left the room. She held Scott's hand, feeling the heat of living flee his body, and could think of nothing now that Scott was gone except her old fear that, without him, Johnny would lose his luminance, that without Scott she would no longer know Johnny.

Scott's favorite place to sit by the river had been under a large willow whose branches drooped down to the water to play on the surface there. Because of the way the branches hung, the spot had not been visible from the house, the dock, or the water. The shade kept it cool even on hot days, and from this place Scott had watched the water, birds, and boats, and had been alone, especially during that summer when he had never been allowed time to himself. It was his own hidden room, hung with a tapestry of leaves, swaying, hanging, swaying. He liked it for its silence.

Scott had discovered the tree not long after the four of them had bought the house; though it wasn't difficult to get to (he'd managed to navigate his way even with his cane), you had to step through some weeds and smaller trees to find the spot, a little south of the dock and picnic table where Kathryn liked to write. Scott had made sure to visit this place each time he came to the house, even if he could stand among the branches for only a minute. It was like saying a prayer, a pact he'd made with himself. Near the end of that last summer, he'd found it difficult to be true to the pact, had felt far too feeble to make it out to that area by himself, as his body wasted away. On an ocean beach, the sort of place he'd always loathed, when you stand in the way of the tide the ocean water comes in and deposits sand on top of your feet while it digs other sand from beneath your heels and pulls that foundation out to sea. This was how Scott had thought of his body. It was falling out from under him and burying him at the same time.

Scott had vastly preferred the flow of the river: inland, far from the big storms, slow and serene. The river flowed to the ocean, that place of little calm, where storms arose as Johnny's temper had from time to time, subsiding just as quickly, leaving behind broken feelings. Not that Johnny had gotten angry often until Scott became sicker, but then a storm could rise out of an empty sea to batter and smash anything in the way of Scott's comfort. Scott had preferred the river. A river was blithe, could be droll even, as required. A river had moods. A river could be blue, could be dappled with facets of reflected sky, hills, and sun, could be magenta and pink; a river could be dolorous, gray with fog and the smoke-blue shadows of the other shore; a river could be iridescent as an oil slick or, better, as uncannily iridescent as the body of a dragonfly; a river could be choppy in the wind, torn by a boat's wake. And a river could be smooth in the morning, a smear of molten glass, an ominous, deeply orange gold. Most of the time, to Scott, the river had been heartbreaking. Little hadn't been heartbreaking when he sat there, watching.

Johnny, of course, Johnny had been wonderful; and friends such as Jesse and Kathryn, whom one could never understand how they fit so well into each other, whom one might read about in a story, had been a source of strength for Scott. He'd loved watching them some Sundays napping together on the gazebo lounge, molding into each other in their sleep. They were a couple everyone envied. Scott had never felt like a voyeur, seeing them sleep like that, Jesse's arm drawing Kathryn close, never felt like he was intruding. Instead, he'd felt at ease within their comfort with each other; it seemed to enclose him. He had most admired their ability to quarrel, which they did as only women do, with an almost Zen-like respect for the anger of the other. Scott had only gotten angry when he felt Johnny's rage blow across him like hot wind off a fire. That was an anger Scott felt he couldn't respect, even when the anger arose for Scott's sake, because it only burned to please itself, to burn up, burn out, producing nothing but charred wood and ash, and what good was that?

Johnny had been wonderful, though. He had tried bravely to hide his anxiety about Scott's dying, which only made Scott love him more, that and the tender way he had asked Scott if he wanted to smoke marijuana again. Sometimes Scott had come here, smoked a joint, and cried. For no reason, really. He had been thirty-seven that summer, and though he hadn't quite been done with living, Scott had long before made peace with dying young, especially since life had always felt so very, very long to him. This was a privilege, and he had recognized it as such. Life was long, and it had taken so much time for him to reach thirty that each birthday surprised him. ("Oh, is it that time again?" he'd said one year when Kathryn and Jesse emerged with a cake alight with candles.) That date had become a number on his driver's license, something to enumerate under those ridiculous checkboxes for "Mr." and "Single" that he always felt obliged to leave unmarked.

Scott had had few regrets, for life is long. Since his family had money, he'd been rather untroubled in many ways—except for dying young, which he'd supposed was a trade-off that wasn't particularly unfair. After watching others die before him, friends and non-friends, Scott had surmised that some people loved pain. So Scott had waited to see, wondering when that moment would arise, when he would discover some new, ascetic pleasure in suffering. A pleasure that would reveal itself the way a familiar piece of music one day discloses a structure always there but too simple to have been noticed before; the way a poem one day describes a new, intimate meaning that comes to you in a murmur. Scott had been able to imagine the experience, but had never felt it, and he had decided that it was the expectation itself that had warded away this, well, this ecstasy.

Dying was ugly; he'd learned that. He'd believed that he was ignoring the startled looks people gave him when he'd started losing weight. He'd wondered if it was shame he felt, or pride at the physical changes in his body; at some point in his last month of life the distinction had become impossible to discern. (Is this ecstasy? he'd thought.) Johnny had been good with all the drudgery of caregiving: the meds, the diets, the shit, the blood in the shit. Johnny had guarded Scott solemnly, sometimes ferociously, as though he were guarding a little Pentecostal flame against being extinguished—a little boy with an adult task, carried out with great seriousness.

Sitting under his tree, Scott had sometimes contemplated the ways his body had become harder to move even as there was less of it. He'd wondered how his life might have been different. He would have liked to fall in love again. He'd known for a while that if he hadn't gotten sick, he would have left Johnny. He'd supposed that this was selfish. Johnny would fall in love again, after all, as many times as he might like to, after Scott were gone. Whatever their relationship, Scott had no longer felt that throb, that lump in his throat, for Johnny; and he'd believed that if Johnny still had that vertiginous tumbling it was because he'd guessed that he, Scott, had not been in love with him for some time. The fact that he would never fall in love again made Scott feel like someone was scraping out his insides, leaving him hollow, like a melon shell with all the good stuff gone. Never again to see how silly someone looks in the morning, with their eyes, their hair, full of sleep. Never to fight again with someone you adore, fight so hard that you think of ending the relationship. Now breaking up with someone sounded so heartbreakingly sweet to him, so human and hard, so simple. To never break up again, never cry over someone again, never fight the urge to call someone you hate to love. Scott hadn't cried when thinking these things in his secret spot; the only weeping then had been that of the tree itself, in the long, heavy bend of the branches. To live as a matter of waiting. To no longer wake up to breakfast on a tray and Johnny's killer Gene Kelly grin. During what he knew had become his last summer, Scott had sat by the river thinking the thoughts that dying people think, thoughts that die when they die, are therefore unthought by the rest of us, unthinkable without them.

After brunch, while Kathryn went to retrieve Jesse from the train station, Johnny and Sam decided to take in the river. Sam held Johnny's hand as they went. The sun was climbing high into the sky, pouring heat all over the river and the hills across the river; the air was ripe with it. Johnny steered them to a cascade of small white trumpet-shaped flowers hanging doubtfully on a wall of viny green.

"Watch this," he said. Johnny pulled a flower off with great delicacy—his hands were big—pinched the place at the very bottom where the trumpet ended, gently piercing the tube so as not to break the stamens hidden inside, and pulled. The stamens slipped into the wide trumpet mouth and threaded through the narrow base, and a drop of pale gold appeared at the hole, hanging precariously along the thread as Johnny pulled it through the bottom of the flower. "Close your eyes and stick out your tongue," he whispered. Sam looked unsure. "Hurry!" So Sam did, and Johnny touched the golden drop onto the end of Sam's tongue.

Sam smiled. "Oh," he said.

"Honeysuckle," Johnny said with the finality of a professor, and pulled another trumpet off the bush to taste the watery sweetness himself. (When he was a child, he and his best friend had pulled honeysuckle flowers off the shrub in his backyard till it was bare, and then were sick to the stomach from the nectar.) Sam snapped the bottom off a flower along with the base of the stamens, leaving him nothing to pull.

"See?" Johnny demonstrated again. "You have to be careful not to break off the stamen—this is the tricky part—then you slide the long part through the asshole you've made." And he slid the thread out. The nectar collected dutifully at the hole and he touched his tongue to it. The taste was quickly followed by that of Sam's mouth, orange from French toast and faintly honeysuckle again.

"You're a hot guy," he said to Johnny when they stopped kissing.

"You, too," Johnny said, grabbing a bunch of Sam's pectoral between his thumb and index finger.

They continued through the yard and down the gentle hill to the dock, holding hands again.

Sam yawned, "You said there's a gym up here?"

"Yeah. We can go later this afternoon."

At the beginning of the summer, Johnny had joined a cheap Bally's in a strip mall one town over. The gym was stocked with many StairMaster machines for the local housewives who comprised the larger part of the population and were worked on by the pumping machine pedals, not the other way around, like taffy on spindles. The meager constellation of free weights and benches on a slightly raised area in the back provided a small stage for one, two, or three blue-collar guys to perform their own little show in the mirror, for themselves or whoever was looking. Were they husbands or single guys? Johnny couldn't tell. He noticed, though, that the two populations ignored each other, making it impossible to tell what, if any, relationship they might have. How baffling the straight world could be.

Because Johnny was big (and getting bigger), the one or two other men doing a midday workout (always alone: no gym pals here) were sure to ask him for a spot at some point. "Thanks, buddy," they would say manfully to Johnny. They did not turn it into an opportunity for conversation, but acted as though the spot were expected, as though they (and Johnny, clearly), as men, deserved it somehow, as though there were some unspoken bond among men, among "real" men. If, in the passing off of a weight, Johnny's hand were to touch the other man's, he took no notice (though Johnny was hyperaware of it), as though to be squeamish were simply another version of a womanish (which is to say faggy) overattention to detail. To even notice such a detail was beneath them. Their ignorance of such things, of social detail itself, which are feelings, Johnny found brutal, and therefore attractive, because it was therefore authentic.

Johnny and Sam stood looking over the water for a minute before Sam sat down on the end of the dock, his legs dangling over the side. Johnny sat, too and saw that Sam, who was shirtless, had pulled from his pocket a tiny brown glass bottle, which he proceeded to unscrew and dip into with a microscopic spoon attached to the lid.

"What is that? Coke?"

"Nah," Sam said as he snorted the smallest spoonful up a nostril before pinching his nose closed. Through pinched nose, he said, "It's K."

"Really. What other letters do you have?"

"Come on, you're going to tell me that a big sexy guy like you doesn't know what this is?"

"It looks that way."

Sam didn't seem to be noticing Johnny's surprise through his own surprise. He snorted another bump into his other nostril, then offered the bottle to Johnny.

"It's horse tranquilizer."

"Oh, this is too weird."

"C'mon, it's fun," Sam urged.

"No, thanks. I don't feel like being tranquilized right now."

Sam kissed Johnny on the cheek (it was more of a smooch, actually). "You goof, it isn't like that."

Johnny stared at the other shore as Sam's hand gently explored his belly and moved upward, eventually finding a nipple and kindling it to life in just the way Johnny liked. His penis responded

accordingly. Soon they were kissing, their mouths tasting of powdered sugar, maple syrup, and orange. Sam smelled of sweat, they
both smelled of sweat, and, hidden from view under a T-shirt, Sam's
cum was scaled over and dry on Johnny's stomach, the scent of which
now was also aroused again.

The heat and brightness of the midday sun drove them off the
dock, into the shade trees near the picnic table. In the fall, they would
prop the table up against a tree so water and snow wouldn't collect in
its grooves and grain. This image always reminded Johnny of childhood games, the table enshrouding its head in its arms against the
tree like that, counting through the winter.

Johnny followed Sam into the overgrown strip of their property
along the shoreline, keeping an eye out for poison ivy as they stepped
among younger trees and ferns, knowing it was likely some would be
lurking. The property extended farther north along the shore and
ended abruptly just south of their dock, so it had been decided to let
nature green and bramble as it wished at the southern corner. It
didn't hurt that their neighbors to the south were a cranky old couple
who resisted all attempts at contact and kindness. (Anyone who
didn't like Kathryn clearly had something wrong, to Johnny's way of
thinking.) To separate the properties, they'd built a high wooden
fence, which lanced down the hill and into the trees along the shore
before ending at the point where the ground thickened with roots.
("Fuck it," Jesse had declared, "and fuck those old fucks.") The fence
pointed like a finger at a big ugly willow, hidden from view, which
Johnny had always disliked. The tree marked the southern corner of
their property, and it was here that Sam and Johnny emerged, stum-
bling through some green into a cozy well-shaded clearing underneath the heavy branches.

The place was cool, and it was pleasant to be out of the sun, sweet
for Johnny to be here with this big man whose lips were so soft and
warm against his neck, whose arms were smooth and thick, who liked

all the things Johnny liked. Sam laid Johnny back, pulled up his shirt, and began kissing Johnny's belly and licking Johnny's sweat and his own dried semen; when he climbed onto Johnny to kiss him, his own lips and tongue carried those smells of being a man. Johnny kissed Sam feverishly, taking Sam's full lower lip between his teeth, feeling the roughness of Sam's tongue with his own, inhaling Sam deep into himself—the sweat of the man, the smell and taste of cum in his mouth and nose, that salt, that copper, that breadlike smell. Johnny turned so that Sam was under him now, Johnny tugging at Sam's shorts, his own erection so painful, his teeth at Sam's neck, sinking into the corded muscle there, into Sam's traps, Johnny's need becoming frantic, furnace-hot, a fire fed by the wind. The wind was Sam; the wind Johnny wanted him to be. As he spit into his own hand and fell into that warm sliding, that delicious opening and filling, with a gentle push of Sam's hips, Johnny felt himself wanting to tell Sam he loved him. He kept the words inside himself somehow as he stared into Sam's brown eyes, as he tried to look deep into Sam, as he kissed Sam, as they do in the movies, with a hand on either side of his head.

The fast lane was clear as Kathryn drove home on Sunday, Jess snoozing next to her in the passenger seat. Johnny and Sam were staying at the house for another day, but a meeting had summoned Kathryn back to the city and Jesse didn't feel like staying behind. They'd left after an early dinner, and now the sun was setting somewhere beyond the trees to the right. A clearing every few miles revealed the sun to be a carmine hole in the sky, light pouring out of it and brushing the clouds with the same color. For most of the journey, however, Kathryn had been contemplating the gentle blue wash of the twilight overhead, which extended into darker hues toward the left and behind another bank of trees. With the windows open, the air, damp and slightly cooled, circulating around the car reminded Kathryn of the way summers end—how midsummer sometimes feels like late summer. July is hot, but not the rolling boil of August, which cools on the back burner into something like July again, ready to be served; sitting at the table, you are stunned as red leaves blow across your plate and autumn is upon you again. How does this happen?

Work on Friday had proved exhausting for Jess, and the train ride upstate on Saturday had not helped to relax her. As they drove to the house, Kathryn had explained that Johnny had brought a guest. "It'll be nice to have someone new around," Jesse had said, but within an hour of being in the house she'd told Kathryn that it seemed like the two men were already a couple.

"It's sort of odd, don't you think?" she'd said.

"What does it have to do with you?"

Jesse had shrugged. "This is my home, too."

Kathryn had spent the rest of Saturday keeping herself and Jesse busy, weeding the garden in silence, cutting back the wisteria while Johnny and Sam sunned themselves, farther down the lawn. When the men went to the gym, Kathryn and Jess had prowled around each other in the heat for an hour before getting naked and loving in the gazebo. How sweet it had been to be alone again. How like last summer. Why did it feel most like last summer when the men had gone?

At dinner, there had been a discussion of some recent film, the sort of pretentious trash that tends to pass for art these days. A general thrashing of its merits went on for some time, and as Johnny described his surprise ("despite all that") at the way a pivotal scene turned out, Sam had replied, "I wasn't surprised." With his grin, "But nothing surprises me." He was grinning and chewing his food.

"Aw, that's too bad," Jesse had said from across the table, her first contribution to the discussion.

"Why's that?"

"Because it means you can't learn anything," She'd paced the words carefully, using each syllable like a scalpel.

Then something strange had happened. A tension descended on

the table; Sam, who continued eating happily, had said, "This steak is good." He wasn't changing the subject; it was just that Jess was throwing her words off a cliff. The tension had dissipated like the steam coming off the green beans, extended out into the room, dissolved out into the air, found its way out the windows and doors, into the sky, into nothing.

It's impossible to get inside someone's head, yet so easy to dismiss her and all those complicated feelings and reasons we can't see. Kathryn felt disrespectful when she decided she knew a person; as soon as she was sure she had someone down, on the heels of that certainty Kathryn felt ashamed. It embarrassed her to be so reductive. That knowledge of someone where you begin to see her as predictable, when you believe you know her better than she knows herself, that kind of automatic clocking of repetition—something any child can do—was a trap; Make ye no graven images. But what was the labyrinth of feelings that brought about a repetition in someone so that that person never noticed it? How beautiful. Whatever that is, that is a person's knowledge: the things she thinks and feels so she doesn't know what she's doing. And we on the outside can't know such a treasure, which is buried fathoms deep under all our own expectations and wishes—everyone is an emptiness at which we cast the slim volume of our self-knowledge.

As she drove, Kathryn thought about last summer, which she hadn't thought of since the season began. Suddenly she even missed mowing the lawn and watching the wisteria wind tighter into the gazebo, the deep light of the late-day sun on Jesse's brown skin, in her hair, within her wide brown eyes, finding flecks of gold and green there. She longed to swim naked at night off the dock and sleep late the next day. She missed taking extra days off work to stay up at the house. The things she'd always enjoyed at the house seemed so keenly gone as crimson light poked holes in the black mass of trees next to their car. The sun was very low in the sky now.

Was this summer tentative, after all, despite its familiarity; had they been waiting to see what would happen? Kathryn couldn't tell, but she'd never thought before this moment that they had been doing anything but living their mundane lives. She, Jess, and Johnny had contented themselves with maintaining the division of labor they'd had when Scott was alive—the tasks and order of tasks they had always performed—taking refuge, without realizing it, in the sureness. *I won't feel any difference if I perform these same five tasks in the same ways I've always done—in this way nothing will change, when everything has changed.* Kathryn had worried that she wouldn't know a Johnny without a Scott, and now she saw that the person she no longer knew was, after all, herself.

They had been driving between these two masses of trees that were either burdening or supporting the purpling blue overhead; whichever, Kathryn couldn't tell. The trees stretched behind her, before her. Did they touch the sky; did the sky ever notice trees? On this road there were herself, her car, and her lover in the passenger seat, and the world had become these trees and this twilight. Kathryn felt Scott surge forth—a scent, a sensation of the air—surge and drop out from under her, reminding her of when she'd watched him walk down the lawn, away from her, making his way out to the tree by the river where he liked to sit whenever Johnny was napping. Kathryn had felt his desire to be alone, as clear to her as his back, which was receding, which was leaving them, which had gone. And she pulled the car over to the side of the road to catch her breath and to hold Jesse's hand, sleeping in her own.

3

The leaves on the ginkgo outside the window were blushing, through some sort of alchemy, into a pale gold as Johnny lay in his bed. They had all changed color after a teasing few days as the green fled first some leaves, then others, then all. And it was a cheap yellow, too, the same as the youth's golden hair in the illustrated *Iron Hans* story Johnny had loved so much as a child, now remembered as abbreviated images, pages, and somewhat confused with the story of King Midas, whose touch turned all things into gold. At the end of that tale, Midas's impulsive daughter, who could stand no longer to go unembraced by her beloved father, kissed the king and turned instantly into a statue of metal, her lips going cold against his cheek. The fan-shaped leaves outside his window, their bellies upturned by the wind, brought these stories back to Johnny as the touch of the sun worked a transubstantiation all its own on the clouds over the building across the street.

The night before had been a late one spent clubbing with Sam, in the middle of the dance floor with the other shirtless boys gathered like a colony, their skin pulled tight over muscle, taut, wet with salt. It was Monday, so Sam, who had gone home for a shower, would be at work soon, with a vial of crystal meth for when he felt himself fading. ("Better living through chemistry," he'd whispered against Johnny's lips.)

Johnny loved dancing with Sam, a hand on the other's hip, foreheads pressed together. When Sam had produced the little brown bottle and held that tiny spoon under Johnny's nose, Johnny had snorted the stuff into his head with an ironic "What the fuck?" The lights and music had made him delirious with their shifting, their turning, the way the light conjured a small room of bodies one moment, a flashing series of fragments—chests, arms, faces, eyes—the next. Eyes closed, tongue sliding and tracing back over Sam's tongue in Sam's mouth, Johnny had entered some other place without moving, become aware of a small room in which a tiny basin held water. (Was the room inside him?) He'd watched a fountain fill with water from no source, the smooth liquid rise from the basin's bottom, slide back down to empty as he and Sam kissed. Johnny couldn't be sure if the font was inside Sam, either, and its room with the marble basin like a baptismal font he'd been set to guard over, required to guard, forced to watch with his eyes closed as he'd kissed Sam. The water rose—was it water?—and Johnny had felt tension, a filling up, like getting fucked, maybe. But he wasn't sure if he or someone else was feeling this; perhaps Sam. Inexplicably, the sensation had backed away, almost recoiled, as the little pool—he was almost sure now it was inside Sam—had emptied again, down, down, and he had become aware, almost at once, of the music, of kissing, and, though he couldn't be sure his eyes were open, of white-hot snapshot images of shirtless men flashing all around him. And then the little vial, the spoon again, his nose. After hours of dancing, of kissing a couple of other guys who weren't Sam while Sam kissed guys who weren't Johnny (though he wasn't sure he wasn't always kissing Sam, no matter whom he was kissing), Johnny's legs had become heavy, as though they were very far away; he wasn't sure he could move them, wasn't sure they were part of him, though (he'd found this alarming) they moved anyway, moved as though they remembered how to dance when he could not, and Johnny had learned to trust them. At one point, Sam had tapped him; Johnny swung around to look and Sam shouted in his ear, more than once, to be heard over the recursive thud-thunder of the music. Finally, Johnny had heard Sam's words, telegraphically: *Am I dancing? What? Yes!* How they'd laughed in the cab later when Johnny recounted this on their way home.

Briefly, as though on a movie screen, all the images at the club had passed before his enchanted eyes. Johnny had spotted the guy he'd fucked around with a few times in the spring, who'd faded from the screen after Sam entered the scene. Josh. His blond hair stuck up as if he'd just gotten out of bed, a couple of strands sweat-fixed to his forehead. Now Josh seemed to Johnny like a coal grown cold, a cool stone remembering its heat. Josh had touched him on the shoulder and flashed that big smile, conjuring a grin from Johnny's mouth against his will. He hadn't recognized Josh right away. He'd seemed so small, his body slim-hipped and grotesquely boyish except for the subtle spread of dark blond hair washing gently across his pecs, gathering around, magnetically drawn to, his nipples; if he shaved the chest hair off, there might be more muscle there. Johnny's smile had dropped from his mouth as the scales fell from his eyes and he realized he was away from Sam and their posse, talking to this pale little person. Josh had felt the coldness instantly and made his exit, squeezing Johnny's shoulder, smiling, the sadness in his eyes as he said good-bye, filling Johnny with loathing.

Johnny and Sam saw each other several times a week. They'd started working out together, which amplified Johnny's already-muscular frame, giving more rounded heft to his chest, bringing out his traps, and etching each rib along his torso as though it had been sculpted there, they were so perfect—and amplified his desire for Sam, too. His own appeal (which Johnny had never worried too much about anyway) seemed to increase in kind; he was picking up men on the street with a regularity he hadn't known before. At the end of the summer, wearing a tank top so tight you could make out every oblique on his torso, he'd left a bar only to have a man hurry out after him and beg, "What do I have to say to get you to give me your number?" This fucking around was fun; but, more importantly, it created a counterpoint to his relationship with Sam, whose elusiveness had become maddening, an elusiveness Sam maintained despite the many hours they spent together. The wind blows harder, the fire burns hotter.

Johnny orchestrated every moment they were together. When Sam called to cancel a workout, saying his job was keeping him, Johnny suggested that Sam drop by his place afterward, then greeted him at the door naked, holding two martinis. Johnny loved doing this sort of thing, loved romance. For his part, Sam accepted what was offered and seemed pleased enough to wait for the next time. But

Johnny noticed that there were no whispered thank-yous in the dark
as they drifted to sleep, which only made his fire burn more fervid.

Johnny tried therefore to do more: make more romantic dinners,
suggest more road trips, throw a birthday party for Sam in September. Then he told Sam he loved him. Sam nodded and smiled,
looked as though he would say something, looked away. Johnny
decided, he told Kathryn one day on the phone, that all he wanted
was for Sam to admit he was Johnny's boyfriend. Johnny didn't want
to get married again, he insisted; he certainly didn't want monogamy,
didn't want Sam to move in with him, for God's sake. He just needed
to know that there was something there.

"There must be something there," Kathryn suggested, "or he
wouldn't stick around. Maybe you're giving too much."

That had occurred to Johnny, of course, grudgingly. How could he
keep his mind on that, though? To think it was like fingers thinking
sand. Instead, Johnny lay awake at night anatomizing Sam, imagining
the next event or exchange that would close the gap and finally anthol-
ogize them. What should he say that he hadn't already said? What
could he do? He rehearsed speeches to the ceiling in the dark, refining
the logic, and all the while Sam's impertinent cock, especially the meaty
swell of the head when it got fully erect, would nose its way into his
plans. Or the shape of Sam's heavy-lidded profile would impose itself
against the blue rectangle of the window shade, and Johnny would be
forced to consider which he loved more: that shape, set against the glow
of the streetlamp, or the brightening light that came with it, like a realization of something, a glow working itself into a burning. Sometimes,
inadvertently, Johnny wondered about his past, its distance from him,
its depth and strata, and all those years with Scott, which rarely came to
mind now. And sometimes, lying in his bed staring at the ceiling,
unable to sleep after hours spent explicating Sam's brown nipples
almost hanging off his heavy pecs, Sam's openmouthed smile, Sam's
wretched look when saying good-bye, Sam's lips—sometimes Johnny
wondered if he'd ever really loved Scott.

About the Contributors

Michael Carroll's work has appeared most recently in such literary journals as *Boulevard* and *Ontario Review*, as well as the anthologies *The New Penguin Book of Gay Short Stories* (edited by David Leavitt and Mark Mitchell), *M2M, Men on Men 7* and *Boys Like Us: Gay Writers Tell Their Coming-Out Stories*. He lives in New York.

Jaime Cortez is an artist, writer and cultural worker based in San Francisco. His writing has appeared in numerous anthologies. He is the editor of the anthology *Virgins, Guerrillas & Loca* (Cleis Press, 1999). Jaime's visual art has been exhibited at numerous venues including the Oakland Museum of California, Huntington Beach Center for the Arts, Southern Exposure, The Lab, Galería de la Raza and Intersection for the Arts. He has lectured on art and activism at Stanford University, UC Berkeley, UC Santa Barbara, the University of Pennsylvania and the Yerba Buena Center for the Arts. He is currently pursuing his MFA in Art Practice at UC Berkeley.

Jim Cory, a Philadelphia poet with seven chapbooks to his credit, began writing fiction in 2000 when a long poem he was working on transformed itself into a story. Stories have since appeared or are forthcoming in *James White Review, Skidrow Penthouse and Harrington Gay Men's Fiction Quarterly.* "An Ideal Couple" was the first winner of the Richard Hall Memorial Short Story Award. He is at work on a novel, set in Philadelphia.

Ted Gideonse is a contributing editor and film critic at the Canadian magazine *Maisonneuve,* and his journalism has appeared in *Newsweek, Rolling Stone, Salon.com, Out,* and *The Advocate.* He is a PhD candidate in Anthropology at the University of California, San Diego. He is married to the writer Rob Williams, and they have three cats. "The Lost Coast" is Ted's first published work of fiction.

James Grissom has written for Martha Stewart, *Penthouse* magazine, and Jimmy Swaggart. As he attempted to make a living—and a name—writing literary fiction, he instead wrote for a number of television programs, which has left him capable of a fusillade of quips with only a breast of chicken and some blank tapes as incentive. Mr. Grissom studied at Louisiana State University, the University of Pennsylvania, and Brown University, and has some lovely sweatshirts from all three institutions. Mr. Grissom was born in Baton Rouge, Louisiana, and now has almost no resentment concerning this fact. This is his first published short story. He can be easily had. Ask anybody.

As a journalist, **Wayne Hoffman** has written for such publications as the *Washington Post*, the *Village Voice, The Nation, Billboard* and the *Forward*. His essays have appeared in several collections, including *Generation Q, Boy Meets Boy* and *Mama's Boy,* and he is co-editor of the collection *Policing Public Sex: Queer Politics and the Future of AIDS Activism*. "Sucker" is his first published piece of fiction. His debut novel, *Hard,* is due out next year.

John Mancuso's story, "Psychic Rosemary," was selected by Felice Picano as the winner of the Richard Hall Memorial Short Story Contest and later revised under Patrick Merla's meticulous and wise direction. John's work has appeared in *Fourteen Hills, Punk Planet, The James White Review,* and *For Here or To Go: Stories of the Service Industry.* Additionally, he has garnered a Pushcart Prize nomination, a residency at the Vermont Studio Center and served on the staff of the Bread Loaf Writer's Conference. He teaches writing and literature in Philadelphia but lives in Manhattan. He welcomes comments at john_mancuso@breadnet.middlebury.edu.

Robert Marshall, a writer and visual artist, lives in New York City. His novel, *Ixtlan,* is forthcoming from Carroll and Graf. His work has appeared in *Blithe House Quarterly* and in the anthologies *Afterwords* and *Queer 13*, and his artwork has been exhibited widely throughout the United States, Europe, and South America. He is the recipient of a 2005 New York Foundation for the Arts fellowship. His website is www.robertmarshall.net.

Alistair McCartney's writing has appeared in numerous places, including *Fence, Fourth Street, The James White Review, Wonderlands: Gay Travel Writing, Aroused* (edited by Karen Finley) and *Mirage #4 Periodical* (edited by Kevin Killian and Dodie Bellamy.) He is currently finishing a book of fiction, *The End of The World Book,* to be published by the University of Wisconsin Press. He teaches creative writing and literature at Antioch University in Los Angeles. Originally from Australia, he now lives in Los Angeles with his partner Tim Miller.

Samoan American writer, painter and filmmaker, **Dan Taulapapa McMullin**, has engaged audiences in the South Pacific, North America and Europe, with stories that take place in Samoa, American Samoa, and among the Samoan diaspora in the United States. His 2004 illustrated poetry chapbook, *A Drag Queen Named Pipi* continued a line of work around the 1996 poem "The Bat" and other early works, earning McMullin a 1997 *Poets &Writers* Award from The Loft. His political essays on colonization in American Samoa contributed to the 1999 Gustavus Meyers Humanitarian Book Award-winning *Resistance in Paradise* and his first children's book in the Samoan language *'O lo'u Igoa 'o Laloifi* was published in 2005. Currently he is completing a book of short stories for Hawai'i-Aotearoa co-publication. More on his recent work is at www.taulapapa.com.

Aaron Nielsen holds a BA in English Literature from San Francisco State University, where he is currently pursuing an MFA in creative writing. His fiction and poetry have previously appeared in velvetmafia.com, outsiderink.com, *The Chabot Review, Instant City, Mirage (period)ical #4* and the UK magazine *The Egg Box*. He has also interviewed Poppy Z. Brite for the 'zine *Serendipity* and Dennis Cooper for suspectthoughts.com.

David Pratt has published short stories in *Lodestar Quarterly, Blithe House Quarterly, Velvet Mafia, The James White Review, Harrington Gay Men's Fiction Quarterly,* and in the anthologies *Men Seeking Men* and *His3*. His has written, directed, produced, and/or performed his own works for theater in New York City at HERE Arts Center, Dixon Place, the Cornelia Street Cafe, the Flea Theater, the Dramatists Guild, and at Pace University as part of the eighth annual New York International Fringe Festival. Please visit www.davidprattarts.com.

Lawrence Rinder is Dean of Graduate Studies at the California College of the Arts in San Francisco. Previously, he was Curator of Contemporary Art at the Whitney Museum of American Art where he served as Chief Curator for the 2002 Biennial. In addition to his academic and curatorial work, Mr. Rinder's criticism, poetry, and fiction have appeared in *Artforum, Parkett, Zyzzyva,* and *The James White Review*. A book of his essays, *Art Life: Selected Writings 1991–2005* will be published by Gregory R. Miller & Company in 2005.

Randy Romano is a graduate of Queens College/CUNY, where he majored in English and won the Silverstein-Peiser Award for Fiction. He was raised and lives on Long Island. "Yesterday's Nihilist" is his first published fiction.

Seth Rudetsky has played piano in the pit of twenty Broadway shows as well as writing and starring Off Broadway in *Rhapsody in Seth*. As a comic he was voted "The Funniest Gay Male in New York" and as an actor he has appeared in *Law and Order* and *All My Children*. He was a comedy writer on *The Rosie O'Donnell Show* and is currently a D.J. on Sirius Satellite Radio.

Rakesh Satyal is an editor at Random House. He lives in New York City.

Ohio-born writer **L. Steve Schmersal** writes poetry, fiction, and plays. He lives in New York City.

Stefen Styrsky's stories have appeared in *The James White Review* and *Harrington Gay Men's Fiction Quarterly*. He has published reviews and articles in the *Lambda Book Report* and *Gay City News*. He lives in Washington, D.C. with his partner Michael and their son Richard.

Michael Van Devere is an author, painter and filmmaker. He learned fine arts at Houston's acclaimed High School for the Performing and Visual Arts and studied filmmaking in New York at the School of Visual Arts. Currently studying literature, his short fiction has appeared in *Harrington Gay Men's Fiction Quarterly*. A former resident of Hell's Kitchen, Mr. Van Devere wrote "Man-boobs" as a love letter to Midtown Manhattan, where he came of age in the 90s and met a young man who suprised him.

Michael Wynne has had fiction anthologized in Ireland, Britain, the US and Canada. He is currently reading Philosophy at Trinity College, Dublin.